T0362983

# From
# Courtship
## To Crown

**CLARE CONNELLY**

**SHARON KENDRICK**

**LUCY MONROE**

**MILLS & BOON**

Published by
Mills & Boon
An imprint of Harlequin Enterprises (Australia) Pty Limited (ABN 47 001 180 918), a subsidiary of HarperCollins Publishers Australia Pty Limited (ABN 36 009 913 517)
Level 19, 201 Elizabeth Street
SYDNEY NSW 2000
AUSTRALIA

Printed and bound in Australia by McPherson's Printing Group

# CONTENTS

# CONTENTS

# The Secret Kept From The King

*Clare Connelly*

**Books by Clare Connelly**

**Harlequin Modern**

*Bought for the Billionaire's Revenge*
*Innocent in the Billionaire's Bed*
*Her Wedding Night Surrender*
*Bound by the Billionaire's Vows*
*Spaniard's Baby of Revenge*
*Redemption of the Untamed Italian*

**Secret Heirs of Billionaires**

*Shock Heir for the King*

**Christmas Seductions**

*Bound by Their Christmas Baby*
*The Season to Sin*

**Crazy Rich Greek Weddings**

*The Greek's Billion-Dollar Baby*
*Bride Behind the Billion-Dollar Veil*

Visit the Author Profile page
at millsandboon.com.au for more titles.

**Clare Connelly** was raised in small-town Australia among a family of avid readers. She spent much of her childhood up a tree, Harlequin romance book in hand. Clare is married to her own real-life hero and they live in a bungalow near the sea with their two children. She is frequently found staring into space—a surefire sign she is in the world of her characters. She has a penchant for French food and ice-cold champagne, and Harlequin novels continue to be her favorite-ever books. Writing for Harlequin Modern is a long-held dream. Clare can be contacted via clareconnelly.com or on her Facebook page.

This book's for you—a romance reader who, just like me, loves to be swept up in a passionate, escapist story with a guaranteed happily-ever-after.

# CHAPTER ONE

WHEN HE CLOSED his eyes he saw only his father's, so he tried not to close them much at all. Not because he didn't want to see the Exalted Sheikh Kadir Al Antarah again; he did, more than anything. But seeing his eyes as they'd been at the end, so clouded by pain and unconscious of the world that swirled around him, so robbed of the strength and vibrancy that had been hallmarks of his life and rule, made Sariq's chest compress in a way that robbed him of breath and had him gasping for air.

The King was dead. His father was dead. He was now completely alone in this world, and the inescapable reality he had been aware of all his life was wrapping around him like a cable.

He had been crowned. The job of steering the Royal Kingdom of Haleth fell to him. Just as he'd always known it would, just as he'd spent a lifetime preparing for.

'Your Highness? Malik has asked me to remind you of the time.'

Sariq didn't respond at first. He continued to stare out at the glittering vista of Manhattan. From this vantage point, it was easy to pick out the key buildings that were considered the most well-known landmarks of New York. The Empire State building shone like a beacon. The Chrysler with its art deco detailing, and, far in the distance, the spire of One World Trade

Centre. And in another direction, not far from this hotel, if he followed a straight line, he'd reach the United Nations, where he'd be expected to make his first official speech since the death of Sheikh Kadir. In the morning, he'd address leaders and delegates from dozens of countries, aiming to assure them that his father's death was not an end to the peace that had, finally, been established between the RKH and the west.

'Emir?'

'Yes.' He spoke more harshly than he'd intended. He closed his eyes—and there was his father. He returned his attention to the view, his features locked in a grim mask. 'Tell Malik I am aware of the hour.'

Still, the servant hovered. 'Can I get you anything else, sir?'

Briefly, Sariq turned to face the servant. He was little more than a boy—sixteen or seventeen perhaps. He wore the same uniform Sariq had donned at that age, black with gold detailing. The insignia indicated he was an ensign. 'What is your name?'

The boy's eyes widened.

'Kaleth.'

Sariq forced a smile to his face. It felt odd, heavy and wooden. 'Thank you for your attention, Kaleth, but you may go now.'

Kaleth paused, as though he wished to say something further.

'Tell Malik it was at my insistence.'

This seemed to appease the young officer because he nodded and bowed low. 'Goodnight, sir.'

He turned back to the view without responding. It was after midnight and his day had been long. Starting with meetings in Washington and then the flight to New York, where he'd had dinner with his ambassador to America—also installed in this hotel while the major renovations to the embassy were completed. And all day long, he'd pushed his grief aside, knowing he needed to act strong and unaffected by the fact he'd buried his father a little over three weeks ago.

The man had been a behemoth. Strength personified. His absence left a gaping hole—not just for Sariq but for the country. It was one Sariq would endeavour to fill, but there would only ever be one King Kadir.

He moved towards the view, pushing one of the sliding glass doors open so he could step onto the large, private terrace, his eyes continuing to trace the skyline of New York. The background noise of horns beeping, sirens wailing and engines revving was a constant here, and somehow that made it fade into nothing. It was so loud it became a sort of white noise, and yet it made him long for the silence of the desert to the east of his palace, a place where he could erect a tent and be surrounded by silence, and the ancient sands of his kingdom. There was wisdom in those grains of sand: each and every one of them had stood sentinel to the people of his kingdom. Their wars, their famines, their pains, their hopes, their beliefs and, in the last forty years, their peace, their prosperity, their modernisation and acceptance onto the world's stage.

It was his father's legacy and Sariq would do all that he could to preserve it. No, not simply to preserve it: to improve it. To grow it, to strengthen it, to better his country's standing and make peace so unequivocal that the trailing fingers of civil war could no longer touch a single soul of his country.

Sariq was not his father, but he was of him, he was cast from his soul, his bones and strength, and he had spent a lifetime watching, learning, and preparing for this.

In the morning, it would begin. He was ready.

Daisy stared at the flashing light with a small frown on her cupid's bow lips, then consulted the clock on the wall. It was three in the morning, and the alarm for the Presidential suite was on. She reached for the phone, tucking it under her ear.

'Concierge, how may I help you?'

It had only been a matter of hours since the delegation from the Royal Kingdom of Haleth had been installed in this five-star hotel's most prestigious suite—as well as a whole floor of rooms for servants and security guards—but Daisy had already had multiple dealings with a man named Malik, who seemed to coordinate the life of the Sheikh. As the hotel's VIP concierge, this was her job—she alone was responsible for taking care of every little thing the most prestigious guests wanted. Whether it was organising parties for after their concerts at Madison Square Garden, or, in the case of a Queen from a Scandinavian country, organising a small couture fashion parade in her suite so she could choose what to wear to the Met gala, Daisy prided herself on being able to cope with just about anything that was asked of her.

So when the phone rang, despite the hour, she was calm and prepared. Malik must need something and she would ensure he got it.

What she wasn't prepared for was the timbre of the voice that came down the line, so deep and throaty, accented with spice and an exotic lilt that showed English was his second language. 'I would like some persimmon tea.'

The RKH ambassador had been staying in the hotel for three months while the embassy was being renovated. They now had a permanent supply of delicacies from that country on hand, including persimmon tea.

'Yes, sir. Would you like some *balajari* as well?' she offered, the almond and lemon zest biscuits something the ambassador always took with his tea.

There was a slight pause. 'Fine.' The call was disconnected and Daisy inwardly bristled, though she showed no sign of that. Very few of the guests she'd hosted in the Presidential suite had exhibited particularly good manners. There were a few exceptions: an Australian actor who'd apologised every time he'd 'disturbed' her, a Scottish woman who'd won one of those television singing competitions and seemed unable to comprehend that she'd been jettisoned in the global superstar arena and seemed to want to be treated as normally as possible, and a Japanese artist who had wanted directions to the nearest Whole Foods so she could stock her own fridge.

Daisy called the order through to the kitchen then moved to the service elevator. There was a full-length mirror there—the hotel manager insisted that each staff member check their appearance before going out on the floor, and Daisy did so now, tucking a curl of her blonde hair back into its bun, pinching her cheeks to bring a bit of colour to them, and even though her shirt was tucked in, she pushed it in a little more firmly, straightening her pencil skirt and spinning to have a look over her shoulder at her behind.

Neat, professional, nondescript. Her job wasn't to be noticed, it was to fly beneath the radar. She was a facilitator, and nothing more. A ghost of the hotel, there whenever she was required, but in an unseen kind of way.

By the time she reached the kitchen in the basement, the order was ready. She double-checked the tray herself, inspecting plates for fingerprints, the teapot for heat, then thanked the staff, carrying the tray on one hand as she pressed the call button for the lift.

The Presidential suite was on the top floor and only she and the hotel manager had a staff access card for it. She swiped it as she entered then moved the tray to both hands, holding it in front of her as the lift shot up towards the sky.

When she'd first started working here, two years ago, the elevator had made her tummy ache every time, but she was used to it now and barely batted an eyelid.

The doors pinged open into a small service corridor with a glossy white door on one end. In the presidential apartment, the door was concealed by wall panelling. She knocked discreetly and, despite the absence of a greeting, unlocked the door and pushed into the suite.

The lights were out but several lamps had been turned on, giving the apartment an almost eerie glow.

She loved these rooms, with their sumptuous décor, their stunning views, the promise of luxury and grandeur. Of course, she loved them most of all when they were empty, particularly of the more demanding and disrespectful guests who had a tendency to treat the delicate furniture as though it were cheap, plastic tat.

The coffee table in the middle of the sofas was low-set and a shining timber. She placed the tea tray down on it, then straightened to look around the room. At first, she didn't see him. It took her eyes a moment to adjust to the darkened room. But then, the silhouette of a man stood out, a void against the Manhattan skyline.

The Sheikh.

She'd caught a glimpse of him at a distance, earlier that day, and he was instantly recognisable now. It wasn't just his frame, which was tall and broad, muscled in a way that spoke of fitness and strength. It was his long hair, dark, which he wore in a bun on top of his head. She was used to dealing with powerful, important people and yet that didn't mean she was an automaton. In moments like this, a hint of anxiety always bristled through her. She ignored it, keeping her voice neutral when she addressed him.

'Good evening, sir. I have your tea.' A pause, in which he didn't speak, nor did he turn to face her. 'Would you like me to pour it for you?'

Another pause, a silence that stretched between them for several seconds. She waited with the appearance of impassivity, watching him, so she saw the moment he dipped his head forward in what she took to be a nod.

Her fingertips trembled betrayingly as she reached for the teapot, lifting it silently, pressing down on the lid to avoid any spills, filling the tea to near the top of the cup, then silently replacing the pot on the tray.

She took a step backward then, preparing to leave. Except he still didn't move and something inside her sparked with curiosity. Not just curiosity: duty. He had asked for tea; her job was to provide him with it. She moved back to the coffee table, lifting the teacup and saucer, carrying them across the room towards him.

'Here you are, sir,' she murmured at his side. Now, finally, he did turn to look at her, and she had to grip the teacup and saucer more tightly to stop them from shaking. Her fingers felt as though they'd been filled with jelly. She'd seen him from a distance and she'd seen photographs of him, when she'd been preparing for his visit, but nothing really did justice to his magnificence. In person, he was so much more vital than any still image could convey. His features were harsh, symmetrical and almost jagged. A jaw that was square, cheekbones that appeared to have been slashed into his face at birth, a nose that had a bump halfway down its length, as if it had been broken at some point. His eyes were the darkest black, and his brows were thick and straight. His skin was a swarthy tan, and his chin was covered in stubble. Yes, up close he was quite mesmerising, so she forced herself to look away. Being mesmerised wasn't part of her job description.

'It's supposed to help you sleep.' His voice was unlike anything she'd ever known. If you could find a way to bottle it, you'd be a millionaire.

'I've heard that.' She nodded, crisply, already preparing to fade into the background, to disappear discreetly through the concealed doorway, feeling almost as though her disappearing now was essential to her sanity.

'Have you tried it before?'

'No.' She swallowed; her throat felt quite dry. 'But your ambassador favours it.'

'It is very common in my country.'

His eyes roamed her face in a way that set her pulse firing. Escape was essential. 'Do you need anything else?'

A small frown quirked at his lips. He looked back towards the view. 'Malik would say I need to sleep.'

'And you have the tea for that.'

'Scotch might work better.'

'Would you like me to organise some for you?'

He tilted his head to hers again. 'It's after three.'

His words made little sense.

'It's after three and you're working.'

'Oh, right. Yes. That's my job.'

He lifted a brow. 'To work through the night?'

'To work when you need me,' she said with a lift of her shoulders. Then, with a swift correction, 'Or when any guest of the Presidential suite requires me. I'm assigned to this suite exclusively.'

'And you have to do whatever I ask?' he prompted.

A small smile lifted her lips. 'Well, not quite.' She couldn't suppress the teasing quality from her voice. 'I can't cook and I don't know any jokes, but when it comes to facilitating your requests, then yes, I do whatever is humanly possible to make them happen.'

'And that's your employment.'

'Yes.'

He sipped the tea without taking his dark eyes off her. Ordinarily, she would have taken that opportunity to leave, but there was a contradiction within this man that had her saying, 'I would have thought you'd be used to that degree of service.'

'Why do you say that?'

'Because you travel with an entourage of forty men, all of whom it would appear exist to serve your every whim?'

Another sip of his tea. 'Yes, this is their job. I am King, and in my country serving the royal family is a great honour.'

Something tweaked in the back of her brain. A memory from a news article she'd read a couple of weeks ago. His father had died. Recently.

Compassion moved through her, and empathy, because she could vividly remember the pain of that loss. Five years ago, when her mother had died, she had felt as if she'd never be whole again. In time, day by day, she'd begun to feel more like herself, but it was still a work in progress. She felt her mother's absence every day.

It was that understanding that had her saying something she would normally not have dared. 'I'm sorry, about your father. Losing a parent is…we know it's something we should expect, but I don't think anything really prepares us for what life without them will be like.'

His eyes jolted to hers, widening in his face, so she immediately regretted her familiarity. He was a king, for goodness' sake, and her job was to bring the tea!

Dipping her head forward, she found she couldn't meet his eyes. 'If that's all, sir, goodnight.' She didn't wait for his answer; turning away from him, she strode to the concealed door. Her hand was on it when he spoke.

'Wait.'

She paused, her heart slamming against her ribcage.

She didn't turn around, though.

'Come back here.'

Her pulse was like a torrent in her veins.

She turned to face him. He was watching her. Her heart rate accelerated to the point of, surely, danger.

'Yes, sir?'

A frown etched itself across his face. 'Sit.' He gestured to the sofas. 'Drink tea with me.'

A million reasons to say 'no' came to her. Not once in all the time she'd held this job had she come close to socialising with a guest. For one thing, it was completely forbidden in her contract.

*This is a professional establishment. They are not our friends. They are guests at the most exclusive hotel in the world.*

But that wasn't the only reason she was resisting his invitation.

He was too much. Too charming, too handsome, too completely masculine, and if her first, epic failure of a marriage had taught her anything, it was that men who were too handsome for their own good were not to be trusted.

'I insist.' His words cut through her hesitations, because, ultimately, he was asking her to join him for tea and surely that was within her job description? What the guests wanted, the guests got—within reason.

'I don't see how that will help you sleep,' she reminded him, gently.

His expression was like a whip cracking. 'Are you refusing?'

Panic had her shaking her head.

*Keep the guest happy, at all costs.*

'Of course not, sir.' She was already walking through the room, towards the sofas. Only one cup had been on the tray—besides, she didn't feel like persimmon tea. But she took a seat near the tray, her hands clasped neatly in her lap. And she waited for him to speak, her nerves stretching tighter and tighter with every silent beat that passed.

'Good.' His nod showed approval but it was hardly relaxing. The differences in their situations were apparent in every way. He was a king, his country renowned for its natural source of both oil and diamonds, making it hugely prosperous, with a chequered history of power-play as foreign forces sought to control both these natural resources for their own financial gain. Perhaps that explained the natural sense of power that exuded from every pore of his; he was a man born to rule a country that required a strong leader.

'Would you like a tea?'

'I think it would be rude to refuse,' she said quietly, but he heard, if the quirk of his brow was anything to go by.

'I have no interest in force-feeding you drinks native to my country. Would you prefer something else? Room service?'

The idea of anyone else seeing her sitting on the sofa talking to the Sheikh was impossible to contemplate.

'I'm fine.'

'You're sitting there as though you're half afraid I'm going to bite you.'

A small smile lifted Daisy's mouth. 'How should I be sitting, sir?'

He took the seat opposite, his own body language relaxed. His legs, long and muscled, were spread wide, and he lifted one arm along the back of the sofa. He looked so completely at home here, in this world of extreme luxury. That was hardly surprising, given he'd undoubtedly been raised in this kind of environment.

'However you would usually sit,' he prompted.

'I'm sorry,' she said, the words quizzical rather than apologetic. 'It's just this has never happened before.'

'No?'

'My job is to provide for your every need without actually being noticed.'

At that, his eyes flared wider, speculation colouring his irises for a heart-racing moment. 'I'm reasonably certain it would be impossible for you to escape anyone's notice.'

Heat rose in her cheeks, colouring them a pale pink that perfectly offset the golden tan of her complexion. She wasn't sure what to say to that, so she stayed quiet.

'Have you worked here long?'

She compressed her lips then stopped when his eyes followed the gesture, tracing the outline of her mouth in a way that made her tummy flip and flop.

'A few years.' She didn't add how hard that had been for her—to finally accept that her long-held dream of attending the Juilliard was beyond reach, once and for all.

'And always in this capacity?'

'I started in general concierge.' She crossed her legs, relaxing back into the seat a little. 'But about six months later, I was promoted to this position.'

'And you enjoy it?'

Of their own accord, her eyes drifted to the view of New York and her fingers tapped her knee, as if playing across the keys of the beloved piano she'd been forced to sell. 'I'm good at it.' She didn't catch the way his features shifted, respect moving over his face.

'How old are you?'

She turned back to face him, wondering how long he intended to keep her sitting there, knowing that it was very much within her job description to humour him even when this felt like an utterly bizarre way to spend her time.

'Twenty-four.'

'And you've always lived in America?'

'Yes.' She bit down on her lower lip thoughtfully. 'I've actually never even been overseas.'

His brows lifted. 'That's unusual, isn't it?'

She laughed softly. 'I don't know. You tell me?'

'It is.'

'Then I guess I'm unusual. Guilty as charged.'

'You don't have any interest in travelling?'

'Not having done something doesn't necessarily equate to a lack of interest,' she pointed out.

'So it's a lack of opportunity, then?'

He was rapier sharp, quickly able to read between the lines of anything she said.

'Yes.' Because there was no point in denying it.

'You work too much?'

'I work a lot,' she confirmed, without elaborating. There was no need to tell this man that she had more debt to her name than she'd likely ever be able to clear. Briefly, anger simmered in her veins, the kind of anger she only ever felt when she thought about one person: her waste-of-space ex-husband Max and the trouble he'd got her into.

'I thought you were guaranteed vacation time in the United States?'

Her smile was carefully constructed to dissuade further questioning along these lines, but, for good measure, she turned the tables on him. 'And you, sir? You travel frequently, I presume?'

His eyes narrowed as he studied her, and she had the strangest feeling he was pulling her apart, little by little, until he could see all the pieces that made her whole.

She held her breath, wondering if he was going to let the matter drop, and was relieved when he did.

'I do. Though never for long, and not lately.' His own features showed a tightness that she instinctively understood spoke of a desire not to be pressed on that matter.

But despite that, she heard herself say gently, 'Your father was ill for a while, before he died?'

The man's face paled briefly. He stood up, walking towards the window, his back rigid, his body tense. Daisy swallowed a curse. What was she thinking, asking something so personal? His father had just died—not even a month ago. She had no business inviting him to open that wound—and for a virtual stranger.

'I'm so sorry.' She stood, following him, bitterly regretting her big mouth. 'I had no right to ask you that. I'm sorry.' When he didn't speak, she swallowed, and said quietly, 'I'll leave you in peace now, Your Highness.'

# CHAPTER TWO

MANHATTAN WAS A vibrant hive of activity beyond the windows of his limousine. He kept his head back against the leather cushioning of his seat, his eyes focussed on nothing in particular.

'That could not have gone better, Your Highness.'

Malik was right. The speech to the United Nations had been a success. As he was talking, he realised that he wasn't the only one in the room who'd experienced anxiety about the importance of this. There was an air of tension, a fear that perhaps with the death of the great Kadir Al Antarah, they were to be plunged back into the days of war and violence that had marked too much of his country's history.

But Sariq was progressive, and Sariq was persuasive. He spoke of Shajarah, the capital of RKH, that had been born from the sands of the desert, its ancient soul nestled amongst the steel and glass monoliths that spoke of a place of the future, a place of promise. He spoke of his country's educational institutions which were free and world-class, of his belief that education was the best prevention for war and violence, that a literate and informed people were less likely to care for ancient wounds. He highlighted what the people of RKH had in common with the rest of the world and when he was finished, there was widespread applause.

Yes, the speech had been a success, but still there was a kernel of discontent within his gut. A feeling of dissatisfaction he couldn't explain.

'Your father would have been proud of you, sir.'

Malik was right about that too.

'When we return to the hotel, have the concierge come to me,' Sariq told Malik. He didn't know her name. That was an oversight he would remedy.

'Is there something you require?'

'She will see to it.'

If Malik thought the request strange, he didn't say anything. The limousine cut east across Manhattan, snagging in traffic near Bryant Park, so Sariq stared from his window at the happy scene there. The day had been warm and New Yorkers had taken to the park to feel the brief respite from the temperature offered by the lush surrounds. He watched as a child reached into the fountain and scooped some water out, splashing it at his older brother, and his chest panged with a sense of acceptance.

Children were as much a part of his future as ruling was. He was the last heir of the Al Antarah line of Kings, a line that had begun at the turn of the last millennia. When he returned to his kingdom and his people, he would focus more seriously on that. He knew the risks if he didn't, the likelihood of civil war that would result from a dangerous fight for the throne of the country.

Marriage, children, these things would absolve him of that worry and would secure his country's future for generations to come.

'You wanted to see me, Your Highness?' Her heart was in her throat. She'd barely slept since she'd left his apartment the night before, despite the fact she'd been rostered off during the day, while he was engaged on official business. That was how it worked when she had high-profile guests. She knew their schedules intimately so she could form her day around their movements, thus ensuring her availability when they were likely to need her.

He was not alone, and he was not as he'd been the night before—dressed simply in jeans and a shirt. Now, he wore a white robe, flowing and long, with gold embellishments on the sleeve, and on his head there was a traditional *keffiyeh* headdress, white and fastened in place with a gold cord. It was daunting and powerful and she found her mouth was completely dry as she regarded him with what she hoped was an impassive expression. That was hard to manage when her knees seemed to have a desire to knock together.

'Yes. One moment.'

His advisors wore similar outfits, though less embellished. It was clear that his had a distinction of royal rank. She stood where she was as they continued speaking in their own language, the words beautiful and musical, the Sheikh's voice discernible amongst all others. It was ten minutes before they began to disband, moving away from the Sheikh, each with a low bow of respect, which he acknowledged with a small nod sometimes, and other times not at all.

His fingers were long and tanned, and on one finger he wore a gold ring with a small, rounded face, like a Super Bowl ring, she thought out of nowhere and smiled at the idea of this man on the football field. He'd probably take to it like a duck to water, if his physique was anything to go by. Beneath those robes, she knew he had the build of a natural athlete.

Great.

Her mouth was dry all over again but this time he was sweeping towards her, his robes flowing behind him. She had only a few seconds to attempt to calm her racing pulse.

When he was a few feet away from her, he paused, so she was caught up in the masculinity of his fragrance, the exotic addictiveness of it—citrus and pine needles, spice and sunshine.

'You were offended last night.'

His words were the last thing she'd expected. Heat bloomed in her cheeks.

'I was too familiar, sir.' She dropped her eyes to the view, unable to look at him, a thousand and one butterflies rampaging wildly inside her belly.

'I invited you to be familiar,' he reminded her so the butterflies gave way to a roller coaster.

'Still…' she lifted her shoulders, risking a glance at him then wishing she hadn't when she discovered his eyes were piercing her own '… I shouldn't have…'

'He had been sick. It was unpleasant to witness. I wished, more than anything, that I could do something to alleviate his pain.' A muscle jerked in his jaw and his eyes didn't shift from hers. 'I have been raised to believe in the full extent of my power, and yet I was impotent against the ravages of his disease. No doctor anywhere could save him, nor really help him.' He didn't move and yet somehow she felt closer to him, as though she'd swayed forward without realising it.

'Your question last night is difficult for me to answer.'

'I'm sorry.'

'Don't be. You didn't do anything wrong.'

Her body was in overdrive, every single sense pulling through her, and she was aware, in the small part of her brain that was capable of rational thought, that this was a completely foreign territory to be in. He was a guest of the hotel—their boundaries were clearly established.

She had to find a way to get them back onto more familiar territory.

'I work for the hotel,' she said quietly. 'Asking you personal questions isn't within my job description, and it's certainly not appropriate. It won't happen again.'

He didn't react to that. He stayed exactly where he was, completely still, like a sentinel, watching her, his eyes trained on her face in a way that made her pulse stutter.

'I asked you to talk with me,' he reminded her finally.

'But I should have declined.'

'Your job is to facilitate my needs, is it not?'

Her heart began to pound against her ribs. 'Within reason.'

His smile showed a hint of something she couldn't interpret. Cynicism? Mockery? Frustration?

'Are you saying that if I ask you to come and sit with me again tonight, you'll refuse?'

Her body was filled with lava, so hot she could barely breathe.

Her eyes were awash with uncertainty. 'I'm not sure it's appropriate.'

'What are you afraid of?'

'Honestly?'

He was watchful.

'I'm afraid of saying the wrong thing. Of offending you. My job is to silently…'

'Yes, yes, you have told me this. To escape notice. And I told you that's not possible. I have already noticed you, Daisy. And having had the pleasure of speaking with you once, I would like to repeat that—with a less abrupt conclusion this time. Are you saying therefore that you won't sit with me?'

Her chest felt as though it had been cracked open. 'Um, yes, I am, I think.' She dropped her eyes to the shining floor.

Because I enjoyed talking to you, too, she amended inwardly, fully aware that she was moving into a territory that was lined with danger.

'But if you're worried you offended me, let me assure you, I am not easily offended,' he offered, and now he smiled, in a way that was like forcing sunshine into a darkened room. Her breath burned in her lungs.

'Frankly, I'd be surprised if you were.'

'Then you can bring me tea tonight. I have a dinner but Malik will send for you when it's done.'

He had no idea what he was doing. The American woman was beautiful, but it had been a long time since Sariq had considered beauty to be a requirement in a woman he was interested in. Besides, he couldn't be seriously interested in her. His duty was clear: to return to the RKH and marry, so that he could begin the process of shoring up his lineage. There were two women whom it would make sense to marry and he would need to choose one, and promptly.

Enjoying the companionship of his hotel's concierge seemed pointless and futile, and yet he found himself turning his attention to his watch every few minutes throughout the state dinner, willing it to be over so he could call for a tray of tea and the woman with eyes the colour of the sky on a winter's morning.

She had asked the kitchen to prepare tea for two, with no further explanation. And even though they had no way of knowing the Sheikh wasn't entertaining in his suite, she felt a flush of guilt as she took the tray, as though surely everyone must know that she was about to cross an invisible line in the sand and socialise with a guest.

Calm down, she insisted to herself as the elevator sped towards the top of the building. It's just tea and conversation, hardly a hanging offence. He was grieving and despite the fact he was surrounded by an entourage, she could easily imagine how lonely his position must be, how refreshing to meet someone who hadn't been indoctrinated into the ways of worshipping at his feet by virtue of the fact that he ruled the land from which they heralded.

This was no different from the other unusual requests she had been asked to fulfil, it was just a lot harder to delegate. He wanted *her*. To talk to her. She couldn't say why—she wasn't particularly interesting, which filled her with anxiety at the job before her, but, for whatever reason, he had been insistent.

She knocked at the door then pushed it inwards. He was standing almost exactly where he'd been the night before, still wearing the robes he had been in earlier that day, though he'd removed the headpiece, so her heart rate trebled. Because he looked so impossibly handsome, so striking with his tanned skin and strong body encased in the crisp white and gold.

It brought out a hint of blond in his hair that she hadn't noticed at first, just a little at the ends, which spoke of a tendency to spend time outdoors.

He walked towards her so she stood completely still, as though her legs were planted to the floor, and when his hands curved around the edges of the tray, it was impossible for them not to brush hers. A jolt of electricity burst through her, splitting her into a thousand pieces so she had to work hard not to visibly react.

'I'm pleased you came.'

He stood there, watching her, for a beat too long and then took the tray, placing it on the coffee table.

'The first reference to persimmon tea comes from one of our earliest texts. In the year forty-seven AD, a Bedouin tribe brought it as a gift to the people of the west of my country. Their skill with harvesting the fruit late in the season and drying them in such a way as to preserve the flavour made them popular with traders.'

He poured some into a cup and held it in front of him, waiting, a small smile on his lips that did funny things to her tummy.

She forced her legs to carry her across the room, a tight smile of her own crossing her expression as she took the teacup. 'Thank you.'

He was watching her and so she took a small sip, her eyes widening at the flavour. 'It's so sweet. Like honey.'

He made a throaty noise of agreement. 'Picked at the right time, persimmons are sweet. Dried slowly, that intensifies, until you get this.'

She took another sip, her insides warming to the flavour. It was like drinking happiness. Why had she resisted so long?

'Are you going to have some?'

'I don't feel like sleeping tonight.'

Her stomach lurched and she chattered the cup against the

saucer a little too loudly, shooting him a look that was half apology, half warning.

She had to keep this professional. It was imperative that she not forget who she was, who he was, and why her job mattered so much to her. She was lucky with this position. She earned a salary that was above and beyond what she could have hoped, by virtue of her untarnished ability to provide exemplary customer service. One wrong move and her reputation would suffer, so too would her job, potentially, and she couldn't jeopardise that.

It helped to imagine her manager in the room, observing their conversation. If she pictured Henry watching, she could keep things professional and light, she could avoid the gravitational pull that seemed to be dragging on her.

'You were at the United Nations today, sir?'

A quirk shifted his lips, but he nodded. 'It was my first official speech as ruler of the RKH.'

'How did it go?'

He gestured towards the sofa, inviting her to sit. She chose one side, crossing her legs primly and placing the cup and saucer on her knee, holding it with both hands.

He took the seat beside her, not opposite, so she was aware of his every movement, the shift of his body dragging on the cushions on the sofa, inadvertently pulling her towards him.

'I was pleased with the reception.'

She sipped her tea, forcing herself to relax. 'I can't imagine having to do that,' she confided with a small smile. After all, he wanted to talk to her—sitting there like a petrified automaton wasn't particularly conversational. 'I'm terrible at public speaking. I hate it. I feel everyone's eyes burning me and just want to curl up in a ball for ever.'

'It's a skill you can learn.'

'Perhaps. But fortunately for me, I don't need to.'

Silence prickled at their sides.

She spoke to fill it. 'I don't feel like you would have needed to do much learning there.'

He frowned. 'I don't understand.'

'Sorry, that wasn't clear.' She shook her head. 'I just mean you were probably born with this innate ability to stand in front of a group of people and enthral them.'

She clamped her mouth shut, wishing she hadn't come so close to admitting that she was a little bit enthralled by him.

He smiled though, in a way that relaxed her and warmed her. 'I was born knowing my destiny. I was born to be Sheikh, ruler of my people, and, as such, never imagined what it would be like to...avoid notice.' His eyes ran over her face speculatively, so even as she was relaxing, she was also vibrating in a way that was energising and demanding.

'I don't think you'd be very good at it.'

'At being Sheikh?'

'At avoiding notice.'

'Nor are you, so this we have in common.'

Heat spread through her veins like wildfire.

'I don't think you see me clearly,' she said after a moment.

'No?'

'I'm very good at not being seen.'

His laugh was husky. 'It's quite charming that you think so.'

She shook her head a little. 'I don't really understand...'

'You are a beautiful young woman with hair the colour of desert sand and eyes like the sky. Even in this boxy uniform, you are very, very noticeable.'

She stared at him for several seconds, pleasure at war with uncertainty. Remember Max, she reminded herself. He'd noticed her. He'd praised her, flattered her, and she'd fallen for it so fast she hadn't stopped to heed any of the warning signs. And look how that had turned out!

'Thank you.' It was stiff, an admonishment.

He laughed. 'You are not good with compliments.'

She bit down on her lip, their situation troubling her, pulling on her. 'I should go.'

He reached a hand out, pressing it to her knee. Her skin

glowed where he'd touched her, filling her with a scattering sensation of pins and needles. 'No more compliments,' he promised. 'Tell me about yourself, Daisy Carrington.'

Her eyes flared wide. 'How do you know my surname?'

'I asked my chief of security.'

'How…?'

'All hotel staff are independently vetted by my agencies,' he explained, as though that were no big deal.

Her lips parted. 'Then I suspect you know more about me than I realised.'

'It's not comprehensive,' he clarified. 'Your name, date of birth, any links to criminal activity.' He winked. 'You were clear, by the way.'

Despite herself, she smiled. 'I'm pleased to hear it.'

'May I call you Daisy?'

'So long as you don't expect me to call you anything other than Your Highness,' she quipped.

'Very well. So, Daisy? Before you started working here, what did you do?'

Her stomach clenched. Remembered pain was there, pushing against her. She thought of her marriage, her divorce, her acceptance to the Juilliard, and pushed them all away. 'This and that.' A tight smile, showing more than she realised.

'Which tells me precisely nothing.'

'I worked in hospitality.'

'And it's what you have always wanted to do?'

The question hurt. She didn't talk about her music. It was too full of pain—pain remembering her father, and the way he'd sat beside her, moving her fingers over the keys until they learned the path themselves, the way she'd stopped playing the day he'd left. And then, when her mother was in her low patches, the way Daisy had begun to play again—it was the only thing she had responded to.

'It's what I gravitated to.'

'Another answer that tells me nothing.'

Because she was trying to obfuscate but he was too clever for that. What was the harm in being honest with him? He had reserved this suite for four nights—this was his second. He would be gone soon and she'd never see him again.

'I wanted to be a concert pianist, actually.'

He went very still, his eyes hooked to hers, waiting, watching. And she found the words spilling out of her even when she generally made a habit of not speaking them. After all, what good could come from reliving a fantasy lost?

'My father was a jazz musician. He taught me to play almost from infancy. I would sit beside him and he would arrange my fingers, and when we weren't playing, we would listen to music, so I was filled with its unique language, all the beats that mixed together to make a song, to tell a story and weave a narrative with their melody. I love all types of music, but classical is my favourite. I lose myself in Chopin and Mozart, so that I'm barely conscious of the passage of time.'

He stared at her, his surprise evident, and with little wonder. It was as though the words had burst from her, so full of passion and memory, so alive with her love and regrets.

'Do you play?'

A beat passed, a silence, as he contemplated this. 'No. My mother did, and very well.' Another pause, and, though his expression didn't shift, she had a feeling he was choosing his words with care. 'After she died, my father had all the pianos removed from the palace. He couldn't bear to hear them played. Music was not a big part of my upbringing.'

Her heart twisted in her chest. The pain of losing a mother was one she was familiar with. 'How old were you?'

A tight smile. 'Seven.'

The tightness in her chest increased. 'I'm sorry.'

He nodded. 'As am I. Her death was a grief from which my father never recovered.'

'The flipside to a great love.'

'Speaking from experience?'

Her denial was swift and visceral. 'No.'

Though she'd been married, she could see now that she'd never loved Max. She'd felt grateful to him, glad to have someone in her life after her mother's death.

'My mom died five years ago, and not a day passes when I don't think of her in some small way. At this time of year, when the sunflowers in the street are all in bloom, I ache to take photos for her. She loved that, you know. *"Only in New York would you get sunflowers as street plantings."*' Her smile was wistful.

'How did she…?'

Daisy's throat thickened unexpectedly. 'A car accident.' She didn't elaborate—that her mother had been responsible. That she'd driven into a lamppost after drinking half a bottle of gin.

They sat in silence for several moments, but it was no longer a prickly, uncomfortable silence. On the contrary, Daisy felt an odd sense of peace wrap around her, a comfortable fog that made her want to stay exactly where she was.

It was the warning she needed, and she jolted herself out of her silent reflection, forcing herself to stand.

'I really should go, sir. It's late and I'm sure you have more important things to do than talk to me.'

As with the night before, he didn't try to stop her. She ignored the kernel of disappointment and stalked to the door, pulling it inwards. But before leaving him, she turned back to regard him over her shoulder.

'Goodnight, Your Highness. Sleep well.'

# CHAPTER THREE

'HE'S ASKING FOR YOU.'

Daisy had just walked in through the door of the hotel, and she shot a glance at her watch. It was after ten o'clock at night. The Sheikh was supposed to be at a party until midnight. She'd come in early to settle her nerves, and to mentally prepare her excuses in case he called for her to come and talk to him again.

Henry grimaced apologetically. 'He seems more demanding than most.'

'No, he's not really.'

'You sure? You could get Amy to take care of him. She's already been up there a few times today.'

Daisy thought of the woman who'd been recruited to shadow Daisy, taking care of Daisy's clients when Daisy couldn't. Instinctively, she pushed the idea aside.

'He's a very important guest, Henry. It should be me. You should have called.'

'I don't want you getting burned out, love. You can't work around the clock. We can't afford to lose you.'

'I'm fine.' Her heart twisted in her chest. She'd been buzzing with a heady sense of anticipation all day, waiting to see him, wondering if he'd call for her, or if wisdom and sense would have prevailed so that he woke up and wondered why the heck he was bothering to spend so much time talking to a servant.

'When did he call?'

'An hour ago.'

Panic lurched through her. 'Why didn't you page me?'

'He said to tell you to go up when you arrived. I knew you wouldn't be long…'

'Henry,' she wailed, shaking her head. 'What if it was something urgent?'

'Then that Malik man would have made himself known.' Henry exaggerated a shudder. 'He has no problems demanding whatever the hell he wants, when he wants it.'

That was true. Up until recently, all the requests had come from Malik. 'I'll go up now.'

She reached for the buzzer, to order some persimmon tea, but the kitchen informed her the Presidential suite had already requested dinner. 'It should only be another few minutes.'

'I thought he was at a function.'

'Dunno,' came the unhelpful response, so Daisy frowned as she disconnected the call. Double-checking her appearance in the mirror, she wished her cheeks weren't so pink, nor her eyes so shining with obvious pleasure. The truth was, she couldn't wait to see him, and that was dangerous.

Because he was going home soon, and, even if he weren't, he was just a client. A client who was developing a habit of asking for her in the evenings.

She took the service elevator to the top floor, so the doors whooshed inwards and she knocked once. Before she could step inside, the door was pulled inwards and Sariq stood on the other side. He was wearing more familiar clothes this time—a pair of dark jeans and a white tee shirt with a vee at the neck that revealed a hint of curls at his throat.

Damn it, out of nowhere she found herself wondering how far down his hair went, imagining him without his shirt, and that made it almost impossible to keep a veneer of professionalism on her face.

'Thank you for coming.'

'It's my job,' she reminded him.

He didn't move, but his eyes glowed with something that could have been amusement and could have been cynicism. If it was the latter, she didn't have to wonder at why: it was pretty obvious that her being there had very little to do with her professional obligations.

'I thought you had something on tonight.'

'It didn't last as long as the schedule had allowed,' he said simply, drawing the door open without stepping far enough aside, so in order to enter the suite, she had to brush past him, and the second their bodies connected she felt a rush of awareness that was impossible to ignore. Instinctively, her face lifted to his and she saw the raw speculation there; the same interest that flooded her veins was rushing through his. Her knees shuddered and heat pooled between her legs, making thought, speech and movement almost impossible.

He stood so close, their bodies were touching. Just lightly, but enough, and even when Daisy knew she should move, or say something, she couldn't. She could only stare at him. His face was like thunder, but his eyes were all flame. She could feel the war being raged within him, a battle to control his desire, and she didn't want him to. This was madness. It was sheer, uncontrollable madness—and she had a billion reasons to resist. Max was the main one—her experience with him had warned her off tempestuous affairs for life. But she'd married Max, she'd pledged to love him and trust him, to spend the rest of her life with him. That had been her mistake. The Sheikh was only in New York for two more nights, including this one.

But he was a guest in the hotel! A seriously important guest, and she couldn't afford to have anything go wrong. She swallowed, taking a step backwards, except she forgot there was a piece of furniture there and her hip jabbed into it, shunting her sideways, so she might have fallen if he hadn't pushed a hand out, confidently, easily righting her. Her eyes were alarmed as they lifted to his and stuck there like glue, and when he took a step towards her, she couldn't look away.

Her heart was hammering against her ribs so hard and fast that she was surprised he couldn't see its frantic movements against her breasts. If she pushed up onto the tips of her toes, if she lifted her face, oh, God, she wanted to kiss him. The realisation was like fire, even when she knew it should have doused her desire, that it should have dragged her back to reality and put a halt to this foolishness.

But was it so foolish? Daisy had played it safe for so long and, suddenly, she was sick of it. Sick of playing it safe, of being careful with whom she trusted. It was as though she second-guessed her instincts so often that they'd grown blunt.

'Your Highness...' She wasn't sure what she wanted to say, only that they were standing so close, staring at one another, sensual heat heavy in the air around them, and she wanted to act on it. She wanted him.

But he frowned, his eyes darkening, even as he dropped his head closer. 'I asked you here to show you something.'

Neither of them moved.

'What is it?'

He lifted a hand, as though he couldn't resist, pressing his thumb and forefinger to her chin so he could hold her face where it was, lifted towards him. The contact was so personal, it felt as though they'd crossed a line they couldn't uncross. They could no longer pretend this wasn't happening. They were acknowledging the pull that ran between them.

'I wasn't going to do this.'

'Do what?'

With his body in the door frame, he dropped his head by a matter of degrees, so there was ample time for her to move, to say something, to stop this. She didn't. She stayed where she was, her face held in his fingers, her body swaying a little closer to his so her breasts brushed his chest and, through the fine fabric of his shirt and her blouse, she was sure he must feel the hardening of her nipples, the way they strained against her lace bra.

'I swore I wouldn't.' And then, his mouth claimed hers, his kiss fierce, filled with all the passion of having fought this, of having felt desire and resisted it for as long as he was able.

It was a kiss born of need and it surged inside her, his lips pushing hers apart, his tongue driving into her mouth, his other hand lifting and pushing into her hair, his fingers cradling her head, holding her against him so he could plunder her mouth, tasting her, his body so big and broad compared to hers that she felt utterly enveloped by him, swallowed by his strength and power, her senses subsumed completely by this.

It was a kiss of oblivion, so consuming that she didn't hear the dinging of the lift doors. She was lost completely in this moment but he wasn't. He broke the kiss swiftly, his body in the door frame concealing her. 'Go to my room.' His eyes held a warning that she heeded even when nothing made sense and her body could scarcely move. She'd been in the suite enough times to know where the master bedroom was. She ran there, pushing the door shut except for an inch, so she could peer out.

She saw members of the kitchen team walk into the apartment, each pausing to bow for the Sheikh, before moving to the table and setting it. Sariq's eyes chased hers, down the corridor, so she moved away from the door, pressing her back against a wall and closing her eyes, needing her heart to slow down, her breathing to return to normal. She lifted her fingers to her lips; they were sensitive to the touch.

She was grateful beyond belief for his quick thinking. If it had been up to her, she would have stayed where she was, and someone from the staff would have seen her and rumours would have been flying. His quick response had saved her from that embarrassment. What would Henry say? Mortified, she fanned her face and tucked her shirt in more tightly—it had become loose at her waist, and she paced the room as she waited. It didn't take long. A few minutes and then she heard the click of a door, the turning of a lock, and they were alone once more.

She pulled the door to his bedroom open, moving into the lounge area to find him uncorking a bottle of wine and pouring two glasses. His eyes, when they met hers, were loaded with speculation.

'I ordered us dinner.'

Her eyes moved to the table. Surprise usurped whatever she'd been feeling a moment ago. 'You did? Why?'

His smile was without humour. 'Because we have to eat.'

She sighed heavily. 'I don't have to eat with you, though, Your Highness.'

'I can taste your kiss in my mouth,' he murmured. 'Don't you think it's time you called me something else?'

His words were so evocative but she shook her head. 'You're my client. That should never have happened…'

He paced across the room, handing her the wine glass. She took it without taking a drink. He stayed close to her, his body's contact intimate and loaded with promise. 'It shouldn't,' he agreed, after a moment. 'But it did, and I think we both know it will happen again. And again. So let's stop pretending we don't want this.'

Her eyes flared wide. Need punctured sense almost completely—but not quite. 'I can't afford to lose my job.'

She felt his naked speculation. 'Do you think I'm going to jeopardise that?'

'Socialising with clients is strictly forbidden. It's actually in my contract. And what we just did goes way beyond socialising.'

'I have my own reasons for requiring discretion,' he said firmly. 'Whatever happens between us, no one will know.'

*Whatever happens between us.* The words glowed with promise. Her insides quivered.

'Nothing can happen.'

'Why not?'

'I told you, my job…' but she wasn't even convincing herself.

'And I told you, no one will find out. Do you have a boyfriend?'

'No.' How long had it been since she'd been with a man? That was easy. Max. He was her only lover. He'd been her first, and when they'd divorced three years ago, she thought he'd be her last.

'I think you want me.' His words held a challenge. He took her wine glass from her, sipping from it and then placing it on the table to his left. His eyes glowed with the same challenge as he lifted his fingers to the top button of her blouse.

'I am going to undo these buttons very slowly, giving you plenty of time to ask me to stop. If you say the word, then it's over. You can go away again.' He did as he'd promised, his fingers working deftly to undo the first button, so she felt a brush of air against her skin. Then the next, exposing the top of her lace bra. The next revealed the midsection of the bra and, with the next button, the shirt gaped enough to reveal it completely. At the last button, his fingers slowed.

'You haven't asked me to stop.'

Her eyes were awash with feelings. 'I know that.'

'I want to make love to you.'

'I know that too.'

He turned towards the table. 'Are you hungry?'

She shook her head.

'You don't want anything to eat?'

Another shift of her head to indicate 'no'.

'What do you want, Daisy?'

The final button was separated, so her shirt fell apart completely.

She opened her mouth, but found it hard to frame any words.

'Do you want to know what I want?' he murmured, dropping his head to whisper the words against the sensitive flesh at the base of her throat.

'I think I can guess.' And despite the heavy pulsing of emotion that was filling the room, she smiled, because it was easy to smile in that moment.

He smiled back, but it was dredged from deep within him, so it cut across his face, his lips like a blade.

His grief was palpable. It had been since the first moment they'd met and it was there now, tormenting him, so that this physical act of sensuality took on a new imperative. She understood the power sex held, the power to obliterate grief and pain, even if only for a moment.

Wasn't it her own grief that had made her so vulnerable to Max? He'd promised respite from her sadness and she'd ignored all the warning signs to grab that respite. Was Sariq doing the same thing now?

Should she be putting a halt to this to save him from regret?

His fingers were on the straps of her bra, easing them down her arms so tiny goose bumps danced where his fingertips touched, and his eyes were on her breasts as he pushed aside the scrap of lace, so she felt a burning heat in her chest and a tingling in her nipples, an ache that begged him to touch her, to feel the weight of her breasts in his palms, to touch her nipples, to kiss them.

Her back swayed forward, the invitation silent but imperative, and he understood, lifting his hands to her hips first, bracing her waist as he drew his touch upwards, along her sides until his thumbs swept beneath her breasts and she tipped her head back a little on a plea, biting down on her lip to stop what she knew would be incoherent babbling, the kind of babbling brought on by a form of madness.

'I need you to tell me you want this.' He drew his kiss from her lips to her throat, flicking the pulse point there, dragging his stubbled jaw across her sensitive flesh. She pushed her body forward, her hips moving from side to side, her hands pushing his shirt up so her fingertips could run over his chest. God, his chiselled, firm chest. Her nails drew along the ridges of each muscular bump, running higher so her hands curved over his shoulders, feeling the warmth of his flesh and the beating of his heart against her forearm.

'Daisy?' It was a groan and a plea. His body was tense. He was waiting for her to say that she wanted this and something inside her trembled, because it was such a mark of respect and decency. It wasn't that she hadn't expected it from Sariq, it was that she hadn't known to expect it from anybody. Max had been… She didn't want to think about Max in that moment. He'd already taken so much from her, she wasn't going to give him this moment too. It was hers, hers and Sariq's.

'I want this.' The words blurted out of her. And then, more gently, but the same bone-melting urgency. 'I want *you.*' She couldn't resist adding, with an impish smile: 'Your Highness.'

He lifted a brow, his lips quirking in a smile that was impulsive and so sexy. But he swallowed and the smile disappeared, his expression serious once more. 'I have to go back to the RKH as scheduled. I cannot offer more than this.'

Another sign of respect. Her heart felt all warm and gooey and her voice was husky. 'I know that.' She showed her acceptance by pushing up and kissing him, by wrapping her arms around his waist, holding him close to her body so she could feel the force of his urgent need through their clothing. 'Take me to bed, sir.'

*'Take me to bed, sir.'*

He didn't need to be asked again. He lifted her up, cradling her against his chest as he carried her through the suite and into the master bedroom. He didn't pause to turn on a light, though he would love to have revelled in her beauty, staring at her as he pleasured her: there'd be time for that. Having abandoned himself to this, he intended to enjoy her all night. He knew this would be the last time he acted on impulses such as this, the last time he allowed himself to be simply a man and not a king. Soon he would announce his engagement and he would be faithful to the bride of his choosing.

Until then though, there was this, and he was going to enjoy it. He disposed of her clothes quickly, no longer able to pace himself; he needed to feel every inch of her beneath him. Her legs were smooth and slender. He ran his palms over her flesh as he stripped her of the uniform she wore, acknowledging to himself he'd wanted to do exactly that from the first moment he'd seen her. His own clothes followed next so he stood above her naked. The room was dark but he could make out her silhouette against the bed, her blonde hair shimmering gold in the darkness. He brought the full weight of his body down on hers, his arousal pressing between her legs so, for the briefest moment, he fantasised about taking her like that. No protection, no preamble, just white-hot possession.

She arched her back and lifted her legs around his waist, drawing him towards her, as though she wanted that too. He kissed her, hard, his tongue doing to her mouth what his body wished it could do in that moment, and she met his kiss with every stroke, pushing her body up onto her elbows, wanting more of him, needing him in the way he needed her. Her feet at his back were insistent, pushing him towards her, so he let just his tip press to her sex, her hot, wet body welcoming him in a way he knew he had to control. He swore in his own language, pulling away from her with effort, his breathing ragged.

'Wait.' He stood up and her cry was an animalistic sound of disbelief, her need reaching out and wrapping around him. 'One moment,' he reassured her, moving to the adjoining bathroom and pulling a condom out of a travel bag. He didn't make a habit of this—he couldn't remember the last time he'd slept with a woman he'd just met—but he was always prepared, regardless.

Striding back into the room, he pushed the rubber over his length as he went, inviting no further delay to this. Her eyes were difficult to make out in this darkness but he thought he saw a hint of apology in the light thrown from the bathroom.

'I forgot,' she explained, reaching for him.

'I almost did too.'

'Thank you. For remembering.'

He kissed her more gently, reassuringly, parting her thighs with his palm and locking himself against her, as he had been before. She lifted her hips and this time, he didn't hold himself back. He drove his cock into her, his hands digging into her hips to hold her steady as he took control of her body and made her, completely, his.

# CHAPTER FOUR

IT WAS A pleasure unlike any she'd ever known. Her breathing was heavy as she lay on his bed, waiting for sanity, normality, reason to intrude. Her orgasm—no, her *orgasms*, because he'd driven her over the edge of pleasure several times in a row—was still dissipating, her body felt heavy and weak at the same time as strong beyond belief, and his body, spent at last, was heavy on hers, his own breathing torn from him with silent torment. She ran her fingernails down his back, his skin warm and smooth, curving over his buttocks, and she smiled like the cat that'd got the cream.

Professionally, this had the potential to be a complete disaster, but in that moment, she didn't care. She pushed up and kissed his shoulder, tasting salt there and moaning softly. He was still inside her and she felt him respond, his beautiful cock jerking at her kiss. A sense of power swelled inside her, because he was as much of a slave to this as she was.

'I…didn't think that would happen when I came here tonight,' she said, when finally her breathing had slowed sufficiently to enable her to speak.

He pushed up on one elbow, so she could make out the features of his face against the darkness of the room. 'Do you regret it?'

'Nope.'

His teeth were white, so she could see them in his smile. 'Me neither.' He dropped a kiss to one of her temples and then pushed away from her, standing and striding towards the bathroom. When he opened the door, more light flooded the room. She was so familiar with its décor but now she saw it through new eyes—and always would. He would leave soon, and someone else would occupy this suite of rooms, but the rooms would be overlaid with ghosts of her time with the Sheikh of the RKH for ever.

'I've never done this before,' she blurted out, hating the thought of him believing this was a regular occurrence for her. He reappeared, a towel wrapped around his waist, and now he reached for the wall and flicked a light on, so she was stark naked against the crisp white hotel sheets. She reached for the quilt, at the foot of the bed, pulling it up to cover herself.

'Don't.' And he was imperious, a ruler of a country, his command used to being obeyed. She stilled, her eyes lifting to his. 'I want to see you.'

Her mouth went dry, her throat completely thick, as he stood where he was but let his eyes feast upon her body. And she let him, remaining where she was, naked and exposed, her flesh marked with patches of red from where his stubbled jaw had grated against her, or where his mouth had kissed and sucked her flesh until it grew pink. Her cheeks were warm but still she stayed where she was, grateful there was no mirror within eye line that could show her the picture she made, or self-consciousness might have dictated that she ignore him and seek cover.

But she wouldn't have anyway, because the look in his face was so loaded with admiration and pleasure, with need and desire, that she could do nothing but lie there and watch him enjoy her. It was ridiculous, given how completely he'd satisfied her, but desire began to roll through her like an unrelenting wave, so she was full of want for him all over again.

It was so different from how she'd felt about Max. When

they'd made love it had been…nice, at best. He hadn't ever driven her to orgasm, and he sure as heck hadn't seemed to care. But the closeness had been welcome, and she'd been too caught up in his lies by then to question whether it was enough for her.

'I didn't know it could be like this,' she whispered, unable to hold his eyes at the admission. She heard him approaching her, then felt his hands reaching for hers, pulling her to a sitting position first then to stand in front of him.

'No?' A gravelled question, his eyes roaming her face. She kept her gaze focussed to the right of his shoulder.

She didn't feel any need to obfuscate the truth with this man, even when the difference in their experience level might have rationally caused her to feel a little immature and embarrassed. 'My ex…my ex-husband…and I weren't exactly…we never… it wasn't like this.' She finished with a frustrated shake of her head. 'Now I get what all the fuss is about.'

He was very still, his Adam's apple jerking in his throat. 'You were married?'

'A long time ago.'

'You're twenty-four years old. It can't have been that long…'

'I left him a week after my twenty-first birthday.' Some present. Finding that her bank accounts had been emptied, and a mortgage taken out on her mother's home. All the security she'd thought she'd had, after her mother's death, had evaporated alongside the marriage she'd believed to be a decent one.

He lifted his hands, cupping her cheeks, and now when she looked at him he was staring at her in that magical way of his, as though he could read her mind when she wasn't speaking.

'Do you want to talk about it?'

'No.' She smiled to soften the blunt refusal. 'He took enough from me. I don't want to let him into this, with you.'

Curiosity flared in his gaze, and anger too, but not directed at her. It was the opposite. She felt his anger directed at Max and it was somehow bonding and reassuring—in that the whole 'enemy of my enemy is my friend' kind of way.

'He was a bastard,' she said, the small elaboration a courtesy, more than anything. 'I'm better off without him.'

His nod was short. 'The food will be cold. Are you hungry?'

'I have no objection to cold food,' she assured him quickly. 'Besides, I'd rather not be interrupted.'

He expelled a slow breath, a sound of relief. 'I'm glad you're not planning on running away again.'

She lifted a brow. 'I think you've given me incentive to stick around. At least for a little while.'

His laugh was husky. He weaved his fingers through hers and drew her towards the door of the bedroom but she stopped walking. 'My clothes.' He was, after all, wearing a towel around his hips.

He paused, turning to face her thoughtfully before dropping her hand and pacing to the pile of fabric on the floor. He liberated her silk underpants, crossing to her and crouching at her feet, holding them for her to step into. She pressed a hand to his shoulder to steady herself, and he eased the underwear up her legs. But at her thighs, he paused, bringing his head forward and pressing a kiss to the top, so she trembled against him and might have lost her balance were it not for the grip on his shoulder. She felt his smile against her flesh.

Another kiss, nearer her womanhood, and then his mouth was there, his tongue pressing against her sex until he found her most sensitive cluster of nerves and tormented it with his ministrations, tasting her, teasing her, sucking her until she exploded in a blinding explosion. She dug her nails into his skin and she cried into the room, pleasure making her incoherent.

He lifted his head, his eyes on hers, his expression impossible to discern, and then he lifted her underpants into place, standing as he did so.

'No more clothes.'

Her heart was racing too fast to permit her to speak.

'I like looking at you.'

The words were delivered with the power that she knew came

instinctively to him, and even when there was a part of her that might have felt self-conscious, his obvious admiration drove that away, so she shrugged, incapable of speaking.

'Good.' His approval warmed her. 'Come and eat.'

She was surprisingly hungry, so the feast he'd ordered was a welcome surprise. She hadn't seen it being delivered and unpacked, but it looked as though he'd had a feast of foods prepared, their exotic fragrance making her mouth water.

'Delicacies from the RKH,' he explained. 'Fish with okra and spice.' He pointed to one dish. 'Lamb with olives and couscous, chicken and pomegranate, spinach and raisin flat bread, and aubergine and citrus tagine.'

'Wow.' She stared at the banquet. 'This was just for you?'

'I suspected you'd join me.'

She laughed softly. 'Am I that predictable?'

'I'm that determined,' he corrected softly, running a finger over her arm so she trembled with sensations. 'I wanted you from the moment I saw you.'

'And you always get what you want?'

Darkness coloured his expression for a moment and she could have kicked herself. He was grieving his father's premature death—obviously that wasn't the case.

'Not always, no.'

She nodded, glad he didn't elaborate. 'What should I try first?'

'The lamb is a favourite of mine.' He gestured towards the plate. She moved towards it, inhaling the heady mix of fragrances the table conveyed. Contrary to his prediction, the food was only warm, not cold, which made it easier to taste. She scooped a small heaping of each onto her plate, only remembering she was naked when she sat down and her breasts pressed against the edge of the table. Heat flushed through her and she jerked her gaze to his to find him watching her intently.

She shovelled some food into her mouth to hide the flush of self-consciousness, and sharply forgot to feel anything except admiration for this meal. 'It's delicious,' she murmured, as soon as she'd swallowed.

'I'm glad you think so.'

'I don't know much about your country,' she apologised. 'And I had no idea the food was so good.'

'There are two RKH restaurants in Manhattan,' he said with a lift of one brow.

'Really?'

He nodded. 'One off Wall Street and one in mid-town. This food came from the latter.'

'It wasn't prepared here?'

'No offence to your hotel staff, but RKH cooking is a slow process. Much done in the tagine, which takes hours. There are also a range of spices used that don't tend to be readily available in your kitchens.'

'Still, if we know in advance we can generally arrange anything.'

'RKH food cannot be easily faked.' He winked. 'Better to stick to chefs who prepare it as a matter of course, rather than try to imitate it.'

'You sound incredibly patriotic,' she murmured with a small grin.

'I'm the King—that's my job.'

'Right.' *The King.* A curse filled her brain as the enormity of what she'd done flooded her.

'Don't run away.' He spoke quietly, but with that same tone of command she'd heard from him a few times now. It was instinctive to him—a man who'd been born to rule.

'I'm...not.'

'You were thinking about it.'

She didn't bother denying it. 'It's just...you're a king. I can't... even imagine what your life is like.' She looked around the apartment, a small frown on her face. 'I guess it's like this, but on crack.'

'On crack?'

'You know, to the nth degree.'

He followed her gaze thoughtfully. 'My palace bears little resemblance to this apartment.'

'No?'

'For one thing, there is not a ceiling in the palace that is so low.'

A smile quirked his lips and her heart stammered. He was teasing her. She took another bite of the dinner, this time sampling the fish and okra. He was right. Now that she paid a little more attention, she could taste the difference. The spices were unusual—unlike anything she'd ever known. She doubted even the kitchens in this prestigious hotel could replicate these flavours.

'What is it like?'

'The palace?'

'The palace, the country. I know very little about where you're from,' she confessed. 'Only the basics I researched prior to your arrival.'

'Is this a normal part of your job?'

She nodded. 'I research what I think might be necessary before any guest's arrival. Sometimes that's just their favourite foods or hotel habits, other times it's who they have restraining orders against.' She smiled. 'It depends.'

'And for me?'

Her stomach squeezed as she remembered looking at his photo on the Internet. Even then, she'd desired him. 'The basics,' she said vaguely. 'But nothing that told me of your country or your duties.'

He nodded, apparently satisfied. 'The RKH is one of the most beautiful places you could ever see. Ancient, but in a way that is visible everywhere you look. Our cities are built on the foundations of our past and we honour that. Ruins are left where they stand, surrounded by the modernity that is our life now. High-rise office buildings mingle with stone relics, ancient tapestries hang proudly in these new constructions—a reminder that we are of our past.'

A shiver ran down her spine, his language evocative. 'We are of our land, shaped by the trials of our deserts and the faraway ocean. Our people were nomadic for generations and our desert life is still a large pull, culturally. It is not unusual to take months out of your routine to go into the desert and live nomadically for a time.'

'Do you do this?'

'I cannot,' he admitted. 'Not for months at a time, but yes, Daisy, for days I will escape the palace and move into the wild, untamed desert. There is something energising about pitting myself against its organic tests. Out there, I am just a man; my rank counts for nothing.'

His eyes dropped to her breasts and she felt, very strongly, that he was a man—all man. Desire slicked through her, and her knees trembled beneath the tabletop. She pushed some more food into her mouth, not meeting his eyes.

'Our people were peaceful for centuries, but globalisation and trade brought a new value to resources we took for granted. The RKH stands on one of the greatest oil sources in the world, and there are caves to the west that abound with diamonds and other rare and precious gems. The world's interest in these resources carried a toll, and took a long time to adapt to. We were mired in civil war for a hundred years, and that war led to hostilities with the west.' His face was tense; she felt the weight of his worries, the strength of his concern.

'My father was instrumental in bringing peace to my people. He worked tirelessly to contain our armed forces, to unify our military under his banner, to bring about loyalty from the most powerful families who had historically tilted for the rule of the country. He commanded loyalty.' He paused, sipping his water. 'He was…irreplaceable.'

She considered that. 'But peace has been long-established in the RKH. Surely you don't feel that there's a risk of war now?'

'There is always a risk of war,' he responded quickly, with a quiet edge to his voice. And she felt the weight of responsibility he carried on his shoulders. 'But I was raised to avert it. My whole life has been geared towards a peacemaking process, both within the borders of my land and on the world stage.'

'How does one man do that?'

He was reflective and, when he spoke, there was a grim setting to his handsome features. 'In many different ways.' He regarded her thoughtfully. 'Why didn't you become a concert pianist?'

The change of subject was swift but she allowed it. 'Reality intervened.' She said it with a smile, careful to keep the crushing disappointment from her voice—a disappointment that still had the power to rob her of breath.

'Oh?'

She took another bite of her meal—the last on her plate—and waited until she'd finished before answering. 'The Juilliard is expensive. Even on the partial scholarship I was offered, there's New York's cost of living.'

'And you couldn't afford it?'

Before Max, she could have. Easily. Her mother's inheritance had made sure of that. 'No.' A smile that cost her to dredge up. 'It was a pipe dream, in the end.'

He nodded, frowning, then stood. 'I asked you here tonight because I wanted to show you something.'

'Not because you wanted to drag me to bed?' She teased, glad to move the conversation to a more level ground.

'Well, that too.' He held a hand out to her. 'Come.'

It didn't even occur to her not to do as he said. She stood, putting her hand in his, aware of how well they fitted together, moving behind him, her near-nakedness only adding to her awareness of him. The Presidential suite was, as you might expect, enormous. In addition to the main living and dining area, there was a saloon and bar, furnished with the finest alcohol, a wall of classic literature titles, several in German and Japanese to cater to the international guests and now, a baby grand piano in its centre. Her heart began to speed for an entirely different reason now. Anxiety, longing, remorse. She lifted her gaze to him to find that he was watching her.

'That's a Kleshnër.'

He lifted a brow.

'The type of piano.' She moved towards it, as if drawn by an invisible piece of string. 'They're made in Berlin, only forty or so a year. They're considered to be the gold standard.' She ran her finger over the lid, the wood smooth and glossy. Her heart skipped a beat.

'Play something for me.'

She jolted her eyes to his.

'I want to hear you.'

She bit down on her lip, letting her finger touch the keys. How long had it been? Too long. Her insides ached to do as he said, to make music from ivory and ebony, to create sound in this room. But the legacy of her past held her where she was, the pain that was so intrinsic to her piano playing all bound together.

'You are afraid.'

The words inspired a complex response. She shook her head a little. 'Not really. It's just…been a very long time.'

His eyes narrowed speculatively, laced with an unspoken question. 'Play for me.'

She moved around behind the piano, staring first at the keys and then at his face, and it was the speculation she saw there that had her taking a seat behind the piano, her fingers hovering above the keys for several seconds.

'What would you like to hear?'

'Surprise me.'

She nodded again, and then, a small smile curved her mouth. 'This will be a first.'

'Oh?'

'Playing in only my underwear.'

His smile set flames alight inside her body. 'I could get you

something, if you're cold, though I should tell you it is likely
to decrease my enjoyment of your playing.'

'It's fine.' She winked. 'Just for you.'

He crossed his arms over his chest, waiting. She ran through
a catalogue of songs, each of them embedded in her brain like
speech and movement. Her fingers found the keys and she
closed her eyes for a moment, breathing in deeply, straightening her spine, centring herself to the instrument, and then she
began to play. Slowly at first, her interpretation of the Beethoven
piece more tempered and gentle than many others. She kept
her eyes closed as she played, the strength of the piece building inside her, and as she reached the midpoint and the tempo
crescendoed, she tilted her head back, lost completely to the
beauty of this form of communication.

The piece was not long—a little over four minutes. She
played and when she hit the last notes, both hands pressed to
the keys, she opened her eyes to find that the Sheikh had moved
closer. He stood right in front of her, his eyes boring through her.

When he spoke, his voice was husky. 'Play something else.'

She lifted a brow, a teasing smile on her lips, but the look
was somewhat undermined by the film of tears that had moistened her eyes.

'It's a beautiful instrument.' She ran her fingers over the
keys. 'Did you have this brought up today?'

'I wanted to hear you.'

'A keyboard would have done.'

He shook his head. 'Show me something else.'

She did, this time, her favourite Liszt piece, the *étude* one
she'd mastered only a week before her father had left home. She
vividly recalled because she'd never got a chance to play it for
him, and she had been practising so hard, preparing to surprise
him with how she'd mastered the difficult finger movements.

'You play as well as you breathe,' he said softly, after she'd
finished.

She blinked up at him, her eyes still suspiciously moist. When he pulled her to standing, she went willingly, and when he lifted her against his chest, carrying her back to bed, she felt only intense relief.

# CHAPTER FIVE

'YOUR HIGHNESS.'

The voice was coming to Daisy from a long way away. She shifted in bed a little, lifting a hand to run through her hair and connecting with something warm and firm. And it all came flooding back to her, so her eyes burst open and landed on a man she'd only ever seen in a professional capacity. Malik.

Oh, no!

She'd fallen asleep in the Sheikh's bed—she must have—and now it was morning and his suite was teeming with staff. It wasn't a particularly mature thing to do but she dragged the sheet up higher, covering her face, hiding from the servant.

'Privacy, Malik.' Sariq's voice was firm, and, yes, there was irritation there too.

'Yes, sir. Only you have a breakfast meeting with the President. The helicopter is ready to take you to Washington.'

'It will wait for me.'

'Yes, of course.'

A moment later, the door clipped shut.

'You can come out now.' His voice, so stern a moment ago, showed amusement now.

But it wasn't funny. She pushed at the sheet roughly, and her voice matched it. 'This is so not funny,' she said with a shake of her head, pushing her feet out of the bed and looking for her uniform. 'Oh, God. This is a disaster.'

His frown was way sexier than it should have been. 'Why?'

'Why? Because I told you, no one could know about this, and now that guy, Malik, has seen me *naked* in your bed! Oh, God.' She paced across the room, pulling her shirt on as she went, snagging a nail on one of the buttons and wincing.

'Malik can be trusted,' Sariq assured her.

'Says you, but what if he can't? What if he tells my boss?' She shook her head. 'I can't lose this job, Your Highness.'

At this, he barked a short, sharp laugh into the room. 'Your Highness? Daisy, I have made love to you almost the entire night. Can you call me Sariq now?'

She knew it was absurd, given that she'd already crossed a major professional line, but using his first name felt a thousand kinds of wrong.

'Daisy,' he insisted, moving out of bed, his nakedness glorious and distracting and inducing a panic attack because she'd slept with her client—a lot—and now it was daylight and the magic of the night before had evaporated and she had to face the music. 'Relax. We are two consenting adults who happen to have had sex. This is not something you need to panic about.'

'You don't get it. I'm contractually forbidden from doing this,' she muttered, his amusement only making everything worse. 'It doesn't matter that we're consenting. You're off-limits to me, or should have been.'

'It was one night,' he insisted calmly, coming to fold her in his arms and bring her to his chest. 'Two nights, if you count tonight. And I am counting tonight, Daisy, because I fully expect you to be here with me.'

'What if he tells—?'

He held a hand up imperiously, silencing her with the single gesture. 'If Malik hadn't interrupted us, would you be feeling like this?'

She bit down on her lip, staring at him, and, finally, shook her head.

'Good. Then this problem is easily solved. I will order him to forget he saw you and it will be done.'

She rolled her eyes. 'Nice try, but it's not actually that easy to remove a piece of someone's memory.'

'Malik will do as I say. Put him out of your mind. I have.'

She looked up at him, doubts fading in the face of his confidence. 'I mean it,' she insisted. 'Tomorrow, you go back to your kingdom and nothing changes for you, but I need this job. My life has to go on as it did before, Sariq.' His name—the first time she'd said it—felt like magic. She liked the way it tasted in her mouth, and she especially liked the way he responded, the colour in his eyes deepening in silent recognition.

'And it will.' He dropped his head, his mouth claiming hers, so that thought became, momentarily, impossible. His kiss was heaven and his body weight pushed her backwards until she connected with the wall, so she was trapped between the rock hardness of him, and the wall, and her body was aflame with needs she knew she should resist.

But he lifted her, dispensing with the sheet and pressing her to the wall, his arousal nudging the heat of her sex, so she pushed down, welcoming him deep inside her as though it had been days, not hours, since they'd made love. His possession sent shockwaves of heat flaming through her and he hitched his hips forward and backwards, driving himself into her in a way that had her climaxing within a minute. Her nails scored marks down his back and she almost drew blood from her lip with the effort of not screaming, in case he had other members of staff on the other side of the door.

It was the most sublime feeling, and whatever worries she had seemed far away now. He stilled, holding her, his expression taut, his arousal still hard inside her. She rolled her hips but he dug his hands into her flesh, holding her still.

'What is it?'

'I'm not wearing a condom.' He bit the words out, and she gasped.

'Oh, crap. I didn't even think…'

'Nor did I.' He lifted her from him, easing her to the ground gently, keeping his hands on her waist. 'Shower with me, *habibte*.'

Perhaps she should have declined, but she'd hours ago lost her ability to do what she ought and had abandoned herself, apparently, to doing only what she wanted.

'I suppose it is my job to cater to all your needs,' she purred, earning a small laugh from him. As she stepped into the shower and got the water going, she saw him remove a small foil square from the bathroom drawer and smiled to herself.

Half an hour later, still smiling, she blinked up at him. 'Didn't Malik say the President was waiting?'

Sariq's eyes narrowed. 'He can wait.'

'Your betrothal is all but confirmed.'

Sariq fixed his long-term aide with a cool stare. 'And so?'

'The American—'

'Daisy.' He couldn't help the smile that came to him. Her name was so perfect for her, with her pale blonde hair and ready smile. 'Her name is Daisy.'

'The timing of this could be very bad, if it were to be in the papers in the RKH.'

'It won't be.'

'You are the Emir now, Sariq. More is expected of you than was a month ago. The affairs you once indulged in must become a part of your past.' Malik shook his head. 'Or if you must, allow me to engage suitable women for you, women who are vetted by me, by the palace, who sign confidentiality agreements and are certain not to sell their story to the highest bidder.'

'Daisy won't do that,' he murmured dismissively. 'And the days of palace concubines are long gone. I have no interest in reinvigorating that habit of my forebears.'

'Your father—'

'My father was a lonely man—' Sariq's voice held a warning '—who was determined to mourn my mother until the day he died. How he chose to relieve his bodily impulses is of little interest to me.'

'My point is that these things can be arranged with a maximum of discretion.'

'Daisy is discreet. There are three people who know about this, and it will stay that way.'

'If either of your prospective brides were to find out…'

Sariq tightened one hand into a fist on top of his knee, keeping his gaze carefully focussed on the view beneath him. The White House was just a spec in the distance now, the day's meetings concluded with success.

'They won't.'

'I don't need to tell you how important it is that your marriage settle any potential fallout from your father's death.'

Now, Sariq turned his head slowly, pinning his advisor with a steely gaze. 'No, you don't. So let it go, Malik. This conversation is at an end.'

'He's protective of me, of the kingdom. I've known him since I was a boy.'

Daisy lifted a hand, running the voluminous bubbles between her fingers. The warm bath water lapped at her breasts and, beneath the surface, she brushed an ankle against his nakedness, heat shifting through her. Midnight had come and gone and yet both were wide awake, as though trying to cram everything into this—their last night together.

'He won't say anything?'

'He's more concerned you will,' Sariq said with a shake of his head.

'Me?' Daisy's brows shot up. 'Why in the world…?'

'For money.' Sariq lifted his shoulders.

'Who would pay me for that information?'

His eyes showed amusement. 'Any number of tabloid outlets? Believe it or not, my love life is somewhat newsworthy.'

A shudder of revulsion moved down Daisy's spine. 'You can't be serious?'

'Unfortunately, I am. Malik feels this indiscretion could be disastrous for my country, and, in some ways, there's truth in that.'

'I'll try not to take that personally.'

'You shouldn't. It's not about you so much as it is the women I'm supposed to marry.'

She froze. 'What?'

'I'm not engaged,' he reassured her quietly. 'And I will marry only one. But there are two candidates, both daughters of the powerful families who would have, decades ago, made a claim for the throne. The thinking is that in marrying one of them, I will unify our country further, bonding powerful families, allaying any prospective civil uprising.'

She absorbed that thoughtfully. 'Do you like these women?'

'I've met them a handful of times; it's hard to say.'

'You took me to bed after meeting me only a handful of times,' she pointed out.

'Then I like them considerably less than I like you,' he said, pushing some water towards her so it splashed to her chin.

She smiled back at him, but there was a heaviness inside her. 'What if you're not suited?'

'It's of little importance. The marriage is more about appearances than anything else.'

'You don't think you should care for your bride?'

Something darkened in his features and there was a look of determination there. 'Absolutely not.'

She shook her head. 'Why is that so ridiculous?'

'When it comes to royal marriages, arrangements of convenience make far more sense.'

'It's your life though. Surely you want to live it with someone that you have something in common with?'

'I will have something in common with my wife: she will love our country as I do, enough to marry a stranger to strengthen its peace.'

'And over time, you may come to love her?'

'No, *habibte*. I will never love my wife.' His eyes bore into hers. 'My father loved my mother and it destroyed him. Her death left him bereft and broken. I will never make that mistake.'

She was quiet. 'Do you think he felt it was a mistake to love her?'

'I cannot say. I think at times he wished he hadn't loved her, yes. He missed her in a way that was truly awful to watch.'

'I'm sorry.'

He shrugged. 'I have always known my own marriage would be nothing like his. If it weren't for the fact that I need a child— and as quickly as possible—then I would never marry.'

Something tightened in her chest—a fierce, primal rejection of that. In order to have children, to beget an heir, he would need to have sex, and, though she had no reason to presume he wouldn't, the idea of him going to bed with anyone else turned parts of her cold in a way she suspected would be permanent.

'Children? So soon?'

'I am the last of my family. It's not an ideal situation. Yes, I need an heir. My marriage will be organised within months.' His eyes assumed a more serious look. 'I have to leave here in the morning. I won't be back.'

Inexplicably, a lump formed in her throat. 'I know that.'

'And you, Daisy? What will your future hold? Will you stay working here, servicing guests of this suite of rooms for the rest of your life?'

Her lips twisted. 'I hope not.'

'The way you play the piano is mesmerising. You have a rare talent. It's wrong of you not to pursue it.'

Her smile was lopsided, his praise pulling at her in a way that was painful and pleasurable all at once. 'Like I said, it was a pipe dream.'

'Why?'

'My circumstances wouldn't allow me to study. Becoming a concert pianist isn't exactly something you click your fingers and do. It's hard and it's competitive and I had to get a job.'

'Why? When you had a scholarship...'

'I couldn't do it.'

He compressed his lips. 'If money was the only issue, then let me do as Malik suggested and offer you a settlement. He wanted me to ensure it was more profitable for you to keep your silence than not...'

She sent him a look of disbelief. 'I'm not going to tell anyone about this, believe me.'

'I know that. But I'd like to help you.'

'No.' She shook her head, tilting her chin defiantly. 'Absolutely not. You might be richer than Croesus but I'm not taking a cent from you, Sariq. I absolutely refuse.'

And while he might have been used to being obeyed, there was more than a hint of respect in his eyes when he met her gaze. 'Very well, Daisy. But if you should ever reconsider, the offer has no expiry date.'

She nodded, knowing she wouldn't. Once Sariq left, she would set about the difficult job of forgetting he ever existed. For her own sanity, she needed to do that, or missing him could very well be the end of her.

It was six weeks after he left that she put two and two together and realised the significance of the dates. A loud gasp escaped her lips.

'What is it?' Henry, beside her, turned to regard her curiously.

She shook her head, but the calendar on the counter wouldn't be silenced. She scanned through the guests she'd hosted in the last month and a half, since Sariq had left, and her pulse quickened.

Yes, she'd definitely missed a cycle. Instinctively, her hand curved over her flat stomach as the reality of this situation hit home.

She couldn't possibly be pregnant, though. They'd used protection. Every time? Yes, every time! Except that once, against the wall, but he hadn't climaxed, he'd been so careful. Surely that wasn't enough…

But there was no other explanation. Her cycle was as regular as clockwork; missing a period had to mean that somehow she'd conceived Sariq's baby.

She groaned, spinning away from Henry, uncertainty making it impossible to know what to say or do. First of all she needed proper confirmation.

'Do you mind if I clock out? I just remembered something.'

'Not at all. Make the most of the quiet days, I say.'

She bit down on her lip, grabbing her handbag. 'Thanks, Henry.'

There was a drugstore just down the block, but she walked past it, taking the subway across town instead. It was safer here, away from the possibility of bumping into anyone from the hotel. She bought three pregnancy tests, each from a different manufacturer, knowing that it was overkill and not caring, and a huge bottle of water, which she drank in one sitting. Once back at her small apartment in the basement of the hotel, she pulled a test from its packaging, taking it into the bathroom and following the instructions to the letter.

It took almost no time for two blue lines to appear on the test patch.

She swore under her breath, staring at the lines, a hardness filling out her heart.

What the heck could she do? Sariq had left America six weeks earlier. She hadn't heard from him and she had no expectation she would. He'd made it very clear that he needed to marry one of the women who would promise a greater hope of lasting peace for his people. He would make a match of duty, of national importance, and he'd need to have a legitimate heir with whomever he chose.

This baby would be a disaster for him, and, by extension, for his people. What if the sheer fact that she was pregnant somehow led to an all-out war in his country?

Nausea rose inside her. She cupped her hands over the toilet bowl, bending forward and losing all the water she'd hastily consumed. Her brow was covered in perspiration. She pressed her head to the ceramic tiles of the wall and counted to ten, telling herself it wasn't that bad, that things would work out. She could raise a child on her own. No one ever needed to know.

Daisy re-read the email for the hundredth time before sending it.

Sariq, I've reconsidered. Tuition for the Juilliard is in the attachment. Anything you can do to help...

There was nothing in there that could possibly give away the truth of her situation. No way would he be able to intuit from the few brief lines that there had been an unexpected consequence of their brief, passionate affair.

And that was what she wanted, wasn't it? To do this on her own? She bit down on her lip, her eyes scanning her phone screen, panic lifting through her. Because in all honesty, she couldn't have said *what* she wanted. Their baby, yes, absolutely. Already, she loved the little human growing inside her.

She'd begun to feel the tiniest movements, like little bubbles popping in her belly, and she'd known it was her son or daughter swimming around, finding their feet and getting stronger every day.

Time was passing too quickly. In only five months she'd have to stop working, and then what? Panic made her act. She needed help and Sariq had willingly offered it. Lying to him wasn't exactly comfortable for Daisy but she had to make her peace with that. Sariq had explained what he needed most—a wife and a legitimate heir to inherit his throne.

He'd be grateful to Daisy for this, in the long run, surely.

She read the email once more, her finger hovering over the 'send' arrow. She'd tried everything else she could think of. Thanks to her ex, her credit rating had tanked. She couldn't get a loan, and, even if she could, what in the world would she pay it back with?

For their child, she would do anything, even offer a tiny white lie, via email, to the man she'd had two passionate nights with months earlier. The end justified the means. The email made a whooshing sound as she finally sent it, but Daisy didn't hear it over the thunderous tsunami of her blood.

He stared at the email with an expression that was impossible to decipher. Three and a half months after leaving New York he had begun to think he would never hear from her again.

He re-read the email and a smile lifted his face. He had prayed she would come to her senses, but instinctively known not to push it. It wasn't his place to run her life. Daisy had to decide what she wanted. He wished he could give her more. He wished he could see her again. But knowing he could give her this small gift was enough.

Except it wasn't.

He awoke the next morning with a yearning deep in his soul and he had every intention of indulging it.

Malik was, naturally, against another trip to America.

'I am going,' Sariq insisted firmly, putting a hand on his advisor's forearm. 'Arrange the jet, call the embassy, notify them I'll be there for the weekend.'

'But, sir...'

'No, Malik. No. I'm doing this.'

He felt a thousand times lighter than he had the day before. It was only a temporary reprieve but, suddenly, seeing Daisy again felt like the right thing to do, and he was going to enjoy this last weekend before he made the official betrothal announcements.

Her email was a gift, and he had no intention of ignoring it.

# CHAPTER SIX

To say the building was imposing would be to say the sky was vast. She stared at the RKH embassy, just off Park Avenue, her heart hammering against her ribs.

I'm in Manhattan for the weekend. Come and see me.

A map had been attached to the email with directions to this building, and she'd been staring at it for the last twenty minutes, her central nervous system in overdrive as she tried to brace herself for this.

Keeping the truth of this from Sariq over email had been hard enough! But now? Keeping the secret from him when they were face to face? Daisy suspected it was going to take all the courage she possessed to go through with it.

Every instinct she possessed railed against it. She hated the idea! But what was the alternative? If she told him, then what? He'd be devastated.

She knew what was at stake for him, and why he needed to marry one of the women who would help him keep the peace in his country. The fact she'd fallen pregnant wasn't his fault and he didn't deserve to have to deal with this complication. More importantly, he wouldn't want to deal with it. He'd made that perfectly clear during their time together. It had been a brief passionate affair, nothing more. He'd gone back to the RKH and moved on with his life—the last thing he'd be expecting was the news that, actually, they'd made a baby together.

But didn't he have a right to know? This was his child. When she stripped away the fact he was a powerful sheikh, he was a man who had the same biological claim on this developing baby as she did. She made a noise of frustration, so a woman walking past stopped for a moment, shooting Daisy a quizzical look. She smiled, a terse movement of her lips, then turned away, drawing in a deep gulp of air. It tasted cold, or perhaps that was Daisy's blood.

The fact of the matter was, she couldn't strip his title away from his person. He wasn't just a man, he was a sheikh, and with his position came obligations she couldn't even imagine. One day, when he had the wife and heirs he'd explained to her were necessary, she might feel differently. Maybe then this child would be less of a problem for him. Maybe then he'd even want to know their son or daughter. But for now, she was better to assume all the responsibilities, to raise their child on her own.

It was the right decision, but she simply hadn't banked on how hard it would be to keep something of this magnitude a secret when she was going to see him. With him in the RKH, he was an abstract figure. While she dreamed of him at night and was startled by memories of his touch during the day, he was far away, and it was easy to believe he didn't think of her at all. For the sake of their child, she had to plan for her future knowing he wouldn't be a part of it.

Digging her nails into her palm and sucking in a deep breath for courage, she looked to the right and dipped her head forward as she crossed the street, approaching the embassy as though she were calm and relaxed when inside a wild kaleidoscope of butterflies had taken over her body.

Four guards stood on the steps, each heavily armed and

wearing a distinctive army uniform. She swallowed as she approached the closest.

'Madam? What is it?' The guard studied her with an expression that gave nothing away.

'I have an appointment.' Her voice was soft. She cleared her throat. 'His Highness Sariq Al Antarah asked me here.'

The guard's expression showed a hint of scepticism. 'What is your name?'

'Daisy Carrington.'

He spoke into a small receiver on his wrist and a moment later, a crackled voice issued onto the street. The guard nodded, and gestured to the door. 'Go on.'

Go on. So simple. If only her legs would obey. She stared at the shiny black doors, her pulse leaping wildly through her body, and concentrated on pushing one leg forward, then the next, until she was at the doors. On her approach, they swept inwards. More guards stood here but she barely noticed them at first, for the grandeur of this entranceway.

Walls and ceiling were all made of enormous marble blocks, cream with grey rippling through them. The floor was marble too, except gold lines ran along the edges. At several points along the walls there were pillars—marble—and atop them sat enormous arrangements of flowers, but unlike any she'd ever seen, vibrant, fragrant and stunning. She wanted to stop time and stare at them, to learn the names of these blooms she'd never seen before, to breathe each in and commit its unique scent to memory.

'Identification?' The guard's deep voice jolted her back to the present.

She held out her passport—it had been specified as the only suitable form of identification on the directions she'd received. Her passport had no stamps in it, and in fact she probably wouldn't have had a passport at all if it hadn't been necessary for the vetting process at the hotel.

The guard took it, opening it to the photo page and comparing the image to the real thing, then nodded without handing the passport back. 'Go through security.'

'My passport?'

'I need to make a copy.'

She frowned, uneasiness lifting in her belly. But Sariq was here, and so she wasn't afraid. She trusted him, and these were his people.

The security checkpoint was like any in an airport. She pushed her handbag and shoes through the conveyor belt then walked through an arch before collecting her things.

'His Highness is on the third floor,' a man to her right advised. He wasn't a security guard. At least, he wasn't wearing a military uniform. He wore robes that were white, just like Sariq's, but the detailing at his wrist was in cream. 'There is an elevator, or the central stairs.'

She opted for the latter. The opportunity to observe this building was one she wanted to take advantage of. Besides, it would give her longer to steady her nerves and to brace herself for seeing Sariq again.

A hand curved over her stomach instinctively and she dropped it almost immediately. She had to be careful. No gestures that could reveal a hint of her condition.

The stairs were made of marble as well, but at the first floor, the landing gave way on either side to shining timber floors. The walls here were cream, and enormous pieces of art in gold gilt frames lined the hallway. There were more flowers, each arrangement as elaborate as the ones downstairs.

She bit down on her lip and kept moving. The next floor was just the same—polished timber, flowers, art, and high ceilings adorned with chandeliers that cast the early afternoon light through the building, creating shimmering droplets of refraction across the walls.

She held her breath as she climbed the next set of steps. This floor was like the others except there was a noticeable increase in security presence. Two guards at the top of the stairs, and at least ten in either direction, at each door.

'Miss Carrington?' A man in a robe approached her. She thought he looked vaguely familiar, perhaps from Sariq's stay at the hotel. 'This way.'

She fell into step beside him, incapable of speech. Anticipation had made it impossible. She was vividly aware of every system in her body. Lungs that were working overtime to pump air, veins that were taxed with the effort of moving blood, skin that was punctured by goose bumps, lips that were parted, eyes that were sore for looking for him.

At the end of the corridor, two polished timber doors were closed. There was a brass knocker on one. The man hit it twice and then, she heard him.

'Come.'

That one word set every system into rampant overdrive. She felt faint. But she had to do this. She hated having to ask him for money. She hated it with every fibre of her being, but what else could she do? She was already in a financially parlous state, but adding a baby to the mix and her inability to work? Neither of them would cope, and the comfort and survival of her child was more important than anything—even her pride.

The doors swung open and, after a brief pause, she stepped inside, looking around. The room was enormous. Large windows with heavy velvet drapes framed a view towards Bryant Park. She could just make out the tops of the trees from here. The furniture was heavy and wooden, dark leather sofas, and on the walls, the ancient tapestries Sariq had described. She took a step towards one, and it was then that she saw him.

Her heart almost gave way. She froze, unable to move, to speak, barely able to breathe.

Sariq.

Dressed in the traditional robes of his people, except in a more ornate fashion, this time he had a piece of gold fabric that went across his shoulders and fell down his front. On his head he wore the *keffiyeh*, and she stood there and stared at him dressed like this: every bit the imposing ruler. It was almost impossible to reconcile this man with the man who'd delighted her body, kissing her all over, tasting her, taking her again and again until she couldn't form words or thoughts. He looked so grand, so untouchable.

'Daisy.' Her name on his lips sent arrows through her body. She stayed where she was, drinking him in with her eyes.

'Your Highness.' She forced a smile to her lips, and was ridiculously grateful she'd taken care with her appearance. Her stomach was still flat but she'd chosen to wear all black—a simple pair of jeans and a flowing top, teamed with a brightly coloured necklace to break up the darkness of the outfit. She'd left her hair out and applied the minimum of make-up. His eyes dropped to her feet then lifted slowly over her body, so she felt warmth where he looked, as though he were touching her.

'I feel like I should curtsy or something.'

His look was impossible to decipher. 'That's not necessary.' He stayed where he was, and she did the same, so there was a room between them. The silence crackled.

'Thank you for seeing me,' she said, after a moment. God, this was impossible. She didn't want to ask him for money and, now that she saw him, the idea of having his baby and not telling him was like poison. All the very sensible reasons she'd used to justify that course of action fled from her mind.

He deserved to know. Even if he chose not to acknowledge the child? Even if he turned her away? Even if…the possibilities spun through her, each of them scary and real and alarming.

Her stomach was in knots, indecision eating her alive. She knew only one thing for certain: she had to decide what to do, and quickly. If she was going to tell him, it should be now. Shouldn't it?

She was every bit as beautiful as he remembered. More so. There was something about her today—she was glowing. Her skin was lustrous, her eyes shimmering, her lips, God, her lips. He wanted to pull them between his teeth, to drag her body to his and kiss her hard, to push her against the wall and make love to her as he'd done freely that weekend.

But that had been different somehow. They'd had an agreement. They'd known what they were to each other. Now? He was on the brink of announcing his marriage. Surely he couldn't still be fantasising about another woman?

But he was. He wanted Daisy. Not for one night, not for two. He wanted her for as long as he could have her.

*'Sire, you cannot see her again.'*

*Malik's warning had rung through the embassy.*

*'You were far from discreet last time. With your engagement due to be announced any day now, if word of this were to get out—'*

*'It won't. And I'm relying on you to make sure of that.'*

But Malik's reaction had been a good barometer. He was worried about Daisy, worried about what the people of the RKH would think if the affair became public, and with good reason. Sariq was no longer free to follow his passions wherever they took him. He was now the ruler. He'd been crowned, and the weight of a country rested on his shoulders.

He needed to remember that, and yet, faced with Daisy, he couldn't. He was not a man to throw caution to the wind. All his life he'd been trained for this, he knew what his responsibilities were, but suddenly he wondered if he could have his cake and eat it too.

His engagement hadn't been announced…yet. He had a little time. And he knew just how he wanted to spend it. He regarded her thoughtfully, something pulling at his gut, given how she was looking at him—as though she was remembering every single moment they'd shared, every kiss, whisper, pleasure.

He could postpone his trip, stay in New York a few more nights. Would she stay with him here, at the embassy? It was hard to read her, hard to know what she'd say if he suggested that. Besides, it wasn't enough. A few nights would satisfy him temporarily, but if the fourteen weeks since he'd last seen Daisy had taught him anything, it was that his need for her was insatiable, and not likely to be easily dispensed with. He wanted longer. As long as she could give him.

There was only one solution, and suddenly Sariq knew that if he didn't reach for it with both hands, he'd regret it for the rest of his life.

'I have a proposition for you. One I think you'll like.'

She stood completely still except for her fingers, which she fidgeted behind her back. 'Oh?'

'Have a seat.' He gestured towards the dark leather sofas and she followed his gaze, but shook her head.

'I'd prefer to stand.'

'Would you like a drink?'

'No, thank you.'

He nodded.

'What is this proposition?'

'When is your admission set for the Juilliard?'

Darn it. She should have researched this. 'Mid-January,' she guessed, glad the words came out with such authority.

'In three months.' He ran a palm over his chin, as though contemplating this.

'Yes.'

'Then here is what I would like to propose. I want you to come to the RKH with me, Daisy.'

Her eyes flew wide and her lips parted. She stared at him, wondering if she'd imagined the words. 'But you're…aren't you getting married?'

He nodded. 'My situation is as it was before. I have chosen my bride, but the wedding date is not set.' Now he moved, closing the distance between them, until he was standing right in front of her. 'I will not marry her until you leave.'

A shiver ran down her spine, and she hated that heat was

building low in her abdomen, filling her with a need that was instantly familiar even as revulsion gripped her, making her want to shout and stamp.

'No one could know you were there.' His jaw tightened, as though he were grinding his teeth. 'It would be a disaster if anyone were to find out, so we would have to be very, very careful.' He paused once more, and, for no reason she could fathom, Daisy held her breath. 'Malik would arrange it so that you were installed in an apartment in the capital. He would manage your security, ensure you were not seen by anyone but me. And I would visit you often.' He lifted a finger, tracing a line down her cheek towards her lips. She shivered again. 'It would be just like it was here, in New York. You would have a piano, and you would have me, and anything else you could want. And at the end of it, you would return to study, your tuition paid in full, a house provided for you in New York. Anything you wanted, Daisy.'

She stared at him, her heart dropping to her toes. Pain lashed her. What he was offering was little more than prostitution! Well? What had she expected? She'd come here, cap in hand, after the weekend they'd shared. Could he be blamed for thinking her attention could be bought? Her knees felt weak and her stomach hurt.

'You're asking me to come and be your secret mistress,' she repeated, incredulity ringing through her.

'I'm asking you to be my lover for as long as possible.'

'Before you get married.' She nodded, numb to the core.

He dipped his head in silent agreement.

'And in exchange, you'd give me money.'

Her insides lit up. Nausea crested through her.

'I will give you money anyway,' he assured her, as though just realising how mercenary the proposition sounded. She closed her eyes, wanting to blank him out for a moment, but even then, he was everywhere. His intoxicatingly masculine fragrance filled her. She was drowning in his presence and she desperately needed to think rationally and calmly.

'I cannot offer you more than this,' he said slowly, the words filled with the authority that came naturally to him, so she jerked her eyes open and looked at him once more. 'My duties to my country come first. I could never openly date you. A divorced American? My people wouldn't tolerate it. I know this isn't sensible. In fact, it's the opposite of that. If you were discovered, it would pose a real risk to my rule, but I don't care. Daisy, I want you to come home with me. I want you to be my mistress more than I've ever wanted anything in my life.'

*A divorced American. His mistress!*

She felt so dirty! As though she was somehow lesser than him, and it brought back so many awful memories of her marriage, when Max had so cleverly undermined her confidence in herself until she saw her only value as being His Wife, rather than a person all her own. A shiver of revulsion ran down her spine, because she wasn't that woman any more.

'I can't believe you'd even suggest this.'

He moved forward, his body pressed to hers so weakness threatened to reduce her anger when she needed it most. 'How is it any different from that weekend?'

'You're getting married.'

'And I was getting married that weekend, too.'

'I had no idea the fact I was divorced and an American were such issues for you.'

He frowned, but it was swallowed quickly, as he dropped his head, his lips brushing hers. 'It isn't.'

'Not for your "mistress", anyway. I dare say someone like me is the perfect candidate for that role.'

His hands found the bottom of her shirt, lifting it so he could hold her bare hips, his lips more determined at hers now so a whimper filled her mouth and she felt herself kissing him back, needing him in a way that infuriated her.

'You are the perfect candidate to be in my bed, yes,' he agreed, but it hurt. God, it hurt. She'd never felt so…cheap.

She lifted her hands, pushing at his chest, putting some vital distance between them. 'Damn you, Sariq, no.' She shouted the words and then lowered her voice, aware that there were dozens of guards on this level. 'No.' A whisper. She wrapped her arms around her chest, moving away from him towards the sofas. Her knees were trembling but still she didn't sit. Her eyes were on him, showing her pain and hurt.

'I cannot offer you more than this,' he said again. 'You know what expectations are upon me. My marriage is a bargaining chip; my bride an important part of my political strategy. I cannot bring you to the palace as my mistress—it would offend my future Emira and it would offend my people. I'm sorry if this hurts you, but it is the truth.'

Her heart looped through her. Offend his bride. Offend his people. 'And what about me, Your Highness? Do you care that I am offended by this offer?'

He had the decency to look—for a brief moment—ashamed. But he rallied quickly, his expression shifting to a mask of determination. 'You shouldn't be. I'm offering us a way to both get what we want.'

She made a scoffing noise.

'Money aside, think about how good this could be. How much fun we'd have…'

She closed her eyes, the temptation of that warming her, because if she weren't so horrendously offended, she could see the appeal of his offer. On one level, he was offering her something she desperately wanted. More of Sariq? But everything about the way he'd made his offer filled her with disgust and loathing. He had somehow managed to cheapen what they'd shared so it felt tawdry and meaningless. And he didn't seem to get that!

'I thought you actually *liked* me,' she said with a small shake of her head. 'I thought you enjoyed spending time with me.

That you valued me as a person.' Pain lashed her, because he didn't. He was just like her ex. The realisation was awful and horrifying.

'I do,' he promised immediately, crossing towards her. 'But I'm a realist and I see the limitations of this.'

'Which is sex,' she said crudely, lifting her brows, waiting for him to acknowledge it.

'As it was in New York,' he said firmly.

Her heart dropped. Her stomach ached and tears filled her eyes. It had just been about sex for him? She wracked her brain, trying desperately to remember anything he'd said or done that indicated otherwise, but no. There was nothing. He'd wanted her. He'd made a point of saying that over and over, but that was all.

She'd been a fool to think there was more to it, that they were in some way friends or something.

'I shouldn't have come here. I shouldn't have asked you for money. It was a mistake. Please forget...'

'No.' He held onto her wrist as though he could tell she was about to run from the room. 'Stop.'

Her eyes lifted to his and she jerked on her wrist so she could lift her fingers to her eyes and brush away her tears. Panic was filling her, panic and disbelief at the mess she found herself in.

'How is this upsetting to you?' he asked more gently, pressing his hands to her shoulders, stroking his thumbs over her collarbone. 'We agreed at the hotel that we could only have two nights together, and you were fine with that. I'm offering you three months, on exactly those same terms, and you're acting as though I've asked you to parade naked through the streets of Shajarah.'

'You're ashamed of me,' she said simply. 'In New York we were two people who wanted to be together. What you're proposing turns me into your possession. Worse, it turns me into your prostitute.'

He stared at her, his eyes narrowed. 'The money I will give you is beside the point.'

More tears sparkled on her lashes. 'Not to me it's not.'

'Then don't take the money,' he said urgently. 'Come to the RKH and be my lover because you want to be with me.'

'I can't.' Tears fell freely down her face now. 'I need that money. I need it.'

A muscle jerked in his jaw. 'So have both.'

'No, you don't understand.'

She was a live wire of panic but she had to tell him, so that he understood why his offer was so revolting to her. She pulled away from him, pacing towards the windows, looking out on this city she loved. The trees at Bryant Park whistled in the fall breeze and she watched them for a moment, remembering the first time she'd seen them. She'd been a little girl, five, maybe six, and her dad had been performing at the restaurant on the fringes of the park. She'd worn her Very Best dress, and, despite the heat, she'd worn tights that were so uncomfortable she could vividly remember that feeling now. But the park had been beautiful and her dad's music had, as always, filled her heart with pleasure and joy.

Sariq was behind her now, she felt him, but didn't turn to look at him.

'I'm glad you were so honest with me today.' Her voice was hollow. 'It makes it easier for me, in a way, because I know exactly how you feel, how you see me, and what you want from me.' Her voice was hollow, completely devoid of emotion when she had a thousand throbbing inside her.

He said nothing. He didn't try to deny it. Good. Just as she'd said, it was easier when things were black and white.

'I don't want money so I can attend the Juilliard, Your Highness.' It pleased her to use his title, to use that as a point of difference, to put a line between them that neither of them could cross.

Silence. Heavy, loaded with questions. And finally, 'Then what do you need such a sum for?'

She bit down on her lip, her tummy squeezing tight. 'I'm pregnant. And you're the father.'

# CHAPTER SEVEN

WHEN HIS MOTHER had died, Sariq had been speechless. Perhaps his father had expected grief. Tears. Anger. Something rent with emotion. Instead, Sariq had listened to the news.

*'She died, Riq. So did the baby.'*

He'd stood there, all of seven years old, his face like stone, his body slowing down so that blood barely pumped, heart barely moved, breath hardly formed, and he'd stared out of a window. Then it had been a desert view—the sands of the Alkajar range stretching as far as the eye could see, heat forming a haze in the distance that had always reminded Sariq of some kind of magic.

Now, he stared out at New York, streets that were crammed with taxis and trucks, the ever-present honking of horns filling him with a growing sense of disbelief. There were trees in the distance, blowing in the light autumnal breeze. His heart barely moved. His blood didn't pump. He could scarcely breathe.

Time passed. Minutes? Hours? He couldn't have said. He was conscious of the ticking of the clock—a gift from a long-ago American president to his father, on the signing of the Treaty of Lashar. He was conscious of the colour of her hair, so gold it matched the thread of his robes. The fragrance she brought with her, delicate and floral. He was conscious, somehow, of the beating of her heart. In contrast to his, it was firing frantically.

It was beating for two people. Their unborn child was nestled in her belly, growing with every second that passed.

He closed his eyes, needing to block the world out, needing to block Daisy out in particular.

His breathing was ragged as he went back in time, calculating the dates. It had been what?—almost four months?—since his visit to America. When had she found out? And why had she waited until now to tell him?

Except, she hadn't come here to tell him.

His eyes flared open and flew to her with renewed speculation and his heart burst back to life, pushing blood through his body almost too fast for his veins to cope. The torrent was an assault.

'You weren't going to tell me.'

A strangled noise was all the confirmation he needed. He stood perfectly still, but that was no reflection of his temperament or feelings.

'You came here today to collect a cheque. If I hadn't suggested you join me in the RKH, you would have taken the money and left. True?'

She didn't turn to face him and suddenly that was infuriating and insupportable. He gripped her shoulders and spun her around. Tears sparkled on her lashes and his gut rolled, because he hated seeing her like this but his own shock and anger and disbelief made it impossible for him to comfort her.

'This baby is a disaster for you.'

She was right. His eyes swept shut once more as he tried to make sense of the political ramifications of having conceived a child with a divorced American—a woman he spent approximately forty-eight hours of his life with, if that.

'I didn't come here to tell you, because I understand your position. You have to get married and have children with someone who will strengthen your position, not weaken it. This baby was a mistake.' Her face paled. 'No, not a mistake,' she quickly corrected, her hand curving over her stomach so his eyes dropped to the gesture, something different moving through him now. Was that joy? In the midst of this? Surely not.

'A surprise,' he substituted, his voice gravelled by the emotions that were strangling him.

'You could say that.' Her short laugh lacked humour.

'So what was your plan?'

'Plan?' She bit down on her lip. 'I wouldn't say I have a plan.'

'You came to take money from me under false pretences? And then what?' It was unreasonable, and not an accurate representation of how he felt. He wasn't sure why he had chosen to hone in on that. The money was beside the point, but her duplicity wasn't.

She flinched but nodded, as though his accusation had some kind of merit. 'Believe me, I hate that I came here with my hand out. I hate having to ask you for anything. But I can't afford a child, Sariq. I can't afford this.' Tears ran down her cheeks now and his chest compressed almost painfully.

'The hotel doesn't pay you well?'

'My salary's fine.' She dashed at her tears, her eyes showing outrage. Outrage that she was crying. Outrage that she had to explain her situation to him. But he needed to understand...

'I lost a lot of money in my divorce. I have a mountain of debt with interest rates that are truly eye-watering. My salary lets me chip maybe five thousand dollars a year off the total owed. I should be out from under that in about, oh, I don't know, seventy or eighty years?' She shook her head. 'I can't afford to stop working. The hotel provides my accommodation so once I stop working, I'll need to find somewhere to live, which I can't afford. Benefits won't cut it. I hate that I'm asking you for money,' she repeated, and he felt it, every single shred of her hate and fury and fear, too. 'But we're having a baby and I need to do what I can for her or him.'

'Yes.' It was an immediate acquiescence. He turned away from Daisy, stalking towards the door, staring at it for a moment. His mind was spinning at a thousand miles per hour. His marriage was important. Unifying his country further mattered. But so did begetting an heir. His situation as the last in his family's line had troubled him for a long time, but never more so than since losing his father. He was conscious of how much rested on his survival, how vulnerable that made him. And if there was one thing he hated, it was feeling vulnerable.

This child alleviated that.

He had an heir—or he would, in six months' time.

'Look at me, Sariq.' Her voice cut through him, the grief there, the pain. He turned and his heart jolted inside him, because she was clearly terrified. If he stopped for a moment and saw this from her perspective, he could see how unsettling the discovery of her pregnancy must have been. Neither of them had wanted complications from that weekend. It had been a stolen time of passion, short and brief. And definitely over.

But it wasn't.

This baby would bind them for ever.

'I can't afford to do this on my own, and I hate that, but the alternatives don't bear considering.' A shiver moved her slender frame. Her too-slender frame. Had she *lost* weight since he'd seen her last?

A frown pulled at his mouth. 'You're slim.'

She blinked, the statement apparently making no sense.

'You haven't gained weight. In fact, the opposite appears to be true.'

'Oh.' She nodded jerkily. 'Yes. I haven't felt well. The doctor at the free clinic says that will probably pass soon enough.'

His frown deepened. He didn't feel that was it. Was it possible that she hadn't been eating? That she hadn't been eating well enough? Because she was worried about money?

And as for a *free clinic*? She was carrying the sole heir to the throne of the RKH, one of the most prosperous countries in the Middle East—and the world! She should have top-level medical care. He needed to fix this—he needed to find a way to make this work, for everyone.

'The baby's healthy,' she said quietly. 'I'm fine, apart from the all-day nausea and complete lack of appetite.'

He nodded slowly, fixing his eyes to her. There was only one solution, and he needed it to happen immediately. 'I'm glad you came to me today, Daisy. I'm glad you told me.'

She let out a whoosh of breath, her relief apparent. 'You are?'

A simple nod. 'But we must move quickly in order to avoid a major diplomatic incident.'

She blinked. 'Oh, I'm not going to tell anyone about this, Your Highness.'

He laughed then, a deranged sound. 'For God's sake, we've conceived a child together. We're going to be parents. Call me Sariq.'

She bristled, her eyes showing strength and determination. 'We are *not* going to be parents together.' She spoke with a cool authority that was belied by the quivering of her fingers. 'You're going to be in another country, far away. I'm going to raise our child.'

His eyes narrowed imperceptibly. 'You know what this baby means to me.'

She froze.

'You know how imperative it is that I have an heir.'

'But this baby *isn't* your heir,' she mumbled after a moment. 'We're not married. It can't be…'

'We're not married, *yet*.'

Her eyes flared wide in her beautiful face, and her lips dropped to reveal her glossy white teeth. She didn't speak. She couldn't. Good. He needed a moment to organise this. He crossed to his desk, picking up the phone. 'Have Malik call me.'

He disconnected the receiver once more and turned to face her. She was standing where he'd left her, shaking her head.

'Sit down, *habibte*.'

She shook her head harder. 'I'm not marrying you.'

Determination flooded him as he saw the only path before them clearly, and knew he had to guide them down it. 'There is no alternative, Daisy, so I suggest you move past shock to acceptance. The sooner you do so the better, for both of us.'

She stared at him, her insides awash with uncertainty and disbelief. 'You can't be serious?'

'Does it sound like something I'd joke about? This child has more value to my people and me than I can possibly describe. You are carrying my royal heir. There is no option but for us to marry.'

'I beg your pardon,' she spat, crossing her arms over her chest, wishing his eyes didn't drop to her cleavage in that way that reminded her of everything they'd shared that weekend. 'There is one option, and it's the one we're going to take. I'm going to leave here now, with a cheque that will help me cover medical expenses and rent in some kind of home in which to spend the first year of our child's life, until I can go back to work—'

'Go back to work?' His laugh was a caustic sound of derision. 'And who will be raising the crown prince of the RKH?'

'Or princess,' she snapped caustically. 'And I don't know. I'll find a family day care.'

'Family day care?' he repeated, and she nodded, though she could understand his reaction to that. It was a little haphazard and ill-thought-out.

'I don't know, okay? I haven't gotten that far. I just know that I can do this on my own.' She lifted her chin, breathing in deeply in an attempt to calm her nerves. 'I haven't told anyone anything about what happened between us and I don't intend to. I won't say a word about the fact you're this baby's father. Your name won't appear on the birth certificate. It will remain untraceable.'

His jaw clenched. 'You think this will please me? For my own child not to bear my name?' His nostrils flared with the force of his exhalation. 'Honestly, Daisy, your naivety would almost be adorable if it weren't so inappropriate.'

Anger flared inside her. 'I beg your pardon?'

'How hard do you think it would be for someone to piece this together?' He held her gaze with obvious contempt. 'You cannot imagine the scrutiny my life is subject to. You are acting as though I am any other man, as though this child is like any other love child.'

'I'm sorry, it's my first time being pregnant after a one-night stand,' she muttered sarcastically. 'I have no idea how I'm supposed to act.'

'You're supposed to be reasonable,' he responded flatly. 'There is no way I'm having my child raised anywhere besides my palace and I think you knew that when you told me about your pregnancy.'

His words hit her like a mallet. She shook her head again, feeling like one of those bobble-head dolls.

'Listen to me, Daisy.' He began to move closer to her so she braced instinctively. Not out of fear of him so much as fear of her reaction. How, even in that moment, could she be aware of trivial matters such as the breadth of his shoulders and the strength of his arms?

'I need an heir. You know this, and you understand why it's an urgent concern. As the last remaining heir of my family's line, I am in a vulnerable position...'

She jerked her head in an aggressive nod. 'Which is why you're marrying and planning to have a child as soon as—'

'I have a child.' The words cut through the room, loud and insistent. He paused, visibly calming himself. 'We are having a child.' And now, he closed the distance, gripping her hands and lifting them between them, his eyes boring into hers with the force of a thousand suns.

'You're wrong. I didn't come here to tell you about this. I understand your position, which is precisely why I intended to do this on my own. You don't want to marry me. You don't want to raise a child with me. Your people need you to do what's best for them, and that includes marrying a woman who will secure the peace of your kingdom. I can't do that.' She was trembling, she realised belatedly. He squeezed her hands tighter. 'I won't marry you.' Oh, no. Her teeth were chattering. Panic was setting in.

'You must.'

'No.' Fear strangled her words. 'I've already been married, and it was a disaster. I swore I'd never do that again. I can't.' Tears fell from her eyes. How angry they made her! How frustrated with herself she felt. This was not a time to cry!

She ripped her hands free and wiped at her face, hard, turning away from him and grabbing her handbag. She didn't even remember discarding it but she must have placed it on the chair near the door when she'd entered this room, because it sat there, looking at her in a matter that felt accusatory.

'I want you to forget I came here.'

'I can't do that.'

She spoke as though he hadn't. 'I want you to forget I'm pregnant. No, I want you to forget we ever met.'

'You are not leaving here.'

'Oh, yeah?' She pushed the strap of her bag over her shoulder and whirled around to face him. She felt like a wild animal, all emotion, no civility. 'Try and stop me.'

'I do not need to try to stop you.' He was so infuriatingly calm! It only flared her anger further. 'Have you forgotten where you are, *habibte*?'

'I'm in New York City. You might be King of all you survey in the RKH, but here in America we believe in the rule of law, which means no one, regardless of their position or station, has more legal rights than another.'

'I know what the rule of law is.' He crossed his arms over his chest. 'I'm sorry to say it won't help you here.'

It was like being hit with a sledgehammer. Cold, claw-like fingers began to wrap around her as the enormity of her own stupidity hit her like an anvil.

She wasn't in America any more. Not really. She'd willingly

stepped into his embassy, buried herself in the thick of dozens of his guards and surrendered her passport.

'Oh, my God.' She stared at him, her face heating to the point of boiling, her eyes showing her comprehension. 'You…bastard.'

His head jerked a little, as though she'd slapped him.

'You tricked me.'

His eyes flashed with impatience. 'I did no such thing. I invited you here because I wanted to see you again—'

'To proposition me,' she corrected witheringly, but her voice shook, panic making it impossible to speak clearly, much less think straight. 'That's why you lured me here to your embassy?'

And despite the tension, he laughed, and it did something to her insides, reminding her of the warmth they'd shared, of his easy affection. Her stomach squeezed and she reached behind her, feeling for the chair that had, until a moment ago, held her handbag.

'Do you think I have to resort to kidnap in order to get a woman into my bed?'

His eyes lanced her and she felt angry, stupid and jealous as all heck, all at once.

He softened his tone. 'And I didn't lure you here. This is where I live when I'm in the States. Up until a month ago, it was being renovated and wasn't fit for habitation, hence I stayed at your hotel. As it's now restored to its usual condition, I'm here. This was not a trap.'

'It sure feels like it.'

He dipped his head forward in silent acceptance of that. 'I'm sorry.' His eyes pinned to hers and she was powerless to look away. He strode across the room, crouching before her, clasping her hands in her lap. 'I am sorry.' His expression showed the truth of his words. 'I'm sorry I didn't prevent you from falling pregnant. I'm sorry that my position makes our marriage a necessity. But I am sorriest of all for the fact that I cannot take the time to slowly convince you this is the right thing for us to do. I cannot risk letting you walk out of here because we *must* marry.

It is imperative.' He stroked her hand and her heart ached, because she wasn't sure how she felt and what she wanted but she could see, so clearly, what this meant to him and his people.

But what about her and her needs? Memories of Max had her shaking her head from side to side, needing him to understand. 'I don't want to get married. I can't.'

'I understand that. Put that to one side for the moment and think about our child.' His hand shifted, moving from her wrists to her stomach, pressing against it, and for a moment he appeared to lose his train of thought as he lost himself in the realisation that inside her belly was their own baby.

'Don't you think our child deserves this?'

She bit down on her lip. 'Our child deserves us to love it,' she said quietly. 'To do the best for it, always.'

'And raising him or her together is the best.'

'My mother raised me on her own after my father left,' she insisted, tilting her chin with pride for the job her mother had done even when she'd struggled with her health for years.

'I didn't know that.'

'Why would you? We don't know each other, Sariq. We don't know each other.'

'Don't we?' The question laid her bare and forced her to look inside herself. They might not know one another's biographical details back to front, but she would have said that despite that, after their time together, she *did* know him. But that he was capable of this? Of holding her prisoner in his embassy?

It renewed her anger and disbelief, so she stood a little shakily, moving towards the door. 'You're not going to keep me prisoner here until I agree to marry you.'

'No,' he acquiesced, and relief burst through her. 'We are getting married this evening, Daisy. There is no point fighting over the inevitable.'

He watched her from the mezzanine, and he felt many things. Desire. Shock. Certainty. Admiration. But most of all, he felt a sense of guilt. Her displeasure with this was understandable. She'd arrived at the embassy with no concept of how he would react, and he'd wielded his power like a sledgehammer.

He hated this.

He hated what he was doing, he hated that he was doing it to Daisy, and yet he knew he had no alternative. Not only was their child incredibly politically powerful, if he didn't marry her and bring her to the RKH there was a very real threat to both of them. Only in his palace, with the royal guards at his disposal, could he adequately protect them.

He hadn't wanted to hit her over the head, metaphorically speaking, with the truth of that. It felt like the last thing you should say to a pregnant woman, and yet undeniably there were some factions within his country who would strike out at his heir. And particularly an illegitimate yet rightful heir who could, at any point, return to the RKH and claim power.

For years, he'd believed his mother had died in childbirth. His father had wanted it that way. But when Sariq was fifteen, he'd learned the truth. She'd been murdered. When she was heavily pregnant, while on a private vacation, someone had killed her. Sariq should have been there. He was part of the plan, too, but at the last moment he'd come down with a virus and his father had insisted he stay home to avoid making his mother sick in her delicate state.

He knew, better than anyone, what some factions were capable of and there was no way he was seeing history repeat itself. He would protect Daisy and their unborn child with his dying breath.

No, he had to do this, even when it left a sour taste in his mouth. As to her suitability? He had no doubts on that score; she'd be a fish out of water at first. Who wouldn't? She wasn't raised with these pressures; she had no concept of what would be expected of her. She'd never even travelled outside America, for Christ's sake. His advisors would question his judgement, and they'd be right to do so. There would be political ramifications, but he was counting on the spectre of a royal baby on the horizon to quell those.

At the end of the day he had made his decision and there was no one on earth who could shake him from his sense of duty and purpose. She was angry now, but once they arrived in the RKH and she saw the luxury and financial freedom that awaited her, surely that would ease? In time, when she realised that their marriage was really in name only, a legal arrangement, more than anything, to bind them as parents and to right their child's claim to the throne.

And the fact he couldn't look at her without wanting to tear her clothes from her body?

It was irrelevant. He had a duty to marry her, to protect her with his life. Everything else was beside the point.

# CHAPTER EIGHT

THE DRESS WAS STUNNING. It was perfect for a princess. A pale cream with beads that she was terrified to discover were actual diamonds, stitched around the neckline, the wrists and at the hem, so that the dress itself was heavy and substantial. It nipped in at her waist to reveal the still-flat stomach. On her feet she wore simple silk slippers, for which she was grateful—the last thing she wanted was to be impeded by high heels.

They'd make it far more difficult to run away.

Except she wasn't going to run away. She caught her reflection in the windows across the room. Evening had fallen, meaning she could see herself more clearly. And more importantly, New York was gone. There were lights, in the distance, and the tooting of cars, but the trees of Bryant Park were no longer visible. She lifted a finger to her throat, toying with the necklace her mother had given her, running the simple silver locket from side to side distractedly.

There were guards everywhere. Escape wasn't an option. But even if it were, Daisy wasn't sure she would take it. She knew there were many, many single parents out there doing an amazing job, and perhaps if Daisy hadn't already been worn down by extreme poverty, hunger, and the fear of living pay cheque to pay cheque, she might have had more faith in her abilities.

But the truth was, she knew what it was like to be poor, to be broke, to have enormous debts nipping at her heels, and she wanted so much more for her baby.

It wasn't just the financial concerns though. It was the certainty that if she didn't marry Sariq she would need to go back to work as soon as possible, and already she hated the idea of leaving her baby.

Still, marriage felt extreme.

So why wasn't she fighting? Insisting that she be allowed to call a lawyer?

Was it possible that on some level she actually wanted this? That her body's traitorous need for his was pushing her towards this fate, even when she wanted to rail against it?

She couldn't say. But she knew a thousand and one feelings were rushing through her and not all of them were bad. Which made her some kind of traitor to the sisterhood, surely?

She ground her teeth together, looking around this enormous space idly until her eyes landed on a figure on the mezzanine level and she froze.

'Sariq.' His name escaped her lips without her consent. Then again, it was preposterous to keep calling him by his title. He was watching her like a hawk, his eyes trained on her in a way that made her stomach clench with white-hot need, so fierce it pushed her lips apart and forced a huge breath from her body. She spun away, ashamed of her base reaction. A moment later, he had descended the steps and was behind her, his hands on her shoulders, turning her to face him.

He didn't speak. His eyes held hers, and he studied her for several seconds. 'Are you ready?'

Her heart began to tremble. 'If I said "no", would it make any difference?'

He eyed her for several seconds. 'Yes.'

Her pulse raced. Disappointment was unmistakable and that only made her angrier.

'So you'll let me go?'

'No.' He shook his head. 'But I will delay. We can wait a day or two to let you get used to this. We can talk until you understand. I can prepare you better for what's in store once we arrive in the RKH...'

'But you won't let me leave this embassy?'

Silence prickled between them. 'I cannot.'

'Then I see no point in delay, except to assuage your conscience, which I have no intention of doing.'

He stared at her, surprise obvious on his features. She knew she was lashing out at him out of fear, and that it wasn't fair. He had been as caught off guard by this as she was. He was acting out of duty for his country, and she understood that. But becoming a commodity didn't sit well with her, and her desire for him was making everything else murky and uncertain.

'You're forcing me to marry you, Sariq. I'm not going to let you think otherwise.' His face paled beneath his tanned skin, and she was glad. Hurting him, arousing his conscience, made her feel a hell of a lot better. She struck again: 'You should know that. I'm marrying you because I have to—not because I want to—and I will never forgive you for this. Tonight I'm going to become your wife and I may appear to accept that, I may appear to accept *you*, but I will always hate you for this.' She glared at him with undisguised fury so it was easy for Sariq to believe her. 'I love our child, and, for him or her, I will try to make our marriage amicable, at least on the surface, but don't you ever doubt how I really feel.'

His eyes swept shut for a moment, the only movement on his stone-like face the furious beating of a muscle in his jaw. 'I wish we had an alternative.'

'You do,' she said quietly.

His eyes glittered with something like fire and he reached into his robes, removing a phone. It was a familiar brand but the back was pure gold. He loaded something up on the screen then handed it to her.

She stared at it, her own photo looking back at her, beside

his picture, and beneath a headline that screamed *Secret Royal Wedding!*

She read the article quickly.

> *News broke overnight that the Emir of the Royal King-dom of Haleth married American Daisy Carrington when he was last in the United States in July.*
>
> *The wedding, conducted in secret, means the unknown woman is now Emira to one of the world's most prosper-ous nations.*
>
> *Little is known of the woman who stole the famously closed-off ruler's heart, or of how their romance began.*
>
> *More details to follow.*

'We're not married.' She handed the phone back to him, wish-ing her fingertips weren't trembling.

'Our marriage certificate will be backdated, to remove any doubts as to my paternity.'

Her eyes narrowed. 'This is your child.'

'I know that.' He pocketed his phone once more. 'I have no doubt on that score. It makes things easier, that's all.'

'But...'

'Your name is in the papers, Daisy.' There was urgency in his tone. 'The whole world will know that you are carrying my baby before the morning. And that baby is the heir to my throne. Can you not see how vulnerable that makes you both?'

She stared at him in disbelief, and desire died, just like that. Now, her feels were not unambiguous at all. Anger sparked through her, overtaking everything else.

'You are such a bastard. You did this on purpose, so I'd go through with this?'

'I didn't need to,' he murmured. 'Our marriage is a *fait ac-compli*.'

'But this is insurance,' she insisted. 'Because if I somehow managed to walk out of here, my life would never be the same again, right?'

He didn't respond. He didn't need to. He'd manoeuvred her into a position that made her agreement essential. She wasn't as naïve as he seemed to think. She knew what this baby would mean for her, she knew that there'd be a stream of paparazzi wanting to capture their child's first everything, following her around mercilessly.

'I need you both in the RKH where I can protect you.' He spoke simply, the words so final they sent a shiver down her spine. 'I'm sorry for the necessity of this, but I am not prepared to take any chances with your life.'

'You're being melodramatic.'

His eyes narrowed. 'My mother was killed by terrorists. She was eight months pregnant. I was supposed to be with her that day.' Each sentence was delivered with a staccato-style finality but that didn't make it any easier to digest. 'I will not let anyone harm you.'

Her heart slowed down. Pity swarmed her and, despite the situation she found herself in, she lifted a hand and pressed it to his chest. 'I'm so sorry, Sariq. I had no idea.'

He angled his face away, his jaw clenched. 'It was kept quiet. My father was determined to maintain the peace process and so news was released that she died in childbirth.' His features were like granite. 'The perpetrators were found and convicted in a court convened for the purpose of conducting the trial away from the media's eyes.'

She sucked in a breath, with no idea what to say. A shiver ran down her spine. She was deeply sorry for him, for the boy he'd been and the man he was now, and yet she had to make him see things were different. 'I'm in America, not the RKH, and if you hadn't released this, no one would even know who I am.'

'You underestimate the power and hatred of these people.' He lifted a hand, touching the back of his fingers to her cheek so lightly that she had to fight an impulse to press into his touch.

'But no one knew me.'

'They would have found you. Both of you. Believe me.'

His hand dropped to her stomach. 'I know we each want what is best for our child, Daisy.'

He was right. On that point, they were in total agreement.

'Tell me what you want from me, when we are married,' he said quietly. 'What will make this easier for you?'

It was an attempt at a concession. She bit down on her lip, with no idea how to answer. The truth was, she really couldn't have said. She had so many questions but they were all jumbling around her head forming a net rather than a rope, so she couldn't easily grasp any single point.

'I just need space,' she said simply. 'Once we're married, I need you to leave me alone and let me get my head around all this. And then, we'll have this conversation.'

He looked as though he wanted to say something but then, after a moment, he nodded. 'Fine. This, I can do.'

Daisy's head was spinning in a way she doubted would ever stop. From the short wedding ceremony at the embassy to a helicopter that had flown them to a private terminal at JFK, to a plane that was the largest she'd ever been on that was fully private. It bore the markings of the RKH and was, inside, like a palace. Just like the embassy, it was fitted with an unparalleled degree of luxury and grandeur. A formal lounge area with large leather seats opened into a corridor on one side of the plane. Sariq had guided Daisy towards it and then gestured to the first room. 'My office, when I fly.' A cursory inspection showed a large desk, two computer screens and a pair of sofas.

'A boardroom, a cinema,' he continued the inventory as they moved down the plane. 'A bathroom.' But not like any plane bathroom she'd ever been on. Then again, they'd been short domestic flights from one state to the next, never anything like this. A full-sized bath, a shower, and all as you'd find in a hotel; nothing about it screamed 'airline'.

'Here.' He'd paused three doors from the end of the plane. 'It's a twelve-hour flight to Shajarah. Rest.'

She'd looked into the room to see a bed—king-size—made up sumptuously with cream bed linen and brightly coloured cushions. She still wore the dress in which she'd said her wedding vows—in English, out of deference to her, but at the end in the language of Haleth. She'd stumbled while repeating the words and her cheeks had grown pink and her heart heavy at the enormity of what was ahead of her. She would need to learn this language, to speak it with fluency, to be able to communicate with her child, who would grow up hearing it and forming it naturally.

'I'm not tired.'

Except she was. Bone tired and overwhelmed.

'There are clothes in there.' He gestured towards a small piece of furniture across the room, but made no effort to leave her. His eyes were locked to hers and her pulse began to fire as feelings were swamped by instinct and she wanted, more than anything, to close her eyes and have things go back to the way they used to be between them. She remembered the feeling of being held by him, his strong arms wrapping around her and making her feel whole and safe. But there was no sense seeking refuge from the man who had turned her life upside down.

'Thank you.' A prim acknowledgement. She stepped into the room, looking around, then finally back to facing him. Just in time to see him pull the door closed—with him on the other side of it.

Alone once more, she still refused to give in to the tears that had been threatening her all day. She blinked furiously, her spine ramrod straight as she walked across the room, pulling open the top drawer of the dressing table and lifting out the first thing she laid her hands on. It was a pair of pants, and, despite the fact they were a comfortable drawstring pair, they were made of the finest silk. Black, they shimmered as she held them, and at their feet there was a fine gold thread, just like the robes he wore. A matching shirt was beneath the pants. With long sleeves and a dip at the neck, it was like wearing water— so comfortable against her skin that she sighed. The engines began to whir as she pulled the blankets back and climbed into bed. She was asleep before the plane took off.

Daisy would have said she was too tired to sleep, but she slept hard, almost the entire way to the RKH. She might have kept sleeping had a perfunctory knock at the door not sounded, wrenching her from dreams that were irritatingly full of Sariq. His smile when they'd talked, his laugh when she'd made a joke. His eyes on her in that way of his, so thoughtful and watchful, intent and possessive, so her blood felt like lava and her abdomen rolled with desire.

And then, the man himself stood framed in the door of her room and her dreams were so tangible that she almost smiled and held a hand out to him, pulling him towards her. Almost. Thank goodness sanity intervened before she could do anything so stupid.

'Yes?' The word was cold. Crisp. He didn't react.

'In two hours, we will land. There is some preparation you will need to undergo, first.' His eyes dropped lower, to her décolletage, and she was conscious of the way the shirt dipped revealing her flesh there, showing a hint of her cleavage. 'You must be hungry.'

The last words were said in a voice that was throaty.

'I'm not.'

Disapproval flared in his features but for such a brief moment that it was gone again almost immediately, so she thought she'd imagined it. 'Come and join me while I eat, then.'

'A command, Your Highness?'

Silence. Barbed and painful. Her stomach squeezed. 'If that's what it takes.' He looked at her for a moment longer. 'Two minutes, Daisy.'

* * *

He pulled the door shut before his frustration could become apparent. But he *was* frustrated. In his entire life, he'd never known someone to be so argumentative just for the sake of it. Sariq was used to being obeyed at all times, yet Daisy seemed to enjoy countermanding his words.

And when they were in the RKH? While the country was famously progressive in the region, there was no getting away from the fact it was still patriarchal and mired in many of the ways of the past. Her flagrant flouting of his wishes would raise questions he'd prefer not to have to answer.

Couldn't she see that their situation required special handling? It was as undesirable to him as it was to her—but what choice did either of them have? She was carrying his child, the heir to the RKH. This marriage, living together as man and wife, was the only solution to that situation.

He had to make her understand the difficulties inherent to her situation without terrifying her. He pressed his back against the door, closing his eyes for a moment, so that he saw his father again and a darkness filled him. He didn't want to think about what his father might say about this. Sariq was Emir now. The safety and prosperity of the kingdom lay on his shoulders, and his alone.

Alone again, Daisy flopped onto her back and stared at the ceiling, his command wrapping around her, making breathing difficult. She wasn't hungry, but she was thirsty—the thought of coffee was deeply motivating—and yet she stayed where she was, an emptiness inside her. And she knew why.

The Sariq of her dreams had been the man she'd fallen into bed with, the man who had bewitched and made her feel alive for the first time since Max. But he was gone, and there was only this Sheikh in his place. All command and duty. The juxtaposition was inherently painful.

She bit down on her lip, not moving, the emptiness like a

black hole, carrying mass of its own, weighing her down, holding her to the bed. She lay there for a long time, certainly past the allotted two minutes, and at some point, she heard the door open.

She didn't realise she'd been crying until he said something, a curse, and crossed to the edge of the bed, sitting down on it heavily and moving his hand to her cheek, gently wiping away the moisture there. His expression was grim, his eyes impossible to read, but his fingertips were soft and determined, moving to remove the physical signs of her emotions.

'I would do anything in the world not to have had to do this,' he finally said, the words dragged from him.

She knew that to be the truth. This marriage wasn't what he wanted either. He was as trapped by their baby as she was. 'I know that.' She pushed up to sitting, dislodging his touch, lifting her own hands to wipe at the rest of her cheeks.

'I'm fine.' She was glad her voice sounded clear. 'I've just been more prone to emotions since I got pregnant. It's out of my control.'

It didn't exonerate him. He continued to look at her as though he were fighting a battle with a superhuman force. He hated this. She was openly expressing her disbelief, he was holding his deep inside him, but there was no doubting that both of their lives had been torn open by this pregnancy.

'What did you want to talk about?'

His jaw clenched. 'Will you eat something?'

His words were so reminiscent of the version of him she'd known in New York that for a moment she let herself slip back through the cracks of time, cracks that yearning had opened wider. 'I'd kill for a coffee.'

'Murder is not necessary,' he responded immediately. 'Though I could understand if you felt a little driven to it.' A joke. A smile teased the corner of her lips but her mouth and heart were too heavy to oblige.

'Come.' He stood and her stomach rolled.

She nodded slowly. 'I'll just be a moment.'

He hesitated.

'I'm coming. Honestly.'

A crisp nod. 'Fine. This preparation is important, Daisy. It's for your sake, so you know what to expect.'

Anxiety shifted through her. 'Okay.'

In the bathroom—smaller than the main one she'd passed—she took a moment to freshen up, brushing her hair and teeth, washing her face and applying a little gloss to lips that felt dry courtesy of the aeroplane's air conditioning. But she worked quickly, aware that time was passing, bringing them closer to the RKH and her future as its queen.

He was in the main living space of the plane, but he wasn't alone. Six men and three women were sitting with him, each dressed in suits, so that in contrast Sariq in his robe looked impossibly regal and forbidding. When she entered, all eyes turned to her, yet she felt only the slow burn of Sariq's.

'Leave us.'

Their response was automatic. Everyone stood, moving past Daisy, pausing briefly to dip their heads in a bow that was deferential and unsettling. When she turned back to Sariq, he was standing, still watching her.

'Some members of my government,' he explained.

'Women?' She moved to the table, deliberately choosing a seat that was several away from him, preferring a little physical separation even though it did little to quell the butterflies that were rampaging through her system.

'This surprises you?'

'I guess so.'

'The RKH is not so out of step with the west. Women hold the same rights as men.'

A woman appeared then, carrying a tray, which she placed in front of Daisy. The aroma of coffee almost brought a fresh wave of tears to her eyes. It was so familiar, so comforting, that she smiled with genuine pleasure at the attendant.

'Thank you.'

'*Ha shalam.*' The attendant smiled back, encouragingly.

'*Ha shalam* means thank you,' Sariq explained.

Daisy repeated it.

'This is Zahrah. She will be your primary aide.'

'I am pleased to meet you, Your Highness.' Zahrah bowed as the others had, but lower, and she lifted Daisy's hand in her own, squeezing it. Her eyes were kind, her smile gentle and friendly. The woman was beautiful, with glossy dark hair, long, elegant fingers, and nails painted a matte black. Daisy's heart swelled. Something like relief flooded her.

'She will help you ease into this,' Sariq continued. 'To learn the language and customs of my people, coordinate your schedule, oversee your needs.'

'I think I'll need a lot of help,' Daisy murmured, lifting her brows, the words directed towards Zahrah.

'You're too modest, Your Highness.'

'Please, call me Daisy,' she insisted.

In response, Zahrah smiled and bowed once more before leaving the cabin.

'She won't do that.'

It took Daisy a moment to understand what he meant.

'Do you remember in New York, how hard you found it to use my name?'

Daisy sipped her coffee without answering.

'And you are a foreigner with very little understanding of royalty and its power. Imagine having been raised to serve the royal family, as Zahrah was. Deference is ingrained in her. Do not let it unsettle you. Being treated like this is something you will have to become accustomed to.'

'I don't know if I can—I'm just a normal person. I can't imagine being treated as anything other than that.'

'In the RKH, you are equal to only one person. Me. To everyone else, you are like a goddess.'

A shiver ran down her spine. 'And this is how you were raised? To see yourself as a god?'

'I don't see myself that way.' His response was swift and there was a heaviness to the words. 'Gods have unlimited power. I do not.'

'I'm glad you realise that.' The words were delivered drily but a smile flicked across his lips, widening the cracks into the past. She gripped onto the present with both hands, refusing to let herself remember what that weekend had been like. It was a lifetime ago, and they were two different people. Then, they'd been together by choice. Now? Circumstances required it, that was all.

'When we land, there will be a small group of photographers, vetted by the palace. You will step out of the aircraft first, onto a platform, where you will stand alone a moment and wave. It will be morning in Haleth, and not too warm yet. I will join you once they have had a moment to take a photograph of you alone. Protocol dictates that we do not touch, publicly.'

She lifted a brow. 'That seems somewhat arcane, given I'm pregnant with your baby.'

'It is as it is.' He lifted his shoulders.

'Fine by me.' She sipped her coffee, closing her eyes for a moment as the flavour reached inside her, comforting her, bringing peace to her fractured soul. 'I'd prefer it that way, anyway.'

His eyes flashed with something she couldn't interpret. Mockery? Frustration? Pain? She blinked away.

'You are afraid.'

'Of you? No.'

'Not of me.' He didn't move, but his words seemed to wrap around her. 'Of yourself.'

'What?' She took a gulp of coffee.

'You are afraid of wanting me, even after what's just happened.'

Her heart began to thud inside her. She couldn't tear her eyes away from him, and there was a silent plea on her features, a look of confusion and uncertainty, and, yes, of want. Of need.

He stood then, bringing himself to the space beside her, propping his bottom on the edge of the table and spinning her chair, so she was facing him. 'We should not have slept together.' His hand lifted to her hair, running over its find gold ends as though he couldn't help himself. 'I knew I wanted you the moment I saw you, and yet you should have been off-limits to me.' His hand dropped to her cheek. 'Just as I should have been to you. And yet we couldn't stop this.'

She swallowed, her throat shifting with the movement. His hand dropped to her shoulder, his thumb padding across the exposed bone there. 'I want to promise you I won't touch you again, but I am afraid too, Daisy.'

The admission surprised her.

'I am terrified of how much I want you, even now. Even when I know you must hate me for bringing you here, for railroading you into this marriage.'

Her mouth was so dry. She could only stare up at him, but his confession was tangling her into a thousand knots.

'I do hate what you did,' was all she could say.

His eyes swept shut, briefly, his lashes thick and dark against his caramel skin. Her stomach hurt. Her heart ached. Her body was alive with fire and flames and yet inside there was a kernel of ice that refused to budge.

'I can conquer this,' he said simply, dropping his hand and standing. 'I had no choice but to marry you, but I will not sleep with you again. You have my word.' His hand formed a fist at his side as though even then he was having to force himself to rail against his instincts and not touch her. 'You do not need to fear this.'

Oh, but she did. She was terrified of how she wanted him. Hearing him be so honest about his own struggles made her acknowledge her own—inwardly at least. Yes, she wanted him. Even as they'd said their vows her insides had been heating up, her body acknowledging that, in him, she had met her perfect match.

But she could barely admit that to herself, let alone to him. 'Thank you. I appreciate that.'

So prim! So formal! Good. Let him think she was grateful for this reprieve instead of desperately wanting to contradict his edict.

If he was disappointed, he didn't show it. 'Let's keep going. There is much you need to know before we land.'

# CHAPTER NINE

In New York, he'd made a promise to her. Space. Time. Freedom to think, away from him. And he intended to uphold it even when the knowledge that she was in the palace, only a wall separating them, had him wanting to go to her, to speak to her, to see her, to assure himself she was okay. Yet he had made this promise and it seemed small, in the scheme of all that he was asking of her, and therefore vital that he respect it.

In the three weeks since they'd arrived in the RKH, he'd upheld his promise. Maintaining his distance, receiving his updates from Zahrah to assure himself that Daisy was coping, and that she was well. He'd organised medical appointments to ascertain her physical health, and that of the baby. And he'd managed the politics of their marriage like a bull at a gate. A top PR firm was engaged to sell the message in the media. This was a new age for the country and his marriage to Daisy Carrington symbolised a step forward with the west. Reaction had been, for the most part, positive. Though there were some quarters that publicly questioned his choice and voiced great offence that the Sheikh of the RKH should turn his nose up at the two women who had widely been known to be candidates as his prospective Emira.

As for those women, he'd met with each privately, and to them he'd sold it as a love story.

*'I was not prepared for how I would feel to meet her. I wish I had been able to resist, but there were greater forces at play.'*

It had been easy to sell that message. It hadn't been love at first sight with Daisy, but it had been infatuation, and that was equally blinding.

There were those who seemed to accept his choice to marry an American, but not Daisy. Stories about her had run in the press. Fewer in the RKH papers, which were generally respectful of the palace and its privacy, but, in the blogs and cheaper tabloids, derisive pieces about her status as a divorced woman had been printed. Someone had found photos of her first wedding, so he'd seen her smiling up at her first husband, and something inside him had fired to life, filling him with darkness and questions. He wanted to know about this man she'd married—by choice. The man she must have loved at some point, even if she didn't now.

And he'd wanted to silence the stories that speculated on all sorts of things in Daisy's life before him, things he knew to be false without having had the conversations. Rumours that she'd travelled across America with a rock band, the inference being that she'd slept with the whole slew of musicians. Suggestions that her role at the hotel had been to appease guests in whatever manner she found suitable. And yes, the inevitable suggestion that this baby wasn't actually his.

He had read them with fury at first and, as the weeks went by, with muted anger and disbelief and, finally, with guilt and regret. She didn't deserve this.

'Has she read them?' he'd asked Zahrah on the fifth morning.

'I believe so, Your Highness.'

A grim line had lodged on his lips and it hadn't lifted since, and after three weeks of feeling as if he wanted to see her, to ensure she was okay, but resisting that impulse because she'd asked it of him, he was close to the breaking point.

So it wasn't precisely Malik's fault that they argued. Sariq had been ready to unleash his fury at anyone who looked at him the wrong way, let alone what Malik said.

'You cannot blame these people, sir. She is not suitable and it will take time for the country to adjust their expectations.'

Fire had filled Sariq's blood. 'In what way is your Emira not suitable?'

Malik hadn't appeared to realise he was on dangerous ground. 'Her nationality. Her marital status. Her pedigree.'

'If I have no issue with these things, how dare you?'

Malik's head jerked back. 'I beg your pardon, sir, I did not mean to offend you. I have spent my life protecting your interests...'

'My interests are now her interests.'

Malik was silent.

'You will organise a ball. Invite the parliament and foreign diplomats. It's time for the people of Haleth to meet my wife.'

Malik dipped his head but it showed scepticism.

'She is pregnant with my child.' Malik scraped his chair back and moved towards the open doors that led to the balcony. A light breeze was lifting off the desert, bringing with it the fragrance of sand and ash, and a hint of relief from the day's warmth. 'I wish, more than anything, that it hadn't been necessary to marry her.' His shoulders were squared as he remembered the way he'd had to bully Daisy into this. Regret perforated his being. 'She is now my wife. That's all there is to it.'

It was another baking-hot day. Daisy stood where she was, on the balcony that wrapped around this segment of the palace, staring out at the shimmering blue sky and desert sands that seemed to glow in the midday sun until a raised voice caught her attention. She turned in that direction right as a door pushed open and Sariq strode out, his frame magnetic to her gaze, his expression like thunder.

She stayed right where she was, frozen to the spot, her eyes feasting on him, her brain telling her to move, her blood insisting that she stay. It had been three weeks since she'd seen him. True to his word, he'd left her in peace, and she knew she should have been gratified that he'd respected her wishes, but deep down she felt so lonely, and so afraid.

Emotions she'd never show him, though. She tilted her chin in defiance. At least he looked as surprised to see her as she felt to see him. His chest moved with the force of his breathing; it was clear he was in a bad temper.

But why?

The raised voices—had one belonged to him?

Her mouth felt dry, and that had nothing to do with the arid desert climate.

He stared at her as though he was trying to frame words and she stared back until the silence became unbearable. What did she have to say to this man, anyway?

His eyes roamed her face in a way that sparked fires in her blood. How she resented his easy ability to do that! She felt her nipples pucker against the lace of her bra and her abdomen clenched hard with unmistakable lust. A biological response that she had no intention of obeying.

A bird flapped overhead, its wingspan enormous, drawing Daisy's gaze. She watched as it circled the desert and then began to drift downwards, its descent controlled and elegant.

It flew beyond her sight and so she looked away, back to Sariq. He was frowning now, but still regarding her with the full force of his attention, as though he could understand her if only he looked for long enough. But she didn't want to be understood.

Swallowing to bring much-needed moisture back to her mouth, she said quietly, 'Excuse me,' before turning and heading into the blessed cool of the tiled sitting room of the palace. Her heart though wouldn't stop hammering. She knew their suites of rooms were in close proximity, but she hadn't realised this balcony was shared by both. It seemed to create a greater intimacy than she was comfortable with. She used this space often, particularly in the evenings when the sting of the day's heat had dropped, and she was able to sit beneath the blanket of jewels dotted through the inky night sky, reading or simply existing, quiet and contemplative.

'Daisy.' His voice held a command. She ignored it. 'Daisy.'

Damn it. He was closer now, his voice right behind her. She stopped walking and turned, but she was unprepared for this— the full force of attraction that would assail her at his proximity. But attraction was beside the point—she wouldn't give in to that again.

'Yes, sir?'

He closed his eyes, his nostrils flaring as he inhaled. 'Sariq.'

'Yes, Sariq?'

He latched his gaze to hers and her pulse throbbed through her. Still, he stared, and for so long that she wondered if he had any intention of speaking. She was about to turn away from him anew when his gaze dropped to her stomach and a hint of guilt peppered her mood. She was pregnant with his child, and he'd spent three weeks away from her. Naturally he was curious.

'I'm fine. The baby's fine, too. We had a scan two weeks ago.'

'I know.'

'You do?'

And then, a smile lifted one corner of his lips, a grudging smile that wasn't exactly born of happiness. 'Did you think I wouldn't involve myself in the medical care of our child?'

Their child. This had nothing to do with her.

'How are you?'

'This wasn't included in your report?'

'Basic health information.' He shrugged with ingrained arrogance. 'Nothing more.'

'What more is there of consequence?'

His brows knitted together. Her tone was unmistakably caustic. 'You're happy?'

She couldn't help the sceptical laugh that burst from her. 'Really?'

'Zahrah says you're settling into your routine well?'

Daisy ignored the prickle of betrayal that shifted inside her. Everyone in this palace reported to Sariq. It shouldn't surprise her that the servant she'd begun to think of as a friend was doing likewise. 'My routine involves being pampered around the clock. I don't imagine many people would struggle with that.'

Frustration, though, weaved through her words.

'But you do,' he insisted. 'You don't like it.'

Her expression was a grimace. 'I'm more comfortable doing the pampering than I am being spoiled. I don't need all this.' She lifted a hand to her head, where her blonde hair had been braided and styled into an elaborate up-do. 'I'm not used to it.'

'You'll become used to it.'

A mutinous expression crossed her face. 'Do I have to?'

'Yes.' And then, more softly, 'You're aware of the media stories?'

Pain sliced inside her being. She wrenched her face away, unable to meet his eyes. Some of the stories—most, in fact— had been absolutely appalling. 'Are you wondering how many are true?'

He said a word in his own language that, going by the tone and inflection, was a bitter curse. 'I am asking how these preposterous stories have affected you. This has nothing to do with me.'

'You don't care that I'm a rock star groupie?'

'I don't care about any of it.' But something in his eyes showed that to be a lie. He wasn't being completely honest to her, and she hated that. She hated that he might have read the headlines and believed them, that he might believe she'd made a habit of sleeping with guests of the hotel. After everything she'd been through with Max, Daisy had made a point of remaining guarded with members of the opposite sex.

The irony of these stories—when she'd been a virgin on her wedding night, and slept with no one since her divorce—filled her with a desire to defend herself. Except Sariq didn't deserve that. What did it matter if he thought her promiscuous? Who cared? As if he hadn't had his share of lovers in the past?

There was only one element of the stories that she cared to contradict. 'You are the father.'

A look of anger slashed his features. 'I know this.'

She bit down on her lip then, staring out at the desert. 'We were together two nights, but it was enough for me to see inside your soul, Daisy Al Antarah.' It was the first time her new name had been spoken aloud to her and it sent a *frisson* of response shuttling down her spine. 'I saw you and I wanted you. I seduced you. There was nothing practised about your responses to me. I am aware that I put you in the position of doing something outside your usual comfort zone.'

Which meant what? That she was bad in bed? Great. It was a silly thing to care about in that moment. A thought not worthy of her, so she relegated it to the back of her mind.

'I should have seen the signs. Perhaps I did, and chose to ignore them.'

'What signs?'

'Your inexperience, your innocence.' He shook his head, as though he were angry at himself. 'I knew you were out of your depth and I ignored that because it suited me, because I wanted you, and now we must both pay the price for that.'

Something like pain clenched her heart, because his regret was heavy in the tone of his words, but, more than that, she could feel it emanating off his frame. 'You don't want me here.'

He shifted his gaze to hers without speaking.

'You wish this hadn't happened, that we weren't married.'

A muscle jerked in his jaw and he regarded her silently. When the air between them was unbearably thick with tension, Daisy took a small step backwards, intending to leave, but his hand on hers stilled her.

She froze, her body screaming at her for something she couldn't fathom. 'Don't *you* wish that, Daisy?'

Wish what? She swept her eyes shut for a moment, gathering thoughts that had been scattered by his simple touch. As she stood there, his thumb began to move slowly over her inner wrist, sending pins and needles scuttling through her veins.

'I...' She darted her tongue out to moisten her lower lip at the same moment she opened her eyes, so she saw the way his attention was drawn to her mouth and the flame of desire began to spark harder.

'This marriage is the last thing either of us wanted.' The words were soft, and yet they cut something deep inside her. 'When we met in New York, I was in a deep state of grief.' Her heart softened. 'I was weak, where you were concerned. I wanted someone to take the pain of loss away, and you did. When you came to my bed, it obliterated everything besides my need for you.'

She stared up at him, her heart thudding in her chest. Her head and her emotions were at war with one another. Everything she knew she felt about men and love and sex demanded that she pull away from him, but instincts and feelings were holding her right where she was, a flash of sympathy making her want to comfort him and reassure him even when she doubted he deserved that.

'I wanted to be with you,' she said quietly, absolving him of the guilt of feeling that he'd overruled her in some way. 'Believe me, if I hadn't, I would have been perfectly capable of shutting down your advances.'

He lifted his other hand, reaching it around behind her head to the pins that kept her style in place. 'You had to do so many times, I suppose.'

Pain shifted inside her. 'The articles aren't true.'

'We've covered that.' Each pin he removed, he dropped to the ground, so there was a quiet tinkling sound before he moved on to the next. 'That doesn't mean you weren't the object of interest from many guests before me.'

A hint of heat coloured her cheeks, because he was right.

'From time to time. But I've always found it easy to deflect unwanted attention.'

'To fade into the background,' he remembered, moving to the fourth pin, loosening it so a braid began to fall from her crown.

'As my job required of me.' Why did her voice sound so husky, so coarse?

'And you tried to do this with me.' Another pin dropped.

It shouldn't have been biologically possible, but somehow Daisy's heart had moved position, taking up real estate in the column of her throat. 'Not hard enough.'

His eyes narrowed by the smallest amount. Another pin dropped. And another. When he spoke, he was so close his breath warmed her temple. One braid fell completely. His gaze moved to the side as his fingers worked at freeing it completely, so half her hair hung loose about her face. 'Do you think you could have done anything that would have put a stop to what we shared?'

It was hard to speak with her heart in her throat. 'Are you saying you wouldn't have taken "no" for an answer?'

The other braid fell. 'I'm saying you weren't capable of resisting what was happening between us.'

She wanted to defy him, to deny that fiercely, but there was a part of her that knew he spoke the truth. 'You're wrong.' The words were feeble.

He ignored them. 'So step away from me now.' He loosened the braid. She held her breath, staring up at him, fierce needs locking her to the spot when her brain was shouting at her to draw back, to show him that he was wrong about her, that she was very much in control of her responses to him.

But she wasn't and never had been, and she hated that.

Challenge lay between them, sharp like a blade. The air was thick and nothing could ease it. Breathing hurt.

'I told you I wouldn't touch you.' His fingers loosened her hair. A breeze lifted it so some ran across her cheek. 'I intend to honour that promise until you release me from it.'

Her harsh intake of breath sounded between them. That wasn't fair. She couldn't want him—she sure as heck shouldn't—but her knees were trembling and heat was building between her thighs, whispering promises she desperately wanted to obey.

'Sariq.' She didn't know what she wanted to say, but his name seemed like a good place holder, and she liked the way it felt on her lips, as though it were a promise. But of what?

'If I kissed you...' he moved his hand to her lips, padding his thumb over her flesh '...we'd be in bed within minutes. If we even made it that far.'

Her temperature spiked at the vivid imagery.

'Just like in New York.'

Her lips parted.

'You see, your body tells me a story, *habibte*. I see desire in your eyes, with how wide they flare and how dark your pupils are. Your cheeks are pink, your breathing rushed as though you have run a marathon. Your breasts move quickly as you try to fill your lungs, and your nipples...' he dropped his gaze '...have been begging for my attention since I stopped you from leaving this room. If I touched your most intimate places, I would feel your heat and need for me against my palm, just as I did in New York.'

She sucked in a ragged breath.

'It would be easy for me to kiss you and make you forget the path you've chosen, just as I did in America. It would be easy for me to override your instincts and make you mine. But you would hate me for that, wouldn't you?'

Would she? She couldn't say. She was a mess.

'You think forcing me to marry you isn't already sufficient grounds for hate?'

The anger of her statement surprised her, though it shouldn't. She felt backed into a corner—lashing out was a normal response.

'It's ample,' he agreed with a small shift of his head, but his eyes were dark and they bore into hers.

'Why are you doing this?' she whispered quietly. 'You don't want this to be a real marriage. You told me that at the embassy that night.'

He pulled a face. 'I wasn't referring to sex.'

'No?'

His features shifted for a moment. 'I have known, all my life, that I would never love whomever I married. That's what I was referring to that night. So far as I'm concerned, sex is just a biological act. It can be shared without any true danger of intimacy.'

She felt as though her chest were being cleaved in two. She stared up at him, unable to explain the pain that was lashing her, or its source. But on some level, she found his assertion to be repugnant.

'And intimacy is bad?'

'It's not bad. It's simply not part of the equation for me. I accepted a long time ago that my duty to my country would require me to choose this path.'

He brought his body closer, so his broad chest was pressed to her breasts, and her nipples tingled painfully in anticipation. 'But sex? Sex without emotion, without love, can still be amazing.' He lifted a hand to her face, holding her still, and she caught her breath, waiting for him to kiss her, certain he would.

She felt his needs as surely as she did her own, his desire palpable, his body hardening against hers. Nothing moved, even the very air of the desert stood still, waiting, expectant.

'However, I swore I would keep my distance.' He dropped his hand and, with obvious regret, moved away from her. 'And I intend to honour that promise.'

It took several moments for her breathing to achieve anything close to normal.

'I have given you space, since you came to Haleth.'

Still, she couldn't speak.

'But three weeks without a sighting of the new Queen has

left a hole for the media to fill. It's time for my people to begin a relationship with you.'

Her heart began to speed for a different reason now and anxiety caused a fine bead of perspiration to break out on her forehead. It took her several moments to remember how to form words. 'Do you mean…like an interview or something?'

'An interview is a good idea.' He nodded, no sign of the conversation they'd just had, which had left her all kinds of shaken up, in his handsome face. 'But initially, there is to be a ball. My parliament and foreign diplomats will attend. The event will be held in your honour.'

Whatever she'd been feeling moments ago was gone completely. 'Is that necessary?'

'Do you intend to stay hidden here for ever?'

She considered that. Did she? These last three weeks had been blessedly quiet but she'd been cognisant of the fact she was dodging her responsibilities, hiding from the world she knew to be out there.

'Do you care? About the rumours?'

He frowned. 'No.'

'So why does it matter?'

'Rumours in foreign papers that speculate on matters I know to be false? This is laughable. But you are the Emira of the RKH and my people must respect you; they must accept our child as their future ruler.'

A prickle of danger shifted through her. 'You're worried they might not? That this baby might not be accepted as your heir?'

'I'm not worried.' Nor did he look it. 'But I do not wish your life, or his, to be harder because of steps we could easily take now to smooth the way of this transition.'

It all made so much sense. She knew she should agree, but agreeing with Sariq stuck in her craw, so she maintained a somewhat dubious silence.

'Malik is organising the ball. I'll have Zahrah notify you of the details in due course.'

\* \* \*

He couldn't sleep. Hours after he'd last seen Daisy, and he felt a curdling sense of foreboding, a kernel of worry he couldn't dispel. Telling himself he was being melodramatic, he threw his sheet back and stood, pacing to the small timber piece of furniture against the wall, lifting the ancient pewter jug and pouring himself a glass of water. In the distance, through the open doors of his bedroom, he could hear the familiar call of the *nuusha* bird, the night creature's song a cross between a bell and a whip. It was delicate and resounding, reaching across the desert from their nesting grounds in the cliffs of sand to the west of the palace.

He'd promised her he wouldn't touch her, but, oh, how he'd ached to do exactly that. When he'd seen her that afternoon, her cheeks pink from the heat, her hair so beautifully intricate but in a way he'd needed to loosen, so that he could remember the way it had fallen around her face when they'd made love…

He shouldn't think about that. He couldn't. Those nights were from a different lifetime, when he was free to act on impulse and she to indulge her desire.

He'd promised he wouldn't touch her and yet he'd come so close that day. He'd ached to kiss her. He very nearly had. And now, memories of her kept him awake, tormenting him, so he had a keening sense to go for a run, or a ride, to leave this gilded cage of a palace, to throw off the expectations incumbent upon him and be his own man. For one night. He strode onto the balcony, his eyes finding the looming shape of the caves, tracing their outline, wondering if he could absent himself from the palace for the four days it would take to make the round trip. There was an oasis there; he'd camped at its edges often.

Her strangled sound of surprise was barely audible at first, swallowed by the gentle breeze and the bird's cries.

It was as though he'd thought of her so hard and so often that she'd miraculously appeared before him. She wore a simple cream shift, barely covering her beautiful body, so he strained to keep his eyes on her face rather than allowing them to dip to the swell of cleavage revealed there. After their contact that day, seeing her like this was the last thing he needed. Knowing he had to be strong didn't alter the fact he wanted, more than anything, to drag her against him and make love to her.

'I…' Her tongue darted out, moistening her lips, just as it had earlier that day. His cock hardened.

'You couldn't sleep,' he murmured, knowing he should stay where he was, even when other forces were pushing him forwards, closing the distance between them.

She shook her head. Her hair was loose now, just as he'd wished it to be, and the breeze caught at the lengths, lifting them so a skein of the moon's light cut through it. Silver against gold. Magic and captivating.

When he'd read the articles, only one had caught his attention, only one had played on his mind as being worthy of examination. 'Tell me about your ex-husband.'

Even in the scarce light thrown by the full moon, he could make out the shift in her features, their arrangement into a mask of surprise, at first, and then hesitation.

'Max? Why do you want to know about him?'

'Did you love him?'

Her smile was cynical. 'I'm not like you, Sariq. Love is the only reason I would have ever married anyone.' And then, quickly, with a look of mortification, 'Present circumstances excluded, obviously.'

'Obviously.'

She turned away from him then, but her profile was all the more alluring for she was hiding herself from him. He had to move closer to see her better. He caught a hint of her delicate fragrance and his body tightened. His fingers ached to reach for her.

'And what happened to this great love, then?'

She angled her face to his, her clear eyes analytical, studying him in a way few had ever dared. It was unusual for Sariq to have an equal. Most people feared his power even when he wielded it so rarely, but Daisy was unflinching in his presence, and always had been.

'We got divorced. End of story.'

'I don't think so.'

'What do you want to know?' Her voice rang with discontent. 'All the gory details?'

'The pertinent ones at least.'

'Why?'

'You don't want to tell me?'

A flicker of a frown. He wanted to smudge his finger over her lips, but didn't. 'Is it relevant?'

'It's...of interest.'

She turned back to the view, her eyes following the sound of the bird in the distance. For a long time, she was quiet, and it was easy for Sariq to believe she had no intention of speaking. But then, finally, after a long exhalation, as if gearing herself up to discuss the matter: 'We met shortly after my mother died. I inherited. Not a lot—our house and her small investment portfolio. Enough for me not to have to worry about money for a while. It was her dearest wish that I pursue my musical career and I promised her—' Daisy paused, her voice becoming gravelled, her throat moving beneath his gaze as she swallowed fiercely so he felt a surprising urge to comfort her. 'I promised her I would. It was one of the last things I said to her.'

She was going to cry. He held himself rigid, adhering to his promise, but, oh, how that cost him when his arms were heavy with a need to drag her against him, to offer her physical comfort to her emotional wounds.

'After my father left, I stopped playing. I couldn't bear to any more. It was something we shared.' Her smile lacked warmth; it was a grimace of pain masquerading as something else, something brave when he could feel her pain. 'But then Mom got sick—' she frowned '—and it was one of the only things I could do to get through to her, to help her, so I played and I played and when she was well, she'd beg me never to give up. She'd beg me to play so everyone heard.'

Every answer spawned a new question. What had happened to her mother? Where had her father gone? They'd been so open and honest in New York, it had been easy to ask her whatever he wished, and he'd been confident she would answer. But there were barriers between them now, necessary and impenetrable, so he didn't ask. He stayed on topic even when a part of him wanted to digress.

'And your husband?'

'Max loved my playing too.' Her words were scrubbed raw. 'And I loved to play for him.'

Something moved in Sariq, and he wasn't naïve enough to pretend he didn't know what it was. Jealousy. He had listened to Daisy play and wished, on some level, that she were playing just for him.

'Max had a lot of big dreams. But they were… I helped him as much as I could. I trusted him implicitly. He was my husband, why wouldn't I? I wouldn't have married him if I hadn't.' Her eyes lifted to his and the strength of the ghosts there almost knocked the breath from his lungs.

'And?' His word held a command, there was that imperative he was used to employing, but it was born now not of regal title so much as a desperate hunger to comprehend. Something terrible had happened between them, he could feel it, and it was vital that he understand it.

'He lied to me.' The words were filled with bitterness. 'He didn't love me, he loved my inheritance and the implicit trust I had in him. Trust that led me to add him as a signatory to my accounts, that meant I never questioned his transactions. It wasn't until I began to prepare for the Juilliard that I realised he'd taken everything. *Everything.*'

Sariq was completely silent but inside, her explanation was exploding like the shattering of fine glass.

'Not only had he cleared my accounts, he'd taken out a mortgage on Mom's home, which I had owned clear of debt. I had to sell it, but that debt is still there, so I'm chipping away at it as best I can but...'

'It's onerous,' he supplied, after a moment, sympathy expressing itself in his tone.

'You could say that.' A bitter laugh. Then, her hand lifted to her throat, where a delicate line of diamonds ran across the detailing at the neckline of her nightgown. 'I suppose that's not one of my problems now.'

'Of course not.' Relief spread through him, because this was something real and palpable he could do, to relieve at least one of her worries. 'Have Zahrah provide Malik with the details and he shall clear this debt.'

'Have my people call your people?' she murmured, shifting to face him, so their bodies were only two or three inches apart.

'Something like that.'

Her features compressed with exasperation, and then her eyes lifted over his shoulder, so he wanted to reach out and drag her face to his, to look into her soul through their green depths. 'I thought I loved him, but, over the years, I've given it a lot of thought and, honestly, I think I was just so grateful.' The words were laced with self-directed anger.

'Why grateful?'

'When my dad left, it was easy to believe it had been my fault, that I was in some way unlovable. Then Mom died and I was all alone, and it was terrifying and empty and quiet. When Max appeared, he seemed to worship me. He was so full of praise and flattery and couldn't bear to be away from me.' She shook her head. 'It cooled once we were married. Now I see why: he got what he needed from me, but I was so grateful still, and I kept telling myself everything would be okay when my instincts were warning me all along.'

'Were you able to recoup any of the money?'

'He lost it.' She gripped the railing with one hand; the other remained at her side, as if weighted there by the burdensome diamond wedding ring he'd placed on her finger. 'Or hid it so well I didn't have the means to find it.'

'And so you took a job working at a hotel, trying to chip down a massive debt by waiting on demanding guests?'

'They weren't all demanding,' she corrected.

'If the debt is the size you're implying, surely that would have been a fool's errand?'

'What were my other options?' she pushed, a hint of steel touching the words. 'To accept defeat? To let him win?'

Her fierce fire stirred something to life in him.

'Many would have.'

'Not me.'

'No, not you.'

She swayed forward a little, but not enough. He remembered the way she'd felt that afternoon, her soft curves against his hard edges, and he wanted, more than anything, to feel that again. And then what?

The flicker of flames would convert to so much more. They would touch and he would kiss her, and then carry her to his bed where he'd spend the entire night reminding her that, aside from her pregnancy and their marriage, there was something between them that was all their own. But there couldn't be. All his life he'd understood the danger that came from caring for one's spouse. His father had been destroyed by his mother's death. Sariq would never care for anyone enough to feel their loss so keenly. His country deserved such sacrifice—his duty demanded that of him.

And perhaps she intuited the strengthening of his resolve, because she blinked, her huge eyes shifting to his with a look he couldn't comprehend, and then she stepped backwards, wrapping a single arm across her torso. 'It's late and I'm tired. Goodnight, Your Highness.'

She was gone before he could remind her to call him Sariq.

# CHAPTER TEN

HE READ THE intelligence report with a frown on his face that gave little of his anger away. But inside, a fury was unravelling that would know no bounds. 'And they were arrested at the border this morning?'

'Two security agents intercepted their vehicle as it crossed into the old town of Rika.'

'Armed?'

'To the teeth.'

Sariq's expression was grim. 'Where are they being held?'

'In the catacombs.'

'Fine.' He scraped his chair back. 'We shall go there now.'

Malik's displeasure was obvious. 'But, sir, the ball begins in an hour…'

'The ball will wait.' The words were louder—harsher—than he'd intended. With an effort, he brought his temper under control. 'These men were intending to kill my wife, were they not?'

'That is the charge, yes, Your Highness.'

'Then before I parade my wife in front of a slew of people, I would like to ascertain, beyond a shadow of a doubt, that they have no links to anyone in attendance this evening.'

'The guards will investigate this.'

Sariq held a hand up to silence his oldest, most loyal advisor.

'That is not sufficient. In this, I will not delegate.' He stalked towards the door. 'Come, Malik.'

Daisy wasn't sure what she'd expected. In the hotel in America, the ballroom was impossibly grand, with tall columns and exceptional art, but even that was nothing to this. A wing of the palace stood vacant of all furniture. The walls were gold, and each was decorated with an ancient piece of art. Flower arrangements were placed on marble pillars at regular intervals, so the air was rent with sweetness. At the end of the enormous room, glass doors had been thrown open to reveal a dance floor made of white marble tiles. While there were fairy lights strung across it, nothing dimmed the beauty of the desert night, the brightness of the stars that shone down on them. The music was traditional, lyre, flute and sitar combining to create an atmospheric and intriguing piece.

Daisy hovered above it all, waiting in the wings, safe from being seen, her anxiety at the role she must play increasing with every moment that passed.

'He won't be much longer,' Zahrah, standing a little way away, murmured soothingly.

Daisy made an effort to relax her expression, even attempting a smile. 'It's fine.'

The music continued and, below her, beautifully dressed guests milled, champagne in some hands, iced tea in others. Some of the women wore western-style ball gowns with enormous diamonds and jewels at their throats. Others wore ornate gowns and robes, the delicate, bright scarves arranged over their hair, adding mystery and intrigue to their appearance.

Daisy had worn what Zahrah had provided her with. 'It was the Emira's,' Zahrah had explained.

'Who?'

'His Highness's mother.'

'Oh.' She'd dressed with a sense of reverence, careful not to break any of the delicate fabric that made up the ceremo-

nial gown. White with gold, just as Sariq often wore, it was
heavier than it looked courtesy of the yellow diamonds that
were stitched into the neckline and waist. It glittered from every
angle. At her throat, she wore a single yellow diamond, easily
the size of a milk-bottle cap, and on top of her head, a tiara.

Her hands were covered by white satin gloves that came to
her elbows. 'They're hot,' she'd murmured to Zahrah, when
she'd pulled them on. 'Perhaps I'll give gloves a miss.'

'You must wear them. It's protocol.'

'Gloves?'

She'd made a noise of agreement. 'No one is allowed to touch
your hand but the Sheikh.'

Daisy's brows had lifted.

'You're not serious?'

'It's tradition.'

'So I'm meant to wear gloves my whole life?'

'Well...' Zahrah had smiled kindly '... I think we can relax
the traditions behind closed doors, just as much as you'd like to.
But when on state business, it will be expected that you do this.'

Daisy had compressed her lips, biting back an observation
about the silliness of such a requirement. Haleth was an ancient and proud country. There were many habits and rituals
that were new to her, but that didn't mean she could stand in
judgement of them.

The guests swirled beneath them, an array of fabulous colour and finery. Twenty minutes later, Daisy looked to Zahrah.
'This is becoming rude.'

Zahrah frowned. 'Madam?'

'Keeping all these people waiting. Where on earth is he?'

'The message I received just referred to urgent business,
I'm sorry.'

'I hate the idea of going down there on my own, but surely
that's preferable to ignoring the guests?'

Zahrah's alarm was obvious. 'You can't. Not for your first
function. His Highness would never approve.'

Daisy's interest was piqued. 'Oh, wouldn't he?' The idea of flaunting his authority was wildly tempting and she couldn't really say why.

'Of what would I not approve?'

Daisy whirled around, her eyes catching those of her husband immediately. He wore another spectacular robe, this one emphasising the strength and virility of his frame, the darkness of his complexion. On the balcony, he was the man she'd met in New York, but like this, he was an untouchable ruler. There was something unusually forbidding in his appearance, a tightness in his frame that had her brows drawing together.

Zahrah bowed low at his entrance and before she could straighten, Sariq had dismissed her. 'Leave us. Allow no one to enter.'

'Yes, sir.'

Alone, Daisy gave her husband the full force of her attention. 'Where have you been? People have been here an hour. *I've* been here an hour.'

He wasn't accustomed to being questioned by anyone, but somehow he'd become so used to that with Daisy that it no longer surprised him. He shouldn't have come here straight from the prison. It would have been far wiser to give his temper time to cool down, but the plans that he'd discovered on the would-be assassins had chilled him to the core. Seeing Daisy now, knowing he was the reason her life had potentially been in danger, filled him with a deep and immovable anger.

'An urgent matter called me away. Are you ready?' His voice was curt. He couldn't help it, though he knew he must. Daisy didn't deserve to feel the brunt of his anger. Even though the threat had been contained—his expert security teams had done just what they were supposed to and perceived a threat before it could come to the fore—the knowledge of what these men had planned sent a shiver down his spine.

'Sure.' Her smile was brave, but he detected her hesitation beneath it. Something pulled at his gut—guilt—a desire to absolve her from this life, to set her free from all of this. But even as he thought that, there was an answering certainty that he never would. That he couldn't. She was the mother of his child and her place was here with him. If this evening's arrests had taught him anything it was that her position as the mother to the heir of the RKH put her at grave risk. He intended to do what he could to protect her from that.

But at the doors that led to the wide, sweeping marble stairs that created the entrance to the room, she stopped. 'Wait.'

'What is it?'

When he angled his face to look at her, he saw that she was pale and alarm filled him. 'You're well?'

'I'm fine. I'm fine. I'm just...' She lifted a hand to her throat, pressing her gloved fingers to the enormous jewel there. 'You said they'd never accept me. A divorced American. Why do you think tonight will be any different?'

Her anxiety was palpable, and of his making. And yet, he'd been speaking the truth. 'You're my wife now. It *is* different.'

'But it's not. You were talking about why you couldn't marry me, about what was expected of you. No one wants me to be here with you.' She curved a hand over her stomach and his eyes dropped, following the gesture. Something moved inside him then because, without his notice, her stomach had become rounded. Not hugely, but enough. His child was growing inside her. Something locked into place within him, making words difficult to form for a moment.

'No one wants me to be pregnant with your child.'

The threat was contained. There was no danger to Daisy in this crowd. And yet he put a hand on her forearm and turned her to face him. 'Would you rather avoid tonight?'

Her eyes lifted to his, surprise in their depths, but it was squashed by defiance. 'No.' She looked towards the crowds once more. 'This ball has been organised in my honour, like you said. The least I can do is turn up, right?'

Admiration shifted through him. 'We won't stay long.'

Daisy was surprised when she realised she was enjoying herself. She wasn't sure what she'd expected. Hostility? Open dislike? And there had been some people who'd regarded her with obvious scepticism and misgiving, though she was shepherded away from those people by an attentive Sariq, who hadn't left her side all evening. For the most part, though, the crowd had been welcoming and generous. Most of the women she'd spoken to had conversed in English in deference to her. Sariq had translated for people who spoke only the native language.

Yes, she was enjoying herself but, after an hour of making small talk with strangers, her energy was flagging.

As if he could read her thoughts, Sariq leaned towards her, whispering in her ear so his warm breath filled her soul. 'There is a dance, and then we can leave.'

'A dance?' Of its own accord, her heart began to move faster, beating against her bones as though it were trying to rattle free.

'Just one.' His smile was alarming, because it reminded her so strongly of the way he'd been in New York. Seeing him like this surrounded by his people, she was in awe of not only his charisma, but also his strength and intellect. In every conversation, he was able to demonstrate a complete understanding of matters that affected his people. Whether it was irrigating agricultural areas to the north or challenges facing the country's education system, he was informed, nimble and considered. She listened to him and saw how easy it had been for him to work his way into her being.

It hadn't purely been a physical connection between them. While she found him attractive, it was so much more than that. And suddenly, out of nowhere, she was struck by a desire to be alone with Sariq, to have the full force of his attention on her as it had been in New York, and briefly on the balcony that evening several weeks ago.

'Ready?'

She bit down on her lip and nodded slowly, her heart slowing down to a gentle thud. 'Okay.'

'Don't look so afraid,' he murmured in her ear, so only she could hear. 'We have a deal, remember? This is just for show.'

Her heart turned over in her chest and she pulled back, so she could look in his eyes. Just for show.

This marriage was the last thing he wanted. She needed to remember that. While it was inevitable that they'd get to know one another, she'd be a fool to hope for more.

To hope for more?

Her insides squirmed. What was she thinking? She was the one who'd sworn off marriage. She'd promised herself she'd never again be stupid enough to get so caught up in a fantasy that she lost who she was. No one deserved that, least of all this man, who'd insinuated she was good enough to take to his bed as a mistress but not good enough to marry. The man who'd told her, point blank, that he'd never love his wife. That, for him, sex and intimacy were two separate considerations.

She straightened her spine, thrilled to have remembered such pertinent facts before his body enfolded hers, drawing her close to him. And as if by some silent cue, the music paused and another piece began to play, slow and lilting. With the stars shining overhead, the dance floor cleared so it was only Sariq and Daisy, their bodies moving as if one.

'You dance well.'

She wasn't sure she could take the compliment. He led, she followed—it was effortless and easy. They matched one another's movements as though they'd been designed to do just that. But they were silent and, after a few moments, that began to pull at her nerves.

'This is such an incredible courtyard.' For now, from this

vantage point, she could see that the dance floor was surrounded on three sides of the palace. On the fourth, the view opened up to a manicured garden in the foreground and, beyond it, the desert. The wildness of the outlook, juxtaposed with the grandeur of this ancient building, created a striking effect.

'It was one of the first parts of the palace. In the eleventh century, these walls were erected. This courtyard was, then, the court, where the Emir presided over official matters.'

'Really?'

He made a sound of agreement. 'Over there—' he gestured with his hand, so she followed the gesture '—you can see the relics of the throne.'

And indeed, she could. It was made of marble, only a leg remained, but it was cordoned off, as though it were an object of great value. 'The walls provided defence—from enemies and sandstorms that are rife in this region.'

She looked around the courtyard with renewed interest, making a mental note to come back and study it in more detail in daylight.

'Where is your court now?'

'I have an office,' he responded with a smile that was lightly teasing. Her belly flopped. 'Here, at the palace, and one in the city. There are state rooms for conducting the *rukbar*.'

'What's the *rukbar*?' She repeated the foreign-sounding word, imitating his accent.

'Very good.'

His approval warmed her.

'Literally translated, it means "relief". It is a day each month when the palace doors are thrown open and anyone, regardless of their wealth and stature, may come to the palace.'

'What for?'

'To eat and be seen.' His smile deepened, and a kaleidoscope of butterflies launched itself through her belly. 'The tradition began in my great-grandfather's day, when poverty and famine were crippling in this country. The palace provided a banquet for any who could make it, and, more than this, he sat in and listened to people's needs from dawn until nightfall, helping where he could.'

Daisy had slowed down without realising it. Sariq shifted, moving her with him. 'You still do this?'

He dipped his head in silent agreement.

'How do you help people?'

'It varies. Sometimes it's a question of a child not being able to get into school, in which case Malik has the education secretary look into matters. Other times, it's a family where the father has died and the mother cannot work, in which case we grant a stipend to help support her.' He lifted his shoulders in a gesture of nonchalance but there was an expression in his face that robbed Daisy of breath. 'In Haleth, you would never have struggled as you have.'

Daisy's feet stopped obeying her altogether. She was moving purely under Sariq's guidance. 'No?'

'No.' He lifted a hand, brushing his fingertips across her cheek as though he couldn't help himself. 'Here in Haleth, you would have come to me and I would have had Max held for questioning before he could "lose" your money.'

'Just like that?'

'Just like that.'

Her smile was lopsided. 'So you're the knight in shining armour for every distressed person in Haleth?'

'It's not possible to help everyone. We have social security agencies in place but the *rukbar* provides a catch-all. An additional layer for the people.' He paused. 'The RKH is a phenomenally wealthy country. Distributing wealth wisely is one of the purviews of my role, and I intend to see the resources of this country benefit the people of the land.'

She felt the strength of his convictions and understood. She knew what his position meant to him. Admiration shifted inside her, and it brought with it a dark sense of foreboding. She didn't want to admire him; she didn't want to like him. But dancing beneath the stars in the arms of the man she'd married, Daisy felt as though a spell were being cast, and there was no antidote to it.

Sariq didn't believe in fate. He didn't believe in destiny. But dancing with his wife in the ancient courtyard, beneath a blanket of stars, he knew one thing: there was perfection in how they fitted together. Not only in the physical sense, but, more than that, in the way they thought.

He liked speaking with her. He liked hearing her thoughts, her answers. She fascinated him and intrigued him, and it was easy to see how he could become addicted to that.

'I'd like to see it.'

He didn't follow.

'The *rukbar*.'

Hearing her use his ancient language was an aphrodisiac. He kept moving, careful not to display the effect she had on him, even as his body was stirring to the beat of an ancient drum.

'It convenes in one week. I will advise Malik you shall join me.'

'Really?'

Her happiness stitched something in his gut. He nodded once. 'But I should warn you, Daisy, it can be harrowing. Some of the people who attend have nothing. Their stories are distressing.'

Her lips twisted in a way that made him want to drop his head and capture them with his own. He might have, to hell with the complications of that, if they hadn't been surrounded by hundreds of dignitaries.

'I can cope.' There was steel in her words, and he wondered at the cause of it. There was so much about her he didn't know, and yet he felt that on some level he understood every cell of her being. That wasn't enough though. The gaps in his knowledge of her seemed insupportable all of a sudden. There was an urgency shifting through him.

'Has anyone told you about the *tawhaj* tower?'

She frowned. 'No?'

He moved his fingers by a matter of degrees, stroking them lightly over the flesh at her back. He felt her body tremble in response. Desire kicked up a notch.

'No.' Her voice was soft, husky. 'What is it?'

'Look.' He stopped dancing so he could gesture behind her. She shifted her gaze, her neck swanlike as she followed the direction he'd indicated. 'Do you see it?' He couldn't stop looking at her. He had to get a hold of this. They were being watched and the seduction they were enjoying was palpable. Surely everyone would be aware of the heat that was moving between them.

'No?'

'There.' It was an excuse to move closer. His arm brushed her nipples as he pointed more clearly and he felt her response. It was imperative that he remove them from this environment. He no longer wished to be surrounded by a hoard of onlookers. He needed his wife all to himself.

'Oh! Yes, I think so?'

It was, indeed, difficult to make out the tower in the moonlight. The spindly structure, forged from marble and stone many hundreds of years ago, was slender and elegant.

'Would you like to see it?'

She shifted to face him just as the music slowed to a stop. Her eyes held his and it was as though a question was moving from him to her, silent and unspoken, but heard nonetheless. 'Yes, Sariq. I would.'

# CHAPTER ELEVEN

HIS HAND IN the small of her back was addictive. They didn't speak as they moved through the ancient corridors of this palace. Floors of marble, walls of stone, tapestries, flowers, gold, jewels. It all passed in a blur. All Daisy was conscious of was the man beside her. His nearness, his touch, his warmth, his strength. She could feel his breathing as though it were her own.

It took several minutes for the noise of the party to fade from earshot completely and then there was silence, save for the sound of their footfalls and the pervasive throb of anticipation.

'In the thirteenth century, Haleth was made up of three separate kingdoms. War was frequent and bloody. The tower was built, initially, as a lookout. It is the highest point of palace land, and has a vantage point that, on a clear day, extends to the sea. It gave the Emir's forces the ability to detect a likely skirmish from a great distance.' He guided her through a pair of enormous timber doors, each carefully carved with scenes she would like to come back and study, another time.

'It meant that most of the approaches to the palace took place during sandstorms, when visibility was poor.'

She shivered. 'Such violence.'

'Yes.' He looked down at her, something unreadable in his

expression. There was a tightening to his features that spoke of words unsaid.

'What is it?'

'Nothing.' He shook his head, as if to clear the thought. 'Here.'

They approached another set of doors. These were gold, and guarded on either side by two members of the RKH military, dressed as the guards in the embassy had been.

Sariq spoke in his own language, a short command. Each bowed low and then the guard on the left pulled a ring of brass keys from his pocket, inserted one into the door. Both guards worked in unison to open them.

Inside, there was a marble staircase, but it wasn't possible to see more than the first two steps. One of the guards moved ahead, and when Daisy and Sariq followed, she saw that the guard was lighting heavy lamps attached to the walls. The staircase smelled of kerosene and damp.

On they went, each tread worn down in the centre by the thousands of steps that had come before theirs, until finally the air grew clear, the stars shone overhead, and they emerged into an open room right at the top of the tower.

The guard was lighting the lamps, giving the space a warm glow, but Daisy barely noticed. She was too busy taking in the details of this spectacular tower. The walls were open, just spindly supports every few metres, to create the impression of windows where there were none. Those same spindles rose like the branches of a tree towards the sky, curving inwards at great height, stopping well before they reached the centre so the roof was open, showcasing the night sky in a way that was breathtaking. The moon was full and it caught the pale marble in such a way that it seemed to shine against the inky black of the heavens.

'Wow.'

The guard was leaving. They were alone.

'These pillars are incredible.' She moved to one, running her hands over the carefully carved shapes. 'They must have been made by talented craftsmen.'

His expression was rueful. 'They were carved by prisoners. I used to come here a lot, as a child.' His features grew serious and, without any elaboration, she understood what he was alluding to.

'After your mother died?'

Surprise flashed in the depths of his dark eyes. 'Yes.'

She nodded slowly. 'Losing a parent at seven must have been incredibly difficult. Were you and she close?'

His jaw clenched, and he stared out from the tower, his body rigid, as though he weren't going to speak.

'She was my mother.'

Daisy considered this. 'That's not an answer.'

His gaze pivoted to hers. 'Isn't it?'

She traced her finger over a line in the marble, following the swirling texture contemplatively. 'I loved my mother, but we weren't close. That didn't stop it from hurting like anything when she died. I think a relationship with your parents can be complex.'

'Why were you not close?'

She was conscious that he was moving their conversation to her, and perhaps it was a technique for deflection, a way of moving the spotlight off him. She allowed that, with every intention of returning to her question in a moment.

'My mother was bipolar.' It was amazing how easy she found that coming from her lips, when for years she'd grappled with discussing the truth of her home life. 'When she was in a manic phase, she was the most incredible fun.' Daisy shook her head, her brow furrowed as she looked up at the stars across the night sky. The view from here showcased the incredible silver of the desert sands, filling her with a desire to lift her wings and fly across its wide expanse.

'But there were times when that wasn't the case?'

'Oh, yes. Many times. As a child, I didn't understand it. I

mean, one day she'd be pulling me out of school so we could go to the movies, or feeding me ice cream for breakfast, and then the next she wouldn't get out of bed.' She shook her head. 'Our house was either scrubbed to within an inch of its life, the smell of bleach on every surface, or completely abandoned. Milk cartons left out, dishes not washed, floors filthy.'

Sariq didn't say anything, but she felt the purpose for his silence. He was drawing her out, letting her keep talking, and despite the fact she generally kept her past to herself, she found the words tumbling from her now.

'There were times—when she stayed on her medication— when things were okay. But not really, because the medication just seemed to hollow her out. I don't think she really persisted in finding a good doctor and getting the right prescription. She hated the feeling of being "stable". Without the lows, she couldn't have the highs.'

'And your father?' Sariq prompted after a moment.

Daisy felt her throat thickening, as it often did when she thought of that time in her life. 'Dad couldn't deal with it. He tried to get Mom help but she was beyond that. He left home when I was ten.'

'Without you?'

'He wanted to take me. I refused. I knew my mom wouldn't cope.' She frowned. 'I was so angry with him, Sariq. To leave her just because she was sick? He failed her, and he failed me.'

'He did.' The words held a scathing indictment that was somehow buoying.

'Towards the end, Mom's manic phases grew fewer, her depression deeper. She began to self-medicate. Marijuana at first, then alcohol. Lots of alcohol.' Daisy closed her eyes, trying to blot out the pain. 'She was drunk when she crashed her car. Thankfully without hurting anyone else.'

He was quiet beside her but she felt his closeness and his strength and both were the balms to a soul that would always carry heavy wounds of her past. Silence sat between them, but it was a pleasant silence, wrapping around her, filling her with warmth. She blinked up at him and even though their eyes locked, she didn't look away.

He was staring at her and she felt something pass from him to her. There was magic in this tower, a great, appreciable force that weaved between them.

'When my mother died…' he spoke, finally '…my father sent me away. Partly for my own protection, but mainly, because I reminded him of her. He couldn't bear to spend time with me.'

She frowned. 'I thought…'

'Yes?' He prompted, when her voice trailed off into nothing.

'I just, the way you speak about him, I presumed you thought the world of your father.'

'He was an exceptional ruler. I admired him greatly. I feel his absence every day.' Sariq's gaze moved, returning to the desert beyond them. 'He loved only one person, his whole life. My mother. When she died, he lost a part of himself with her and he learned a valuable lesson.'

'What lesson?'

'That love leads to hurt.'

'Not always.'

'Really?' He lifted one brow, his scepticism obvious. 'You can say this after your own experience? Your father? Your husband?'

She bit down on her lip, wondering at his perspective.

'Dance with me?'

She blinked, looking around them. 'Here?'

'Why not?'

She was about to point out the absence of music, but she didn't. Because her heart was creating a beat in her ears, and it was all she needed. Wordlessly, she nodded, so he brought his arms around her waist, shaping her body to his.

They moved without speaking for several moments, but his revelations were playing through her mind. 'I think,' she murmured softly, 'that you don't know your own heart.'

He didn't respond, but that didn't matter. Deep in her own thoughts, she continued. 'Losing someone you love hurts. Betrayal hurts. But I don't think knowing there's a risk of that inures you to caring for another person. You think your father didn't love you? That you didn't love him? I think that's biologically impossible.'

'Your father didn't love you,' he pointed out after a beat had passed.

'Well, my dad's a somewhat deficient human. And anyway, he did love me. He just loved himself more.' She shook her head. 'Your father pushed you away because he was scared of being hurt again—because he knew that he loved you so much hurt was inevitable, if anything were to happen to you.'

He stroked her back in such a way that made it hard to hold onto a single ribbon of thought.

'Being afraid doesn't mean an absence of affection.'

'You're a romantic.' His words were murmured across her hair, teasing and light, pulling at her.

Was she? Daisy had never considered this to be the case. 'I think I'm more realist than romantic.'

'Not going by what you've just said.'

'Love is a reality of the human condition. You can't deny it's within you. You can't close yourself off to it. You loved your father and he died. The night we met, you weren't simply mourning a leader. You were grieving for the loss of your dad—something that goes beyond position and title. He was your father—the man who gave you life.'

Sariq stilled for a moment and then began to move, his steps drawing her towards the middle of the marble floor. 'It's different.'

'How? Why?'

He expelled a sigh. 'A royal child isn't… I was his heir. Not only his son. My purpose was always the continuation of the family.'

'You make it sound as though you were property rather than a person.'

'I was required.'

Daisy considered that a moment. 'Just like our child is "required"?'

A slight pause. 'Yes.'

The confirmation knotted her stomach in a way that was unpleasant. 'And so you won't love our child?'

'You are fixated on the notion of love.' The words were said lightly but they did nothing to ease the seriousness of her thoughts.

'I didn't have a father in my life for very long. I don't want my child to know the pain of an absent parent.'

'I was the one who insisted we raise our child together, wasn't I?'

'No.' She stopped dancing and looked up at him, her eyes sparking with emotions she couldn't contain. 'You insisted that I move here so your child would be in the RKH. Your heir. There's a difference.'

'What do you want me to say?'

She bit down on her lip, unable to put that into words. 'I don't want you to keep our child at an emotional distance,' she said, after several moments had passed. But it wasn't all-encompassing. She felt so much more.

*I don't want* you *to keep me at an emotional distance.*

'I won't.' The assurance was swiftly given, but it did little to assuage her concerns.

'Because I'd rather take my chances in America, regardless of what you say, than expose our child to the kind of upbringing you've described.'

He froze, his body completely still, his arms locked around her waist. There was such contrast—the strength and warmth of him juxtaposed to the rigid cool of his stance. 'America is not an option.'

Something flashed inside her. Anger! And it was so welcome. In the swirling, raging emotions she felt, anger was one she could grasp. It made sense. She liked it.

'You don't get to command me.'

His nostrils flared as he stared down at her, his attempt to control his temper obvious. 'You're wrong.'

'No, I'm not. You told me I was coming to the RKH as your equal. Well—' she pushed her hands onto her hips, glaring right back at him '—if I want to go to America then there's nothing you can do about it.'

His laugh lacked humour.

'I'm serious.'

'As am I. Deadly serious.' He brought his body closer to hers, but it seemed accidental, as though he were simply moving without conscious thought. 'Do you know why I was late this evening?'

She shook her head.

'I was in the catacombs that run beneath the city. They were converted to prison cells a few decades ago. Two men are detained there, right now, who were planning on hurting you, Daisy.'

She froze, his words slamming into her like bricks. Out of nowhere, she began to tremble. Her ears rang with a high-pitched squealing sound. 'You're making that up.' She wanted to reject it. It couldn't be true.

'I wish I were.'

The shaking wouldn't stop.

Sariq swore under his breath, then his big, masculine hands were cupping her face, holding her steady for his inspection. 'Here, I can protect you. My guards can protect you. And believe me, Daisy, nothing matters more to me than your safety.' Neither of them moved. 'You and our child will have the full force of my army at your disposal. You must remain in the RKH. Can you see that?'

She nodded quickly. Fear—not for herself so much as for the life of her unborn child—was instinctive and swift. 'But why?'

His lips were a grim slash in his face. 'Because of what you represent. Because of the stability our child will bring.'

'I… Why didn't you tell me?'

'I just did.'

'I mean sooner.'

'I dealt with it.'

A shiver ran down her spine. 'What does that mean?'

'These men will not harm you.'

Her eyes flashed with fear. 'What did you do?'

His laugh was gruff. 'Not what I wished, believe me. They will spend a long time in prison for this though.'

'So if the threat is gone…'

'There are always madmen, Daisy, with political agendas.'

'You can't protect me from everything for ever.'

'No.' A muscle jerked in his jaw. 'But I can try.'

She thought of his mother then, who was murdered by madmen such as those apprehended this evening. His mother who had been pregnant with another child, and whose death had caused the beginning of the end for Sariq's relationship with his father. And a part of Daisy wanted, more than anything, to console Sariq. It was a selfish need though, because she also needed consoling. She needed distracting. She wanted to feel alive and safe, and present in the moment.

Reaching to her face, she pulled his hands away, stepping back from him to give them a little space. Then, slowly, deliberately, she reached for the straps of the dress, guiding them down her arms slowly, her eyes on his the whole time.

'What are you doing?' There was an expression of panic on his features, as though he knew that if she started this, he wouldn't be able to stop it.

'What does it look like?'

His eyes closed for a moment, then pierced her with their intensity. 'Daisy…'

She shook her head then, and the desert breeze lifted some of her fair blonde hair, blowing it across her cheeks.

'I don't want to think right now. I don't want to think about plots to kill me, threats, nothing. I don't want to think about dangers and politics.' The dress dropped to the floor at her feet. She stepped out of it, mindful of the beautiful silk lingerie she wore, grateful Zahrah had presented her with the set that evening.

'I just want to feel.' She stood where she was, her eyes fixed to his, her lips parted a little. 'Will you make me feel, Your Highness?'

Invoking that formal title made his eyes flare wider. He released a low, growling sound, then shook his head, but it was obvious he was holding on by a thread. 'You'll regret this.'

'Perhaps.' She lifted her shoulders. 'But that doesn't mean I don't want it to happen right now.'

He took a step towards her and her breath hissed from between her teeth, sharp and intense. 'You don't know what you're asking of me.'

She lifted a brow. 'Really? Do you need me to spell it out?'

He didn't react to her attempt at humour.

'Make love to me, Sariq. Please.'

He cursed every word he knew in all the languages he spoke, but nothing helped. His wife—his beautiful, pregnant, desirable wife—was asking him to sleep with her and, despite the promise he'd made on the plane, he felt his resolve weakening.

He wanted her every bit as much as always. There was no absolving himself of this desire even when he knew it was fraught with potential dangers. They were married, true, but not for any reason other than this child. Becoming lovers could complicate that.

He needed to be clear.

He was a man of honour, and he had no intention of misleading his wife. 'Just sex.' He lifted a finger to her lips, pressing there gently. 'And just tonight.'

Her eyes flared wide and he held his breath, needing her to

agree to his terms. He couldn't confuse what they were with physical desire. It had no part in this.

'If you say so.' Her eyelids fluttered and then she was pushing towards him, so he caught her in his hands, holding her to his body as he dropped his mouth and did what he'd been craving since the moment she'd walked into his embassy.

He kissed her, hard, hungrily, and it was like coming home.

Her eyes were heavy, her body too. She was warm, safe. Cradled against Sariq's chest, his heart beating beneath her ear. Steps, marble, kerosene. A door. She nuzzled closer. Something warm was wrapped around her, a robe? His robe? She inhaled. Yes, it smelled of him. Another door, footsteps. She closed her eyes. His heartbeat was steady, loud.

Another door. Something soft was beneath her. She forced her eyes open and looked around. Her room. Sariq, beside her bed.

'Don't go.' She lifted a hand, holding it towards him. 'Please.'

If he were a man of honour, he would leave her now. For hours they'd pleasured one another, his body answering the call of hers, instincts driving them together, making it impossible to remember anything except the sense of what they each craved from the other. But in a few short hours the sun would crest over the desert dunes and reality would intrude.

She didn't want this, and nor did he. It was an illusion. A snatch out of time.

Danger lay before him. If he joined her in bed, he'd fall asleep. They'd wake up together, facing a new day as lovers.

His eyes dropped to her belly, rounded with his child, and a paternalistic pride fired in his belly. He owed it to their child not to mess this up. Sleeping with Daisy tonight had been, undeniably, perfect but it was also problematic. He wanted her.

He wanted her in a way that was addictive, that could threaten his legendary self-control if he didn't take care.

'It's late.' The words were crisp and he saw her flinch in response. He was already ruining this. Just as he'd said in the tower, pain brought pleasure and pleasure brought pain. 'Go to sleep.'

He left before she could respond.

# CHAPTER TWELVE

HE BARELY SLEPT. Just as the sun lifted above the desert, he pushed the sheet from his body and strode, naked except for a pair of boxer shorts, onto the balcony. Frustration gnawed at his gut. Dissatisfaction too.

He shouldn't have left her without an explanation.

He'd panicked, but she'd deserved better.

Without intending to, he moved along the balcony, towards the doors that led to her apartment. If she was asleep, which she surely would be at this hour, he would leave her. And if she was awake?

He stood on the other side of the glass, looking in at his wife's room, wondering at the thundering inside his chest. The morning was perfect. Clear and cool, none of the day's stinging temperature apparent yet.

Daisy slept. She was so peaceful like this, so beautiful. Memories flashed through his mind. New York. Her smile. Her laugh. The fascination he'd felt with her from the beginning.

Her face when he'd propositioned her to become his mistress.

The obvious shock. Despite the normality of such an arrangement, she'd been offended. Her fire when she'd thrown her pregnancy at him, with no idea what that revelation would mean.

And finally, her words on the night they'd married.

*'I'm marrying you because I have to—not because I want to—and I will never forgive you for this. Tonight I'm going to become your wife and I may appear to accept that, I may appear to accept you, but I will always hate you for this. I love our child, and, for him or her, I will try to make our marriage amicable, at least on the surface, but don't you ever doubt how I really feel.'*

She'd begged him to make love to her in the tower, the night before. Their physical connection was real and raw. There was no questioning that. But beyond it? She hated him. She despised him, as she had every reason to.

Did she still though? Even after time had passed and they'd grown...what? Closer? Did he really think that? Did he really *want* that?

His heart thumped.

Yes.

He wanted it, and yes, they had. He'd shared more of himself with Daisy in the short course of their marriage than he had any other soul in his entire life. He'd felt painfully lonely when they'd met and now?

He didn't want to examine it because the answer terrified him.

He would never allow himself to love her. No woman, ever, but especially not Daisy. There was far too much risk there. If he ever really let himself care for her, he suspected he'd lose himself completely. When he'd confronted the prisoners in the catacombs the night before, he'd wanted to kill them with his bare hands. The impulse had assailed him from nowhere but it had been strong and desperate. The idea of anyone hurting Daisy had been anathema to him.

He stood up straighter, his breathing forced.

For Daisy, he would give up his kingdom, his crown. Anything she asked of him. Revulsion flooded him, and a heavy sense of guilt. Being Sheikh of Haleth was his purpose in life.

He had been born and raised for this, and desire for a woman wasn't anywhere close to a good enough reason to doubt his duty.

Except it wasn't just desire, a voice niggled inside him. There was a complexity of considerations here, but none of these could permit him to forget what he owed his country.

He cursed under his breath and spun away, stalking back into his own room and dressing quickly. What he needed was to think.

All his life, Sariq's life had followed a path, a plan, and now he was stepping into the unknown. It wouldn't work. He didn't want it. He needed a new plan, one that would work for him, Daisy, and their child.

He needed to think without the knowledge that Daisy was only a wall away.

'Have a horse prepared. I'm going to the desert.'

He would never love her.

Daisy lay on her back, one hand on her stomach, patting the rounded shape there, her eyes chasing the detailing in the ceiling. Her body bore the marks of his lovemaking but it was all a lie. Sex and intimacy were not connected for Sariq.

How many times and in how many ways had he said this? Even at the embassy, when she'd first arrived and he'd asked her to become his mistress.

Why had that hurt so badly?

Her stomach dropped, because an answer was beating through her, demanding her attention. In New York, she'd been drawn to him because she'd never known anyone like him. And at the embassy, she'd been furious with him, but also, she'd felt a thousand and one things—good things.

And now?

She closed her eyes and remembered all of their conversations, shared moments, desire, need, a tangle of wants, impulses that had been pushing her towards him even when she wanted to dislike him so, so badly.

But for him?

*Just sex. And just tonight.*

Nothing had changed. It was the same parameters he'd established in New York, the same parameters he'd tried to enforce when he'd asked her to come to the RKH as his mistress. And every time he'd reminded her of those limitations, it had twisted inside her, like a snake's writhing. Pain, discontent. Why?

'Oh, crap.' She sat up, her throat thick with emotion. 'No.' She'd thought she loved Max when she'd married him, but she hadn't. She'd had no idea what love felt like—until now. It wasn't something you decided to do. It was all-consuming, a firestorm that ravaged your body. It was lighting her up now, making her feel…feel everything.

She'd fallen in love with her husband and that might ordinarily have been considered a good thing but, for Daisy, she couldn't see any way to make this work. He didn't love her. He never would. That was his one proviso.

Her stomach looped fiercely. Her heart contracted.

And suddenly, this marriage, this palace, the prospect of raising a child with him, felt like cement weighting her down. Living here with him had been scary enough, when he'd insisted on this marriage. She'd thought her fear came from the unknown, the pressure of being the mother to the royal heir. But it was so much more than that now.

She'd fallen in love with him, and he could never know. She couldn't tell him. She wouldn't.

But how could she keep it secret? Flashes of their night together came back to her. It might have been sex for him but every touch, every moment, had been a connection, a moment of love. She communicated her feelings in everything she did.

How could he not know?

And then what? If he realised how she felt?

Mortification curled her toes. He would become the third man in her life she'd offered herself to, the third man she'd loved or purported to love, who'd found it easy to withhold those same feelings. After her father, she'd been wary with men, but Max had found a way under her defences. After Max, she'd been wary to the extreme, but Sariq… It wasn't even that he'd charmed her. He hadn't. He'd been himself but there was something in his manner that had made it impossible for Daisy to forget.

But the idea of having *this* love rejected was anathema to her. It would hurt too much. She knew how he felt—she didn't need him to spell it out to her. No good could come from having this conversation.

Maybe she could make him love her? Her heart began to stammer. But she was being a fantasist. You couldn't make anyone who wasn't so inclined fall in love with you—as her first marriage had taught her.

At no point had Sariq given her even the slightest reason to hope. This feeling was her fault. Her mistake.

She had to conquer it.

He rode for hours, until the heat of the day, so familiar against his back, was almost unbearable. He rode towards the caves, knowing he would not make it there on this occasion. Knowing even as he set out from the palace that cowering from this wasn't worthy of him. He was not a man to run from anything, and he wouldn't run from this.

Last night was a mistake.

He couldn't blur the lines of what he wanted from Daisy. She was right to insist on boundaries being in place. With every fast-moving step of the steed beneath him, his certainty grew that their marriage would only succeed if he insisted on structure. Formality. He'd been mistaken to let his interest in Daisy as a woman cloud what he needed from her.

Before he met her, he'd been preparing to marry, and his wife, whomever he chose, would have simply been a ceremonial addition to his life. Someone with whom he would have perfunctory sex for the sake of continuing the family line and then leave to her own devices.

He'd had no intention of having his bride installed in the apartment beside his own. That had been for Daisy, because to have her in his palace but any further from him felt wrong. His first instinct—and it had been a failure.

She was beautiful and desirable but how he felt about her personal charms was irrelevant now she was pregnant with his child. He wouldn't make the same mistake his father did. He wouldn't let affection for a woman weaken him.

He rode on, his face a mask of resolve. With every day that passed, he would conquer this.

It was some time around three when Daisy began to feel the exhaustion from the early start. Zahrah had woken her for the *rukbar* before day's break, so she could dress in a special ceremonial robe and be prepared for the procedures of the day.

'You'll sit beside Sariq. You won't need to say anything, though people will no doubt be very excited to see you. Some might ask to touch your belly—it is considered extreme good fortune to do so to any pregnant woman here in Haleth. But you, carrying the royal heir, your stomach would be seen as very fortunate.'

Daisy had found it hard to smile since the morning after she'd slept with Sariq. Having not seen him since then, she found that smile had felt even heavier, but she lifted it now, turning to see Zahrah. 'You haven't asked to touch my stomach.'

'I presumed you wouldn't want me to.'

Daisy lifted her shoulders. 'It's just a tummy.'

Zahrah extended a hand, her fingertips shaking a little, and it was in that moment Daisy understood the momentousness of this child she was carrying. Any child was special and important, but their baby meant so much to the entire country. Sariq had said as much at the embassy in Manhattan but she *could see that for herself* now. For Zahrah and she had become friends, yet the enormity of touching Daisy's pregnant belly was obviously overwhelming for Zahrah.

The sky was still dark when Zahrah led her towards the ancient rooms that bordered the courtyard where they'd had the ball a few nights earlier. Her eyes found the spot where they'd danced and ghosts of his touch lifted goose bumps over her skin.

'Here,' Zahrah murmured. It was only as Daisy approached she saw Sariq locked in serious conversation with Malik. He turned towards her, so she had only a moment to still her heart and calm her features. It was the first time she'd seen him since he'd carried her back to her bed. Since she'd asked him to stay and he'd left.

*Just sex. Just tonight.*

He'd been true to his word.

'Your Highness.' Malik bowed low.

Sariq said nothing.

Uncertainty squeezed her gut. 'Good morning.'

At that, Sariq nodded, his eyes holding hers for a moment too long before he turned back to Malik and finished his conversation. Daisy felt as though she were on a roller coaster, hurtling over the highest point at great speed.

'I'll be fine,' she assured Zahrah. 'You should go back to bed.'

Zahrah's smile was so normal. Daisy wished it could tether her back to her real self, to the woman she'd been before she realised how she felt. 'I'll be to the side of the room,' Zahrah murmured. 'If there's anything you need, just turn to me and I will come.'

Daisy nodded, but having this kind of attention bestowed on her still felt unusual. 'You're so kind to me.'

Zahrah smiled. 'You're easy to be kind to.' And she reached down and squeezed Daisy's hand. 'You'll be good at this. Have courage.'

It was a relief that Daisy's nervousness could be attributed to the *rukbar* she was about to take part in and not the first sighting of her husband in days.

Sariq spoke in his native tongue, which she was getting very proficient at understanding, if not speaking. 'Leave us now.'

Zahrah and Malik both moved further along, towards the doors that would lead to the room.

Now, Sariq offered a tight smile that was more like a grimace. 'You remembered.'

It was a strange thing to say. She lifted her eyes to his and felt as though she'd been scorched. 'You're still happy for me to be a part of this?'

Something flashed in his eyes and her stomach dropped. He wasn't happy. She didn't know how she knew it but she did. Waves of uncertainty lashed at her sides. 'The people will be gratified by your attendance.' It was so insufficient. The people. Not him.

A noise sounded, like banging against a door. 'That's our signal. Ready?'

And so it began. Once they were seated at two enormous, elaborate thrones made of gold and black metal, she'd heard the din from the external doors of the palace. A sense of fear and awe filled her when the doors were thrown open, but there was no stampede. An orderly queue had formed, and she learned, when they'd taken a small break to eat lunch, that security screening had been implemented, for the first time in the *rukbar*'s history, on the other side of the doors. Because of her?

Undoubtedly.

She'd seen his determination to keep her safe. For a moment that lifted her spirits until she remembered that her value, at this point, had more to do with her child than it did her.

She couldn't dwell on her own fracturing heart though. Not when the room was filling with people who were, so obviously, doing it tough.

Sariq listened patiently to each who came before him, offering a brief summary of each situation to Daisy in English once they'd finished speaking. Each story was hard—some were almost impossible to bear. Parents who'd lost children touched her the deepest of all. There were no medical bills here, the state provided, but there were other concerns. The cost of the funeral, the legacy of caring for other children while too grief-stricken to return to work.

Daisy felt tears filling her eyes on a number of occasions but worked hard not to show how deeply affected she was by these tragedies.

As the afternoon progressed though, she grew tired, her heart heavy, her mind exploding. And through it all, Sariq continued, looking as fresh as he had that morning, his concentration unwavering. She turned towards Zahrah, who immediately appeared at her side.

'Do you need something, Your Highness?'

'Just a little water.'

'Of course.'

Sariq turned to her, from the other side, and Malik paused proceedings. 'Are you okay?'

It was such a ludicrous question that she almost laughed. Okay? Would she ever be okay again? Did she even deserve to lament such a question in the face of so much suffering? 'I'm fine.' A bright smile and then a nod. 'Just thirsty.'

His eyes roamed her face, his expression unconvinced. 'You're pale.'

'I'm American.'

His impatience was obvious. 'Paler than usual.'

'I'm fine.' She couldn't say why she sounded angry at him, because she wasn't. Her anger was all directed at herself and her own stupidity for falling in love with a man who was so completely determined to be unavailable. 'Let's keep going. It sounds like there are still a tonne of people to see.'

And there were. The line continued until the sun set. 'Traditionally, this is when the *rukbar* concludes. Food is served in the adjoining room. I usually join the guests for a short time. You do not have to.'

'Of course I will,' she insisted, despite the fact she was bone-weary. Pride wouldn't let her show it. 'But do you have to stop now? There are people out there who've waited all day.'

His eyes clung to hers and then he nodded. 'Ten more.'

As Malik turned to the crowd to announce what the Sheikh had decided, Sariq leaned closer. 'Those that were not seen today will be given tickets for the next *rukbar*, so they're seen first. And any that feel they cannot wait have an email address to use to have their matter dealt with more speedily.'

That appeased her. The whole day had been eye-opening and fascinating. She felt, sitting beside Sariq, as though she was truly getting to know the fabric of this country. There was no hostility towards her—a divorced American. In fact, it was quite the opposite. People had been unstintingly kind, curious, polite.

Another hour stretched and then the *rukbar* was declared closed. Daisy was a little woozy when she stood, swaying slightly so that those in the room gasped and Sariq shot out a hand to steady her.

'I'm fine,' she said through a tight smile. 'Just not used to sitting down for so long.' He didn't relinquish his touch though, and her skin burned at the contact, her body throbbed, that same fire ignited, stealing through her soul. He guided her down the steps, away from the thrones, towards doors that led to another room.

'You should go to your room.'

Her gaze shifted. 'Is that an order?'

She saw the way his jaw tightened, and felt the battle raging within him. 'It's a suggestion.'

'Then I politely decline.'

He didn't like that, it was obvious. It wasn't fair to be angry with him. He'd done nothing wrong, nothing whatsoever. All along he'd been honest with her. Loving him was her fault, her problem. And yet she did feel anger towards him, because it simply wasn't fair. How could her heart be full to bursting and his determinedly empty?

'Daisy—'

'Everyone's waiting,' she said through clenched teeth, shifting away from him a little, just enough to dislodge his hand from her waist. 'Let's do this.'

Daisy was charming and lovely. He watched as she spoke to the assembled guests, moving from group to group and using the native language. He hadn't realised how good she'd become. Her accent was excellent and while she paused from time to time to search for a word, she was able to cover more than the basics. He watched the effect she had on his people and a warm sense of pride lifted him.

She was a natural.

No one, regardless of their lineage or birth, would have been a better Emira than Daisy. He turned back to his own conversation, listening to the rainfall statistics for the last quarter, but always he was aware of her location in the room. From time to time he would hear her laugh, soft but imprinted on him in such a way that meant he could pick it out easily. Would he ever lose this fascination with her? Would he have the ability to inhabit the same space and *not* hone in on her with every cell in his body?

Yes.

Of course.

Because that was what he wanted, and Sariq knew that with determination and focus he could do anything he wished. Daisy was beneath his skin at the moment, but he would dispense with that in time. Once the baby was born, he could even contemplate giving her exactly what she wanted, sending her to live away from him.

His body tightened. Rejection, anger, dismissal. Doubt. Disgust. She wasn't a piece of trash he could simply discard once she'd served her purpose. And yet she was the one who'd suggested going to America.

But her security was of paramount concern. The men held in the prison beneath the city were not part of a wider organisation. They were rogue militants with their own agenda. There was no reason to think she was in any greater risk than she had been before, and yet the idea of any harm befalling her, even the slightest harm, filled him with the sense of burning acid.

His eyes found her once more. She was in conversation but she looked as though she wasn't listening. His eyes narrowed. Her skin was so pale, like milk. She nodded, but then she swayed a little, just as she had before, at the end of the *rukbar*.

His chest clutched.

He cursed inwardly. She was going to faint. 'Malik.' His voice cut through the room and Sariq began to stride quickly, just as Daisy stumbled. Another curse, this one said aloud, and he broke into a run, catching her only a moment before her body crumpled. She would have fallen to the floor if his arms hadn't wrapped around her, lifting her and cradling her against his chest.

The room was silent; he barely noticed. Holding her to him, just as he had when they'd left the tower and she'd been exhausted from the lateness of the hour and the way they'd spent their night, he carried her from the room now, his heart slamming against his ribs in a way that told him all he needed to know.

# CHAPTER THIRTEEN

'PLEASE PUT ME DOWN.'

Such stiffness in her voice, cold and hurt, and he winced inwardly because he understood it. He'd disappeared and he'd hurt her. Pleasure turned to pain, always.

'Sariq? I'm okay. It was just hot and I was tired.'

'You should not have stayed so long.'

He wished condemnation didn't ring through his words but, damn it, didn't she see? Protecting her was important.

She didn't say anything and that was wise. He felt worry and a worry that was close to turning to frustration and anger. Panic, too. A team of men stood outside the doors to her room. 'Where is the doctor?'

'Here, Your Highness.'

At this, Daisy scrambled against him, trying to stand, but he held her tight, pushing through the doors. Only when he reached her bed did he loosen his grip, laying her down on the bed, not wanting to remember the last time he'd done that.

'Please.' Her cheeks were pink. 'This is so silly. I'm fine, really.'

'The doctor will confirm that.' Sariq stepped backwards, allowing the doctor room to move.

He could see Daisy wanted to argue so he played the trump

card, which he knew she would listen to. 'Think of the baby, Daisy.'

At that, she stilled and, after a moment, nodded. 'Thank you.' But her gratitude was directed to the doctor. The examination was thorough yet brief. He checked Daisy's blood pressure, heart, temperature, felt the stomach and then listened to the baby's heart using a small handheld device that spilled the noise into the room. And Sariq was frozen to the spot at this small, tangible proof of their child's life. Daisy too lifted her eyes to Sariq's and he saw the emotion in them, the understanding of what they'd done.

Together, they'd made life. It hadn't been planned, and the pregnancy had led to all manner of complications, but it was, nonetheless, a miraculous thing.

'Your blood pressure is a little high, but not alarmingly so. You must rest. Stay hydrated. I'll come back to check on you in an hour.'

'Is that necessary?'

'Yes.' The doctor's smile softened the firmness of his response. 'Absolutely.' He turned to Sariq and bowed, then left.

Sariq stood there for what felt like a very long time, looking at his wife, as the clarity of his situation expanded through his mind. 'Zahrah will sit with you. I'll check on you in the morning.' He stalked towards the door, turned back to look at her as a sinking feeling dropped his stomach to his feet. 'You did well today, Daisy.'

He pulled the door inwards but Daisy was there, moving behind him, grabbing his wrist. 'Don't you dare walk out on me.'

He stared at her, surprise on his features. 'Calm down.'

'No.' And then, she lifted her hands to his chest and pushed him, her expression like fire. 'Damn you, Sariq, stop walking away from me. Can you not even stand to be in the same room with me? Are you worried I'm going to beg you to make love to me again?'

Her anger was so obviously born of hurt. He held her shoulders and lightly guided her from the door, away from the ears of the guards beyond.

'Don't!' She wouldn't be placated.

'I'm not leaving,' he assured her and in that moment he was so desperate to say or do anything that would placate her. 'Just sit down and be calm.'

'I don't want to be calm!'

'For the baby.'

'The baby's fine, you heard the doctor.'

'I heard him say your blood pressure is elevated. Arguing is not going to help that.'

'I don't want to argue with you. I just want you to tell me why you're avoiding me.'

He ground his teeth together, her accusation demanding an answer. But he didn't know what to say—he couldn't frame into words the complexity of his feelings.

'You regret sleeping with me.'

Damn it. He felt caught on the back foot, and it was a new experience, one he didn't like at all. 'It was...unwise.'

'Why?' She thrust her hands onto her hips so even then he was conscious of the jutting of her breasts, the sweetness of her shape, rounded with his baby. What was wrong with him that even in that moment he could want her?

Everything.

That was the problem.

His feelings for Daisy weren't logical. They weren't safe. Nothing about her fitted his usual modus operandi. That was why he had to gain control of this—it was in their mutual interest that he did so.

'I've thought about your request to return to America.' That was true. In the desert, it was all he could focus on. 'That would be unwise and potentially unsafe. I want our child raised here, in Haleth.'

She glowered. 'I'm not asking to go back to America. Not really. I understand why that's not possible.'

He ignored that, continuing with his train of thought as though she hadn't spoken. 'But you do not have to stay here at the palace. There is another palace on the outskirts of the old city. You should move there and live your own life, away from me and the pressures of this royal life.'

She stared at him for several seconds and he had no idea what she was thinking.

'Is that what you want?'

When he thought about what he *wanted*, it was a very dangerous path. So he concentrated instead on what he knew they needed. 'I want our child to be healthy. I want you to be happy. And I want to be able to focus on ruling the RKH, just as I was before.'

'And you can't do that with me here?'

He clenched his jaw, fierce memories burning through him. 'The situation is more complicated than I would like.'

'What does that even mean?'

He expelled a hot sigh. 'You're not like the wife I imagined,' he said, dragging a hand through his hair.

'I'm aware of that.' Her voice was scathing.

Great. He'd offended her once more. 'I mean that we have this history. Even before I knew about your pregnancy, I came to America intending to be with you again. From the moment we met I haven't been able to stop thinking about you. You take up too much space in my brain and I can't have that, Daisy. I can't.'

Her lips parted, her eyes widened, and she was completely still, perhaps replaying his admission.

'You don't want me to leave because you don't like me?'

He frowned. 'Why would you think that?'

'Because you've been ignoring me for a week?'

He was quiet a moment. 'I can't offer you what you need, and it's not fair for me to take what I want from you when I want it—'

'Sex,' she interjected acerbically.

He dipped his head in a silent admission. 'I won't use you like that.'

'So don't use me. Open yourself up to more.'

Her words burst through him, but he was already shaking his head, denying that. 'There's no more. My responsibilities require my full attention.'

'Liar.'

His laugh was a sharp burst. 'I don't think anyone's ever called me that before.'

'Perhaps you've never lied before but you're lying to me now, and to yourself. Why do you think you can't get me out of your head, Sariq? Hmmm?' There was a challenge in her voice, an angry, determined tilt to her chin. 'Why do you think you came to the embassy and propositioned me?'

'Sexual infatuation is one thing,' he said firmly, his tone flat, but she shook her head, dismissing it before he'd even finished.

'If it was sexual infatuation we'd have been sleeping together ever since our marriage. You wanted me, I wanted you. Instead, you've deliberately kept me at arm's length because you're terrified of what this could become. You keep *everyone* at a distance. You have no friends, no family. Malik is the closest person to you and he's a curmudgeonly old man who exists purely to serve you. That's not about your damned duty to Haleth. It's about fear. You don't want to get hurt so you're pushing everyone away. I won't let you do that to me.'

He stared at her, disbelief numbing him. 'You can have no idea what my life is like,' he said, after a moment. 'So do not stand there and judge me, Daisy.'

'I know what your life *could* be like.' She changed tack, her voice lower, softer, working its way into his bloodstream so he had to work hard to hold his course. 'Do you think this is easy for me? I'm terrified! Terrified of telling you how I feel, of opening myself up to you, of opening myself up to yet another disastrous marriage. And yet I'm standing here, saying that I feel—'

'Don't.' He lifted a hand, silencing her. 'Don't say what you cannot take back. I don't want to hear it. I can't. I can't offer you the same, and it will be easier for both of us if we pretend—'

'Coward!' She stamped her foot, and he shifted backwards a little, shocked by her reaction.

'I'm in love with you. There! I've said it! Now what are you going to do? Are you going to admit you love me too? That we fell in love in New York and it's inconvenient and crazy and unpredictable but that doesn't change the fact we're in love? Or are you going to cling to the notion that your life will be better if you stay closed off, completely your own person? Immune from emotional pain but so lonely with it.'

His heart was like a hammer inside him, relentless and powerful. Another challenge, just as she always hit him with. He stared at her, and shook his head slowly, his mind like putty.

Her words threatened to overrun him with joy, but the rational, sensible approach to life he'd fixed on many years earlier was not easy to shake.

'I have never suggested I would love you.'

'Damn it, that's not an answer.' She pushed his chest again, her frustration understandable. 'Tell me you don't love me. Say you'll never love me.'

Say it! Tell her what she needed to hear, if that was how he could put an end to this conversation.

Except he couldn't say those words. Contrary to what she had accused him of, Sariq was not a liar. In fact he was unstintingly honest. 'No.'

Her eyes flared wide.

'I will not talk about you and me in the context of love. That's not what our marriage is predicated on.'

'Yes, it is! You're a fool if you can't see that we fell in love in New York. It's not a one-sided thing. I know, because I've been in a relationship like that and this feels completely different. I believe you love me. And I think you're trying to send me away because love is a complication you're not prepared to deal with.'

A muscle throbbed in his jaw. He stared at her, the stark truth of her words so simple, so right.

'Can't you see how right this is? We could have everything we both want in life. I'm not going to distract you from your responsibilities. I want to help you with them. I want to be your partner in every way.'

'No.' A harsh denial, when his heart was bursting through him, begging him to agree to what she was proposing. But his attitudes were forged from the coal fire of pain and were immovable.

'No? Is that all you've got?'

He glared at her. Damn her fire and spirit. Couldn't she see this wasn't going to work?

'I'm sorry, Daisy. I'm…flattered that you care for me.' She made a scoffing noise. 'But our marriage will work better if we treat it as a business arrangement.'

He began to move to the door but she stalled him with a fierce cry. 'You stop right there.'

He turned to face her, his expression like thunder, matching the strength of his feelings.

'I will not spend the rest of my life in a marriage like you've just described. I should never have agreed to this.'

'But you did, and you're here, and soon our baby will be born.'

'I don't care. If you're telling me our marriage is going to be so cold, then to hell with it. I want a divorce.'

He stared at her, panic strangling him for a moment, making it difficult to frame a response. 'That's not possible.'

'Oh, don't be so ridiculous. Of course it is. It's not what you *want*, but it's absolutely possible. You'll still have your heir. I'll even raise our child here in the RKH so you can be a part of his or her life. But no way am I going to tie myself to you for the rest of my life knowing you'll never accept that you have feelings for me.'

The ultimatum was like an electrical shock, galvanising him.

He stared at her for several moments and then nodded. 'I need to think about that.'

This time, when he left, she didn't try to stop him.

Daisy stared at the closed door with an ache in the region of her heart. She'd done it. She'd laid all her cards on the table and he'd refused to admit he cared for her. She'd been wrong, then. It wasn't love. Not from him, anyway.

And now? He was thinking about granting her a divorce.

God, where had her request come from? Fear? Anger? Had she hoped it would snap him out of his state of denial? That it might wake him up and force him to be brave?

She was trembling all over, the fight knocked out of her by the shock she might get exactly what she'd asked for. Another divorce. Another failed marriage. But this one, so much worse than the first. The idea of not having Sariq in her life in any capacity filled her with a hard lump of pain.

But wasn't it better this way? A lifetime was a long time, and she couldn't see that this would get any easier.

The next day she played the piano Sariq had had brought to the palace the day after she'd arrived. She played Erik Satie because there was a pervasive sadness moving through her and Satie suited that. She played for almost two hours, and didn't hear the door pushing inwards. Nor was she aware of Sariq standing in the door frame, watching her, his eyes running over her as if committing her to memory.

When she finished playing though, he shifted and she turned, her blood pounding through her veins at the sight of him. He wore trousers and a business shirt. She wasn't prepared for that.

'Well?' It was like waiting for the executioner's axe to fall.

He moved towards her, coming to stand by the piano. 'I refuse to keep you here against your will.' His face was grim. 'I was wrong to pressure you into this marriage. I acted on instincts. I panicked. If you were serious about wanting a divorce, I'll grant it.'

Oh, crap. It wasn't what she wanted. But what she needed, he wouldn't give her, so that meant divorce was her only option. 'Fine.' She couldn't meet his eyes. She wanted this over. Like ripping off a plaster.

'You will need to stay in Haleth, as you offered. Once our child is born, we can come to a custody arrangement.'

Was she imagining the emotion in his voice? She didn't know any more. Perhaps her own feelings were so strong, so urgent, that they simply coloured her perception.

She nodded, still not looking at him.

'I apologise to you, from the bottom of my heart.'

Now, her gaze met his, but it hurt too much to hold. The look of pity there was the worst thing. She didn't want him to pity her. She wanted his love.

'I should never have slept with you in Manhattan. I have been selfish this whole time. I hope one day you will forgive me.'

'I can forgive you for almost everything,' she said with a small lift of her chin. 'Manhattan. The embassy. Our marriage. Those were decisions you made because you *felt*.' She pressed a finger into his chest, her eyes like little galaxies. 'Agreeing to divorce me is because you refuse to feel. I don't know if I'll ever get past that.'

'Damn it, Daisy.' He dropped his head then, his forehead to hers, his breathing ragged. 'You ask too much of me.'

'I ask nothing of you,' she corrected. 'Except your heart.' But he wasn't going to give it. Daisy could see that. Slowly, she stood, her fingers finding the keys once more, pressing two together. 'It's a beautiful instrument. Don't make the same mistake your father did—don't shut music from your life once I'm gone.'

Her words chased themselves through his mind for days. They whispered to him overnight, waking him before dawn, they spoke to him at the strangest times. When he was running or working, meeting with foreign politicians. Always that strange parting statement settled around him.

*'Don't make the same mistake your father did.'*

He kept the piano and he went to it often. Every day the sun rose and he went through the motions of his day, just as he had before Daisy. He remained committed to his schedule. He didn't enter her suite of rooms. Nor did he use their adjoining balcony. But the piano he visited. He sat at the stool once, pressed the keys, remembered her fingers in those exact same places, the passion that ran through her.

And he thought about the life she should have been living, and would have been leading had her own plans not been so thoroughly derailed by those who were all too willing to take what they could from her without a second thought for what Daisy needed.

He'd been right to refuse to complicate their marriage. Right to insist he wouldn't use her. How much easier that would have been! To pretend there was hope for them. To sleep with her each night, to fold her into his life only so far as he was willing, but all the while remaining steadfastly committed to his duties as ruler of the RKH.

*'Let me help you.'*

She didn't understand the pressures he lived with. He hadn't been raised to share that burden. Daisy was gone, and he was glad. Not because he wanted her to be anywhere else but because he hoped whatever she thought she felt for him would pass.

Except it wouldn't.

She wasn't like that.

She loved him and she always would.

His gut clenched. Guilt cut through him. He turned away from the piano and stalked to his apartment. Malik was there but Sariq dismissed him quickly. 'Not now.'

Forty sunrises had passed without Daisy. Forty mornings,

forty nights, forty days that each seemed to stretch for weeks. Time practically stopped. Only in sleep, when she filled his dreams, did he relax.

He craved sleep. Each day, he longed for it, and all because of Daisy. But it wasn't enough. Forty days after she left, he felt broken enough by missing her to accept that the solution to their marriage wasn't so simple. He couldn't send her away and forget about her.

He wasn't the same as he'd been before. She'd changed him, and he'd never change back. Everything was different now.

Cursing, he strode from his room. 'Malik? The helicopter. Immediately.'

# CHAPTER FOURTEEN

'YOU ARE NOT EATING.'

Daisy regarded Zahrah over her water glass. 'I am.'

'Not like before,' Zahrah chided affectionately. 'When you first came to Haleth you could not get enough of our food.'

Daisy's smile was thin. She had nothing in common with the woman she'd been then. 'I'm eating.'

Zahrah compressed her lips but Daisy was saved from an argument she couldn't be bothered having by the sound of helicopter rotor blades. At the same time, a knock sounded at the door. Zahrah moved to intercept it, and a moment later, returned.

'His Highness is here.'

Daisy's pulse was like a tsunami. She curved a hand over her stomach, her eyes flying wide open, her lips parting in surprise. It had been over a month since she'd left the palace. Their last conversation was painfully formal. He'd spoken to her as though she were a stranger.

Why was he here now? She couldn't bear the idea of another stilted, businesslike interaction.

She stood uneasily, pacing towards the windows where she might get a glimpse of him. But the doors opened and she turned, her flowing turquoise dress blowing in the breeze created by his entrance. And she stood there and stared at him, her face too disobedient to flatten of all expression completely.

Butterflies beat against her and she hated that. She hated how reliably he could stir her to a response when she wanted to feel *nothing* for him.

'What are you doing here?'

There was no point with civility, was there? Perhaps there was, but she couldn't be bothered. She was tired, so tired.

He didn't speak though. He stared at her and with every second that passed, her blood moved faster and harder so that it was almost strangling her with its intensity.

'Your Highness?' It was like waking him from a dream. He straightened, turning to Zahrah, then back to Daisy.

'I'd like to speak to you. Is now a good time?'

She startled. His uncertainty was completely unusual. 'I'm… yes.' She nodded a little uneasily. 'I suppose so. Zahrah?'

'Yes, Your Highness.' Zahrah bowed low. 'Would you like any refreshments, sir?'

'No.' The word was swift. 'Thank you.'

Zahrah left, and still Sariq didn't move. It unsettled Daisy, so she wiped her hands down her front, drawing his gaze to her belly. In the forty days since she'd left the palace, her bump had 'popped'.

She waited for him to speak but he didn't and the silence was agonising. So eventually, she snapped. 'Please tell me why you're here, Sariq.'

He nodded, moving deeper into the room. 'I came—' He shook his head.

'What is it?'

'I came because…'

Nothing. She ground her teeth together. 'What? Is everything okay?'

Emotion, heavy, obvious emotion, moved on his face. 'No.' So simple. 'It's not.'

Daisy's heart rate doubled. 'Why not?'

He stepped towards her, then froze. 'I came because I couldn't not.'

'You're not making any sense.'

'I know.' His throat shifted as he swallowed. 'I came to apologise, because I cannot live with what I said and I did, with how I made you feel. I came because it occurs to me you're living here believing that I don't love you, that I won't love you, when you were right. I do.' Again he pulled at his hair, shaking his head, his eyes heavy with his emotions.

Daisy couldn't move.

'The night of the ball, when those men were apprehended for what they intended to do to you, I went to see them. I wanted to kill them, Daisy. There was nothing measured or calm in my response. Because of how I feel for you I risked undoing all of my father and grandfather's work and dissolving our entire legal system so I could take my revenge. Even my father didn't do this when my mother was murdered.' He swallowed once more.

Daisy was incapable of speech or movement.

'Loving you terrifies me because there is no limit to what I would do for you if you asked it of me. If anyone hurt so much as a finger on your hand, I would have the kingdom turned upside down until they were found and brought to justice. I'm terrified that I cannot be what my country needs of me when I feel this way for you.'

A strangled noise escaped Daisy's throat.

'But if the last forty days have taught me anything, it's that I cannot live without you either. Perhaps it's the smart thing to do, but I cannot be smart if it means losing you. I won't.' He crossed the room, lifting her face in his palms, staring down at her with such obvious amazement that her heart turned over as though it were being stitched into a new position. 'You are so brave. Fearless and strong, courageous, incredible. You faced up to how you felt about me even after what you've been through.

After what *I* put you through. You are generous and good and I pushed at you, just like you said, pushing you away, unable to see a middle ground with you. Perhaps there isn't one. Perhaps loving you will mean I cannot rule as I otherwise might have. I don't care.'

But a sob burst through her. 'I care. I won't have you choose a life with me if you believe it weakens you.' She lifted a hand to his chest though, softening her statement with a gentle touch. 'I have too much faith in you for that.' Her fingers moved gently across the flesh that concealed his heart. 'You didn't kill those men. You stayed within the bounds of the law, because you are a good sheikh and an excellent man. You will rule this kingdom with all your goodness, and I will be at your side, making sure of that. I have no intention of being your weakness, Sariq. I want to be your biggest support and your greatest strength. Understood?'

He groaned, shaking his head. 'How can you be so good to forgive me after what I put you through?'

She bit down on her lip. 'I didn't say I'd forgiven you.'

His features tightened. 'No, of course not. I misunderstood. I know it will take time for me to make it right between us, but I want to do that, Daisy.'

Her stomach flipped. 'I believe you.'

'And because you are clearly so much wiser than I in these matters, I ask only that you tell me how. What do I do to make amends?'

His hands dropped to her stomach and he closed his eyes, inhaling. 'I want you and our child to be in my life. Please, Daisy.'

And she smiled because she knew he meant it, and because she wanted, more than anything, to grab the dream of this future with both hands.

'Well…' She pretended to think about it. 'Perhaps we should put the divorce on hold. At least while I consider my options.'

He was disappointed, and there was a tiny part of her that

enjoyed that. But she couldn't string it out any longer—it was too cruel.

'There are some things you could do to help me with that, you know.'

Hope flicked in his eyes. 'Oh?' Then, more seriously, his voice gruff, 'Anything.'

She lifted a finger to his lips, silencing him.

'Love me.' That was it. Nothing more complex than that.

'I do.'

'Good.' Her smile beamed from her. 'Love me with all your heart, for all your life, and don't ever stop.'

He pulled her against his chest, holding her tight, breathing her in. Their hearts beat in unison. Happiness burst through her.

'Not only is that something I can manage, it turns out it's completely non-negotiable.'

His kiss sealed that promise, and she surrendered to it, to him and to the future she knew they'd lead.

A year later, she stared out at the packed auditorium, anxiety a drum in her soul that was lessened only by the presence in the front row of her husband, the powerful Sheikh Sariq Al Antarah. Since returning to the palace, he'd insisted she further her piano studies. Leaving to attend a school like the Juilliard wasn't possible—once their son Kadir was born, named for his grandfather, she found she didn't want to go anywhere anyway. But Sariq saw no obstacle to that. He engaged world-famous pianists to come to the palace and work with her.

And now, all that effort had culminated in this. A performance that had sold out within minutes, the proceeds of which were going towards the charitable institution she'd established, helping women with mental health issues. Nerves were like fireflies in her veins but she closed her eyes and lifted her hands to the keyboard.

It was a perfect moment with infinite possibilities. She began to play and felt all the hopes of her childhood, the aspirations she'd nurtured for so long, bearing fruit. Who she'd been then, who she was now, unified in one dazzling, magical moment. She smiled, because she was truly happy, and suspected she would be for ever after.

\* \* \* \* \*

# One Night Before The Royal Wedding

## *Sharon Kendrick*

**Sharon Kendrick** once won a national writing competition by describing her ideal date: being flown to an exotic island by a gorgeous and powerful man. Little did she realize that she'd just wandered into her dream job! Today she writes for Harlequin, and her books feature often stubborn but always to-die-for heroes and the women who bring them to their knees. She believes that the best books are those you never want to end. Just like life...

## Books by Sharon Kendrick

### Harlequin Modern

*Cinderella in the Sicilian's World*
*The Sheikh's Royal Announcement*
*Cinderella's Christmas Secret*

### *Conveniently Wed!*

*His Contract Christmas Bride*

### *The Legendary Argentinian Billionaires*

*Bought Bride for the Argentinian*
*The Argentinian's Baby of Scandal*

Visit the Author Profile page
at millsandboon.com.au for more titles.

For the gorgeous Pete Crone—with thanks for his help and inspiration, particularly in regard to the Marengo Forest.

# CHAPTER ONE

WHO *WAS* SHE?

A puppet, that was who.

Zabrina pulled a face, barely recognising the person she saw reflected back at her. Because the woman in the mirror was an imposter, her usual tomboy self replaced by a stranger wearing unaccustomed silks and finery which swamped her tiny frame. Another wave of panic swept over her. The clock was slowly ticking down towards her wedding and she had no way of stopping it.

'Please don't scowl,' said her mother automatically. 'How many times do I have to tell you? It is not becoming of a princess.'

But at that precise moment Zabrina didn't *feel* like a princess. She felt like an object, not a being. An object who was being treated with all the regard you might show towards a sack of rice being dragged by a donkey and cart towards the marketplace.

Yet wasn't that the story of her life?

Expendable and disposable.

As the oldest child, and a female, she had always been expected to safeguard her family's future, with her hand in marriage offered up to a future king when she was little more than a baby. She alone would be the one able to save the nation from her weak father's mismanagement—that was what she had always been told and she had always accepted it. But now the moment was drawing near and her stomach was tying itself up in knots at the thought of what lay ahead. She turned to face her mother, her expression one of appeal, as if even at this late stage she might be granted some sort of reprieve.

'Please, Mama,' she said in a low voice. 'Don't make me marry him.'

Her mother's smile failed to hide her resolve. 'You know that such a request is impossible, Zabrina—just as you have always known that this is your destiny.'

'But this is supposed to be the twenty-first century! I thought women were supposed to be free?'

'Freedom is a word which has no place in a life such as yours,' protested her mother. 'It is the price you pay for your position in life. You are a princess and the rules which govern royals are different from those of ordinary citizens—a fact which you seem determined to ignore. How many times have you been told that you can't just behave as you wish to behave? These early-morning missions of yours are really going to have to stop, Zabrina. Yes, really. Do you think we aren't aware of them?'

Zabrina stared down at her gleaming silver shoes and tried to compose herself. She'd been in trouble again for sneaking out and travelling to a refuge just outside the city, fired by a determination to use her royal privilege to actually *do* something to help improve the plight of some of the women in her country. Poverty-stricken women, some under the control of cruel men. Her paltry personal savings had almost been eaten away because she had ploughed them into a scheme she really believed in. She repressed a bitter smile. And all the while she was doing that, she was being sold off to the king of a neighbouring country—in her own way just as helpless and as vulnerable as the women she was trying to help. Oh, the irony!

She looked up. 'Well, I'm not going to be able to behave as I please when I marry the King, more's the pity!'

'I don't know why you're objecting so much.' Her mother gave her a speculative look. 'For there are many other positive aspects to this union, other than financial.'

'Like what?'

'Like the fact that King Roman of Petrogoria is one of the most influential and powerful men in the world and—'

'He's got a beard!' Zabrina hissed. 'And I *hate* beards!'

'It has never prevented him from having a legion of admirers among the opposite sex, as far as I can understand.' Her mother's eyes flashed. 'And you will soon get used to it—for many, a beard is a sign of virility and fertility. So accept your fate with open arms and it will reward you well.'

Zabrina bit her lip. 'If only I could be allowed to take one of my own servants with me, at least that might make it feel a bit more like home.'

'You know that can't happen,' said her mother firmly. 'Tradition dictates you must go to your new husband without any trappings from your old life. But it is nothing more than a symbolic gesture. Your father and I shall arrive in Petrogoria with your brother and sisters for the wedding.'

'Which is weeks away!'

'Giving you ample opportunity to settle into your palace home and to prepare for your new role as Queen of Petrogoria. After that, if you still wish to send for some of your own staff, I am certain your new husband will not object.'

'But what if he's a tyrant?' Zabrina whispered. 'Who will disagree with me for the sake of disagreement?'

'Then you will work with those disagreements and adapt your behaviour accordingly. You must remember that Roman is King and he will make all the decisions within your marriage. Your place as his queen is to accept that.' Her mother frowned. 'Didn't you read those marriage manuals I gave you?'

'They were a useful cure for my recent insomnia.'

'Zabrina!'

'No, I read them,' admitted Zabrina a little sulkily. 'Or rather, I tried. They must have been written about a hundred years ago.'

'We can learn much from the past,' replied her mother serenely. 'Now smile, and then let's go. The train will already be waiting at the station to take you to your new home.'

Zabrina sighed. It felt like a trap because it *was* a trap—one from which it seemed there was no escape. Never had she felt so at the mercy of her royal destiny. She'd never been particularly keen to marry anyone, but she was far from ready to marry a man *she'd never even met*.

Yet she had been complicit in accepting her fate, mainly because it had always been expected of her. She'd been all too aware of the financial problems in her own country and the fact that she had the ability to put that right. Maybe because she was the oldest child and she loved her younger brother and sisters, she had convinced herself she could do it. After all, she wouldn't be the only princess in the history of the world to endure an arranged marriage!

So she had carefully learnt her lessons in Petrogorian history and become fluent in its lilting language. She studied the geography of the country which was to be her new home, especially the vast swathe of disputed land—the Marengo Forest—which bordered her own and would pass into the ownership of her new husband after their marriage, in exchange for an eye-watering amount of cash. But all those careful studies now felt unconnected with her real life—almost as if she'd been operating in a dream world which had no connection with reality.

*And suddenly she had woken up.*

Her long gown swished against the polished marble as she followed her mother down the grand palace staircase which descended into an enormous entrance hall, where countless servants began to bow as soon as the two women appeared. Her two sisters came rushing over, a look of disbelief on both their faces.

'Zabrina, is that really you?' breathed Daria.

'Why, it doesn't really look like you at all!' exclaimed little Eva.

Zabrina bit down hard on her lip as she hugged them good-bye, picking up seven-year-old Eva and giving her an extra big hug, for her little sister sometimes felt like a daughter to her. She wanted to cry. To tell them how much she was going to miss them. But that wouldn't be either fair, or wise. She had to be grown-up and mature and concentrate on her new role as Queen, not give in to indulgent emotion.

'I don't know why you don't wear that sort of thing more often,' said Daria as she gazed at the floaty long gown. 'It looks so well on you.'

'Probably because it's not really appropriate clothing for being on the back of a horse,' replied Zabrina wryly. 'Or for running around the palace grounds.'

She hardly ever wore a dress. Even when she was forced into one for some dull state occasion, she wouldn't have dreamed of wearing one like this, with all its heavy embellishments which made it feel as constricting as a suit of armour. The heavy flow of material impeded her naturally athletic movements and she hated the way the embroidered bodice clung to her breasts and emphasised them, when she preferred being strapped securely into a practical sports bra. She liked being wild and free. She liked throwing on a pair of jodhpurs and a loose shirt and jump-ing onto the back of a horse—and the more temperamental, the better. She liked her long hair tied back out of the way in a sim-ple ponytail, not gathered up into an elaborate style of intricate curls and studded with pearls by her mother's stylist.

Her father was standing there and Zabrina automatically sank to the ground, reluctantly conceding that perhaps it was easier to curtsey in a dress, rather than in a pair of jodhpurs.

'How much better it is to see you look like a young woman for a change,' the King said, his rasping voice the result of too many late-night glasses of whisky. 'Rather than like one of the grooms from the stables. I think being Queen of Petrogoria will suit you very well.'

For one brief moment Zabrina wondered how he would react if she told him she couldn't go through with it. But even if her country *didn't* have an outstanding national debt, there was no way the King would offend his nearest neighbour and ally by announcing that the long-awaited wedding would not take place. Imagine the shattered egos and political fallout which would result if he did!

'I hope so, Papa—I really do,' she answered as she turned towards her brother, Alexandru. She could read the troubled expression in his eyes, as if silently acknowledging her status as sacrificial lamb, but despite his obvious reservations what could the young prince possibly do to help her? Nothing. He was barely seventeen years old. A child, really. And she was doing it for him, she reminded herself. Making Albastase great again—even though she suspected that Alexandru had no real desire to be King.

Zabrina walked through the gilded arch towards the car which was parked in the palace courtyard and, climbing into the back of the vintage Rolls-Royce, she envisaged the journey which lay ahead of her. She would be driven to the railway station where King Roman of Petrogoria's royal train was waiting, with his high-powered security team ready to accompany her. On this beautiful spring afternoon, the train would travel in style through the beautiful countryside and the vast and spectacular Marengo Forest, which divided the two countries. By tomorrow, they would be pulling into Petrogoria's capital city of Rosumunte, where she would meet her future husband for the first time, which was a pretty scary thought. It had been drummed into her that she must be sure to project an expression of gentle gratitude when the powerful monarch greeted her, and to curtsey as deeply as possible. She must keep her eyes downcast and only respond when spoken to. Later that night there would be fireworks and feasting as the first of the pre-wedding celebrations took place.

And two strangers would be expected to spend the rest of their lives together.

Zabrina shot a wistful glance across the courtyard in the direction of the stable block and thought about her beloved horse, which she had ridden at dawn that very morning. How long would it take for Midas to miss her? Would he realise that until she was allowed to send for him one of the palace grooms would take him out for his daily exercise instead of her?

She thought about the bearded King and now her cause for concern was much more worrying. What if she found him physically repulsive? What if her flesh recoiled if—presumably when—he laid a finger on her? Despite her jokey remarks, she had read the book gifted to her by her mother, but she had received most of her sexual education from the Internet and an online version of the Kama Sutra. Even some of the lighter films she'd seen didn't leave a lot to the imagination and Zabrina had watched them diligently, fascinated and repelled in equal measure. She had broken out in a cold sweat at the thought of actually *replicating* some of the things the actors on the screens had been doing. Could she really endure the bearded King's unwanted caresses for the rest of her life?

She swallowed.

Especially as she was a total innocent.

A feeling of resignation washed over her. Of course she was. She'd never even been touched by a man, let alone kissed by one, for her virginity played a pivotal role in this arranged marriage. She thought about another of the books she'd ploughed her way through. The one about managing expectations within relationships and living in the real world, rather than in the fantasy version peddled by books and films. It had been a very sobering read but a rather useful one, and it had taught her a lot. Because once you abandoned all those stupid high-flown ideas of love and romance, you freed yourself from the inevitability of disappointment.

The powerful car pulled away to the sound of clapping and cheering from the assembled line of servants, but Zabrina's heart was heavy as she began her journey towards unwanted destiny.

# CHAPTER TWO

'SIR, I URGE you not to go ahead with this madcap scheme.'

Roman's eyes narrowed as he surveyed the worried face of the equerry standing before him, who was practically wringing his hands in concern as they waited in the forecourt of the vast railway station for the Princess to arrive. He wasn't used to opposition and, as King, he rarely encountered any. But then, usually he was the soul of discretion. Of sense. Of reason and of duty.

His mouth hardened.

Just not today.

Today he was listening to the doubts which had been proliferating inside his head for weeks now—doubts which perhaps he should have listened to sooner, if he hadn't been so damned busy with the affairs of state which always demanded so much of his time.

'And what exactly are your objections?' he countered coolly.

Andrei took a deep breath, as if summoning up the courage he needed to confront his ruler. 'Your Majesty, to disguise yourself in this way is a grave security risk.'

Roman raised his brows. 'But surely the royal train will be packed with armed guards who are prepared to give their lives for me, if necessary.'

'Well, yes.'

'So what exactly is your problem, Andrei? Where is the risk in that?'

Andrei cleared his throat and seemed to choose his next words carefully. 'Will the future Queen not be angry to discover that the man she is marrying is masquerading as a commoner and a bodyguard?'

'Why don't you let me be the judge of that?' remonstrated Roman icily. 'For surely the moods of the future Queen are no business of yours.'

His equerry inclined his head. 'No, no, of course not. Forgive me for my presumption. Your wishes, as always, reign supreme, my liege. But, as your most senior aide, I would not be doing my job properly if I failed to point out the possible pitfalls which—'

'Yes, yes, spare me the lecture,' interrupted Roman impatiently as they made their way towards the red carpet where the Petrogorian train was sitting on the platform in all its gleaming and polished splendour of ebony and gold. 'Just reassure me that my wishes have been understood. Are all the other guards up to speed about what they are to do?'

'Indeed they are, my liege. They have been fully briefed.' Andrei cleared his throat. 'For the duration of the train journey from here to Petrogoria, you have taken on the role of chief bodyguard. A role to which you are well suited, with your expertise in the martial arts as well as your undoubted survival skills.'

'Are you trying to flatter me, Andrei?' enquired Roman drily.

'Not at all, sir. I am simply stating the facts—which are that you are perfectly qualified to act as a bodyguard, for your strength and your sword skills are legendary. And that hitherto you will be known as Constantin Izvor and none of the staff will address you as sire, or Your Majesty. They have also been instructed that under no circumstances are they to bow in your presence or give any clue as to your true, royal identity.'

'Good.'

'And they also know that, along with a female servant, you will have sole access to the Princess.'

'Correct.'

'If I may be so bold, it is also a little strange, sire, to see you clean-shaven.'

Roman's lips curved into a smile, for this was a sentiment he shared with his equerry. He had worn a beard since he was nineteen years old and the thick black growth had always defined him, as had his thick black hair. Even when he had ascended to the throne four years ago, he had not conformed by cutting off the luxuriant mane whose ebony waves had brushed against his collar. The press often commented that it made him look like a buccaneer and sometimes referred to him as the conquering King, and he was not averse to such a nickname. But he had been taken aback by how dramatically a shave and a haircut had changed his appearance and when he'd looked in the mirror, he had been a little startled. He had noticed, too, that many of the palace servants had passed him by without recognising him!

And hadn't that sensation filled him with a sudden sense of yearning and sparked off this brainwave of an idea? He'd realised that this was his first ever taste of anonymity—and that, although it was sweet in the extreme, it was poignant, too. Like being given a glimpse of something very beautiful and knowing you would never see it again. Oh, he had travelled incognito before, especially if he was visiting one of his former mistresses in Europe, but he'd never pretended to be anyone other than a king before, and the sense of occupying the skin of a commoner was curiously liberating.

As he awaited Zabrina's arrival, Roman could sense his aide's surprise showing little sign of evaporating and maybe that was understandable, because he was aware he was behaving in a highly uncharacteristic way. For years he had thought nothing of his long-arranged marriage, for such unions were traditional in royal circles, such as his own. In fact, the only time the convention had been broken had been by his own father, and the disastrous results had reverberated down through the years. It was a mistake he was determined never to replicate, for his parents' short-lived marriage had been enough to sour Roman's appetite for anything defined by the word 'love'.

His mouth twisted. Only fools or dreamers believed in love.

He knew he must wed if he wished to continue the noble line of Petrogoria and it was sensible to select a wife who would fit seamlessly into her role as his queen. Just as he knew that the odds were better if his intended bride was also of royal blood—and this marriage had been brokered many years ago. He would acquire the hugely significant Marengo Forest, and Zabrina's homeland would be bankrolled in exchange. It was a deal designed to satisfy the needs of both their countries and, on paper, it had seemed the perfect pairing. In fact, for many years it hadn't even impacted on his personal life, for he had enjoyed brief relationships with carefully selected women who were chosen for their discretion as much as their shining beauty. His arranged marriage had just been something which was there in the background—like a string quartet playing quietly during a state banquet.

Yet lately, the thought of his impending nuptials to someone who supposedly ticked all the right boxes had started to give him cause for disquiet. A wedding which had always seemed an impossibly long way ahead seemed to have arrived with indecent speed. He had started wondering what kind of woman Princess Zabrina really was and the rumours which had reached his ears about her offered him no reassurance. It was said she was a little too fond of her own opinion, and at times could be feisty. It was also said that she was a rule-breaker and there were claims that she sometimes disappeared and nobody knew where she was. And mightn't that create a problem going forward? Because what if the virgin princess proved to be an unsuitable candidate to sit by his side and help rule his beloved country, and raise his children?

He swallowed and his throat suddenly felt as raw as if it had been lined with barbed wire.

What if she was like his own feckless mother?

A bitter darkness invaded his heart but instantly Roman quashed the feeling. Instead he concentrated on the rather faded gleam of the Princess's Rolls-Royce as it made its stately approach onto the station forecourt, its Albastasian flag fluttering in the light breeze. Soon he would no longer have to rely on conjecture and he would discover what kind of woman Zabrina *really* was. Beginning with her appearance—which up until now he had only ever seen in pictures in which she often appeared to be glaring suspiciously at the lens, as if she didn't like having her photo taken.

And there she was. The car door was opened and a woman stepped out, the tip of her silver shoe contrasting vividly against the scarlet carpet which streamed in front of her like a rush of blood. She moved rather awkwardly in her silken gown as if she was uncomfortable within its rich folds, and Roman felt a sudden unexpected rush of adrenalin as he surveyed her in the flesh. Because she was…

He felt the inexplicable thunder of his heart.

She certainly wasn't what he'd expected. Small of stature and very slim, she looked much *younger* than he'd imagined, although he knew for a fact that she was twenty-three—a decade less than himself. But right now she looked little more than a girl. A girl with the cares of the world on her shoulders if her sombre expression was anything to go by, for there were lines of worry around her full lips. Her smile seemed almost *forced* as he began to walk towards her, though surely that could not be so, since she must have been aware that there were countless women who would have wished to be in her situation.

Who would *not* want to marry the King of Petrogoria?

As he grew closer he could see that her skin was glowing— unusually so—and his eyes narrowed. This wasn't the protected flesh of a pampered princess who spent most of her time beneath gilded palace ceilings. In fact, she had the high colour of someone who was far more comfortable being outside. He frowned, because didn't that feed into some of the gossip he'd heard about her? Yet he noticed that her eyes were an unusual shade of deepest green—as dark as the tall trees of the Marengo Forest, which would soon be his—and that they widened as he came to a halt in front of her. They were beautiful eyes, he realised suddenly. Rich and compelling, with a flicker of innocence in their depths. Quelling the brief stab of his conscience at what he was about to do—because surely one day they would laugh together about this—he executed a deep bow and stepped forward.

'Good morning, Your Royal Highness,' he said. Only now he wished he weren't masquerading as anyone—because wouldn't his kingly status have given him licence to lift her hand and press those tanned fingers to his lips? To inhale the sweet scent of her skin and acquaint himself with her own distinctive perfume? He cleared his throat, struck by the sudden quickening of his blood. 'My name is Constantin Izvor and I am the chief bodyguard who will be in charge of your safe passage to Petrogoria.'

'Good morning.'

Zabrina's response was steady but inside she felt anything *but* steady. She inclined her head in greeting, mainly to hide her face, aware of a disconcerting cocktail of emotions flooding through her which she didn't want the King's servant to see. Her initial thought was that the chief bodyguard seemed a little *too* confident and full of himself and her second was that he was…

She swallowed.

The second was that he was *utterly gorgeous*.

Her heart missed a beat. He was beautiful, there was no other way to describe him. And he was powerful. Strong. The most incredible-looking man she'd ever laid eyes on. Not that she had a lot of experience in that department, of course, but she'd certainly never seen anyone like him among the dignitaries at official functions, or the palace servants she'd grown up with.

She tried not to stare but it was difficult, because he was better looking than any Hollywood heart-throb and all she wanted to do was to drink him in with her hungry gaze. Zabrina had been taught from birth never to maintain eye contact with anyone—especially not servants—but suddenly that seemed an impossible task. And, since she was surely permitted a closer look at the man who had been charged with her protection, she continued with her rapid assessment.

Night-black hair was cropped close to his head and his skin gleamed, like softly buffed gold. His features were chiselled and exquisitely sculpted—the faint scar on his jaw the only thing which marred their even perfection. A silky cream shirt hinted at the hard torso beneath and close-fitting trousers were tucked into soft leather boots, emphasising every sinew of his muscular thighs and making the most of his sturdy legs. She could see a sword tucked into a leather belt—and, in his other pocket, the unmistakable outline of a handgun. These two weapons made him look invulnerable. They made her think of danger. So why was that filling her with a wild kind of excitement, rather than a natural wariness, which surely would have served her better?

Remembering her instructions, she forced herself to look down again—as if it were imperative to study the nervous fingertips which were brushing fretfully over her silky gown. But his image remained stubbornly burned into her memory. She wished her heart rate would steady and that his proximity weren't sending her senses so haywire. Senses which until now she hadn't known she possessed. She felt raw. Vulnerable. Her body felt as if a deep layer of skin had ripped away from it, leaving her almost...*naked*.

Yet as she lifted her gaze upwards once more, it was the bodyguard's eyes which unsettled her most—because they were not so easy to look at as the rest of him. They were hard and cold. The coldest eyes she'd ever seen. Steely-grey, they cut through her like the sword which hung from his belt and were fringed by liquorice-dark lashes which made his gaze appear piercing and...brooding. Suddenly it was impossible to keep a flush of self-awareness from flooding her cheeks, making her shift from side to side in her silver shoes, wondering what on earth was happening to her.

Because she wasn't the type of person to be blindsided like this. The only time she could remember having had a crush on someone—and an innocent one at that—had been for her fencing tutor when she'd been just seventeen. Somebody must have noticed her clumsy blushes whenever he was around because the man had been summarily removed from his employment without her even having had the chance to say goodbye to him. Zabrina remembered feeling vaguely sad—a feeling which had been superseded by indignation that her life should be so rigidly controlled by those around her.

But what she was experiencing now was the very opposite of *innocent*. There was a distracting tightening of her breasts and the pulsing of something honeyed and sweet at the base of her stomach. A faint film of perspiration broke out on her forehead and she thought how horrified her mother would be to see her princess daughter sweating like a labourer.

'Is there anything Her Royal Highness desires before we set off?' Constantin Izvor was saying.

And sudden Zabrina was angry at the nature of her jumbled thoughts. Angry at the way her stomach was fluttering with butterflies. With an effort she composed herself, drawing her shoulders back, and determined to inject a suitable note of command into her voice. 'There is nothing I desire, thank you, Izvor. And since I see no reason for further delay, I suggest we get going. We have a long journey ahead of us,' she said crisply, perfectly aware that her observation was actually an order and hoping her brusque words would shatter the debilitating sense of torpor which had suddenly enveloped her.

The bodyguard looked slightly surprised—as if he wasn't

used to being spoken to like that—which alerted Zabrina to a couple of possibilities. Was his employer, the King, especially tolerant with his staff? she wondered. Was Izvor one of those tiresome servants who seemed to think that the trappings of royalty were theirs, too—simply by association? Well, he would quickly learn that he needed to keep his distance from *her*!

'Certainly, Your Royal Highness,' he drawled. 'The train is ready to leave. You have only to say the word and I will ensure we are quickly under way, for I am your most obedient servant.'

Something about his words didn't quite ring true and the hint of a smile playing at the edges of his lips made Zabrina feel as if he were actually *mocking* her, but surely he wouldn't dare do that? Anyway, why was she even giving him a moment's thought, when Constantin Izvor was nothing more than one of the many cogs who kept the royal machine smoothly rolling along?

'Good. Consider the word given. Let's go!' With a quick nod, she began to walk down the red carpet and as the brass band began to play the Albastasian national anthem, Zabrina was surprised by the powerful wave of homesickness which swept over her. From now on she was going to have to listen to the Petrogorian version and, although she had learnt the words by heart, it was not nearly so tuneful.

Constantin Izvor leapt onto the train in front of her, but she refused the helping hand he extended, with a firm shake of her head. Admittedly, it was a very big and old-fashioned train, but she was perfectly capable of negotiating her way up the cumbersome steps into the front carriage without any assistance from the dashing bodyguard. Why, she had spent her life leaping onto the backs of horses which made most people quake!

Yet the thought of him touching her filled her with a disconcerting burst of something which felt like excitement. Why could she suddenly imagine all too vividly how it might feel if those strong fingers tightened around her much smaller hand with a firm grip?

Slightly hampered by the abundant folds of her dress, Zabrina hauled herself up onto the train where a young woman was standing, waiting to greet her. With her blonde hair cut into a neat bob and wearing a simple blue shift dress, she looked more like a member of an airline cabin crew than a royal Petrogorian servant. Constantin Izvor introduced her as Silviana and Zabrina smiled, unable to miss the bodyguard's flicker of surprise when she replied in fluent Petrogorian.

'You speak my language well,' he observed, on a deep and thoughtful note.

'When I am seeking your approval, I will be sure to ask for it!' Zabrina answered coolly and for some reason Silviana winced, as if she had said something untoward.

'I will be sure to remember that in future, Your Royal Highness,' the bodyguard replied gravely. 'And in the meantime, I will escort you to your salon.'

She followed him along the narrow corridor until he threw open a door which led onto a lavishly appointed salon. Zabrina nodded and walked inside but, annoyingly, the bodyguard showed no sign of leaving. He was still standing on the threshold, his steely eyes gleaming, as if he had some God-given *right* to dominate her space and disturb her equilibrium. Zabrina wondered if she should formally dismiss him—yet the stupid thing was that, despite his presumption and his undoubted arrogance, she was strangely unwilling to see him go. It would be like closing the night-time shutters on a spectacular moon—you wouldn't be sure when you'd see all that beauty again.

'How long do you anticipate we'll be travelling for?' she questioned.

He shrugged, a movement which served only to illuminate the powerful ripple of his shoulders beneath his silky shirt.

'Fourteen hours at most, for the train will halt its journey midway, to allow Her Royal Highness a peaceful night of sleep,' he replied smoothly. 'We should reach the capital of Rosumunte before the sun is too high, where the people are already gathering to greet you.'

'Good,' she said, though the word didn't register her sudden rush of nerves at the thought of crowds of people waiting to see her. Would they like her? Would they consider her worthy to be the wife of their King?

'I trust you'll find everything to your satisfaction,' he said.

Zabrina forced herself to look around, trying to take in her surroundings and act as if she cared about them when all she could think about was him. She tried to acknowledge the splendid decoration. The walls were hung with pale lemon silk and several stunning oil landscapes, which she recognised as being of some of Petrogoria's most famous beauty spots. Woven silk rugs were scattered on gleaming wooden floors, and on a polished bureau she could see plenty of writing materials, along with golden pens in a jewelled container. A bowl of fruit stood on a low table and the two sofas which stood nearby were littered with soft and squashy cushions. Through a carved archway was a door leading to what was probably the bathroom and, beyond that, a wide and sumptuous-looking divan bed, scattered with yet more cushions. The bedroom, she thought, painfully aware of the sudden flush of colour to her cheeks as she prayed the bodyguard hadn't noticed.

'This all looks perfect,' she said, but suddenly all she could think of was how strange and alien it seemed. And how alone she was going to be for the next few weeks before the wedding—so far from home and away from everything which was familiar. She might moan about her family from time to time, but they were still her family, and right now they represented stability.

Constantin bowed. 'In that case, I will take my leave of you, Your Royal Highness. Silviana is here to wait on your every need but if there is anything you discover you don't have—'

'I'm sure there won't be,' she said quickly.

'Anything it is within my power to give you,' he continued,

as if she hadn't spoken, 'then please ring. At any time. I will be stationed directly outside your compartment.'

'You will?' questioned Zabrina nervously. 'Right outside?'

'But of course. Your welfare is my sole preoccupation and only a wall will divide us. Nobody will pass me to gain access to the Princess and I will remain awake for as long as the journey lasts.' He paused, his voice dipping. 'It is usually the custom for the chief bodyguard to eat meals with his or her royal subject.'

'Really?' she questioned.

'But of course. I need to taste your food and make sure it has not been poisoned, or tampered with. Which is why I am proposing to join you for dinner this evening, unless you have any objections to that.' Once again he flickered her a steely grey stare. 'Would such a proposition be acceptable, Your Royal Highness?'

Zabrina's mouth grew even dryer. She was expected to *eat meals* with him? She was expected to sit looking at his beautiful face, while all the time attempting to adopt an air of indifference? It sounded like a forbidden kind of heaven, made worse by the fact that Zabrina knew she shouldn't be thinking this way. She was promised to another man, wasn't she? That was the deal. She should be thinking about Roman and only Roman—beard or no beard. 'Why?' she questioned, playing for time. 'Am I such an unpopular choice to be your queen that I am likely to be poisoned?'

'Of course not.' He gave the faintest wave of dismissal. 'It is simply a necessary precaution. A safeguard, if you like, so that you will be delivered to the King unharmed.'

'I see,' said Zabrina slowly, but his use of the expression 'deliver' only reinforced the doubts she'd been experiencing earlier. Was that how *everybody* saw her—as a commodity? She supposed it was. She might be a crack shot who was fluent in four languages and thoroughly at home on the back of a temperamental horse. She might have devoted a huge portion of her time to working for women's charities and trying to get more equality for them in her homeland. But none of these things counted for anything, not really. And perhaps it was that which made a sudden streak of rebellion influence her decision, even though she had vowed to herself she wasn't going to make waves.

She could have told the autocratic bodyguard she wasn't particularly hungry and was quite happy to miss dinner—both of which were true. She could have hidden herself away in here and not seen anyone until they reached Rosumunte. But she wasn't going to. She glanced around at the sumptuous salon and suddenly it resembled nothing but a gilded cage.

Her gaze was drawn to the spring-like countryside outside— a blur of bright green as the train passed through. She was leaving her old life behind. When she returned here—and who knew when that would be?—it would be as the queen of a foreign country. One which had waged war against her ancestors in the past. And she was one of the spoils of that war. The modern-day virgin princess offered to the grisly king in exchange for a small chunk of his sizeable wealth.

Through the train window she caught a tantalising glimpse of an orchard at its very best. The branches of the trees were covered in thick white blossom, as if a mantle of snow had fallen on them. She found herself thinking of sunshine and birdsong and felt the sudden quickening of her blood.

Was it that which made her bold?

She was about to consign herself to a life of duty with the bearded King and, in essence, this was her last day of freedom. Surely she could have a little harmless fun before that happened? Would it be so wrong to mix socially with someone she wouldn't usually have been allowed anywhere near? Constantin Izvor obviously knew her husband-to-be as only a loyal servant could—and certainly a whole lot better than she did. Perhaps she could subtly learn a few tips on how best to handle the powerful King.

At least, that was what Zabrina told herself.

Just as she told herself it had absolutely nothing to do with the bodyguard's steely eyes and hard body.

'Yes, I suppose that will be okay,' she said carelessly, and then turned away before he saw the telltale flush in her cheeks.

# CHAPTER THREE

AS HE STOOD outside the ornate door of the Princess's carriage, Roman felt the powerful thunder of his heart. His throat was dust-dry and his body tense as the train hurtled towards the vast forest which divided Albastase from Petrogoria. He felt excited, yes, but the familiar, blood-pumping sensation of desire which raced through his body was one which filled him with foreboding.

Because Princess Zabrina had thrown his thoughts into disarray and caused him to feel more than a little apprehensive. And, try as he might, he couldn't dispel the feeling that he had been short-changed. That he had somehow been misled about what to expect from his future bride.

He had anticipated a little more modesty from the virgin princess. For downcast lids to cover those forest-green eyes—not a challenging stare to be slanted in his direction, which had made the hairs on the back of his neck stand up. He found himself wondering if he had imagined the powerful sizzle of lust which had passed between them. Or had that simply been wishful thinking on his part—because he had looked at her and wanted her and suspected that she wanted him too, because women were never able to resist him? Had he misinterpreted her acerbic response as one of flirtation, when in reality she was genuinely irritated by him—hard as that might be to believe? He curved his lips into an indulgent smile. He would not judge her too harshly. Of *course* she wouldn't have been flirting with him—she would have known perfectly well that any such flirtation should be reserved solely for the monarch to whom she was promised.

But in a way, the fact he was having to ask these questions justified what he was about to do—for what better way to observe his future bride than through the invisible cloak of the humble servant? And when he revealed his true identity to her, he would do it in such a way that could not possibly offend. Even if she was piqued by his elaborate charade, any displeasure would quickly be smoothed away. He would charm her and shower her with the priceless gems he had brought with him and which were currently concealed within his carriage. Because jewels were always a reliable bargaining tool. He had observed the way women behaved with priceless and glittering baubles and doubted his bride-to-be would be any exception.

And he knew this princess was financially astute. Hadn't she already negotiated a fairly hefty personal settlement for herself within the terms of the marriage contract, which his lawyers had expressed some anxiety about? But her greed did not repel him. Instead, it reassured him. This marriage was nothing but a business deal and the Princess recognised that, too.

He rapped on the door and Silviana opened it. Of course she did. Did he really imagine that Zabrina herself would fling it open and ask him inside? He watched as the servant's brow creased above the line of her veil, and wondered if she was resisting the desire to curtsey to him. Probably. She knew his true identity but was too well trained to offer anything but a polite nod of greeting. Roman smiled. His equerry had obviously done his job well in warning the staff not to 'recognise' him. He glanced across to the other side of the room where a table had been set for dinner, right next to the window and the dusky countryside which was hurtling by. Pale, fragrant roses stood at the centre of the linen cloth and pure white candles had already been lit, casting flickering lights which contrasted with the darkening sky outside.

It was, he realised suddenly, a very romantic scene and now he found himself wondering if that was such a good idea.

Was he worried that temptation would assail him?

'The Princess will be with you shortly,' Silviana said. 'She is getting ready for dinner.'

He nodded, lifting the palm of his hand in a gesture of dismissal. 'Excellent. You may leave now, Silviana. We will ring the bell when we wish the meal to be served and after that I wish to be alone with the Princess for the rest of the evening.'

She hesitated for no more than a fraction of a moment but Roman had seen it and raised his eyebrows at her in arrogant query.

'Was there something else, Silviana?'

'No, no, not at all, Constantin Izvor,' she said hastily. 'Please. F-forgive me.'

But Roman barely registered the servant's stumbled apology or her silent departure. He was much too preoccupied by a growing sense of anticipation—an expectation which was allowed to mount during the thirty long minutes it took for Zabrina to arrive.

He was not used to being kept waiting. Nobody would dare make the King cool his heels in contemplation, and Roman quickly discovered he was not over-fond of the experience. He had often secretly wondered what it would be like to live as an ordinary man but was fast discovering that perhaps he had been guilty of sentimentalising a life of obscurity. Because this was *boring*—standing to attention while Zabrina took all the time in the world to prepare herself for dinner.

During the hours which had passed since she had closed the door on him earlier, he had allowed himself to fantasise about what she might choose to wear tonight. Was she dressing in one of her fine gowns to dine with him? he wondered, unable to prevent the sudden drying of his mouth. Would the soft rustle of silk precede her, and that tanned skin be complemented by the framing of lavish lace and satin? He felt the heavy beat of desire as he imagined her parading around her bedroom in a variety of different outfits, which banished his boredom just long enough to ensure he was genuinely lost in thought when, eventually, he heard a sound behind him. But there was no rustle of silk or waft of fine perfume as he turned round to survey his future queen.

Roman's lips parted in disbelief as the Princess entered the salon.

Was this some kind of joke?

She had certainly changed from the embellished dress she'd had on earlier but she had not replaced it with something similarly splendid, or regal. No, she was wearing a pair of what he believed were called 'sweatpants', teamed with a loose top which effectively concealed her upper body like some kind of monstrous, flapping tent. She had removed the pins from her hair, too, but the intricate styling had not been replaced by a gratifying fall of lustrous unfettered hair. Instead, the thick brown locks were drawn back in a tight ponytail and she looked...

His brow furrowed. She looked like a woman leaving the gym!

She walked in and saw him and he observed the wariness in her eyes. 'Oh,' she said, with that same careless tone she'd used last time she'd spoken. 'You're here.'

'Did you think I wouldn't be?'

She shrugged. 'I wasn't sure.'

'I said I would be eating dinner with you, Your Royal Highness.'

'So you did. So you did. Well, you'd better stand at ease, I suppose.' She flopped down onto one of the sofas and Roman noticed her feet were bare and for some reason his disquiet was replaced by a mounting indignation that she should be so studiedly *casual* in his company. Because although she was ignorant of his royal identity—surely she shouldn't be so relaxed in the presence of a strange *male* bodyguard. Surely she shouldn't be stretching her arms above her head so that he couldn't help but be transfixed by the sudden pert outlining of her breasts beneath that horrible garment. Instantly, he looked out of the window and gave the darkening sky a searching scrutiny, as if scanning the horizon for potential threats. As if reminding himself that he was supposed to be guarding her and not running his gaze lustfully over her small and perfect body.

'Are we waiting for something?' she questioned.

'Not at all. I shall ring for dinner immediately,' he said, resenting the implicit order as he found himself noticing the curving sweep of her dark lashes which shuttered those amazing green eyes.

'You know, I'm almost tempted to ask if we couldn't have a sandwich or something instead,' she continued, huffing out a small sigh. 'At least that way we could cut the evening short.'

Again, people trying to limit the amount of time they spent with him was something Roman wasn't used to. They usually hung on his every word until he took his leave of them, and he wasn't enjoying the sensation of knowing she was there under *sufferance*. No, he wasn't enjoying it one bit!

'A casual snack would of course be possible, Your Royal Highness,' he answered smoothly. 'Though surely you need to keep your strength up for the long days of celebration and preparation which lie ahead? I am certain that the royal chefs would be deeply disappointed if you didn't allow them to offer you a range of typical Petrogorian delicacies.'

The forest-green eyes were suddenly very direct. 'And is that to be my role for the evening?' she questioned quietly. 'That I am to moderate my behaviour in order to please the catering staff?'

'Of course not, Your Royal Highness,' he said stiffly. 'That was not what I meant.'

\* \* \*

Zabrina saw the way the bodyguard's jaw tightened with obvious disapproval and in a way she couldn't blame him, because she probably *was* coming over as spoiled. But her behaviour was motivated more by self-protection, rather than petulance. She had been pacing her room restlessly ever since she had met Constantin Izvor at the beginning of this journey, glad to shut the door on him and mop her hand over her sweating brow. She had peeled herself out of her constricting gown and tried blaming *that* for the acute aching of her breasts and the increased sensitivity around the nipple area, which was making her feel oddly excited but deeply uncomfortable. She had convinced herself that if she dressed down in the comfy clothes she had secreted into her luggage without her mother's knowledge then she would quickly feel as relaxed as she sometimes did when she was gathered together with her sisters and brother, watching American films and eating popcorn in the palace games room.

But she had been wrong.

Despite the slouchy pants and baggy top, all those feelings of earlier were still there, only more so. In fact, she had only to look at the powerful bodyguard for her heart to start racing as if she had been galloping her horse at great speed.

*But it was wrong to feel this way about the brooding servant. She was on her way to marry another man!*

Conditioned by years of inbred royal etiquette, she sat up straight, put her shoulders back, pressed her knees together, and smiled as she tried to ignore the fake intimacy of the candlelit scene beside the window. 'Forgive me,' she said. 'I am not quite myself. This whole situation is so...'

His steely eyes narrowed. 'So what?' he questioned, as her words tailed off.

She shook her head. 'It doesn't matter.'

'But—'

'I said—' her voice was cool now, and properly regal '—it doesn't matter. And I meant it. Really, it doesn't. So why don't you order supper, Izvor, because the sooner you do, the sooner I will be able to retire for the night and you can go back to your guard post?'

It puzzled her that a look of faint irritation crossed his face and she wondered what on earth his agenda was. Was he so arrogant about his undoubted good looks that he found it hard to believe that a woman would want to cut short her time with him? Maybe she had been right in her initial assessment of wondering if his closeness to the King might have given him ideas above his station. Or maybe he was dating one of the chefs and determined that their culinary skills would be properly appreciated by the new Queen! Was that why he seemed so determined to have her eat an elaborate and possibly heavy meal when that was the last thing she wanted?

And then the strangest thing happened and it took her completely by surprise. A dark streak of something she didn't recognise shot through her body like a sweeping arrow and Zabrina felt her chest tighten as she imagined the bodyguard with another woman in his embrace.

Hugging her.

Kissing her.

She swallowed as he reached for the bell, realising that the emotion was one of jealousy and that she'd never felt it before. It unsettled her even more, because surely to feel such an emotion about a servant was very, very wrong. 'I wonder, could you also organise something to drink for me?' she croaked.

'But of course. Is something the matter, Your Royal Highness? You look...' His steely eyes narrowed, as if he was suddenly remembering it was not his place to offer his opinion on how she looked. 'I trust you are not ill?'

'No, of course I'm not ill and nothing is the matter. I would just like a drink, if that's not too much to ask!'

She saw his brow darken with what was almost a scowl, before he replaced it with a bland smile.

'Of course, Your Royal Highness. Your wish is my command. Might I offer a little wine, perhaps? I could recommend a superb Petrogorian vintage, ma'am. Some say it is even finer than the finest of French wine—though obviously the French themselves are not among that number!'

Zabrina rarely drank alcohol—not even on high days and holidays—and, much as she longed for something which might help ease the terrible tension which was spiralling up inside her, she knew it would be foolish to accept a drink from Constantin Izvor. Because alcohol loosened the inhibitions—didn't it?—and instinct was warning her that was the *last* thing she needed to do right now.

'International comparisons between alcoholic beverages do not particularly interest me, if it's all the same to you,' she answered coolly. 'But I *would* like a drink of water.'

'Certainly, Your Royal Highness,' he said, a nerve working in his cheek as he rang the bell, as if he were having difficulty dealing with her testy orders. A manservant answered his summons and took the order, reappearing moments later, carrying drinks on a silver platter, before silently exiting the room.

She watched as Constantin poured sparkling water into a glass, lowered his head and sniffed it as though he were judging a fine wine and then solemnly sipped.

'Perfect,' he murmured, filling another crystal goblet and handing it to her, and as he did so his fingers brushed against her skin.

And Zabrina could do nothing about the shiver which whipped over her body, even though it angered her. Because wasn't it *insane* that such a brief touch could make her breath catch in her throat? How could something so small and so meaningless make her want to sit there gazing at him in rapt and eager wonder? She was behaving like a love-struck schoolgirl! Lifting up the glass, she took a mouthful, but even as the cool liquid quenched her parched throat all she could think about were the bodyguard's lips, which were gleaming in a way which was making her feel strangely stirred-up inside.

It was worrying.

It was more than worrying.

She was on her way to marry another man and all she could think about was the one standing before her.

More servants appeared, carrying plates and covered dishes, which were placed on the table, and once they'd gone Zabrina shot him a questioning look. 'You have dismissed the rest of the staff?'

He shrugged. 'The train carriage is relatively small, ma'am, and I suspected you would feel more relaxed if you were not being observed by your new subjects. Does my action not meet with Your Royal Highness's approval, for I can immediately re-scind it if you would prefer?'

'No, no. That all sounds perfectly…reasonable.' She risked a glance into those pewter eyes and was immediately beguiled by their smokiness. 'Shall we sit?'

'If you don't mind, I would prefer to stand. And after I have sampled each dish, I will serve you.'

'Yes. Yes, of course,' said Zabrina hastily, terrified that she had broken some unknown rule of food-taster's etiquette. 'Thank you.'

Roman watched as she rose from her position on the sofa and slid onto one of the dining chairs, but as she shook out her napkin and placed it on her lap he thought she looked uncomfortable. As well she might, he thought grimly. She had casually invited him to sit opposite her—as if he were her equal! His mouth hardened. Was this how she *regularly* conducted herself when dealing with servants of the opposite sex—or with men in general? Were they unsuitably relaxed about such matters as correct social distancing, back at her palace in Albastase?

Briefly, he wondered if his judgment of her was unnecessarily harsh. He knew he possessed certain strong views about women and he knew, too, their source. But being aware of his own prejudices didn't mean he was going to blind himself to his future bride's obvious deficiencies!

He took his fork and ate some wild rice studded with pome-granates and pine nuts, and afterwards heaped a small amount on her golden plate, thinking that her tiny frame could surely not accommodate a larger portion than that.

He watched as she put a few grains into her mouth and found himself fascinated by the movement of her mouth as she chewed. It would be no hardship to kiss those soft lips, he thought, with a sudden fierce rush of desire, for he had not been intimate with a woman for well over a year, despite the many invitations which had come his way during his last royal tour. But he had resisted any such overtures, no matter how tempting they had been, aware that it would be unfair to the woman he was soon to marry if he had indulged in any pleasures of the flesh so close to their wedding.

But as a result, his sexual appetite was highly honed and keener than he could ever recall and he seemed to be growing harder by the second.

He cleared his throat. 'A little more, Your Royal Highness?'

'No, no. That was plenty.' She surveyed the selection of platters before her with a rueful smile. 'Especially as there appear to be several other courses to follow.'

He allowed himself a brief smile. 'Indeed there are.'

She lifted her head to look at him and, in the flicker of the candlelight, he was aware of feathery shadows on her honeyed skin, cast by her long lashes. 'Look, why don't you sit down for the rest of the meal, Constantin?' she said. 'It's hurting my neck to have to look up at you.'

Roman hesitated, but not for long, because it was a temptation too powerful to resist. It was a break with protocol, that much was true, but since he was planning to surprise her by revealing his identity before too long—and festooning her with a king's ransom in jewels—surely it wasn't too heinous a crime. Carefully, he removed his sword and put it within reach, before lowering his frame into the seat opposite hers. Then he forced himself to try and concentrate on the food he was tasting, rather than thinking how much he would give to free that magnificent mane of hair from its constricting ponytail and see what it looked like when it was tumbling down over her shoulders. But he comforted himself with the knowledge that it would not be too long before she was in his arms and in his bed. A few short weeks until their wedding and they could enjoy the legal consummation of their royal union. And if in the meantime, fuelled by his fierce hunger for her, that time passed with unendurable slowness, well, that wouldn't be the end of the world, would it? For wiser men than he had written that deprivation was a sure-fire guarantee of pleasure.

He forced himself to return his attention to the meal. Thin slivers of cold fish came next, accompanied by a leafy salad, soft with buttery avocado. She ate this with a little more interest and Roman experienced a small pang of compassion as, gradually, he saw her narrow shoulders relax and some of the tension leave her face and her body.

'You haven't eaten in a while,' he observed.

She looked up from her plate, her eyes narrowed and wary. 'How can you possibly know that? Are you a mind-reader or something?'

'That is one gift I suspect would be a double-edged sword,' he said drily. 'No, it's simply instinct. In the past I have commanded an army and can always recognise the signs when the men are hungry.'

'Oh?'

He shrugged, and as she continued to look at him curiously, he elaborated. 'Food is a necessity. A fuel, not a luxury, Your Royal Highness—although women often regard it as the enemy. And you need to eat. You're slim enough not to have to diet to get into your wedding dress and your brain and body need nourishment, especially when you consider what lies ahead.'

She put her fork down and he could see her lips pressing

in on themselves. 'If you don't mind, I'll skip the lecture,' she said. 'Though when I want advice on dieting or nutrition, I'll be sure to come to you.'

'Forgive me for my presumption.'

She bit down on her lip, as if she was itching to say something but trying very hard to hold her words back.

Which made Roman curious. Curious enough to let the silence between them grow into something very real and somehow brittle. He could feel a renewed tension in the air. He could see the distress clouding her forest-green eyes and all of a sudden the words came sliding from her mouth, even though he had not prompted them. Words he had not been expecting to hear, delivered with soft venom, as if she were excising a painful wound and needed all the poison to spill out before she could be healed.

'But what if you have no appetite?' she questioned in a low voice. 'What if you have barely been able to face food for days, because of the fate which awaits you?'

'To which fate do you refer, Your Royal Highness?' he questioned steadily. 'Surely your destiny is one which any princess would envy. Are you not about to become queen of one of the richest lands in the world and to marry its most powerful king?'

'Yes! Yes, I am,' she flared, putting her fork down with a clatter as she jumped to her feet. 'But unfortunately, that's the problem.'

'Problem?' he probed, his brow furrowed with confusion.

And now all semblance of protocol had disappeared and the face she turned towards him was both mulish with pride and pink with passion. 'Yes,' she breathed. 'A problem to which there is no satisfactory solution, for all my high-born position in life. Because I am being forced to marry a man I have no wish to marry!'

# CHAPTER FOUR

ZABRINA WAS SHOCKED to find herself on her feet, staring across the table at Constantin Izvor as the train continued its swaying journey through the countryside. No, that wasn't quite true. She wasn't shocked. She was horrified.

*Horrified.*

Had she really just announced to the King's chief bodyguard that she had no desire to marry his esteemed boss?

Yes, she had. Guilty as charged.

So now what?

Trying to smooth her scrambled thoughts and work out how to get herself out of this bizarre situation, she walked over to the window to survey the darkening landscape outside. High up in the indigo sky the moon was nothing but a thin, almost unobtrusive slither, which meant that you could see the blaze of thousands of stars which bathed the countryside, illuminating the blossom-covered trees with an unworldly silver light. It was the most beautiful scene she could remember seeing in a long time, yet it felt unbearably poignant. She thought about the same stars shining high over her palace in Albastase and her brother and sisters assembled there, and was surprised by another wave of homesickness which swept through her.

But she couldn't be a coward. She must face the music she

had managed to create all by herself. She had just committed what was, in effect, an act of treason. And if Constantin Izvor was determined to denounce her to his boss—which he was perfectly entitled to do—then she would have to accept her punishment and her fate.

Slowly, she turned around and lifted her gaze to his, but to her surprise the bodyguard did not look outraged. In fact, judging by the implacable expression on his devastatingly handsome face, he didn't even seem particularly shocked by what she had just blurted out. Just curious—the way she imagined someone might look if they had just been handed an envelope written in a hand they did not recognise.

'Look, can you forget you heard that?' she began falteringly. 'I was...overwrought. It must have been a lack of blood sugar—like you said.'

'Or not?' he negated.

She looked at him in surprise. 'Not?'

'In my experience, people don't just say things they don't mean. You clearly have some concerns—and concerns should always be addressed. So why don't I ring for these dishes to be taken away, while you go and sit down over there and compose yourself?' His grey eyes narrowed as he lifted the bell and rang it. 'And then perhaps I can put your mind at rest for you.'

He was gesturing towards one of the sofas on the opposite side of the salon and, once again, Zabrina thought he was behaving almost as if *he* were the host, rather than a member of the royal household! But by then a fleet of silent servants had arrived and were taking away all the used dishes, extinguishing candles and lighting soft lamps around the carriage, and by the time they had quietly shut the door behind them, she started thinking quickly. Wondering how she could possibly redeem herself in the light of such an inappropriate outburst, she sank onto the sofa he had indicated, thinking how blissfully comfortable it felt after being seated on that rather hard and ornate chair. Suddenly, the atmosphere seemed attractively inviting and *intimate*. She found herself wishing that the rest of the world would disappear and she could just stay in here, with him, protected and safe from the world. Wasn't that a bizarre thing to be thinking at such a time?

And now Constantin Izvor was moving across the silken rug towards her—this time not apparently requiring any invitation from her—and he sat down on the opposite end of the sofa and turned his head so that she was caught in the penetrating spotlight of that steely gaze.

'So,' he said, his accent sounding pronounced and thoughtful. 'You clearly have reservations about your forthcoming wedding.'

She thought that was probably the understatement of the year. 'Doesn't every bride?' she hedged.

'May I ask why?'

It wasn't really a subject which should be up for discussion but there was something so...so *approachable* about the way he was looking at her that she found herself wanting to tell him, but something held her back. It would be far better to pretend they'd never started this conversation, wouldn't it? She could dismiss him and he would obviously obey and next time she saw him she could act as if nothing had happened. But that wouldn't work for all kinds of reasons. *He* would know what she'd said and he would either pass those words on to his boss, or keep them to himself. If he did the former she would be vilified, and the latter would mean there would be a big secret between the two of them which the King wouldn't be privy to. And both those outcomes would be a disaster.

So couldn't she backtrack a little? Play up her natural worries about marrying a man of the world like Roman, and make out that they were nothing but the natural fears of any innocent bride-to-be?

She lifted up her shoulders and felt her ponytail whispering against her back. 'I realise it came out all wrong—'

The brief shake of his head indicated his lack of agreement.

'It came out the way it did because it was something you were feeling at the time. But please be aware that I am not planning to judge you, Your Royal Highness, for it is not my place to do so. Or to tell tales,' he added coolly. 'I am simply interested in your reaction and thinking that perhaps you need to get something off your chest. Certainly before you arrive at the royal palace,' he concluded softly. 'For I know it can be an intimidating place at the best of times.'

'But I grew up in a palace!' she defended quickly. 'And I'm used to that kind of life.'

'Perhaps you are, but no palace in the world can equal the size or splendour of the Petrogorian citadel,' he said, eyeing her with a shuttered look. 'Look, why don't you consider me like a priest in the confessional, knowing that anything you say to me is bound by the rules of confidentiality and will go no further than these four walls?'

Anyone less like a priest, Zabrina couldn't imagine—because surely holy men weren't supposed to inspire thoughts of…of… She swallowed. Thoughts she didn't understand properly, but which were bubbling away inside her and making her want to squirm uncomfortably beneath his seeking gaze.

Yet hadn't one of her initial thoughts on meeting him been that he would know the King better than anyone? What better person to allay her fears about her future husband and put her mind at rest, than Constantin Izvor?

'I have heard that the King is very…ruthless,' she said at last.

His thin smile was followed by a shrug. 'Some might say that an element of ruthlessness is necessary for any monarch and particularly for a man as successful as Roman the Conqueror. He has increased our country's wealth by some considerable margin since coming to the throne, and brokered peace in a region which has a history of being notoriously unstable. As you know, Petrogoria has often come under siege from its neighbours in the past.' He flicked her a candid look. 'Including from your very own country, Your Royal Highness.'

Zabrina nodded. She wasn't going to defend the actions of her ancestors and their dreams of conquest—how could she, when they had planted the Albastasian flag on disputed territory, which they had claimed as their own and which was now being returned to its rightful owner?

'I know all that,' she burst out. 'I just wish I wasn't being offered up as the human sacrifice in all this! If you really want the truth, I wish I wasn't getting married to anyone—but certainly not to a total stranger.'

The look he shot her was pensive. 'But you will gain a massive financial package as a result of the marriage,' he observed. 'Plus, you understand all the privileges of royal life as well as its constraints. And do not most princesses want to marry a king?'

'It was a decision made for me by someone else.'

'Alas, that is one of the drawbacks and also one of the strengths of an inherited monarchy. That the needs of the country are put ahead of personal need.'

'And the King is perfectly happy with this arrangement?' she questioned tentatively, thinking that *satisfactory* somehow sounded insulting.

'The King is governed by facts, not emotion. He knows perfectly well that a marriage of blue blood is preferable,' said Constantin, a sudden harshness entering his voice.

'The King's father married a commoner, didn't he?' probed Zabrina as she found herself remembering things she'd heard about him, and when he didn't answer, she persisted a little more. 'Was that one of the reasons why they had that terrible divorce? When he was so young? Didn't she leave, or something?'

The bodyguard's mouth twisted, as if he had just tasted something unspeakably sour. 'Something like that,' he agreed bitterly, before his face cleared and he looked at her with that oddly detached expression, as if it had been wiped clean of all emotion. 'Such an experience inevitably scarred him, but some say that boyhood pain makes for a powerful man.'

It was an aspect of the King's reputed character which

Zabrina had never considered before, but there was another one which she had. One which naturally made her wary. 'Is he cruel?' she questioned suddenly.

He didn't answer straight away. His dark brow knitted together and his eyes narrowed, as if he had seen something outside on the horizon he wasn't sure he recognised. 'No.'

'You sound very sure.'

'That's because I am sure and, believe me, I know him better than anyone. It is true that some women have gone to the press and given interviews which imply cruelty,' he said eventually. 'But maybe that's because he has been unable to provide them with what they most desire.'

'And what do women most desire?' she questioned, into the silence which followed, feeling suddenly out of her depth.

'Can't you guess?'

'S-sex?' she questioned, with more boldness than she had ever displayed in her entire life.

'No, not sex,' he said softly, with a short laugh. 'Sex is easy.'

Zabrina blushed. 'What, then?'

'Love,' he said, and when she made no comment, he carried on. 'That nebulous concept which drives so much of the human race in hopeless pursuit and brings so much misery in its wake. I find that women are particularly susceptible to its allure. How about you?' He arched his black eyebrows questioningly. 'Do you rate love very highly, Your Royal Highness?'

'How would I know how to rate it when I have no experience of it?' she said quietly.

'Then you should consider yourself fortunate, for some say it is nothing but a madness and others do not believe in its existence at all,' he asserted, before giving his head a little shake. 'But forgive me, for I digress. I don't know how we got onto this subject. Were we not supposed to be talking about the King?'

'Yes,' she said, a little breathlessly. 'I suppose we were.'

'You will find Roman exacting and demanding at times, as most highly successful men are,' he continued. 'But he asks of people no more than he is prepared to give himself. He certainly drives himself too hard—his people often say that he defined the term *workaholic* before the word became widely used. But, at heart, he is a good man.'

Zabrina was aware that her lips had grown dry and that her heart had begun to skitter and suddenly her lack of desire to meet the King was growing. 'That's hardly the most glowing recommendation I've ever heard.'

'I am trying to be honest with you, Princess. Did you wish for me to spin you a fairy tale—to make him into the kind of man you would wish him to be? You are not being promised rainbows and roses, no, but something far more solid. You will be embarking on the tried and tested situation of the arranged marriage, which offers the highest chance of success.'

'And so, in order to guarantee this "highest chance", I am to be immersed in your culture, without outside influence. I am being taken to Petrogoria, without family or servants to comfort or reassure me. I am being prepared for your ruler, as a chicken would be prepared for the pot.'

She had spoken without thinking but, surprisingly, the comment made him laugh and Zabrina was shocked by how much that sexy sound affected her. It whispered over her skin like rich velvet. It made her want to curl up her toes and sigh.

'Ah, but an uncooked chicken is cold and lifeless,' he said softly as he removed his gun from its holster and laid it on the low coffee table in front of the sofa. 'While you are warm and very, very vibrant.'

The unexpected compliment shocked her and made her react in a way she hadn't been expecting. It made her breasts tighten beneath her sloppy sweatshirt and her heart begin to pound. She knew that what was happening was inappropriate, but somehow Zabrina had absolutely no power over what her body was doing. She looked into the steely gleam of his pewter eyes and felt a clench of something low in her gut. She'd experienced something like this a bit earlier, but this felt different. It was more powerful. It seemed to be eating her up from the inside and suddenly she was overcome with an aching regret that she would never know what it was like to be held within the powerful circle of Constantin Izvor's arms, or to be kissed by him.

She thought of all the photos she'd seen of her future husband. On horseback, wielding a sword. At an official function in New York with presidents and other dignitaries, or wearing a black tie and tuxedo at some glittering charity event. She'd seen images of him dressed in ceremonial robes and army uniform, and others of him working hard at his desk.

And not one of those images had provoked the faintest glimmer of desire in her.

'He's a grisly bear of a man,' she found herself whispering, dimly aware that Constantin's eyes were suddenly very bright and that he was actually sitting much closer to her than she'd thought. 'With a beard. And…'

There was a pause. A heartbeat of a pause.

'And?' he prompted smokily.

Zabrina looked at him and knew it still wasn't too late, even though she had already said far too much. She could send the bodyguard away and retire to her room and take whatever consequences came her way. But she couldn't seem to move. Not only couldn't, but didn't want to, despite the undeniable thrum of danger in the air and the sense that something momentous was about to happen. She just wanted to sit there, drowning in the smoky grey light from his eyes and letting his velvety voice wash over her. 'And I hate beards,' she added, her voice suddenly fierce.

Roman nodded in response to her bitter words. He should have been angry. It was surely his *right* to be angry but that was the last thing he was feeling. Maybe because the defiant face which was turned to his was so irresistible. Maybe because he wasn't used to such candour, not from anyone. He could see the urgent flicker of a pulse beating at the base of her neck and could sense all the latent resentment which had stiffened her slender frame. But there was something else he could see in her eyes and that something was desire—a sexual hunger which surely matched the one which was pulsing around his veins. It had been present from the moment they'd met and now it was plainer than ever.

She didn't want the man she was promised to, he realised—and yet she wanted *him*.

He shook his head slightly, knowing what he should do. He should immediately absent himself from her company and address the disturbing aspects of her character this had raised in the cold, clear light of morning. But he knew he wasn't going to. He was going to kiss her. He *had* to kiss her because she was drawing him to her like a magnet. He was dazzled by the light which shone from her eyes. As he looked into her face his overriding sensation was one of intoxication. Or maybe he had just been celibate for too long and was woefully unprepared for any kind of temptation.

All he could see was the gleam of her lips. The rise and fall of her breasts and the whisper of her unsteady breath as she looked at him, those forest-green eyes soft and molten with hunger. The subtle scent of desire hung like a musky perfume in the air and he felt it wrapping him with silken bonds. He knew he should tell her the truth. Tell her who he really was. But how could he possibly explain his dilemma when right then he wasn't sure *who* he was? No longer an ice-cold monarch or masquerading bodyguard, but a man whose senses had been invaded with a potency which had taken him by surprise, leaving his nerve-endings clamouring and urgent with need.

It felt visceral.

It felt all-consuming.

As if everything he'd ever known before that moment had been forgotten and was focussed in the hard, sweet throbbing at his groin.

He must have moved, for his shadow threw her slender body into shaded relief and his face hovered above her startled, yet hungry expression. And suddenly he was responding to the glint of invitation in her eyes. He was bending to brush his lips over hers, fired up by the groan of pleasure which passed from her mouth to his as he kissed her. He told himself that any moment now she would come to her senses and push him away, but that wasn't happening. Her fingers were on his shoulders. They were digging into his flesh and she was pulling him closer, as if she wanted him to go deeper. And he did. God, he'd never kissed a woman as deeply as this before. The pressure of their seeking mouths was like lighting the touchpaper of a firework. He could feel her breasts pressing against his chest. His tongue laced with hers and she was moaning softly—moaning like someone in the middle of an erotic dream who was just about to come.

Was she?

Or was *he*?

Maybe.

Roman slipped his hand beneath her baggy top and a groan of pleasure escaped him as he cupped her breast in his palm, luxuriating in the lace-covered feel of it. He kneaded the soft flesh, thinking how much more luscious it was than it had appeared beneath her embellished dress of earlier. He grazed a negligent thumb over one pert nipple and heard her little moan of joy.

His lips on her neck, he ran the tip of his tongue over her skin and felt her shiver in response and, as he tasted her flesh, he felt utterly bewitched by her. His hand moved down towards the waistband of her sweatpants and she was circling her hips towards him, like a dancer on a podium inviting men to throw money at her. And all the questions he should have asked— not just of himself, but of her—suddenly seemed to evaporate.

Hadn't he told her that everything which was said would re- main between these four walls for ever—and didn't that count for everything they *did*, as well?

'Princess,' he intoned huskily. But it was more than an un- deniable purr of appreciation. It was also an unspoken question which they both understood as he stared deep into her eyes.

Zabrina stilled as she heard the use of her official title, but even that brief brush with reality wasn't enough to dampen her desire for him, which was off the scale. He was tacitly asking if she wanted to continue and she knew only too well what she ought to say. Despite her inexperience, she could sense that things were getting rapidly out of control, yet she was doing nothing to stop him—and it was pretty obvious why. All during dinner she'd been fascinated by him. She had been deeply attracted to him on a physical level, yes, but there had been a huge element of trust, too.

He had told her she could confide in him and for some reason she had believed him—because the light shining from his grey eyes had looked genuine and honest. So she had. She'd told him more than she'd ever told anyone. But all those confidences now seemed like a double-edged sword. It had been good to get things off her chest and vocalise her doubts to someone outside her immediate family, yet the freedom of doing such an *unroyal* thing had made her feel strangely restless and…incomplete.

It had made her long for the freedom to do more of the same. It had made her wish she weren't a princess who was being sold off to a man she didn't know, but a woman who had the ability to make her own choices about things. Like, about who she would give her body to, when she chose to have sex for the first time. Constantin had tried to put her mind at rest by explaining that Roman was an *exacting* rather than a cruel king—but that didn't cancel out the fact that she didn't fancy him, did it?

But she fancied Constantin.

Her heart pounded almost painfully. She fancied him more than she could say. Especially as he was now peeling back her sweatshirt and bending his mouth to the mound of her breast. She tipped her head back and a helpless shudder ran through her as he sucked at the nipple through the flimsy barrier of her new bra. And now he was beginning to stroke her belly and she wanted more. Much more. She could feel the molten heat building between her thighs, along with a hungry pulse of need which had started flickering there. Her mouth dried to dust because he was igniting a yearning deep inside her and it felt so incredible that every cell of her body was screaming to let him carry on.

So she did.

She told herself it would only be for a minute. Certainly no longer than that.

His hand slipped further down and he pushed aside the centre panel of her panties, which were almost shockingly wet, and Zabrina gave a little cry as he made contact with her aching flesh. She swallowed. Was it so wrong for his finger to be skating urgently over that most intimate part of her? And for that same finger to alight on the exquisitely sensitised nub before beginning to move in delicate rhythm? How could it be wrong when it felt like nothing she'd ever experienced before? When it felt so *good*…

She closed her eyes as the light movement made her catch her breath, then blindly she lifted her face to his, and his responding kiss made her feel as if she were drowning in honey.

'Princess?' he groaned again against her lips.

Again she sensed that some new barrier was about to be crossed and he was seeking her permission. Maybe if he'd said her name then common sense might have prevailed, but his repetition of her title made her feel slightly disconnected and uncaring of the consequences. As if this were not happening to her but to someone else—someone she didn't know very well. A wild stranger who was briefly inhabiting her body and demanding that this fierce sexual hunger be fed.

'Yes,' she said, in her own language, her next words muffled by the sweatshirt he was pulling over her head. 'Yes, please.'

# CHAPTER FIVE

HE WAS UNDRESSING. Or at least, he was freeing himself from his clothes. There was very little ceremony involved. Zabrina watched as Constantin Izvor impatiently removed his long leather boots and kicked them aside, before peeling off his dark trousers and sending them in the same direction, after first extracting a mysterious packet of foil.

His shirt followed, exposing the honed magnificence of his bare chest—but there wasn't really time to appreciate it because the bodyguard was turning his attention to her once more. He splayed his palms over her hips, her slouchy pants were swiftly disposed of and it wasn't until she felt the rush of cool air against her legs that it suddenly occurred to Zabrina that Constantin was completely naked, while she was still wearing her underwear.

His eyes narrowed as if he had suddenly tuned into her thoughts. 'We don't seem to be very equally matched,' he murmured.

It was almost enough to destroy the mood, because Zabrina knew they would *never* be equally matched, because, no matter how vaulted his position, he was still a servant and she a royal. But by then she didn't care, because he was deftly unclipping her bra and her reservations were dissolved by the delicious sensation of her breasts sliding free. She liked the way that made her feel, just as she liked the way his eyes had darkened in response.

His gaze roved to the only remaining barrier to her nakedness—a tiny triangle of pink lace panties, which matched the bra—and she saw his mouth harden with something she didn't recognise. Something which looked faintly disapproving. Surely not—for hadn't part of her pre-wedding sexual education reinforced the fact that men liked provocative lingerie and it was a wife's duty to heed such desires?

Zabrina chewed on her lip. Perhaps he was perplexed by her extravagant underclothes, particularly when worn underneath such a deliberately unglamorous outer layer. She wondered what he'd say if he knew that the flimsy garment was completely unlike the sleek black briefs she normally favoured, which made horse-riding so much easier.

But now was not the time to start thinking about the trousseau which had been acquired by one of her mother's stylists. Not when he was hooking the sides of her panties with his fingers while making a low, growling noise at the back of his throat. For one crazy moment she thought he was about to rip them off and wasn't there an unknown and rather shocking side to her character which actually hoped he *would*? But she had been mistaken, because he was removing them conventionally enough, sliding them down over her knees—though with hands which were slightly unsteady.

His watchful eyes burned into her as he ran a questing finger over her thighs, lightly stroking the goose-pimpled flesh in inciting circles which made them tremble even more. And suddenly Zabrina found herself parting her legs for him, as if his pewter gaze was compelling her to do so—and he was…he was…

She gave a startled gasp as Constantin Izvor bent his head down between her thighs. His tongue began to dart over the exquisitely aroused flesh and he gently hushed her with a single, 'Shh!'

It was an impossible order. How could she possibly stay silent when he was working such magic? When he was making her feel like this—as though she were rapidly soaring towards an unknown destination? Some place of unbelievable sweetness which was beckoning to her with honeyed fingers. It felt shockingly intimate. Decadent and delicious. It felt *perfect*.

Helplessly, Zabrina writhed beneath the featherlight accuracy of his tongue, scarcely able to believe that it could get any better. But it did. It was getting better all the time. It was so good that she felt as if she were going to faint with pleasure. She bit back a cry of disbelief mingled with joy, and just as her body started convulsing he pressed his lips against her pulsating core. Bunching up her fist, she dug her teeth hard into her fingers and bit on them as the flick of his tongue intensified the blistering sensations. One delicious spasm was followed by another and never had she felt quite so vulnerable—or so powerful—as she did in that moment. Time stretched and suspended and she found herself strangely reluctant to float back down to earth.

Her eyelids parting, she saw Constantin opening the foil packet he'd retrieved earlier and Zabrina suddenly understood what it contained. She'd never even seen a contraceptive before—why would she?—and she'd always imagined she might feel a mixture of terror and embarrassment when eventually she did. But the only thing she was experiencing right now was a warm anticipation as he moved to lie on top of her. His flesh was silky and hard. She could feel the muscled weight of his body and his satin tip nudging against the core he had just kissed so intimately. She could detect a faint perfume in the air, and as he lowered his head to kiss her she could taste the scent on his tongue and realised that the taste was *her*.

'Constantin,' she said, almost brokenly.

'What?'

For a moment she felt him grow still against her, as if he was having second thoughts.

Was he?

Should *she* be having them?

*Of course she should.*

A lingering remnant of common sense reminded her of the insanity of what she was about to do—yet her body was so greedy for more of this incredible pleasure that it refused to contemplate any other alternative than what was about to happen.

'What is it?' he demanded again, his voice raw and ragged with need.

'N-nothing.' If she wasn't careful she would start putting doubts in his mind, and the King's servant would realise what a compromising position they were in. And if he decided to call a halt to it could she really bear it? No, she could not. Was that what made her instinctively thrust her pelvis forward, so that his tip entered by a fraction and he gave a soft roar as he thrust into her more deeply?

Zabrina sucked in a disbelieving breath as he filled her and she was amazed at how quickly her body adjusted to his possession—as if she had been waiting all her life for this man to be inside her. She let out a slow shudder as he began to move and, very quickly, could feel an escalation of that now-familiar bliss with each powerful thrust he made. But as his mouth fixed itself on hers and she felt the lace of his tongue again, she suddenly became aware that this was about more than the purely physical. It felt as if the two of them really had become one—in every sense. Did she feel that connection because he'd convinced her to confide in him? Or because he'd made her feel almost normal—less like a princess and more like a woman?

And that had never happened before.

'Oh,' she whimpered.

He raised his dark head, his eyes seeming unfocussed. 'Oh, what?'

'It feels…amazing.'

'I know it does.'

What was that sudden edge to his voice as he drove even deeper? Zabrina wasn't sure but right then she didn't particularly care, because it seemed that instinct was guiding her movements again. Why else did her thighs lock with familiar ease around his back, and why else did she move her pelvis to meet each hard thrust? The low moans of pleasure he gave thrilled her immeasurably. Did that mean he liked the way she was responding to him? She hoped so because she liked everything he was doing to her.

Everything.

She liked the way his teeth teased her nipples into diamond points. The way he smoothed his fingers over her arching flesh, as if discovering every centimetre of her body through touch alone. Each thrust he made took her deeper, and then deeper still, into a new and intoxicating world which was becoming familiar to her. In her befuddled mind she saw the twitch of a colourless curtain, behind which was a glimpse of that rainbow place again. And suddenly it became real, and all those incredible sensations were swamping her in tantalising waves.

It couldn't be happening, Zabrina thought dimly. Not…not again.

But it could, and it was.

Oh, it *was*.

As her body began to clench around him, he drove his mouth down on hers—as if recognising that kissing was the only way of stemming the euphoric cry which was bubbling up inside her. Zabrina yelped softly into his mouth as his movements became more urgent—until at last he jerked inside her, his head tipping back as he shuddered out his own moment of fulfilment.

It felt like an intensely private moment but she was so dazed and spellbound that she risked a glance at his face.

He looked enraptured. There was no other word for it. As if he'd just discovered the most delicious thing imaginable. And for a few silent seconds, Zabrina allowed herself the pointless luxury of fantasy.

What if he'd realised—like her—that this type of connection was rare? So rare that she would be prepared to give up her destiny for it. For him. She could tell him that she'd meant what she'd said about his boss—that she had no desire to marry him, nor even any desire for him. She could renounce her royal title and they could run away together. There would be a terrible scandal, yes, but people would get over it and the world would move on. He was strong and resourceful. He could build them a cottage in the woods and she would bear his children. She would cook meals and grow vegetables and he would come home every night and take her into his arms, and... She frowned. It was true that she'd never cooked anything in her life, but she would soon learn!

'Constantin,' she said softly, and as she said his name an astonishing transformation seemed to come over him.

The first thing he did was to withdraw from her, as if he couldn't wait to put some distance between them. But not before she'd detected the way he had begun to harden inside her once more...and she sensed he was having to fight the urge not to thrust inside her again. She wished he would. She wanted to ask him if something was wrong but her inexperience warned her to wait a little. Because he might be awash with feelings of guilt and regret at what they'd just done—feelings she knew she should share, but somehow she just couldn't. How on earth could she possibly feel guilty or regretful about something which felt as if it had been written in the stars?

His back to her now, he peeled off the condom and dropped it on top of his discarded trousers, as if this was something he had done a million times before. He probably had, Zabrina reasoned, though she needed to understand that his life before he'd met her was none of her business and she must not question him about it. Not when they had more than enough questions of their own they needed to address. In fact, he was probably wondering where the hell they went from here, so surely it was up to her to put his mind at rest and reassure him that she wasn't intending to pull rank.

'Constantin?' she repeated softly.

He turned to face her then and Zabrina almost wished he hadn't, because…

Surely there had to have been some kind of mistake? Surely someone couldn't have travelled from bliss to contempt so quickly. But eyes which had been soft and smoky with lust now resembled chips of grey ice and his face looked as if he had pulled on a dark mask of anger. Was he anticipating the repercussions of what they had done?

She frowned. 'Is…is something wrong?'

'What do you think?' he snapped, his voice as cold as his eyes.

She swallowed. 'I know we shouldn't have—'

Roman shook his head, unable to contain his anger for a second longer. Anger at the naked princess who was still tempting him unbearably, yes, but far more potent was the anger he was directing at himself. How could he have lost control like that? How *could* he? 'Damned right, we shouldn't,' he snarled.

She was sitting up in bed and smoothing down her hair, shiny strands of which were tumbling from its constricting ponytail and falling tantalisingly over her bare breasts.

'Look, I don't have any experience but I do know that these things happen,' she whispered.

Her wide-eyed expression was completely at odds with the foxy euphoria he'd witnessed when she'd been orgasming underneath him and now Roman felt another spear of anger directed at the erection which was stirring at his groin. 'Oh, please. Don't insult my intelligence by playing the wounded innocent, when nothing could be further from the truth!'

She blinked at him in confusion and it almost looked real. She was a good actress, he'd say that for her.

'What are you talking about, Constantin?'

The way she spoke his name made another wave of anger wash over him. 'What do you think I'm talking about?' Furiously, he rose from the bed and grabbed at his clothes, rapidly pulling on his trousers before heading towards the bedroom at the far end of the compartment. From there, he tugged a silken coverlet from the bed and walked back into the salon before tossing it to her. 'Cover yourself up,' he said, striding over to the door and turning the key in the lock.

Thankfully, she did as he asked, concealing her delicious body from his hungry eyes with the aid of the bedspread. That was one less distraction at least, Roman thought grimly as a pert pink nipple was covered by a ripple of silk, though he couldn't deny his faint sense of deprivation. His mind was buzzing but all he could see was the fearful gaze she was directing at the door before looking back at him, as if she had only just realised where they were and what they had been doing.

'Oh, my goodness. We could have been discovered,' she was breathing in horror. 'Anyone could have walked in at any time.'

Roman shook his head. He had been wondering how he could tell her what she needed to know—he just hadn't been sure how to go about it. But now he was. There was a perfectly simple way of alerting her to the simple fact which was going to change her fate for ever. His, too. Yet wasn't there a part of him which felt a kind of *relief* at the prospect that he would no longer need to marry her? No need to marry *anyone*.

'Nobody would have walked in,' he declared, with icy certainty.

She gave a nervous laugh. 'You can't possibly know that.'

'Yes, I can.'

'How?'

The stab of conscience he had all but eliminated made another brief attempt to unsettle him, but Roman quickly quashed it. Because surely her deception was far greater than his? He looked into her forest-green eyes and sucked in a deep breath.

'Because my name is not Constantin Izvor and I am not the chief bodyguard to the royal household. I am—'

'You are the King,' she interrupted suddenly, her face growing as white as a summer cloud. 'You are King Roman of Petrogoria.'

# CHAPTER SIX

'HOW THE HELL do you know who I am?' he demanded.

Zabrina felt a flicker of pleasure that she'd taken him by surprise because surely her sudden realisation of the King's true identity gave her back a modicum of control over this awful situation.

But only a modicum.

Keep cool, she told herself fiercely, as the train continued to rattle through towards the border which divided their two countries. Don't let him guess at your thoughts or your feelings. Because if he does—*if he does*—that will give him even more power than he already possesses. If he realised, for example, that her primary feeling was one of hurt and betrayal, then wouldn't that run the risk of making her appear even more foolish? She shuddered as she forced herself to recall her stupid imaginings. Had she seriously been considering renouncing her title and her life to live in a country cottage with him? She must have been out of her mind.

'How long have you known my true identity?' he questioned coldly.

She forced herself to glare at him instead of drinking in his steely beauty, which she had been doing until just a couple of minutes ago. Why, if she was capable of winding the clock back even by a minute, she would still be in that dazed place of sensual fulfilment, her body all glowing and tingly. And wasn't it crazy that, even now, she was finding it difficult to remain immune to his physical allure? It was very difficult to concentrate on anything when she noticed he'd left the top button of his trousers undone. 'You mean, how long is it since I found out that you've been deceiving me, since even before I boarded this royal train?'

'You dare to talk to me of deception?' he flared back. 'When you were planning to arrive in my country to great fanfare and acclaim and then to marry me, having had sex with someone you believed was my bodyguard?'

Zabrina felt completely wrong-footed by his icy accusation, which was presumably his intention—because everything he'd said was true. She *had* done all those things. But it was all becoming much clearer now. When she had met the man who had introduced himself as Constantin Izvor, she had quickly noticed his autocratic bearing and had thought he was a little full of himself. *Of course he was.* He had been trying to behave like a commoner, when all his life he had occupied one of the most powerful positions in the region. No wonder he had struggled with humility. No wonder he had such strong traces of arrogance. She had thought that at times he seemed almost regal—because he was! Oh, why hadn't she trusted her instincts and found out more about him, instead of taking everything he said at face value? Why the *hell* had she trusted him? Hadn't she learnt ever since she was barely out of the cradle that men were selfish creatures who were not to be trusted?

'You started it!' she declared. 'You started the whole seduction process!'

'How?'

'By telling me…' Oh, how trite it sounded now and how gullible she had been. 'By telling me that my skin was soft and silky—'

'And do you respond to all men who compliment you like

that?' he snapped. 'If, say, one of the servants had admired the colour of your eyes, would he have been allowed to put his head between your thighs and be in the position I now find myself in?'

'How dare you?'

'It's a simple question, Zabrina. All it needs is a yes or a no!'

'I shouldn't even dignify that question by responding, because you know very well what the answer is. The answer is no, of course it is. Because I was an innocent,' she elaborated, when he continued to look at her coldly.

'What the hell,' he iced out, 'are you talking about?'

Zabrina had thought it couldn't possibly get any worse than it already was, but she had been wrong. She looked at the contemptuous curve of his lips and a terrible truth began to dawn on her—one so awful that initially she wouldn't allow herself to believe it. Surely he didn't think…? 'I was a virgin,' she repeated—and wasn't it another stupid side-effect of the situation she now found herself in that she should feel embarrassed about having a clinical discussion about something so personal, when in his arms she had behaved completely without inhibition?

'Oh, please.' His laugh was bitter. 'We may have both committed the sin of deception, but that time has gone, and from now on perhaps we should agree to speak only the truth.'

'That's exactly what I am doing.'

'I'm giving you time to think about what you've just said and to modify it accordingly. You were no virgin, Princess. So please don't insult me by pretending that you were!'

Instinctively, Zabrina's fingers dug into the silken coverlet as his gaze raked over her and she wondered if she had imagined that sudden brief darkening of his eyes. Was that because she was naked underneath it? she wondered. And did he still want her as much as she wanted him? How inconvenient desire could be, she thought bitterly, aware of her hardening nipples in response, and the molten heat which clenched so tantalisingly at the base of her belly. 'Are you saying I *lied* to you about my inexperience?'

'If it makes you feel better, I'll be generous and put it down to you being creative with the facts. I can understand your reasoning because obviously you want to protect your reputation. But it won't make me think any worse of you if you admit to the truth,' he added. 'It certainly won't change the outcome of what I am about to do next.'

Maybe she should have addressed the slightly sinister portent of 'what I am about to do next', but Zabrina was so horrified by his accusation that she briefly forgot his words. 'Why are you saying that?' she whispered, and then, as a sudden horrified thought sprang into her mind, she glanced over at the sofa to quickly put her mind at rest, relieved to see that it was as pristine as before. 'Because there was no evidence? Were you hoping to fly the bloodied sheet from the palace balcony in Rosumunte on our wedding night? Aren't we royals supposed to have moved on from those days?'

'Please do not try to distract me with inappropriate sarcasm!' He glowered at her. 'Because I *know* how a woman behaves when it is her first time with a man. She is shy. She is tentative. She is often overwhelmed by what is happening to her.'

'How encyclopaedic you sound, *Roman*. Which leads me to conclude that you must have had sex with many virgins before?''

'Some.' He shrugged. 'Not many.'

'And is that supposed to make me feel better?'

'I don't imagine anything would be able to do that at the moment,' he commented wryly and gave a sudden, heavy sigh. 'But if it's any consolation, I feel pretty much the same.'

'It isn't!' she snapped. 'I'm not interested in consolation, even if you were capable of providing any, which I suspect you aren't. And as for knowing how a woman behaves when it is her first time—don't you suppose that any shyness on her part might have something to do with the fact that you're a powerful king? Except when you're pretending not to be, of course.' She gave a short laugh. 'Surely your crime was worse than mine, since you knew exactly who I was. Was that your intention all along, *Roman*? To seduce me? Was this some sort of primitive test of my character to see how much temptation I could take before submitting to you?'

'Which I have to say you failed quite comprehensively, Princess.'

'Well, maybe you shouldn't be so skilled at seduction!'

There was silence for a moment before eventually he expelled a long sigh. 'Look, I can see with hindsight that it's unreasonable of me to apportion blame,' he said, lifting the palms of his hands in what looked like a gesture of conciliation.

'Why don't you say that as if you mean it?' she demanded, thinking that here was a man who was a stranger to the word *apology*. But weren't all powerful men like that—especially kings? They only said sorry if they were forced to—the way her father had done in the past, when he'd been found out in his latest dalliance. They might go through the motions, but they never really *meant* it.

'I have had sexual partners before,' he continued. 'So I guess it's not unreasonable that you should have done the same.'

'But?' She raised her eyebrows. 'I sense there's a "but" coming.'

Again, a shrug—but this time there was no accompanying hint of apology. 'We both know that the unwritten clause in our marriage contract is that you should have known no lover other than me, Zabrina. It's how these things work. Sexual equality may be alive and well in most of the world, but it has yet to reach either of our two countries. And I'm certain your grasp of royal history is thorough enough for you to realise that there can be no possible question over the legitimacy of any future progeny, which can only be the case if my bride is pure.'

'*Pure?*' Zabrina stared at him, tugging the band from her hair and giving her ruffled mane an angry shake. 'Look, believe or don't believe that I wasn't the cowering little innocent you were hoping for—I don't particularly care either way. But please don't illustrate your prejudices with such ridiculous euphemisms. You make me sound like a bar of soap!'

For a moment Roman almost smiled at her outburst, until he remembered the gravity of the situation in which he now found himself. A situation which must be resolved as quickly as possible. He shook his head. If only he could just walk out of the salon now and pretend that this had all been like a bad dream.

Or an irresistibly sweet one...

But he couldn't. That was the trouble. Nobody could re-write the past, no matter how much power they possessed at their fingertips. And unfortunately, the past wasn't his only dilemma—not when the present was haunting him in a way he hadn't anticipated. He found himself wishing she were someone else. Someone anonymous, with whom he had no projected future, so that he would have no qualms about going back over to the sofa on which she reclined and ravishing her over and over again as he hungered to do. What wouldn't he give to feel her soft thighs wrapped around his back one more time, and hear her soft moans of joy as he thrust into her with wild abandon? He swallowed, looking into her defiant face and realising she didn't look in the least bit *chastened*—which he might have expected in the circumstances.

Until he forced himself to remember that this was not a virginal princess who was grateful to marry the mighty King who had been selected for her. No, this was a princess who had betrayed, not only him, but both their lands. And now she would pay the ultimate price for her folly.

Yet he remembered what it had felt like to touch her and he felt a bitter regret that he would never experience it again. Sex had never felt like that before. As if he would die if he didn't possess her. As if his very life had depended on being deep inside her. He remembered the battle which had raged within him as he'd fought to conquer the terrible desire she had unleashed in him. To stop what was happening before it reached the point of no return. But he had been unable to turn away from her sweet temptation and prevent himself from stripping them both bare, before losing himself in her delicious honey. As he had entered her, he had looked deep into her eyes and seen a powerful yearning which had matched his own and a random thought had briefly speared his mind. A thought which contradicted everything he had been brought up to believe.

That this woman was his equal.

But he forced himself to focus on the truth instead of fantasy.

Yes, she was a woman who would have made a superb mistress.

But a thoroughly unsuitable wife.

He wondered if she would save face by exiting their embryo relationship with the minimum of fuss or whether she needed him to spell it out for her. He thought perhaps she did since she was studying him with an impassive expression, almost as if nothing had changed. When everything had changed.

But he knew that this was a delicate situation which required careful and diplomatic handling, if the fallout was to be kept to a minimum.

'You have many attributes, Princess,' he said slowly. 'You are a beautiful and intelligent woman and I am certain you will find another man who is willing to marry you. Perhaps not one as highly connected as I am, it is true.' He glimmered her a smile, trying to reassure her, yes, but also trying to convince himself that nothing would be gained from making love to her again. He tried to take his mind off his throbbing groin. 'And you must rest assured that what I said earlier was true. Nothing which has passed between us will go any further than these four walls.' He gave her a swift, businesslike smile. 'Your secret will be safe with me.'

Some of the impassivity left her face. 'My...secret?'

'Nobody will ever know what happened between us, Princess. It will be like closing the chapter of a book.'

Zabrina flinched and not just because his words were filling her with fury, but because they were managing to turn her on at the same time. How did he *do* that? For a few brief seconds she felt almost powerless over the effect his cool stare was having on her. Why else would she find herself recalling how amazing it had felt to have him peeling off her panties? Or remembering the expert flick of his tongue against her throbbing bud until he had brought her to orgasm? She swallowed as she remembered the second orgasm when he'd been deep inside her. Just the thought of what he'd done was making her stomach dissolve and her skin grow heated. Surely, if she wasn't careful, he would guess at the effect he was having on her.

And that was something she simply couldn't afford to let happen.

Setting her mouth into a firm line, she stared at him. 'You mean, you are no longer planning to marry me?' she verified.

His sigh sounded genuinely regretful—it was just a pity the steely glint of relief in his eyes didn't match the sentiment. 'I cannot marry you, Princess—for the reasons I have already expanded upon and which I am sure you understand. Because if you are being honest with yourself, can you really be hypocritical enough to exchange public vows with a man you theoretically betrayed, even before you'd met him?'

'I—'

'The wedding must be called off as quickly as possible. We just need to work out the best way to go about it and how best to return you to your country.' A new and gritty note entered his deep voice. 'A damage-limitation exercise, if you like.'

If she *liked*?

Zabrina could hardly comprehend the audacity of the man. How did he have the nerve to start talking about *damage limitation* and coolly state that he was about to send her back to Albastase like some reprimanded schoolgirl? She bristled with indignation. And wasn't it funny how contrary human nature could be? Earlier that day she would have sold off the few humble jewels she possessed if someone could have guaranteed her a get-out clause for her marriage to the grisly King.

Except that he wasn't grisly.

He was anything but. He was gorgeous enough for her to have eagerly surrendered her virginity to him—a virginity he didn't believe she'd possessed. So not only had he deceived her, he had also accused her of lying! His list of crimes against her was long, but could she afford to dwell on them, or take offence? No, she could not. She needed to keep her eye on the bigger picture and not on whether or not her feelings were hurt, because at the end of the day that didn't matter. Feelings passed. They waxed and waned like the moon whose cold, silver crescent now looked like a scythe hanging outside the train window.

She thought about the different choices which lay ahead of her. She and Roman could agree a joint statement which could be put out by both their countries, stating that the wedding would not take place. They could fudge a reason—although it was difficult to see what that reason might be. Incompatibility was hardly going to work as a believable concept, because the underlying understanding within an arranged marriage was that compatibility had to be *worked* at.

She swallowed. Then there was all the expense involved— all the lavish celebrations which would need to be cancelled— not to mention the disappointment of their subjects, who were looking forward to a three-day holiday of feasting and dancing, once the wedding had taken place. But those things paled into insignificance when she remembered the real purpose behind this union...

Her country badly needed an injection of funds to bring it back from the brink of economic ruin.

*And wasn't she the only person who could do it?*

If the wedding was called off, she would be seen as a failure. No matter how they spun it she would always be known as the Jilted Princess, unwanted by the highly desirable and powerful ruler. She would be the one who would be judged negatively, because in this region men were seen as more important than women. Her father would be furious that she had failed to provide the goose that laid the golden egg, but ultimately wouldn't it be her brother and her sisters who suffered as a result of a cancelled marriage?

Zabrina sucked in a determined breath. No. No matter what the provocation, the luxury of escaping her fate with the arrogant King was simply not an option.

'But I don't want to call off the wedding,' she informed him quietly.

His eyes narrowed, but not before she'd seen the flicker of astonishment glinting in their pewter depths—as though someone disagreeing with him was something he wasn't used to. Zabrina could almost see the cogs of his brain whirling, as if he was trying to decide the best approach to take to kill off her rebellion, before it had a chance to grow.

'I'm sorry to disappoint you, Princess, but that's what's going to happen.'

'No. I think you misunderstand me, Roman. I am not disappointed. This is a decision I have made using my head, not my heart. This has nothing to do with emotion, because emotion has no place in this marriage of ours. It never did. I never particularly wanted it, if the truth were known, but I was willing to accept my fate.'

'Do you realise how much you insult me?' he breathed.

'It was not said with the purpose of insulting you. I said it because it was true. But the past is irrelevant.' She drew in a deep breath. 'The union must still take place. It has long been agreed. My country will benefit. Yours, too. Aren't you forgetting how much you desire that piece of land?'

'And aren't you forgetting something?' he snapped. 'Something less pragmatic than matters of finance and territory? It was always intended that my future queen should be—'

'*Pure?*' she interjected sarcastically. 'So you keep saying. Maybe it was and maybe I should be a lot more offended than

I actually am that you don't believe I was. But I find I'm not offended at all—which I can only put down to the fact that I set the bar very low when it comes to my expectations concerning men!'

'Your negative opinions about men do not interest me. And I don't think you're hearing me properly, Zabrina. You are not what I consider to be a suitable partner and I do not want you as my wife.'

'And you're not hearing *me*,' she countered fiercely. 'You said yourself that my virginity was the unwritten clause in our wedding contract, and anyone who knows even a little bit of law realises that an unwritten clause means nothing!'

His eyes hardened. 'So you wish to force me to marry you? Is that what you really want? A man you have hounded to the altar? And all because your ego can't take perceived rejection.'

'It has nothing to do with my ego and everything to do with securing a prosperous future for my country!'

'And then what?' he demanded. 'Being with someone who doesn't want you is hardly a recipe for life-long contentment, is it?'

For a moment Zabrina was perplexed by his words—because surely he wasn't foolish enough to believe in fairy tales like *life-long contentment.* A relationship of polite civility and tolerance was the best that could be hoped for, because that was how these things worked. A royal marriage was about what the couple *represented* rather than the relationship which existed between them. She had even known she would be expected to turn a blind eye to his behaviour—to the liaisons with other women he would undoubtedly have—and she had been prepared to do that, because that had always been the case for the wives of kings.

She looked at him and thought about his words. 'But in some ways you *do* want me,' she said slowly.

'I'm not talking about sex!' he snapped.

'But isn't that also important? I mean, is what happened between us just then usual?'

'No, it isn't *usual*,' he said. 'You must know that.'

Zabrina nodded. She'd thought that to be the case. Perhaps in a different situation she might have been pleased by his acknowledgement of the powerful chemistry which existed between them, were his words not tinged with such obvious bitterness. And, of course, accusation. That subtle jibe about her supposed sexual experience hadn't escaped her. But she had lived a life where unfairness was something you just learned to live with and there was no reason why this should be any different.

'So why not just go through with it? It's not ideal, I know. But understand this, Roman. I've spent years preparing for my fate and if I hadn't, I might have lived my life very differently. I don't want to go back to Albastase as the Jilted Princess, and when you think about it you'll have to go to all the trouble of finding another bride who can provide you with an heir—that all-important means to securing and continuing your line of inheritance. Someone else who might just happen not to pass your exacting vetting process.'

There was silence for a moment. 'You mean you wish to bear my children?' he questioned slowly.

It had always been a given that she would do so and deep down Zabrina had always longed for children of her own. She thought of the fierce love she felt for her sisters and brother and how much she was going to miss them. Producing a family was an essential part of an arranged royal marriage, when you stopped to think about it, and yet it wasn't the kind of thing you spoke about in polite society. Yet as Roman asked the question, Zabrina felt a surge of something which felt like hope. Something which warmed and stirred her heart in a way she hadn't expected, but she kept her expression deadpan, because she suspected that somehow it would be more appropriate. That passion or eagerness might scare him.

'That has always been part of the deal, hasn't it?' she questioned quietly. 'We could make this marriage work, if we wanted it to. We don't seem to have a problem with communication and maybe that could work in our favour. We don't shy away from discussing things other people might find difficult. And neither of us believe in love, only duty. We have no foolish illusions, do we, Roman? No secret dreams ripe to be shattered. So, if you were to agree, we could continue on this train to the palace at Petrogoria and I could prepare for my life as your queen, as planned.'

There was a long pause before he spoke. 'Just like that?'

'Why not?'

His eyes narrowed, the silver gaze slicing through her like a blade. 'You've got it all worked out, haven't you, Princess?'

She wished he wouldn't use her title in that mocking way, because she liked it. She liked it more than she should. 'Let's just say I'm making the best of a bad situation.'

'And if I refuse? What then?'

His voice was silky but the note underpinning it was anything but. Zabrina imagined that tone might have intimidated many people, but it wasn't going to intimidate her. She shrugged, hearing the rhymical sound of the train as it thundered through the darkness towards Petrogoria. If she had been somebody else she might have threatened to go to the newspapers, because imagine all the money the press would pay for a juicy scoop like this—a respectable king pretending to be someone else and seducing the virgin princess! But she wouldn't do that—and not just because such a disclosure would drag both their names and their reputations through the mud. No. There were some things she would push for and some things she realised were pointless, because on an instinctive level she recognised that a man like Roman the Conqueror would never give in to something like blackmail.

'I don't think you will refuse,' she said, her gaze very steady. 'Because I think you need this marriage as much as I do.'

# CHAPTER SEVEN

THERE WERE FLOWERS EVERYWHERE. Bright flowers which filled the air with their heady scent. Roses and gerbera. Delphinium and lilac. Pink and blue and red and orange and every conceivable shade in between. Swathes of them festooned the railway station at Rosumunte and yet more were waved by the packed crowds lining the roads to the palace. Petals were thrown towards their open-topped car and most fluttered to the ground but some were captured by the inert wipers and lay against the car's windscreen, where already they were beginning to wilt in the warm sunshine.

And there were so many *people*. In the pale blue silk dress which had been specially chosen for this occasion, Zabrina sat bolt upright beside the King, who was raising his hand to his adoring subjects, and she forced herself to follow suit. 'Gosh,' she breathed, her heart missing yet another beat. 'This is…'

He turned to her, his face shadowed and enigmatic despite the bright sunshine. 'What?'

She swallowed but somehow turned the movement into a small smile, the sort of smile her new subjects would expect to see, because she wasn't supposed to be inside her own head, thinking about the man whose thigh was so tantalisingly close to hers. She was supposed to be thinking about other things.

Like that sweet little girl by the roadside, who was waving like crazy in her direction. Zabrina lifted her fingers in response and the child's smile widened.

But it wasn't easy to rid her thoughts of the devastatingly handsome King, because it took some getting used to—seeing him in uniform when before she'd only ever seen him in billowing shirt, trousers and long boots. And naked, of course. She mustn't forget that. But the Petrogorian army uniform was dark and formal and did incredible things for his already impressive physique. It emphasised the hard, honed body, while the peaked cap drew attention to the shadowed jut of his jaw and the proud posture which made his shoulders look so broad. Zabrina cleared her throat. 'It's massive,' she breathed. 'I wasn't expecting all these people to turn out to greet me.'

'You are their future Queen. Of course they wish to welcome you.'

'I know, and I appreciate that. It's just that you can be aware of something intellectually, but, when it happens, it doesn't feel how you thought it would feel.'

'And how does it make you feel? Nervous?'

She folded her hands together in her lap, terrified he would notice the tell-tale dampness of her palms, because hadn't she fought for this? To be Roman's future queen and to bear his children? In which case it would be inappropriate to showcase a quivering mass of uncertainties which seemed to have come at her out of nowhere. 'I was told many years ago that nerves have no place in the life of a princess.'

'And did you believe everything you were told, Zabrina?'

'I suppose I did,' she said carefully, resolutely ignoring the trace of mockery in his voice. 'Doesn't every child put their faith in the adults who form their view of the world?'

His laugh was unexpectedly bitter and the lines around his mouth became deep and tense. 'Not necessarily. Not if they've discovered such an exercise to be futile.'

'Is that what happened to you?'

'I don't dwell on the past, Zabrina. It's pointless.'

She wanted to argue that the past informed the present and to tell him that she needed to get to know him better, but something told her now was not the time and her immediate concerns were of a far more practical nature. Soon they would arrive at the palace and, if her own father's exalted position was anything to go by, the King would quickly be surrounded and swept away by a cohort of aides and equerries. And she would be on her own. Alone in a place where she knew absolutely no one.

Except him.

She moistened her lips with the tip of her tongue. 'So what happens when we reach the palace? What's the set-up there?'

He shrugged. 'The set-up will be exactly as was always planned. You will have your own staff. A private secretary with their own office, plus various ladies-in-waiting who will provide you with anything you need. You will obviously wish to explore as much of Petrogoria as is possible in the run-up to the marriage and to acquaint yourself with your new country and its people. Some of these visits we will do together, some you will perform solo and, once we are married, we will tour nearby Greece.'

She touched one of the waxy blooms of the lily-of-the-valley bouquet she had been presented with on embarkation and fixed her gaze on his. 'I was told that it would be possible for my horse to be brought here. And before you start telling me that you have the finest stable of horses in the world—it's not the same as having a mount you've owned ever since he was a young foal.'

'Of course you can have your horse here. I will set the process in motion,' he said, his eyes narrowing, as if he had picked up some of her apprehension. 'The aim is to make you feel at home, Zabrina, not alienate you, and all efforts have been made to do this. Your suite of rooms is in the southern end of the palace, where the outlook is particularly fine. I am sure you've heard about the fabled gardens here, which have inspired some of the nation's finest poets and—'

'Of course I have,' she interjected quickly, because he was the last person she could imagine enjoying poetry and just the thought of that was more than a little distracting. 'But what about you?'

'Perhaps you could be a little more specific, Princess.' His grey eyes gleamed with yet more mockery. 'What *about* me?'

'Is your...?' A lump seemed to have inconveniently lodged itself in her throat, making her next words come out as a thready whisper. 'Is your own section of the palace nearby?'

'Why, is that what you were hoping for?'

'Of course not,' she said crossly, but her burning cheeks ran the risk of making her words seem like a sham.

'I have decided that there will be no resumption of intimacy until we take our vows, as tradition demands. So I'm afraid you will just have to survive on the memory of how good it can be, Princess.'

'Does anyone know?' she questioned, in a low voice.

'You mean, are my staff aware that we've already had sex?'

'Keep your voice down!' she hissed. 'How...how are you going to explain the fact that you were even *on* my train when it arrived this morning, when I was supposed to meet you for the first time at the station? I could tell the crowds were surprised when they saw you jumping off in front of me and then lifting me down.' She raised her hand to wave to the crowds, her serene smile belying the rapid thunder of her heart. 'A completely over-the-top response, in my opinion.'

Roman expelled a reluctant sigh as the sunlight splashed pale gold streaks over her dark hair, because the reworking of the original plan had given him cause for concern. He had considered having the train make an unscheduled stop just outside the capital, and for one of his grooms to have a horse saddled and ready for him to ride to 'meet' the Princess for the first time. But the thought of any more subterfuge had been wearisome and he couldn't guarantee how Zabrina would react to such a suggestion—negatively, he suspected. And besides, he was the King. If he occasionally broke the rules, so what?

'I've already spoken to my aides and given them a story.'

'A *story*?'

'Don't look so shocked, Princess. Isn't that what everyone does?' He saw an old woman lay her hand across her heart as he passed by and he gave a courteous nod of acknowledgement. 'Reality is just an interpretation of facts,' he continued smoothly. 'And no two people ever see things the same way. I told them I was determined to protect my future bride and the most effective way of ensuring that was to guard her myself.'

'Right. Because the real facts—the true facts—that you were secretly doing a character assassination of me, wouldn't play out very sympathetically for you, would they, Roman?'

'Possibly not,' he mused. A flurry of rose petals drifted into the car and as one of them lodged itself beneath a pearl clip which gleamed in her hair, Roman had the strongest desire to smooth it away with his finger. But he didn't. He didn't trust himself to touch her again. At least, not yet. And certainly not in public, where his every action would be forensically scrutinised. What if some clever camera lens managed to capture his gnawing frustration at the way control seemed to be slipping away from him whenever he was around her?

Because none of this was turning out as he'd expected. He had thought, after deciding to go ahead with the marriage, that they might spend the remainder of the night on the train, blissfully exploring each other's bodies. There had certainly been plenty of sexual tension fizzing between them, after she'd given him all the reasons why they *shouldn't* call off the union. In a way, he had almost admired her dogged determination to get her own way. It had certainly turned him on. And while he was aware that sexual propriety would have to be observed once they reached the palace and they wouldn't be intimate again until their wedding night—surely that was even more reason to have capitalised on the strange circumstances which had led to that first delicious encounter. Silviana the servant could have been dismissed for the night and he could have locked the carriage door and let bliss take over.

But it had seemed that Zabrina had other ideas.

In fact, he had conducted the remainder of the journey standing to attention in the rattling corridor of the train, right outside her salon.

'If you're so determined to pretend to be a bodyguard, then maybe you'd better start acting like one!' she had hissed, before slamming the door in his face—something which had never happened to him, not in all his thirty-three years.

Outside his stint in the Petrogorian army or those heart-knotting times after his mother had deserted him, it had been the longest night of his life—not helped by the thought of Zabrina lying in bed only a few metres away. At the beginning of his long shift, thinking about her and what they had done together had been a welcome distraction—until it had become a self-induced form of torture. He had found himself wondering whether she slept naked. He had begun picturing her tiny frame and the slender curves which had wrapped themselves around him so accommodatingly, and his body had stiffened with such a hard jerk of desire that a passing guard had looked at him with concern and asked if he was okay.

Of course he hadn't been okay! He had been frustrated in more ways than one—furious at having been wrong-footed by the foxy Princess. A part of him still was...

'And do you still think it was a good idea?' she questioned suddenly, her soft voice breaking into the muddle of his thoughts. 'To pretend to be someone you weren't, just to find out what I was really like?'

He looked at her. It would have been easy to say no, that he regretted all the subterfuge and deceit, and surely that would dissolve some of the strain which had tightened her features. But a defining—and possibly redeeming—feature of their relationship had emerged during the short time they had known one another. She had said so herself. They had no illusions of love. No foolish dreams to shatter. Couldn't total honesty elevate this arranged marriage into something which didn't need hollow and placatory words to survive?

'Perhaps the manner of execution wasn't ideal,' he mused. 'But if you're asking whether I regret having got to know you in that way, then the answer would have to be no. If we had been introduced in the traditional way, then all kinds of barriers would have been erected. We would have made polite small talk and been forced to endure a stilted courtship. And yes, it is going to be something of a farce and frustration to deny ourselves physical satisfaction in the run-up to the wedding, but it will certainly hone our mutual desire.' He turned and slanted her a complicit smile. 'Which is presumably why you kicked me out of the carriage last night.'

'I did that because I didn't trust myself not to kick you literally!'

He could feel the flicker of a smile tugging at the edges of his lips. 'If you want me to be perfectly frank, it was something of a relief to discover you were sexually experienced.'

'It was?' she verified, her voice growing a little faint.

'Undoubtedly.' He turned and waved to someone in the crowd who was calling out his name. 'To be honest, virgins are hard work.'

'Hard work?' she echoed dully. 'In what way?'

He shook his head. 'It doesn't matter.'

'Oh, I think it does.'

'You don't want to know.'

'Oh, but that's where you're wrong, Roman. I do. I thought we were going to be frank with one another. I don't want you to spare my feelings.'

He shrugged. 'If you want the truth, virgins need constant reassurance. They don't seem to realise that if you're constantly asking a man whether or not he likes it and whether or not you're doing it properly, it's a bit of a turn-off.'

'I see.' She pressed her lips together in what he was now coming to recognise was one of her determined smiles. 'Well, I'm glad we've got that out of the way! Thanks very much for the enlightenment.'

Roman's eyes narrowed. In many ways she surprised him as well as amused him, but there was something about her which was... He shook his head, unable to define what it was he was feeling and that did not sit comfortably with him. And surely it was simpler to push such feelings aside... He cleared his throat. 'If you look straight ahead,' he said unevenly, 'you'll get your first view of the palace, with the Liliachiun mountains behind.'

The iconic towers of the Petrogorian palace soared into view, but Zabrina could barely focus on the pale-hued magnificence of the ancient building ahead, so great was her anger towards the man by her side. He was...*unbearable*. He was the most unspeakably arrogant man it had ever been her misfortune to meet and if she was now committed to spending the rest of her life with him, she had only herself to blame.

So how come she still fancied him like crazy, even though some of the things he came out with made her want to scream with rage?

His damning assessment of virgins and their *constant need for reassurance* had been unbelievable! Was that how he regarded everyone who came into his orbit? In terms of how they impacted on him? Why, he'd made it sound as if he found some women boring even while he was actually having sex with them! Her heart missed a beat as an annoying flash of jealousy shot through her like a dark flame at the thought of him being intimate with another woman, but, once it had passed, her overriding emotion was one of relief. Thank heavens she hadn't asked him if she was pleasing him! Or if she was 'doing it right'.

But it hadn't been like that, she remembered. There had been no sense of inequality when they had both lain naked on that sofa. It hadn't felt as if he was the super-experienced one—

which he clearly was—while she didn't have a clue, because she had never done it before. Because everything which had happened seemed to have happened so naturally. As if, on a physical level at least, they *knew* one another.

She shook her head a little because thoughts like that were dangerous. Fanciful. If she wasn't careful, she would start believing her own stupid fairy-tale version of what had happened. And Roman had tacitly warned her not to do that. He'd said that reality was just a personal interpretation of facts. So she'd better be careful not to misinterpret them.

Surreptitiously, she wiped her palms over the skirt of her silk dress and looked ahead. She could see even more crowds gathered outside the gilded gates of the palace and a huge cheer went up as the open-topped car began to make its stately progress up the wide, tree-lined boulevard.

'Do you like it?' Roman was saying. 'Your new home?'

Zabrina's eyes narrowed as they grew closer. She had seen pictures of the palace, of course she had, for it was widely acknowledged to be one of the finest examples of imperial architecture to be found anywhere in the world. The walls were the colour of rich cream, the conical towers rose-gold. Arched windows were edged with pale stone and a pair of intricately carved columns stood on either side of the vast main doors. In the distance she could see a glimpse of the famous gardens and parkland and, beyond that, the soaring splendour of the Liliachiun mountains.

'It's…beautiful,' she said truthfully, but then almost regretted the sincerity of her words because they had caused Roman to smile with genuine pleasure, and she was ill prepared for the impact of that smile. Did he realise it was like the sun coming out from behind a thunder-dark cloud? He must do. Someone in the past must have told him that when he smiled like that it was like discovering something you'd never realised existed. As if you'd just looked up into the sky and noticed that a second sun had suddenly made an unexpected appearance.

And then he went and spoiled it.

'So you think you will be able to tolerate your position here?' he questioned coolly. 'As the wealthiest consort on the planet, with untold riches at your disposal.'

'How greedy you make me sound,' she reflected, but the stupid thing was that it hurt. She didn't want it to be all about money. She wanted it to be about feelings.

But his steely gaze was completely lacking in emotion. 'Not greedy, Zabrina,' he said calmly. 'Just practical. We're both going into this marriage because of what we stand to gain. And I think it's wise to acknowledge that, don't you? I read the pre-nuptial contract thoroughly before signing. I saw the clause your lawyer insisted on inserting—that you would be guaranteed a private income of your own.'

His black brows were raised in arrogant query as if demanding an explanation, but Zabrina was damned if she was going to give him one. She had her reasons for wanting that money, but she wasn't ready to share them with him and maybe she never would be. He probably wouldn't believe her anyway. And wasn't there something a bit sad about someone who insisted on pointing out what a do-gooder they were? She didn't trust him, he didn't trust her, so maybe they should just leave it at that.

She shrugged. 'And I noticed your lawyer inserted a rider to that clause, saying that I would only get the money for as long as the marriage lasted.'

'Of course he did. Otherwise there would be no incentive for you to make the marriage work, would there? You could just take the money and run.'

He said something harsh beneath his breath, and Zabrina frowned.

'Did you just say…"*just like my mother*"?' she asked slowly.

She spoke without thinking and must have hit a raw nerve because a flash of something dark ravaged the carved beauty of his face. It was as if he'd put on a savage mask which made him almost unrecognisable, but it was gone in an instant, his features shuttered and emotionless again—as if he was all too aware that the prying lenses of the cameras were trained on them.

'I had forgotten that you spoke fluent Petrogorian,' he bit out. 'Perhaps I would do well to guard my tongue in future. But even so, do you consider this is an appropriate time to ambush me with such questions?'

Zabrina was aware that she had either hurt or angered him but she hadn't meant to do either. It hadn't been intended as a point-scoring exercise, or a desire to catch him off-guard—she'd just wanted to find out more about the man she was to marry.

'Roman—'

'Let's just concentrate on what we're supposed to be doing, shall we?' he interrupted, his lips barely moving as he edged out the words—presumably to foil any would-be lip-readers. 'And smile. No, a *big* smile, Princess. Act like you really mean it. We're here.'

The powerful car drew to a halt in front of the applauding palace staff and Zabrina glanced up to see figures clustered at upstairs windows high above, capturing the image on their cell-phones. Roman leapt from the car and opened her car door himself and as he held out his hand to help her down, Zabrina was aware of two things. Firstly, that the brief touch of his fingers was enough to send soft shivers of desire rippling down her spine, making her wish he would lift them to his lips and kiss them. But he didn't.

Because the second thing she noticed—and this was the one which stayed with her for the rest of the day—was that the grey eyes which were turned in her direction were as empty and as cold as ice.

# CHAPTER EIGHT

SOFT SUNLIGHT FLICKERED over the profuse spill of roses, bathing the famous gardens in a rich golden glow as Zabrina stared out of the vast windows.

But no matter how hard she tried to concentrate on the beauty outside, or on the small dish of fruit on the table in front of her, it was difficult to focus on anything other than the devastatingly handsome man who was seated opposite. The morning light was glinting on his cropped dark hair, making her realise how much it had grown, and his snowy white shirt emphasised the muscular width of his shoulders.

Suddenly he pushed his empty coffee cup away and leaned back in his chair to study her. Was he aware she'd been watching him with a hungry desire which wouldn't seem to go away? And did that fill him with a sense of triumph—and power?

'Today's the big day, isn't it?' he said.

Zabrina gazed at him blankly. The only 'big day' which seemed to be on everyone's lips wasn't for another three weeks—unless somebody had brought the wedding forward and not bothered to tell the bride. She hoped not, because there were still what looked like five million seed pearls to sew onto her traditional Petrogorian wedding dress and sequins which needed to be scattered all over her tulle veil. She picked up her silver spoon, still trying to get used to the enormous emerald and diamond engagement ring which felt too heavy for her finger. 'Big day?' she repeated.

'Your horse,' he said. 'What time does it arrive?'

'He. The horse is a he, not an it,' Zabrina corrected, watching as a servant silently moved forward to refill the King's cup with inky-black coffee. 'And his name is Midas.'

'Ah!' He picked up a sugar cube. 'Named after the king who wished for an excess of gold and almost ruined his life in the process?'

'That's the one.'

He lifted his dark brows in arrogant query. 'Perhaps there is an allegory in that story for us, Zabrina.'

'Let's hope not,' she said darkly.

A brief smile curved the edges of his lips as he dropped the sugar into the cup and began to stir and Zabrina found herself mesmerised by the circular movement of his fingers, wondering how he could make such a simple action look so insanely sexy. But then, he made just about everything he did look sexy. Was that deliberate? Was he taunting her? Reminding her of that heart-punching intimacy they'd shared on the Petrogoria-bound train, which was now being put on hold until they were married?

*Stop it,* she thought. *Just stop it. You are supposed to be having a polite breakfast conversation about the day ahead.*

The kind of measured diary conversation they'd been having every morning since she'd arrived in Petrogoria last week. This was the public face of their formal engagement, as opposed to the private anxieties which plagued her every night when she was alone in bed.

Over coffee, fruit and eggs over easy—for him—they would go through the various royal duties which had been mapped out for them by their private offices—some together and some apart. Solo duties she welcomed. In many ways, it was less distracting when Roman wasn't by her side distracting her with his powerful presence.

Hadn't she thought—hoped—that he would go back on his determination for their nights to be spent separately? But she had been wrong. He hadn't and now she had started to wonder if his reluctance to touch her meant he was having second thoughts about the wedding. But rejection was something she wouldn't countenance—not now—and so she threw herself into her new charities with fervour, hoping that her engagements would make her fit in and feel easier about her place here.

Because Roman had been right. Or rather, Roman when he had been masquerading as Constantin and answering her questions with an alluring frankness, leaving her wondering which of them was the real man. The understanding and passionate bodyguard, or the cold, disciplined king?

It didn't matter.

The fact remained that the royal palace of Petrogoria *was* intimidating, just as he'd warned her.

For a start it was big. Way bigger than she'd imagined and everything was on a much larger scale than what she was used to. It made her childhood home seem like a matchbox lined up next to a shoebox. And it wasn't just the size—it was all the contents. There was more of *everything*. More Old Master paintings, more ancient books and precious artefacts. The scaled-up fountains sprayed bigger and more impressive plumes of water and the corridors seemed endless. And these weren't the familiar corridors of home—the ones which she'd run along and explored and hidden in, from when she'd first learned to walk. These were impossibly wide marble passageways, lined by inscrutable servants who bowed or curtseyed whenever she passed them. Here there were no friendly cooks or grooms who'd known her since babyhood and who had treated her with a slightly modified version of informality, which she'd always found comforting.

Roman had described it as home.

It just didn't feel like *her* home.

Life here was like being part of a beautifully choreographed dance—with the King positioned at its glittering centre. Everything revolved around him. Sometimes Zabrina felt like a satellite to his blazing sun—as if she were an insignificant and very distant star. Each day they took their meals together in different dining rooms, all of them exquisite. They ate breakfast overlooking the fabled rose gardens and lunch was taken in a huge windowed chamber, decorated in a dizzying spectrum of blues. Dinner was served either in the supposedly more low-key Rose Room—which wasn't low-key at all—or, if they had company, in the highly ornate Golden Dining Room. Because if people were coming to eat in a palace as famous as this one, they liked to really feel they'd had the whole palace 'experience'.

After dinner she and Roman might have a nightcap—rare—before retiring to their separate suites, though she gathered from remarks which Silviana had made that the King often worked in his study until the early hours of the morning. Whatever he did, it didn't involve her. In fact, none of his life did. Not physically, at least. Amid the careful carving out of her role as his future queen and the increasingly frenetic arrangements for the wedding, there had been no rerun of that heady sensual episode on the train.

*The King of Petrogoria had not laid a finger on her since she'd walked over the threshold of his glittering golden palace.*

Had she thought it might be different?

Yes, of course she had.

Had she offended him hugely by kicking him out of her carriage that night, when it had been obvious that—after all the dust had settled—he had wanted to stay and carry on with more of what they'd been doing? Probably. She had felt so strong and so sure of herself at the time. She'd been infused with a powerful sense of self brought about by that magical sexual encounter and had felt no qualms about castigating him for his deception, and for refusing to believe that he was her first lover.

Yet the annoying thing was that her show of defiance seemed to have backfired on her—because he had taken her at her word, quite literally! And by keeping his physical distance, he had managed to fill her with a lingering sense of uncertainty. The brief and heady authority she had felt when he had been in her arms had shifted, and now *he* was the one who seemed to possess all the power. She wondered if she had wounded his pride and ego in such a way that he now found the thought of touching her unpalatable. Should she ask him?

*Roman, don't you find me sexually attractive any more?*
*Roman, don't you want to take me to bed?*

No. Because deep down she knew the answer to that, no matter how insecure she sometimes felt. It was made plain by the smoky hunger which flared in his eyes whenever she inadvertently caught him watching her, before quickly composing his handsome face into its more habitual impassive mask. He still wanted her, all right. That mutual desire showed no sign of abating. Predictably and potently, it fizzed between them whenever they were in the same room together. Like a flame, she thought, with equal longing and despair—bright and vital—yet tantalisingly ephemeral.

His grey gaze was fixed on her questioningly. 'So is he gold?'

'Who?' She looked at him in confusion, trying to gather together the scramble of her thoughts. 'Oh, you mean Midas?'

He made no attempt to hide his sardonic smile. 'Isn't that what we've just been talking about?'

She flushed, wondering if he had any idea what had been preoccupying her. She hoped not. Though what did she know? Probably any woman who found herself alone with him spent the majority of their time fantasising about what he was like in bed. It was almost a pity that she had actually experienced it—because didn't that make it harder to shift the tantalising images from her head?

She cleared her throat and forced herself to concentrate on her beloved horse. 'No, he's not really golden. More of a bay. An Akhal Teke, actually. But when I first got him it was my birthday and I was taken down to the stables early in the morning and there he was, with the sunshine glinting off his coat like metal—and he looked…well, he looked magical really. Like a living golden statue.' She paused, the iced mango in her bowl forgotten as an unexpected wave of nostalgia washed over her and she looked at him rather sheepishly, surprised by the narrowed interest in his grey eyes. 'I don't know what made me tell you that.'

But she did know. It was just a long time since she'd allowed herself to think about it.

It had been one of those unusual periods of her upbringing when an air of something like calm had settled over the palace, mostly because her father had returned into the bosom of his family after his latest affair. After one of these interludes, her mother's overriding reaction would always be one of profound relief that everything could be 'normal' again. Often, this would provide the ideal opportunity for the palace to release a photo depicting happy family life. It was also one of the reasons why her father would overcompensate—materially, at least—and overspend even more than usual. Thus, Zabrina had been gifted a beautiful and very expensive horse with a scarlet ribbon tied around his neck and the cake they had all eaten later for her birthday tea had been ridiculously big.

The memory of that monstrous gateau made her feel a little nauseous and she pushed her half-eaten dish of mango away, forcing herself to change the subject. But maybe she should capitalise on the fact that Roman seemed to have let his guard down and this was the most relaxed he'd been. There were a million questions she wanted to ask him but instinct told her that she needed to tread carefully. Maybe he was like a prized thoroughbred, who needed careful handling. 'Can I ask you something, Roman?'

Instantly, his eyes narrowed with caution. 'You can ask. I won't guarantee that I'll answer.'

She wondered if he had been a lawyer in a previous life. 'Are you planning to do anything with the Marengo Forest after our wedding?'

Roman sat back in his chair as he stared into the long-lashed beauty of her green eyes. She could be quite...unexpected, he conceded. He had imagined her mind to be flapping with those tiresome thoughts women so often entertained and had been anticipating her demanding to know how he 'felt' about her. And that was the last thing he wanted to answer. Because the bizarre truth of that was he didn't really know and there was no way he wanted Zabrina to realise that.

She seemed such a contradiction. Sometimes seasoned, sometimes innocent, sometimes spoiled and at others sweetly thoughtful. Her complexity intrigued him and he had no wish to be intrigued, because that wasn't what this union was supposed to be about. She unsettled him and he didn't like being unsettled by a woman. Hadn't he vowed that was never going to happen to him again? That no woman should have any kind of power over his thoughts and his feelings?

That was one of the reasons why he hadn't touched her since he'd brought her to his palace. Why he hadn't given into the silken tug of desire even though every time he saw her he grew exquisitely hard. He swallowed. Before her arrival, she had been allotted a separate suite at the opposite end of the vast palace complex. At the time he had accepted there would be no sex before marriage because the Princess was a virgin and tradition demanded it. And even though her subsequent behaviour had meant there was no reason for such a restriction, he saw no reason to change the existing plan, because he could see a definite advantage to denial—no matter how frustrating he might find it.

Because hadn't Zabrina of Albastase smashed down all his carefully erected defences that night? Hadn't he found himself unable to resist her in a way which had been mind-blowingly unique? His mouth hardened. She had made him lose control in a way which was alien to him, transforming him into a man he didn't recognise, or particularly respect. In her arms he had felt as if he had died and gone to heaven and it had been terrifying and delicious. But he realised it had put her firmly in the driving seat and he wanted to shift the balance of power back in his favour. And *that* was why he continued to distance himself from his future bride, no matter how great the cost to his equilibrium.

She wanted him. Of course she did. Every woman had always wanted him, ever since he'd reached puberty. But what he felt for her was right off the scale. It was as though provocative and carnal invitation thrummed from every pore of her delicious body. At times it became almost too much to bear and he was tempted to throw caution to the winds and take her in his arms. His fantasy involved either the slowest removal of lingerie in the history of the world, or ripping off her panties and plunging deep into her syrupy heat as her little cries of encouragement urged him on.

But he wasn't going to do that. He was going to make her wait, even if he half tortured himself with frustration in the process. He would demonstrate icy control and defer delight until the appropriate time and that would be an invaluable lesson in self-denial. Zabrina would come to him on their wedding night, humbled by his restraint and eager to taste pleasure once again. Because delay heightened hunger.

His mouth twisted.

Or so he'd heard.

He looked at the gleam of wavy dark hair which fell so abundantly over her shoulders. At the green silk dress which matched her eyes and clung so enticingly to the small and perfect breasts. He'd thought about those breasts a lot recently, especially at night when he'd been lying in his lonely bed, sleeplessly staring as the shifting moon painted the walls silver. Just as he'd thought about her strong, slim thighs and the way his head had fitted so perfectly between them.

'Of course I'm planning to *do* something with the Marengo Forest,' he said, reluctantly dragging his thoughts back to the present, knowing he had no one but himself to blame for the hard throb of his erection. He cleared his throat. 'Its return has been in my sights for a long time and I have big plans for it.'

She looked up from where she had begun to pleat her napkin with those tanned fingers which had worked such magic on his shuddering flesh. 'You do?'

He frowned. 'Why else do you think I should go to so much trouble to acquire it? Why I'm prepared to pay such a monumental amount of money for it, in the form of your dowry?'

'I hope you think I'm worth it.'

He saw her cheeks colour and momentarily felt a little bad as she made the sardonic comment, but only for a moment. Hadn't they both agreed to be pragmatic about the situation? 'It's a deal, Zabrina,' he said simply. 'Remember? And this is not just about territory—about me having some hypothetical need to return the Petrogorian flag to its rightful place. I want to build an airport nearby—it's a pristine, natural wilderness which is ripe for sympathetic eco-tourism.'

'Oh.' Her fingers stilled on the napkin, the white linen folds making her skin look like softest gold. 'Oh, I see.'

'So what makes you appear so crestfallen?' he enquired idly. 'The price I'm paying for that piece of land is more than you could have ever hoped of achieving, if you'd sold it on the open market. Even you must realise that.'

'Yes, of course I do. It's not that.'

'What, then?'

'It doesn't matter.' She shook her head. 'It won't be of any possible interest to you.'

'Why don't you let me be the judge of that?' He took a sip of coffee. 'I'm interested to know what's making you bite your lip as if you have all the cares of the world on your shoulders.'

Imprisoned in the grey spotlight of his narrowed eyes, Zabrina hesitated. Should she tell him what she'd been thinking? This was to be nothing but a marriage of 'convenience', which presumably meant they could keep things on a very superficial level. But what was the point of keeping everything buttoned up inside her? Wasn't one of the benefits of a live-in relationship supposed to be that you were at liberty to confide in your partner? And surely it would be good to talk to someone who might actually *listen*, rather than her mother—on whose deaf ears Zabrina's concerns had always fallen, so that she'd given up expressing her fears a long time ago.

'If you must know, I admire your ambitious plans about a region which has lain neglected for so long...'

'But? I suspect there's a "but" coming?'

'I guess I'm also slightly frustrated that my country didn't think of doing it first.'

'Either nobody considered it, or they didn't have the where-withal to carry it out. Presumably the latter.' He looked at her with a steady gaze. 'It usually boils down to hard finance, Zabrina.'

'I know it does.' She puffed out an unsteady breath. 'I suppose I'm also concerned about the amount of money you're pay-ing for the land. And for me,' she finished drily.

He raised his eyebrows. 'You don't think it's enough?'

She gave a short laugh. 'Nobody in the world could think that. It's an extremely generous amount of money. I'm more worried about what's going to happen to it when it lands in my father's bank account.'

'He could spend it wisely. Make sure it's ploughed back into the country.' He gave a shrug. 'You know. Invest in some new infrastructure.'

Zabrina could feel her cheeks colour as she wondered whether it might be wise to close the subject down. Anyone who had been to Albastase knew it was getting very frayed around the edges, but few people knew just how inept the King was at managing finances. Sometimes she wished this money had been transferred directly to the government, bypassing the royal coffers, giving him little opportunity to fritter it away—but she could hardly denounce her own father.

'I hope so.'

'You don't sound very convinced.'

She had obviously failed to inject a tone of enthusiasm into her voice but Roman's perception surprised her. She hadn't thought of him as a student of nuance. Just as she hadn't expected him to continue to regard her with what looked like genuine interest.

And somehow she started telling him about it. Stuff which she never talked about with her family, because there had been no point. Her mother could not or would not act, her sisters were too young and uninterested and her brother... Zabrina swallowed. Her brother was already having difficulty coming to terms with the fact that one day he would be King and she didn't want to be the one to add to those concerns. They had been like the family of someone with an unacknowledged drinking problem...as if by ignoring it, the problem would somehow go away.

'My father can sometimes be...extravagant.'

'That is surely one of the perks of being a king.'

Her jaw worked and somehow all her fears about leaving everyone back home to fend for themselves came tumbling out. 'No. This is more than having a garage full of fancy cars, or a fleet of racehorses which he keeps overseas.'

'I'm glad about that,' he said wryly. 'Or I might find myself the subject of your obvious disapproval.'

She shook her head slightly impatiently. 'It's more than extravagance. He's surrounded by a coterie of stupid advisors and the trouble is that he listens to them. They keep getting him to invest in their friends' supposedly amazing business schemes, only they never quite work out the way they're supposed to and he gets his fingers burned. Every time.'

'Then one has to ask the question as to why he keeps doing it,' said Roman coolly. 'Don't they say that the definition of madness is to keep repeating the same mistake, over and over again?'

'Because he doesn't believe in his own fallibility and when it happens, he needs something to reassure him that he's as clever as he thinks he is,' said Zabrina quietly. 'Which is why, after every failure, he grabs at that guaranteed age-old ego boost so beloved of men.' And wasn't it crazy that she *still* felt a sense of guilt as she admitted the truth to the man she was soon to marry, as if she were wrong to criticise her own father. Yet in the midst of all these misgivings, it felt a huge relief to be able to confide in him like this.

'And you're worried because your country is gradually being run down?' Roman questioned.

'Of course I am. But I'm more worried that by the time my brother Alexandru inherits, there won't be anything left. He's a delicate young man,' she whispered. 'And super-sensitive. I'd hate for him to take on the burden of kingship if he was also saddled by an enormous debt!' she finished, her lips wobbling a little with the impact of expressing all that usually bottled-up emotion. She looked into the King's face but, as usual, its cool impassiveness gave nothing away.

Instead he raised his fingers and the servant brought him another cup of coffee, before Roman indicated he should leave—signalling that this breakfast might go on longer than anticipated. And that surprised Zabrina, because usually these meal times were strictly regulated and chaperoned—as if the man she was to marry couldn't bear to be alone in her company a second more than he needed to.

'I can understand that,' he said slowly. 'But now you've triggered my interest.'

'Oh?'

He lifted his gaze to hers. 'What *exactly* is the age-old ego boost your father always resorts to?'

She guessed they'd always needed to have this discussion, so why not now, even though it wasn't really the kind of thing she'd ever imagined discussing calmly over the muesli? Because Roman was a king and what she was about to talk about was what all kings did. It came with the territory and she was surprised he even needed to ask.

'Affairs,' she said simply. 'He has affairs.'

# CHAPTER NINE

ROMAN STUDIED ZABRINA'S expression with a curiosity he didn't bother to hide, because something about the calm acceptance he read there surprised him. 'Explain,' he clipped out. 'About your father's affairs.'

She shrugged with studied carelessness, but he didn't miss the fleeting look of apprehension which crossed her eyes.

'They usually come about as a reaction to one of his disastrous business investments,' she began slowly. 'You see, he loses huge amounts of money and promises himself it will never happen again.' She stared at the pink roses in the vase at the centre of the table, before lifting her gaze to his again. 'But in the meantime he needs something to make him feel better—to take his mind off what he's done. And women can do that. They can fill that emotional hole—just like a drink or an unnecessary plate of food. And, of course, he's a king. So he can do what the hell he likes.'

'Isn't that a rather sweeping generalisation?'

She laughed. A sound he had heard only infrequently and usually he was forced to steel himself against its soft lure, but now it was edged with the hard ring of cynicism.

'I'm only basing my comments on experience, Roman.'

'Of observing your father, you mean?'

She shook her head. 'No, not just that. Don't forget my mother is a princess herself and she and her sisters all married monarchs and, according to her, they have all "strayed". I always thought that was a funny expression to use,' she added reflectively. 'It reminds me of a horse or a cow somehow managing to get out of its enclosure.'

He guessed that was supposed to be a joke but the brittle note in her voice suggested she wasn't as comfortable with the subject as she wanted him to think.

'So your mother just accepted this state of affairs, if you'll excuse the pun?'

She didn't laugh, just shrugged. 'In a way. She said it was easier to accept than to constantly rail against something she couldn't change. She told me that husbands always returned—eventually. Especially if there was a calm and non-accusatory welcome for them to come back to. And especially if there were children involved.'

He felt the chill of something dark. The indelible shadow of his childhood making itself known without warning. His heart clenched with pain but he was practised enough to be able to eject the thought and corresponding emotion as far from his mind as possible, and to continue to subject Zabrina to a steady stare instead. 'And what about wives?' he questioned softly. 'Do they also stray?'

Either she was genuinely shocked by his question or she was a superb actress, for her lips fell open and she frowned.

'Well, no. She never did.'

'Why not?'

'Because men are different.'

'In other ways than anatomically, you mean?' he challenged, disproportionately pleased to see the blush which made her cheeks colour so thoroughly.

She glared. 'That's not funny. It's a biological thing, or so my mother always said. I'm not saying that infidelity is necessarily a good idea—more that it's understandable. Nature's way of ensuring the human race continues, because men—'

'I get the idea, Zabrina. There's no need to spell it out,' he interrupted drily, taking a final sip of coffee before pushing his cup away. 'So will your extremely liberal views on fidelity impact on our own marriage?'

She paused. For effect, Roman suspected, more than anything else. Because surely she must have given this subject *some* consideration in the light of her own experience.

'This is a duty marriage,' she said at last. 'And I don't have any unrealistic expectations about that side of it. I know that men often get bored when they have been intimate with one woman for any length of time, and that they crave new excitement.'

'Who the hell told you *that*?'

'My mother. She's a very practical person.'

Roman thought these views cynical rather than practical, but he didn't say so. 'I see.'

'What's important to me is providing a secure base for the family we both hope to have.'

'Well, that's something, at least,' he said and maybe some of his own cynicism had become apparent because she shot him a quick and rather worried look.

'You do *want* a family?' she verified. 'I mean, I know we touched on it on the train—'

'We did a lot of touching on the train, Zabrina.'

'That's not funny.'

'No?'

'No.' Her voice was bitter. 'I wish I could forget that trip.'

'So do I,' he said, with more force than he had intended.

'All I ask…'

He could see her throat constricting and she appeared to be conducting a struggle to find the right words. 'Don't upset yourself,' he said, with a sudden wave of empathy which surprised him. 'We don't have to talk about this right now.'

'But we do. We need to get all these things out of the way. All I ask,' she continued stolidly, 'is that you're discreet—both before, during and after any affair you may choose to have. That you don't rub my face in it.'

'This is extraordinary,' he breathed, raking his fingers back through his shorn hair which, thankfully, was beginning to grow a little. 'You're basically giving me carte blanche to be unfaithful?'

She didn't appear to be listening, for her gaze was locked to the movement of his hand and he found himself remembering the way she had pressed her fingers into his scalp when she'd been coming, crying out something softly in her own language. He wondered if she had been remembering it too. Hell. Why think about that *now*? He shifted uncomfortably in his chair, thankful that the sudden jerk of his erection was concealed by the snowy fall of the tablecloth. But his thoughts quickly shifted from desire to evaluation. He tried to imagine how other men in his position would react if confronted with the astounding fact that their wife-to-be was prepared to look the other way, if he were ever unfaithful. But her words gave him no heady rush of freedom or anticipation—in fact, his overriding feeling was one of indignation and a slowly simmering anger.

'Why, Zabrina?' he demanded. 'Are you planning to do the same? To take other men as your lovers and expect me to be understanding in turn?'

'Of course not! If you want the truth, I can't imagine ever wanting any other man but you.'

He sat back in his chair, surprised by her candour. This wasn't the first time this particular sentiment had been expressed to him by a woman—yet instead of his usual irritation he found himself ridiculously pleased by her sweet honesty. 'I see,' he said, again.

'Obviously I would prefer our marriage to be monogamous, because I've seen the havoc these affairs can wreak. I've seen the damage they can inflict on a couple's relationship.' She tore off a fragment of croissant and lifted it to her mouth before seeming to change her mind and putting it back down on the plate again. Her eyes were very dark and very direct. 'And since we're on the subject. You haven't told me anything about your own parents.'

Instantly he was on the defensive. 'There's nothing much to tell. It's all on the record, as I'm sure you know. I imagine you've seen it for yourself.' Roman could feel his throat thicken and cursed the pain one woman's desertion could still cause him. No wonder he never talked about it. No wonder he had closed his mind to it a long time ago. 'My mother left when I was three years old and I never saw her again,' he said baldly. 'My father never remarried.'

'But—'

'But what?' he interrupted, forcing all the bitter emotion from his words and replacing it with a tone of cool finality. He reminded himself that this was a conversation they needed to have only once and he could make it as short as he wanted. 'Those are the facts, Zabrina. I've never gone in for analysis and I don't intend to start now.' He stared down at the inky brew in his coffee cup before lifting his gaze to hers. 'And since we're being so remarkably frank, there's something else we should address. I think we both need to know where we stand on the subject of divorce, don't you?'

Zabrina grew still as his words filtered across the table towards her, stabbing at her like little arrows. She should have been prepared for this question but, stupidly, she wasn't and as a result she found herself filled with another rush of uncertainty. Had she thought that if she was so reasonable on the subject of fidelity, Roman might declare she would be his wife for life? And wasn't there some inexplicable part of her which *wanted* that—because while she might feel unsettled around him, weirdly she felt really *safe*? As if Roman could protect her from some of the terrors of the world. That as long as he was by her side, nothing really bad could happen.

Why think something as irrational as that?

She stared at the sunny gleam of her half-eaten mango, trying to work out what had changed inside her, but it was difficult to put her finger on, mainly because she didn't understand the softening of her feelings towards the man she was soon to marry. It wasn't just the amazing sex they'd shared on the train—although that had obviously been the most incredible thing which had ever happened to her. It was more to do with his subsequent behaviour and the conversations they shared whenever they took their meals together. He spoke to her as if she were his equal. She realised that sometimes Roman could seem as sympathetic as 'Constantin' had been. He made her feel as if her views counted. As if she was an intelligent person worthy of consideration. And nobody had ever done that before.

But that didn't mean she should allow herself to be lulled into a false sense of security, because, although his attitude towards her might sometimes be sympathetic, his feelings hadn't changed. He didn't *have* feelings towards her, remember? Of *course* he would wish to address the subject of divorce, because it was relevant. This wasn't an emotional discussion, she reminded herself, but a practical one. They were a modern monarchy and there wasn't a royal family in the world which hadn't been affected by marital breakdown. Divorce no longer held any real stigma—other than the devastating heartbreak her auntie had told her about after she'd gone through it herself. Perhaps that was what had made her mother so determined to hang onto her own marriage, no matter what. And surely she couldn't be condemned for that.

'I don't know about you,' she said, meeting the question in his eyes, 'but I would prefer to avoid divorce, especially if there are children involved. Though obviously,' she amended hurriedly, 'if circumstances were to change—'

'In what sense?' he questioned coolly.

The words were threatening to stick in the back of her throat, so that each one felt as if it had been coated with tar. 'If, say, you were to meet another woman,' she began. 'And to fall in love with her. Then obviously I wouldn't stand in your way, if you wanted to end the marriage.'

His face was shuttered. 'How very understanding of you, Zabrina. I had no idea I was marrying such a libertarian.'

'Why, what would you prefer me to do?' she demanded. 'Display an undignified rage and rake your cheeks with my fingernails?'

'Honestly?' He gave a short laugh. 'Right now what I would prefer you to do involves being locked in my arms.'

But it was less of a question and more of a statement and the short silence which followed was broken by the smooth glide of his chair against the marble floor. Zabrina's heart began to thunder and she felt the curl of excitement low in her belly as he rose to his feet.

'Roman,' she said—and this too was a statement, because he was walking around the table towards her, moving with a natural grace and stealth which was incredible to watch, and the look of intent on his sensual features cried out to something deep inside her. Something which scared and excited her. She tried to bat the feelings away but somehow it wasn't working. Beneath her silk dress, she could feel her nipples tightening into hard buds and surely he must be able to see that too? There was a syrupy tug in her belly and suddenly she longed for him to touch her there. She swallowed and felt her cheeks colour. Yes, *there*—where the aching was at its most intense. Did he see her blush? Was that why his lips curved into that seeking smile?

He was beside her now. Reaching down and lifting her clean off the chair—or was she reaching up to him? She didn't know, and afterwards she would find it impossible to remember. All she knew was that there were no servants present—for he had dismissed them all—and that this was the first time they had been alone since she had stepped off that train in Rosumunte.

And that they seemed to be in the middle of some crazy sexual power game.

'Roman,' she whispered.

'We're done talking,' he husked. 'Just kiss me.'

It was an uneven request which went straight to her heart but Zabrina needed no such instruction because her lips were already seeking his, and, oh, that first touch of his skin against hers made her gasp. How could a simple kiss feel like this? How come that already she wanted to explode with pleasure? One of his hands was tangled in the fall of her hair while the other was on her peaking breast, his thumb circling the pebbled nipple with dextrous provocation which was making her want to squirm. Sanity implored her to call a halt but she couldn't. She didn't want to.

Her hands explored the width of his powerful shoulders then reacquainted themselves with his chest, her nails scraping hungrily against the fine linen of his shirt. She could feel the faint whorl of hair against his muscular torso and, as he cupped his palms possessively over her buttocks, he deepened the kiss. He was pulling her even closer, so that his body was imprinted on hers. She felt the rocky outline of his erection and remembered what it had been like when he had been naked and proud, and she shuddered in his arms.

'Sweet heaven,' he husked, and never had she thought that a man so powerful could sound so helpless. 'How the hell do you do that?'

'Do what?'

'I don't know,' he grated, almost angrily, as he circled his hips against her, his voice dipping to a silken murmur. 'Do you like that?'

'You know I do,' she whispered back.

The words seemed to stir him into action, for he began to move. He was backing her across the room, his mouth not leaving hers, until she could feel the coolness of the wall pressing against her back. His mouth was on her neck. Her jaw. As she looped her arms around his neck and arched herself into the hardness of his body he gave a low laugh, and the sound of his exultation thrilled her even more. And now his fingers were rucking up her dress and lightly tracking over the goose-pimples which were rippling over her thighs. Any minute now and he would reach her panties, whose moist panel felt like an unbearable barrier, denying him the access she was so desperate to grant him. She squirmed in expectation and he gave an unsteady laugh.

'Do you have any idea of how much I want you, Princess?' he bit out in a tone she'd never heard him use before, and in that moment Zabrina felt a wave of the same heady power which had flooded her the first time he'd made love to her. *She* could make him feel like this.

But that random thought was her undoing—or maybe her salvation.

Because he hadn't 'made love' to her, had he?

He'd had sex with her while pretending to be someone else! He'd thought—and presumably still did—that she had a comprehensive backlist of lovers! He'd tried to wriggle out of marrying her!

Reality shattered the tension like a rock hurled through a window, but she tried to block it because she didn't want to think about those things right now. She didn't want to destroy the pleasure she was feeling. But, infuriatingly, she couldn't keep them at bay any longer—and one thought dominated everything. Wasn't this just another example of Constantin/Roman amusing himself with her as if she were his own, personal plaything? And was she prepared to go along with that?

No, she was not.

Somehow Zabrina untangled herself from his arms and took a step sideways, needing to put some space between them, terrified that any closer and she'd be tempted to carry on. But hot on her frustration came a sudden wave of irritation when she saw just how *composed* Roman looked. Why, he might have been doing nothing more strenuous than reading the financial pages of the newspaper!

'That's enough,' she said, in a low voice.

'So I see. But you're not going to deny how much you were enjoying that, are you?' he challenged softly.

Oh, if only that were the case—but Zabrina was no hypocrite. She wished she knew what she wanted. Or what she didn't want. Deep down she wanted to make a success of this arranged marriage, but everything seemed to be in such a muddle. *She* was in a muddle and she didn't know what do.

She wanted to burst into tears and laugh out loud, all at the same time. She wanted to rush from the breakfast room— yet she wanted him to lock the door and finish what they had started. But she mustn't. She really mustn't. The King of Petrogoria had spent the last week treating her with polite and considered detachment. He hadn't shown a single jot of desire for her. He had behaved as if she were some convalescing relative who'd come to stay at the palace, not the flesh and blood woman he was soon to marry. Only now he seemed to have become bored with that particular course of action—and presumably that was why he had kissed her. Was this all some sort of game to him? Did he think she was like one of those old-fashioned dolls her grandmother used to have—the ones you wound up so they would obediently walk and talk for you?

'You know I was enjoying it. But we both know the rules. Or rather, I thought we did. No...' Her voice trembled a little but she forced herself to say it. Why be shy of saying something they'd actually *done*? 'No sex until we're officially man and wife.'

'That didn't seem to bother you on the train, Zabrina.'

'I wasn't... I wasn't thinking straight on the train,' she said, smoothing the crumpled skirt of her dress with palms which were clammy. 'And we were lucky not to have been caught. We might not be so lucky this time. So if you'll excuse me, I'm going. I want to get down to the stables before my dress fitting and check everything is ready for Midas's arrival.'

'As you wish.' He was looking at her thoughtfully—as if he knew perfectly well that her composure was nothing but a façade. But the hard gleam of his eyes was underpinned with something else and she couldn't quite work out what it was. 'Oh, and I'm going away for a few days.'

And Zabrina was surprised by the sudden sinking of her heart. He was going away without her, leaving her alone in the palace? 'Where?'

'I'm taking a short trip to the Marengo Forest. I want to meet with a few people there so we can get the ball rolling on the airport development as soon as the wedding takes place.'

She nodded her head. Of *course* his mind was fixed on his shiny new acquisition—wasn't that the main reason he would soon be sliding a golden band on her finger? And, while he might have been momentarily distracted by that passionate encounter, he wasn't obsessing about it, like her. He wasn't reading all kinds of things into it which simply didn't exist. So show him how independent you can be. Don't be such a *limpet*. She nodded. 'In that case, I'll see you when you get back. Have a good trip.'

He had started walking ahead and when Zabrina realised he was pulling rank on her, she had to resist a childish urge to race him to the door! But just as he reached the door, he briefly turned his dark head.

'Oh, by the way, you'll find some jewellery waiting when you get back to your suite.'

'What kind of jewellery?'

'Just a necklace. I thought you could wear it to the palace ball on Saturday.'

# CHAPTER TEN

'JUST' A NECKLACE, Roman had said. But this wasn't just any old necklace, Zabrina had quickly realised. This was a glitzy waterfall of sparkling emeralds and diamonds which was too big and too heavy and completely swamped her. But she supposed it was exactly the sort of accessory people would expect a future queen to wear and she had to admit that the jewels matched perfectly her green ball gown. And how strange it was that as she had slithered into the silk creation earlier, she had felt a slow building of anticipation rather than dread. From someone who had hated dresses she had found herself wondering if Roman would approve of her outfit. It came as something of a shock to realise she was dressing for *him*.

The candlelit ballroom was decked with fragrant white roses and now, as the remains of the seven-course banquet were cleared away and the Petrogorian Chamber Orchestra started to play, Roman led her from the table to begin the dancing. The other guests had formed a circle around the dance floor like spectators at a bullfight, to watch the newly engaged couple on their first formal outing. But Zabrina was aware that every eye in the golden ballroom was fixed on *her*. People's gazes were running over her assessingly. Possibly critically. She worried that the high-flown members of Petrogorian society wouldn't approve of the Princess who was shortly to become their Queen. She found herself wishing she'd worn higher shoes because she barely reached Roman's shoulder and surely the discrepancy in their height must make them look faintly bizarre as a couple.

Her sudden attack of anxiety wasn't helped by the recognition that some of the most beautiful women she'd ever seen were gathered in this sumptuous ballroom, along with their powerful husbands. But her smile hadn't faltered as line after line of Roman's loyal subjects had filed in front of her before dinner, and the Prime Minister had seemed favourably impressed when she'd quoted from one of his country's ancient poets.

Zabrina could feel the loud skitter of her pulse as Roman put his arms around her and she tried not to let her inner excitement show too much. The King had been away in the Marengo Forest for three whole days and she was taken aback by how pleased she'd been to see him again. To touch him again. Wasn't it crazy how being on a dance floor allowed you to be intimate with a man in a way which would be forbidden anywhere else? And she had missed him. Missed him more than she should have done, considering she'd barely known him a fortnight. More than anything, she wanted to talk to him because they'd been seated at opposite sides of the table during the sumptuous banquet and had barely exchanged a word all evening.

'So, when did you get back?' she asked a little breathlessly as they began to move in time to the music, because she was acutely aware of the indentation of his fingers at her waist.

'This morning.'

'Oh.' A stupid sense of disappointment washed over her. He'd been here all day and hadn't bothered to let her know? She wanted to say, *Why didn't you come and find me?* Or, *Why didn't you join me for lunch?* But maybe that would have been presumptuous. As if she were laying down terms, or revealing expectations he might stubbornly refuse to meet if he were aware of them. Instead she strove to find just the right, light touch. To sound like the kind of undemanding partner he might wish to spend more time with and not one who was immediately haranguing him with demands. 'I've been with Midas for most of the day.'

'I know you have.' There was a pause. 'I came down to the stables to see you.'

She turned her face upwards, aware of the faintly shadowed jut of his jaw and the sensual curve of his lips. 'But you didn't come over and say hello?'

'You looked as if you were preoccupied. I didn't want to disturb you. I watched you riding for a while and that kept me... entertained. You are quite something on the back of a horse, Zabrina.'

Something in his tone spooked her—but not nearly as much as the thought of Roman quietly observing her, his pewter eyes glinting from within the concealment of the stable yard's many shadows. She wondered how long he had been there for. She wondered if she would have behaved any differently if she'd known he was watching.

'How was the Marengo?' she said, changing the subject.

'The Marengo was fine,' he replied evenly. And then, 'You didn't tell me that your groom was planning on coming to Petrogoria, too.'

She stiffened a little. 'That's because I didn't know.'

'You didn't *know*?'

'Well, that's not strictly true. Not specifically. I knew one of the grooms would travel with him and Stefan has known Midas since he was a foal, so I guess it made sense that he should have been the one to make the journey. But when he got here...well.' She shrugged, feeling the heavy weight of the jewels scratching against her skin and she wished she could just rip them from her neck and drop them to the ground. 'It seemed silly for him to go back immediately, so I gave him permission to stay. Just to get the horse properly settled in, of course.'

'Of course,' echoed Roman, his words non-committal as he spun her round, thinking that she was as light as a cloud.

He glanced down at the loose dark hair which spilled over her shoulders. At the dark green silk which clung to her slender frame, making her appear pristine and perfectly princess-like, especially when adorned by the priceless glitter of his gift. He contrasted that with the carefree image he had seen on horseback earlier, trotting out of the yard with a banner of a ponytail floating behind her. She had tipped back her head and laughed at something her groom had said and something dark and nebulous had invaded his soul. Something which had been eating him up ever since.

Was it jealousy?

No. He felt the slippery silk of her dress beneath his fingertips and his jaw tightened. It couldn't be.

But just because you'd never felt something before, didn't mean you wouldn't be able to recognise it when you did. And if that *were* the case didn't he only have himself to blame? Despite not being the sort of princess he had ever imagined himself marrying, she had persuaded him into going ahead with the union and he had allowed himself to be persuaded, because the pros had outweighed the cons. Or so he had convinced himself. Theirs was to be an unemotional business arrangement. He knew that and she knew that. She had implied that she was prepared to be 'reasonable' if he sought solace in the arms of another woman, as kings had done from the beginning of time, and by implication that meant he couldn't rule out her doing the same, despite her protestations to the contrary. So why did he feel the primitive throb of dark possession when he even considered that option? Why did he want to roar out his anguish at the thought of her ever being in another man's arms?

But his face betrayed nothing, for an implacable countenance had been drummed into him for as long as he could remember. A king must never show his feelings and, in order to guarantee that, it was preferable not to have those feelings in the first place. It had been one of the first things his father had taught him when he had woken on that bleak, black morning to find his mother gone.

It had been a useful lesson in survival.

'Do you want me to ask him to leave?' Zabrina was saying. 'Is that what you want?'

He looked down, steeling himself against the forest-dark beauty of her eyes and resenting the fact that he found her so enchanting, even while inside he was quietly simmering with rage. 'This isn't supposed to be about what *I* want, Zabrina,' he said coolly. 'This is supposed to be your home, not a prison, and if you want your groom to stay on then that, of course, is your prerogative.'

The music came to an end and the Petrogorian Prime Minister stepped in to ask Zabrina to dance and willingly she resumed her progress around the floor with the portly leader, even though she wanted to stay with Roman and ask him...

She swallowed.

Ask him what? He was being perfectly reasonable, wasn't he? Telling her she was free to do as she wished. Telling her Stefan could stay as long as she wanted. She didn't imagine it would go down very well if she started quizzing him about why he was adopting that tone of voice.

What tone of voice was that?

Dark?

Disapproving?

Yes, both those things.

But if he felt that way, then surely that was his problem. If she tried to accommodate him—to gauge his mood and to modify her behaviour accordingly—wouldn't that be setting an awful precedent, turning her into the kind of woman she didn't really like? Or respect. And it wasn't going to be that kind of marriage, she told herself firmly. A meeting of minds and bodies, hopefully, yes, but ultimately it was a transaction. She needed to keep her independence and sense of self-worth, or else she suspected she could easily fall into a deep hole of useless yearning for someone who saw her simply as a means to an end.

She did her best to put on a credible show as a future queen that night—her mother would have been proud of her. She danced with everyone who asked but made sure she conversed with plenty of the women too, admiring their gowns and jewels and talking about various charitable endeavours. But with Roman there was no more dancing. She told herself it wasn't deliberate and that she was imagining his cool and sudden distancing himself from her. But as the clock chimed out midnight, and she and the King left the ballroom to the tumultuous applause of their guests, Zabrina realised that she hadn't really had a chance to talk to him again.

Servants converged on them, walking both ahead and behind as they made their stately progress towards her suite. But when they arrived outside her door, Zabrina turned to the King, licking her lips and slanting him a nervous smile. 'I wonder, shall we have a...nightcap?'

If she had suggested that he suddenly broke into an impromptu rendition of the Petrogorian national anthem, he couldn't have looked more—not *shocked*, exactly, but certainly slightly appalled. As if she had just come out with a highly irregular proposition and had somehow let herself down.

'Unfortunately that will not be possible. I have work which I need to attend to,' he said coolly, briefly lifting her fingers to his lips and bowing his dark head as he kissed them. 'I will see you at breakfast tomorrow.'

The imprint of his mouth on her hand was all too brief and suddenly Silviana was ushering her inside and helping remove her necklace, before undoing all the little buttons at the back of her ball gown.

'Shall I run you a bath before you retire, mistress?' she ventured.

Zabrina shook her head. 'No, thank you. To be honest, I'd just like to be left on my own now.'

'Is something…forgive me for my presumption, Your Royal Highness, but is something *wrong*?'

Zabrina was biting the inside of her lip but she forced herself to smile. Because what if she answered that question honestly? What if she dared to admit even to herself that she was scared of the way Roman could make her feel? She didn't want his disapproval and yet she didn't want to go seeking his approval like some tame puppet. So where did that leave her?

'No, nothing is wrong.' She widened her smile, hoping it looked more reassuring than it felt. 'It's just been a long day and that was my first official introduction as Roman's future bride.'

'All the servants were saying how fine you looked, mistress,' cooed Silviana. 'And that you will make a wonderful queen.'

'That's very sweet of them. Go now and make sure you get a good rest. You've waited up very late.'

But once the servant had left, Zabrina found herself unable to relax and, even though she undressed and climbed into bed, the adrenalin which was rushing around her body made it impossible for her to sleep. She stared at the ceiling. She stared at the necklace which lay discarded on her dressing table, the pile of stones glittering in the moonlight like a handful of shattered glass.

She thought about Roman, working in his office, no doubt. And then she thought about Midas—because that was easier on her heart than thinking about Roman—and was suddenly overcome with an urgent need to see her beloved horse. She could put her arms around his neck and give him the kind of unconditional love she'd never felt comfortable channelling anywhere else apart from to her siblings.

Sliding on a pair of jodhpurs and a fine wool sweater, she slipped silently from her room, listening for a moment as the door opened soundlessly, her gaze darting down the wide marble corridor. But there was nobody around and maybe that wasn't so odd. Servants had to sleep.

She made her way towards the stables, moving as noiselessly

as she could and sticking mainly to the shadows but thankfully encountering nobody along the way. Outside in the fresh air the moon was still waxing—every night getting bigger and brighter—and the stable yard was bathed in ghostly silver. Ignoring the heavy sounds of breathing and occasional snorts coming from the King's thoroughbred horses, Zabrina made her way to Midas's loose box and peered inside.

To her surprise, the horse was lying down, fast asleep—which meant that he must be much more contented in his new home than she'd imagined. But he must have had one ear pricked up and heard her, for he instantly picked himself up and came over to nuzzle her. She petted him for long minutes, murmuring to him in Albastasian sweet talk, and felt much better as a result. It was only when she decided that she really did need to get some sleep and reluctantly began to walk back towards the palace that she saw a silhouette standing motionless on the other side of the yard. She did not jump but carried on walking towards the shadowed figure because she assumed…and that was her first mistake.

'Stefan?' she whispered. 'Is that you?'

'Why, is that who you were hoping for?'

Instantly, Zabrina knew who was speaking and it wasn't Stefan. Because although the groom was young and articulate, he did not speak with a velvety Petrogorian accent, nor have such an aristocratic delivery. Nor would his words ever have been tinged with unmistakable accusation.

'Roman,' she breathed.

He stepped out of the shadows and she was appalled by her body's instant response to all that powerful masculinity, because surely her overwhelming emotion in such a scenario shouldn't be one of desire… He was still wearing the formal suit he'd had on at the ball, though she noticed he had removed his tie and loosened the collar. Just as she noticed the brooding quality of his darkened features and the censure which hardened his sensual lips.

'Surprised?' he taunted softly.

'A little. Have you been spying on me, Roman?'

'You dare to accuse *me*?'

'Too right I do! I want to know what you're doing here. Why you suddenly sprang out of nowhere at this hour.'

'But you weren't scared, were you? You didn't scream and raise the alarm as many women in your situation would have done.'

'So I am to be rebuked for reacting maturely and not like some hysteric?'

'Don't try and change the subject!'

'Then perhaps you could try getting to the point. How did you know where I'd be?'

'Did you really think you could wander the palace at the depths of night without being detected by anyone, Zabrina? That my corridors would go unguarded and my servants not have your welfare at heart?' He gave a bitter laugh as his gaze flicked over her. 'When one of Andrei's aides came rushing to my office and told me that the Princess was out exploring at the dead of night, I knew immediately where you'd be.'

Her heart was thumping painfully but she tried to put a flippant face on it. 'Really? Since you're not a practising clairvoyant as far as I'm aware, perhaps you'd like to let me into the secret of how you "knew" where to find me.'

'Where is he, Zabrina?'

She wanted to say *Who?* but she knew exactly who he meant and to pretend she didn't would surely imply guilt. 'I suppose you're talking about Stefan,' she said slowly. 'What did you imagine, Roman—that I would creep down here to have sex with my groom at the first available opportunity?'

He flinched. 'Did you?' he grated and Zabrina wondered if she had imagined the shudder of pain in his voice.

She stared at him, not bothering to hide her incredulity. Did he really think she'd be interested in a man like Stefan—indeed, in any man—when the only one she had ever wanted was standing right across the yard from her? What kind of women had he dealt with in the past if his level of distrust was so deep and so instant?

'I am hugely insulted,' she said, her voice shaking, 'that you have made so many negative assumptions about me and should believe me capable of such terrible behaviour. What makes you think so badly of me, Roman?'

There was a long pause before he answered, his voice seeming to draw each word out reluctantly. 'I told you. Rumours about you had started reaching me a few months ago—rumours which ignited my curiosity.'

'You mean that I was occasionally guilty of voicing my own opinion?'

'Yes, that.' He narrowed his eyes. 'But I find that trait is not as unappealing as I imagined it would be.'

'Wow,' she said sarcastically. 'This is progress indeed. But much as I would like to applaud your sudden emergence from the Dark Ages, I'm more interested to know what else it was you heard about me.'

He shrugged. 'That you had a habit of disappearing. That the Princess Zabrina would sometimes ride out at first dawn with her groom and not return until the noon sun was high in the sky.'

'And so you came to the conclusion that Stefan and I were galloping off together to enjoy some sort of illicit encounter?'

'Something like that.'

'How dare you? How dare you accuse me of such a thing, Roman?' All pretence at light-heartedness now abandoned, her voice had begun shaking with rage. 'Do you really think I could be so duplicitous that I would agree to marry one man, while being intimate with another?'

'Of course I can!' he flared. 'Because you had sex with Constantin, didn't you, Zabrina? You weren't thinking about Roman then, were you? So how can you explain that?'

She spoke without thinking. She spoke from the heart. 'I can't,' she said simply.

There was a pause. 'Neither can I.'

They stared at each other in silence and all Zabrina could see was the gleam of the moon in his shadowed eyes.

'I tried to resist you,' she said quietly. 'Or rather, I tried to resist Constantin, because I had never met anyone like him before. Surely you must have noticed how deliberately rude and abrupt I was towards you at the beginning?'

'I thought that was a game you were playing.' He gave a short laugh. 'Don't you realise that a headstrong and stubborn woman is exceedingly attractive to a man?'

She shook her head. 'I don't know what happened to me that night and I don't really want to think about it now. But I hold my hands up—I *did* used to ride out with Stefan. If you really want to know what I was doing, then I'll tell you—but we certainly weren't having sex.'

'Really?' He spoke carelessly, but Roman could do nothing about the sudden punch of hope to his heart, even though he despised his visceral reaction to her words.

She nodded and in the moonlight he saw her face assume an expression of fierceness. 'In my country I had a list of charities of which I was patron and which my sister Daria is going to take over, now that I'm no longer there. I was obviously invested in all those charities but there was one in particular which was very close to my heart. It was...' She hesitated. 'It was a refuge on the outskirts of the city. A refuge for women who have suffered domestic violence.'

His eyes narrowed. 'So why all the cloak-and-dagger stuff?'

She nodded, as if this was a topic with which she was familiar. As if she was used to accusation.

'My parents didn't approve of my involvement with these women. It was something else they turned a blind eye to. To admit that women suffered at the hands of men and were made impoverished if ever they chose to escape from abusive relationships—well, they were both of the opinion that the women didn't try hard enough to save their marriages!'

'Good heavens,' said Roman faintly.

The look she threw him was challenging. 'What, is that a bit hardcore old-fashioned, even for you?'

He didn't like being held up as someone completely out of touch with the modern world, just as he didn't like the way she was looking at him. It made him feel...*uncomfortable*. Kings were rarely forced to say they were sorry but Roman knew he needed to say it now. 'I shouldn't have leapt to those conclusions,' he said gruffly. 'Will you forgive me?'

Her absolution wasn't instant. She waited just long enough for him to entertain a little doubt in his mind—and didn't part of him admire her for her strength of character?

Eventually, she nodded. 'Yes, I forgive you,' she said. 'But, going forward, I'd prefer it if you didn't just leap to conclusions. And that it's probably better if you don't just brood about something, but ask me outright.'

She smiled then and the deepening dimple in her cheek drew his gaze, so that suddenly it looked like the most beautiful thing he had ever seen.

Roman swallowed. Her lips were gleaming irresistibly and looking unbearably kissable. He knew what he should do. Escort her back to her suite and bid her goodnight. Just as he knew what he wanted to do, which was to pull her into his arms and then lay her down in one of the dark corners of the stables and make love to her over and over again. And then he thought of all the reasons why he shouldn't—but the one which dominated them all was duty.

Duty.

It was a word which had been drummed into him from the moment he'd been born. A concept which had driven him all his life. It had been duty which had made him focus himself on his lessons and fencing skills, rather than give in to the bitter tears of a deserted child. Duty which had made him fulfil his end of this marriage bargain with the young Albastasian Princess.

Couldn't he—for once—take a break from the crushing

weight of royal expectations? Suddenly, he felt a jolt of his own power as he looked at her. 'I want so badly to make love to you.'

He saw her bite her lip and gaze at the ground, as if seeking an answer amid the strands of silvered straw which lay there, and when she raised her head again, her face was serene and very solemn, as if she had come to some swift conclusion of her own. 'I want that, too.'

He sucked in an unsteady breath, his body warming as he acknowledged her instant capitulation. 'And I suspect that if I drew you into the shadows now and laid my hands and my lips upon your body,' he continued, 'you would again be mine.'

'R-Roman,' she said shakily, but she didn't contradict him.

'But we aren't going to do that.'

'We…aren't?'

Was he wrong to enjoy her obvious disappointment? No, he was not. For didn't her response indicate that the balance of power between them was more equal than he'd thought, and perhaps that was something he needed to address.

'No, we aren't.' He paused just long enough to give *her* a taste of doubt, because wasn't uncertainty one of the most powerful aphrodisiacs of all? 'Instead, I will come to your suite tomorrow. At midnight.'

Her eyes widened. 'But you can't! You know you can't. Tradition states—'

'I don't give a damn what tradition states because *I* am King now and I make the rules.' He lowered his voice, even though there was nobody within earshot. 'I have no intention of broadcasting my movements to palace staff but neither do I intend to have sex with you on a sofa, or rammed up against a wall, or lying on the dusty ground of the stables, even though the prospect of not doing that right now is almost unendurable. I want to share your bed—properly. As Roman, not Constantin. As the man I am and not the man I was pretending to be. But I need you to be certain that this is what you want too, Zabrina.' He paused. 'This is to be no hot-blooded and hasty liaison, fuelled by rampant hormones and frustration, which is why I'm giving you adequate time to think about it. Because if, for any reason, you decide that you would prefer to wait for our wedding night to be intimate with me again then you must send me a signal.'

'How?'

His eyes gleamed like the blade of a sword. 'If you wish me to share your bed, then you should light a lamp in your window tomorrow night, and leave it unshuttered. If the light flares, then I will come to you. But if shutters are closed then I will not, and we will never refer to the matter again. It will be as though we never had this conversation. Do you understand what I'm saying to you, Zabrina?'

'Yes,' she said, in a voice so quiet he could barely hear her response. 'I understand.'

# CHAPTER ELEVEN

ZABRINA SHIVERED AS she positioned the light in the centre of her bedroom window, thinking how strange life was. One minute you could be watching a film about a mermaid and wondering how she could possibly keep her hair looking that shiny when it was constantly immersed in salt-water, and the next...

She licked her dry lips.

Next you could be sending out a secret and silent message as you waited for your lover.

*And she didn't have a clue what she was getting herself into.*

Should she be in bed, waiting for Roman to arrive? Surely it wouldn't be a very attractive sight if she were caught anxiously pacing the floor—even if she *was* clad in a delicate nightgown which she had plucked from her trousseau with trembling fingers. Maybe she ought to be in bed, carefully positioned against the pillows, with her newly washed hair falling artfully over her shoulders. No. No, she couldn't do that. She would feel like a fraud—an imposter—and it would make the situation even more unreal than it already was.

There was a light rap on the door and then, without any prompting from her, it silently opened and closed again and there was Roman in her suite, dominating the space around him, dominating everything with his aura of alpha masculinity. For a moment Zabrina said nothing—but her breathing was so erratic she doubted she'd be able to speak any kind of sense in any case. Because, as always, his brooding beauty stopped her in her tracks. For once his muscular body was clothed in muted colours—presumably so he would melt into the background as he made his way from his part of the palace to hers. But no matter what he wore, his aristocratic bearing always shone through, like a diamond in a pile of rubble.

Yet her own royal status suddenly seemed to count for nothing. She felt like a fraud despite standing before him in her provocative lingerie, which was presumably perfect for an assignation such as this. But how she looked on the outside wasn't how she felt on the inside. Her fluttery excitement kept morphing into worry that she wouldn't be able to handle the way he made her feel, because wasn't the underlying message she was getting from him that this was supposed to be about sex, not emotion?

The King probably thought she knew how these midnight encounters worked, when the truth was she didn't have a clue. So did she have to go through another humiliating disclosure about her lack of experience and hope he'd believe her this time—or did she pretend, and try to pick things up as they went along?

Yet wasn't the whole point of their relationship supposed to be honesty?

'Roman—'

'Shh. Just let me take you to bed, Princess. Because I don't think I can wait for a moment longer.'

His soft words shushed her. They bathed her in silk. The slight cracking of his voice was hugely flattering and suddenly Zabrina was in his arms and his fingers were pushing back through the spill of her hair and he was kissing her as she'd never been kissed before. Stars splintered at the backs of her eyes as she kissed him back, as if they couldn't get enough of each other. He groaned against her mouth and then suddenly he scooped her up into his arms and carried her into the bedroom, the mattress dipping beneath her as he laid her down on the huge divan.

Without taking his eyes from her face he began to unbutton his shirt, but still she said nothing. For hadn't his soft words been a tacit order not to break the spell of what was about to happen—and wasn't the truth that it really *did* feel like magic?

Zabrina watched as he peeled off his clothes until his golden flesh was naked and rippling in the lamplight. Her mouth dried as he joined her on the bed and he pulled her against his powerful frame. He let out a long sigh as his fingers began to reacquaint themselves with her aching body but there seemed a different kind of urgency about him tonight as he kissed her. Her nerves were quickly dissolved by the sweetness of his mouth roving over her neck, her hair and her breasts and Zabrina was writhing with impatience when at last his hand moved beneath the delicate nightgown and began to ruck up the slippery fabric.

'Was this for your honeymoon night?' he murmured.

'Y-yes,' she whispered back, her skin prickling into goosebumps.

Did she imagine the brief darkening of his face before he peeled it off with such infinite care, so that in that moment she felt almost...*treasured*? *Cherished.* Zabrina's heart clenched with something which felt unbearably poignant—as if she'd been given a glimpse of something which could never be hers. Something elusive and fragile and wonderful. Was this what *love* felt like? she found herself wondering wistfully. Until she reminded herself fiercely that love was irrelevant. Emotion was superficial and sensation was key to what was happening. So she turned her attention to the satin of his skin, and his deepening kisses indicated just how much she was pleasing him. The pace began to change and quicken. The air crackled with rising tension and musky desire. She felt him reach for protection, heard the rough tearing of foil before he stroked her thighs apart with beguiling fingers. And then he moved over her and she was lost.

Roman groaned as he entered her. She felt so *tight*. Tighter even than she had done on the train—or was that because he was so unbelievably turned on tonight? He thrust deep inside her honeyed flesh, taking her to the brink again and again, until she cried out his name in a ragged plea and he gave her what she wanted. What she needed. What he needed, too. And didn't a distinctly primeval satisfaction wash over him as he heard her shudder out his name, so that he was forced to silence her frantic cries with another kiss? She was still spasming around him when he started coming himself and never had so much seed spilled from his loins before.

Afterwards, drained and empty, he felt the powerful beat of his heart as she lay slumped against his sweat-sheened shoulder, her own hair damp with exertion. He heard the sudden catch in her breathing and wondered if she was crying. And even though it was definitely not his style to probe a woman's mood, he found himself doing it.

'Zabrina?'

She shook her head as if she didn't want to engage. 'Shh,' she said, the sound mimicking the very one he'd made earlier.

It was a get-out clause. An escape route. But surprisingly, Roman paid it no heed. He rolled on top of her again, smoothing the tousled tendrils of hair away from her flushed cheeks. Her eyes were closed as if she didn't want to have this conversation, which would normally have suited him fine, but he found himself unable to ignore the sudden stab of his conscience.

'Zabrina?'

Her lashes fluttered open and he found himself staring into forest-dark eyes.

'I know,' he said softly and nodded his head resolutely. 'I know I was the first man for you. The only man. And I'm sorry I accused you of all those things.'

She drew back, her eyes wide. 'I don't understand.'

'It's hard for me to understand myself.'

'Well, try.'

He traced his forefinger along the tremble of her lips and resisted the urge to kiss them. 'When I saw you waiting for me tonight, you looked so sweet and so nervous.' He shrugged. 'And so obviously out of your depth. You certainly weren't behaving like an experienced woman of the world. Deep down, I realised that on the train, when you told me—only it was easier to think you weren't. To paint you as someone who was wanton, and free.'

'And why was that, Roman?' she questioned softly.

He shook his head, afraid of what he might say, what he might reveal in an unguarded and totally irrelevant post-orgasmic moment. But he had been the one who had started all this, hadn't he?

'Because it would be easier to keep me at a distance?' she guessed, when still he said nothing.

He furrowed his brow into a frown. He didn't want her to be right, just as he didn't want her to be this perceptive. But he wasn't going to tell a lie. 'Maybe,' he admitted. 'And maybe because it gave me permission to make love to you under the guise of another man. I should never have done that, Zabrina.'

'Maybe you shouldn't,' she said slowly. 'But I wanted you to. I wanted it more than I can ever remember wanting anything.'

It was an unexpected display of candour, but to his surprise it didn't repel him or make him want to run. The look in her eyes seemed to be beguiling him even more than before and Roman tensed. The atmosphere was getting claustrophobic and in danger of suffocating him if he wasn't careful.

He swallowed. So what was he going to do about it?

He reached down to play with one of her nipples and felt himself grow hard as it puckered beneath his touch. He kissed her and guided her hand between his legs, biting back a moan of pleasure as she began to whisper featherlight fingertips up and down his aching shaft.

'I want you to teach me,' she said softly. 'About the things you would like me to do.'

Already, he felt as if he could explode. 'You don't seem to need any advice from me. You're doing just fine,' he growled.

He had been about to show her how to pleasure him but it seemed that his princess was an instinctive expert where his body was concerned and a feeling of anticipation rippled over his body as he reached down and began to finger her in turn.

He closed his eyes.

Because this type of feeling he could cope with, but only this. Maybe that was the only lesson he needed to teach her.

When Zabrina awoke, he had gone. She turned to look at the imprint of his head on the pillow and felt her heart give a wrench. Of course he had gone. That was the deal. He had crept from her bed under the velvety cloak of darkness, to slip back unnoticed through the palace corridors.

Lying amid the warm and rumpled sheets, watching dawn as it filtered through the unshuttered window, she allowed herself a moment of erotic recall.

It had been...

She swallowed.

It had been divine on every level, bar one. She had been nervous about having sex with the King, wondering if it would be the same as having sex with his alter-ego bodyguard. But it had been incredible. Perhaps because so many different layers of their characters had been peeled away, it had felt deeper than what had happened before. It had been intense. Powerful. Almost *transforming*. Every single time. Once, when he had been deep inside her pulsing out his seed, she had wanted to weep from pure joy. She had wanted to trace her fingertips over the shadowed graze of his jaw and thank him for making her feel this way. But instinct had warned her against such an over-the-top reaction and instinct had proved her right. Because just before Roman had returned to his own quarters, rising gloriously and boldly naked from the sheets, she had thought he seemed more...

She frowned as she tried to think of a word to describe it. Remote, yes—that was it. Almost as if the intensity of their physical interaction had made him want to instinctively push her away. Maybe she was reading too much into it. After all, what did *she* know about how men behaved once they had shared a woman's bed? And hadn't his last words been a husky promise that he would come to her later that night? She smiled as she plumped up the pillows and afterwards fell asleep and when next she awoke, the sun was up and Silviana was busying herself in the suite, laying out all her clothes for the day.

Leaving her hair loose, she put on a floaty dress the colour of apple blossoms, but she definitely felt nervous as she walked into the breakfast room, to find Roman already seated and looking at his phone. She wanted him to say something or do something. To send out some secret acknowledgement of what they had shared during the night by slanting her a complicit look. But when he glanced up from his phone and smiled, his face looked nothing except composed.

'Good morning,' he said. 'Did you sleep well?'

Maybe it was irrational but Zabrina was disappointed at the lack of unspoken communication passing between them. She wondered how he'd react if she blurted out the truth. *No, not really. How could I possibly sleep when you were deep inside my body for most of the night?* But, of course, she didn't. She simply sat down while a servant shook out a napkin and placed it on her lap, and attempted to match her fiancé's cool air of self-possession.

'Very well, thank you,' she answered. 'You?'

'Mmm,' he said, non-committal as he put his phone face-down on the table, as if he were making a great sacrifice. 'So, what are you doing today?'

'I have a dress fitting, and I need to finalise the design for the top layer of the wedding cake.' She lifted up her spoon to scoop up a cinnamon-dusted strawberry and shot him a look.

'Would you like to give your input? Any favourite recipes from your childhood?'

His expression suddenly grew stony and shuttered. 'I've never been much of a cake-eater, Zabrina. So why don't I leave that side of it to you?'

She wanted to ask what had made his face darken like that, but she didn't do that either. The mood in the room was too fragile for those sorts of questions. *She* was too fragile—like a piece of honeycomb which had been placed in the path of an approaching pair of feet. The brief insecurity which had washed over her in bed earlier that morning now grew heightened. In a flash it came to her that she wanted more than erotic intimacy. She wanted other intimacies, too. She wanted them to grow close and to be a real couple—not spend her life tiptoeing around his feelings. She looked at the proud jut of his aristocratic jaw.

*So make it happen.*

Don't crowd him.

In public at least, give him space.

Zabrina dug her spoon into another strawberry and nibbled at the fruit delicately, even though she would have preferred to have picked it up with her fingers. But she knew how palace life worked. Beneath the careful scrutiny of the servants she would play the royal game which was expected of her. She would make small talk and discuss generalities about the day ahead and that would have to do for the time being. But there was nothing to stop her from breaking down Roman's barriers whenever she got the opportunity. Surely that was essential if she wanted to discover more about this complex man she was soon to marry.

And where better than when they were alone in bed?

# CHAPTER TWELVE

'YOU NEVER REALLY talk about your past, do you, Roman?'

Roman kept his eyes tightly shut, hoping his forbidding body language would stem the Princess's infuriating line of questioning. Because this wasn't the first time she'd tried to quiz him after one of his delicious midnight visits to her bedroom. Chipping away as she tried to get to know him better, as lovers inevitably did—no matter how many times he discouraged them. He guessed that with Zabrina he had been unusually indulgent—and at least their powerful sexual chemistry meant it had been easy to distract her. He'd been able to deflect her annoying queries with a foray into mutual bliss, but this time he heard the note of stubborn determination in her voice which made him suspect the subject wasn't going away.

It didn't.

'Roman?' Soft fingertips began to stroke distracting little circles on his forearm. 'I know you're not asleep.'

Reluctantly, Roman opened his eyes, his vision instantly captured by the sight of the naked woman lying in bed next to him. He felt the instant thunder of his heart as he drank in her slender curves. If this were anyone else he would simply leave but with Zabrina he couldn't—and not just because he was due to marry her in ten days' time. Because wasn't the truth that he simply couldn't bear the thought of leaving her bed? Not when there were still several hours available to them before daybreak, which he intended to put to the best possible use. Starting with the judicious use of his tongue, which he would trickle down over her belly until her nails were scrabbling against his scalp and she was moaning helplessly and bucking beneath him.

But despite the hungry clamour in his groin, his desire was tinged with the flicker of resentment, because he knew that in many ways he had become unexpectedly addicted to her. Didn't he sometimes despair of the way she effortlessly seemed to weave her spell around him? He gave an impatient sigh. Maybe his attempts at evading her questions were simply delaying the inevitable. Maybe his future wife had the right to ask him things which had been forbidden to other lovers.

'Which particular part of my past particularly interests you, Princess?' he questioned coolly.

Her answer came straight back, as if she'd been rehearsing it.

'Your parents.'

'My parents,' he repeated slowly.

'Everyone has them at some point in their life, Roman. You know all about mine but I know nothing about yours. I mean, I know that your father died four years ago and that your parents got divorced, but I don't know any more than that because you've never said.'

'And don't you think there's a reason for that?'

She wriggled up the bed a little, so that her dark hair shimmered down, rather disappointingly concealing the rosy nipple which had been on display.

'So why don't you tell me what that reason is?' she said.

The look in her eyes was compelling, the expression on her face serene as she calmly returned his gaze. And all at once it felt as if there was no hiding place. No place left to run—and the weirdest thing was that Roman didn't *want* to run. He wanted to confide in her. To tell her things he'd never discussed with another soul. A pulse began to beat at his temple. Why *was* that? Why did he suddenly feel as if he had been carrying around an intolerable burden and this was his chance to put it down for a while?

But it wasn't easy to articulate words he'd spent a lifetime repressing, or to expand on them, and for a while he just listened to the sound of silence, broken only by the distant ticking of a clock.

'My mother left when I was three,' he said at last. 'After that, it was just me and my father.'

'What was she like?'

It was a simple question but something he'd never been asked outright and, stupidly, he wasn't expecting it. Forbidden images of a tall blonde woman with a worried face swam into his mind and Roman realised just how long it had been since he'd thought about her. Since he had *allowed* himself to think about her. 'I don't remember very much about her,' he said. 'Only that she used to read me bedtime stories in a low and drawling voice. She was American. She came from Missouri and she used to wear a necklace with a bluebird on it.'

'What else?'

She looked at him and he wondered if her inquisitiveness was inspired by curiosity or horrified fascination. Because a mother who deserted her child always excited people's interest—particularly women's. A mother who left her child was seen as a monster and the child as unloved and unwanted. His preference would have been to have shut the subject down but suddenly he realised that some day he and Zabrina were going to have to explain the lack of a paternal grandmother to their own children, so maybe she *needed* to know. 'What kind of thing do you want to know?'

'Like, how did they meet?'

He raked back through the things he knew, which were surprisingly sketchy. 'They met when my father was on a world tour. She was working as a waitress and I think he just became obsessed by her and swept her off her feet. He proposed, she accepted and he brought her back here with almost indecent haste.' His voice hardened into flint. 'It's why I became an advocate of arranged marriages, Zabrina. He should never have made her his wife.'

She pushed a strand of hair out of her eyes and blinked at him. 'Because she was a commoner?' she said slowly.

'Almost certainly. She couldn't deal with royal life or all the restrictions which accompany it. Or so my father told me afterwards. She never settled into life here—not even when she had me. I remember that sometimes she seemed too scared to hold me and seemed to leave most of my care to my nurse, Olga.' He flinched as the memories came faster now. A black spill of memories he couldn't seem to hold back. 'Even when she read to me at night, she would slip into my room under cover of darkness. I noticed she started being around less and less and sometimes I would spot her heading towards me in one of the corridors, only she would turn away and pretend she hadn't seen me. Don't look at me that way, Zabrina, because it's true. And then one day, she left. She *left*,' he repeated, angry at the hot twist of pain in his heart. Angry with himself because surely it shouldn't still hurt like this. 'She just walked away and never looked back.'

She didn't respond to that and he heaved a breath of thanks, thinking she'd taken the hint and would ask him no more. He was just about to pull her into his arms and lose himself in the sweetness of her body when she propped herself up on one elbow and screwed up her nose. 'So what happened after that? I mean, how did you find out she'd gone?'

'Is this really necessary?' he demanded.

'I think it's important,' she clarified quietly. 'And I'd like to hear the rest of the story.'

'I'll tell you how I found out.' His voice grew quiet now. So quiet that he saw her lean forward fractionally to hear him. 'I woke up one morning and couldn't find her and when I asked Olga where she was, she told me I must go and speak to my father. So I went downstairs and discovered my father calmly eating breakfast. He looked up and told me my mother had gone and wouldn't be coming back, but I didn't believe him. I remember I ran from the room and he let me go. I remember searching every inch of the palace until I was forced to accept that the King had spoken the truth and she really *had* gone.'

He tried to focus himself back in the present but the memories were too strong and they overwhelmed him like the heavy atmosphere you got just before a storm. He remembered the dry sobs which had heaved from his lungs as he'd hidden himself away in a shadowed corner. He hadn't dared show his heartbreak or his fear, for hadn't his father drummed into him time after time that princes should never show weakness or emotion? Olga had eventually found him, but he had turned his face to the wall as she'd tried to tempt him out with his favourite sweets, still warm from the palace kitchens. But the usually tempting smell of the coconut had been cloying and it had been many hours before he had relented enough to take his nurse's hand and accompany her back to the nursery.

The silence which followed felt like a reprieve, but not for long because Zabrina's soft voice washed over him with yet another question.

'And did you ever hear from your mother again? I mean, surely she must have written to you. Sent a forwarding address so you could contact her.'

'Yes, I had an address for her,' he confirmed bitterly. 'And I used to write her letters. At first they were simple, plaintive notes, asking when she was coming back.' It made him curl up with disgust to think how he had humiliated himself by begging her to return, seeking solace from a woman who had rejected him outright. 'After a while, I just used to send her drawings I'd made, or tell her about my horse, or my fencing lessons.'

'But you never heard back?'

Was that disapproval he could hear in her voice, or incredulity? Or just the loathsome pity he had always refused to tolerate? 'No, I never heard back,' he clipped back and then shrugged. 'So in the end, I just gave up. My father never re-married, and brought me up to the best of his ability. It wasn't great. He wasn't a particularly easy man and it certainly wasn't what you'd call a normal, nuclear family but we adapted, as people do.'

'And, of course, you had Olga.'

He didn't answer straight away, just stared out of the window, noticing that the silver moon was almost full. 'No. Actually, I didn't.'

It was the first time she had looked truly taken aback. 'But—'

'My father sacked her.'

'He *sacked* her?'

The lump in his throat made it hard for him to speak, yet somehow the words just kept coming. 'He thought we were too close. As he explained, Olga was a servant and she didn't seem to know her place where I was concerned. He said you couldn't have a nursemaid who was acting like a quasi-mother and, any-way, he was done with commoners.'

'Oh, Roman, I'm so sorry,' she breathed, and he steeled him-self not to react to the crack of compassion in her voice. 'That's terrible.'

'No, it was not terrible. It was manageable,' he said fiercely, daring her to contradict him, because he didn't want to dwell on the pain of that double rejection or how cold and how empty his life had seemed afterwards. 'After that I had a series of nurses and nannies who looked after me—sometimes men and some-times women—all of them experts in one field or another.' But despite the variety of staff who had been engaged to help with his upbringing, they all had one thing in common. They never hugged him. Rarely touched him. Sometimes he'd suspected they'd been instructed to behave that way, but he didn't investi-gate further because the thought of that made him feel slightly sick. And anyway he didn't care, for in the end it had done him a favour and allowed him to view his brave new world with different eyes. Because at least you knew where you were with those people. *They* would never let you down.

He shot Zabrina a speculative look. 'Satisfied now?' he questioned, not bothering to conceal the note of warning in his voice. 'I don't think there's anything else you need to know.'

Zabrina bit her lip. She was aware he wanted her to leave it—why, his body language couldn't have been more forbidding if he'd tried. But how could she stop asking when there was still so much she didn't know? There were so many gaps in his story and she needed to fill them, because otherwise he would remain a stranger to her and she suspected she might never get another chance like this.

'Is she still alive? Your mother, I mean.'

His body tensed. She thought it looked like rippled marble in the moonlight.

'I have no idea,' he answered coldly. 'I stopped writing when I was thirteen and never heard of her again.'

'And you never tried to have her found, not even when you acceded to the throne? I mean, a king has access to the kind of information which would make that sort of thing easy.'

'Why on earth would I do that, Zabrina?' His lips curved disdainfully. 'Unless you're one of those people who believes that continued exposure to rejection is somehow character forming?'

'And Olga?' she questioned, deciding to ignore his bitter sarcasm. 'What happened to your nurse?'

'That I *did* discover,' he conceded, giving a brief, hard smile. 'She went back to live with her family not far from here, in the mountain town of Posera.'

'And do you—?'

'No! No, that is it!' he interrupted furiously. 'You have tested my patience too long and too far, Zabrina, and I will not be subjected to this any longer!'

Without warning, he rose from the bed and began reaching for the scattered clothes which had been discarded when he had arrived soon after midnight.

'What are you doing?' She was acutely conscious of the note of alarm in her voice but she couldn't seem to keep it at bay.

'What does it look like I'm doing? I'm getting dressed. I'm going back to my own room.'

'But it's still early.'

'I'm perfectly aware what the time is.'

'Roman, there's no need—'

'Oh, but that's where you're wrong, Zabrina. There is every need,' he interjected coldly. 'Because I'm not doing this again. Not ever again.'

'You mean…' She could feel the sudden plummet of her heart. 'You mean you won't be coming to my bed again?'

'I don't know.' There was a pause. 'That's up to you.'

'I don't…' Her fingers dug into the rumpled sheet. 'I don't understand.'

'Don't you?' He waited until he had finished pulling on his soft leather boots before flicking her an emotionless look which had replaced the ravaged expression of before. 'Then let me make it crystal clear for you, just so there won't be any misunderstandings in the future. A future you need to make a decision about, because you need to know which direction you want to take.'

'What are you talking about?' she whispered.

'I'll tell you exactly what I'm talking about. I think we have the makings of a good team,' he said slowly. 'In public we just need to turn up and wave and fulfil the worthwhile causes close to our hearts. And in private I certainly have no complaints about what takes place between us, because I would be the first to admit that you completely blow my mind. But as for the rest.' His face grew dark and brooding again. 'All this other *stuff* you seem intent on dredging up with your endless probing and questioning. That has to stop and it has to stop right now. I'm not interested in analysing the past or its effect on me—because the past has gone. And neither will I contemplate the kind of future where you do nothing but needle away at me. I can't and I won't tolerate such behaviour. Either you accept the man I am today, or the wedding is off. No more questions. No more analysis. Do you understand what I'm saying to you, Zabrina?'

There was a long silence. She could hear the muffled pounding of her pulse as she looked at him. 'That sounds like an ultimatum.'

'Call it what you want. I'm not going to deny it.'

It felt as if someone had taken a heavy, blunt instrument and smashed it into her heart. It was illogical to think he might have reacted any differently, but logic was having no effect on the way his words were making her feel. Zabrina's head was spinning. He had wanted to call off the marriage once before but she had insisted on going through with it because her homeland badly needed this union, and she'd convinced herself they could make the marriage work and produce a family.

But now she could see it wasn't as simple as she'd first thought.

She'd used her parents' marriage as a template for her own behaviour—but she didn't *like* her parents' marriage! Her father's affairs indicated a total lack of respect and regard for his wife and her mother's tacit acceptance of his behaviour was tantamount to a nod of approval. Yet she had calmly told Roman she would be prepared to react in a similar way, because she accepted that was what kings 'did'. Had she been out of her mind? Zabrina's stomach churned. Had she really imagined she'd be content to sit back and watch while Roman behaved that way, when the thought of him having sex with another woman made her want to scream out her horror and her distress?

She realised something else, too. She wanted a real marriage. She wanted to be a wife to Roman in every sense of the word, and for him to be a proper husband. She didn't know if that was possible, but surely she had to give it a try. Because when he had been telling her his sad story about his mother, it had sparked off flickers of recognition inside her. It had made her think of other stories which she had heard so many times before. She might be wrong, but there might be a reason why Roman's mother had disappeared in such a dramatic fashion and maybe she should try to discover if what she suspected was true.

The King was now standing fully dressed in his traditional night-time clothes of jeans and a dark sweater and she could sense the air of impatience radiating from his powerful frame as he waited for her answer. But there was more to Roman than his sometimes intimidating exterior suggested. If she looked beyond his arrogant sense of entitlement, she could detect the deep wound which had been inflicted on him as a boy and which had never been given the chance to heal.

Could she help him do that? Would he accept her help, even if such a thing were possible?

Deliberately she lay back against the pillows. 'I'm not going to address ultimatums—and certainly not when they are delivered in the middle of the night,' she said, with a carelessness she was far from feeling. 'Speak to me about it in the morning.'

She wouldn't have been human if she hadn't enjoyed the very real flash of shock and frustration which gleamed from his eyes—presumably because he was never obstructed quite so openly—before leaving the room without another word. And she suspected he might have slammed the door very loudly, if there hadn't been a continuing need for silence.

# CHAPTER THIRTEEN

'SILVIANA?' ZABRINA MADE a final adjustment to the collar of her silk blouse as, with a raised hand, she waylaid her lady-in-waiting just as she was leaving the dressing room. 'Did you ever hear of a palace nurse called Olga?'

The servant lifted her head, her thick, blonde bob swinging around her chin as she did so. Did Zabrina imagine the caution she saw written on her lovely face or was she just getting paranoid?

'Of course I have heard of her, Your Royal Highness. My own mother knew her very well.'

Zabrina nodded. 'I understand she lives in a place called Posera. Is that very far from here?'

Silviana shook her head. 'No, Your Royal Highness. It is a little village nestled in the foothills of the Liliachiun mountains.'

'I was wondering...' Zabrina swallowed, nervous about saying this, but she *needed* to say it. For Roman's sake. For all their sakes. She forced a smile. 'I would like to visit her. This morning. Right now, in fact.'

'Now?' Silviana looked alarmed. 'But you are already late for breakfast with His Imperial Majesty.'

Zabrina shook her head. 'I won't be taking breakfast this

morning. Perhaps you could have someone send word to that effect to the King.' And it wasn't just the thought of food which was making her throat close up. She couldn't face walking into the breakfast room under Roman's indifferent gaze and pretend that last night had never happened. Because it had. He had basically told her that if she wasn't prepared to accept the most superficial of marriages, then the wedding was off. *And that was a decision she wasn't prepared to make just yet. Not until she was fully equipped with all the facts.* 'I would like to set off immediately. I'm sure that can be arranged?'

'No doubt the King would be happy to—'

'No,' Zabrina interrupted firmly. 'I don't… I don't want the King to know about this. I need you to arrange a car to take me there, Silviana, and for the driver to be sworn to secrecy. You can tell him that I am arranging a surprise for His Majesty.' Which was true, she thought grimly. The only trouble was that she had no idea if her hunch was correct—or how it would be received if it was.

Her heart was pounding hard in her chest as she accompanied Silviana through the palace and she didn't begin to breathe normally again until she and her lady-in-waiting were driving through the streets of Rosumunte, towards the famous mountain range which dominated the capital city.

Zabrina tried to concentrate on what she was seeing but found herself not *wanting* to love the elegant trees and lush foliage as the car skimmed through the green countryside. Because what if she was exiled after all this? What if the wedding was called off because Roman was angered by her taking such a bold initiative? Could she cope with the emotional and financial fallout of not securing a marriage deal?

She was going to have to.

Before too long, they drew up in front of an old-fashioned cottage with a thatched roof, just like the ones she'd seen in a book she'd once had, all about England. To the front there was a beautiful garden and in the distance was a goat grazing in a meadow. A young woman came running out of the house when she heard the car, her look of curiosity changing to one of shock as Zabrina stepped from the car, and hastily she sank into a deep curtsey.

'Your Royal Highness!' she gasped. 'This is indeed an unexpected honour.'

'Forgive me for this unannounced intrusion,' replied Zabrina. 'But I was wondering if I might have a word with your…grandmother? Alone, if I may.'

'Of…of course, Your Royal Highness. If you would just give me a moment to inform my *bunica* and quickly prepare the cottage.'

Zabrina could hear the murmur of voices and the clattering of china before being ushered inside the surprisingly large and very comfortable cottage, and minutes later she was sitting opposite a sprightly looking old lady in a chair which rocked before a blazing fire, despite the sunshine of the day outside.

'When you get old, you get cold,' the old lady said.

Zabrina nodded. 'I hope to have the good fortune to discover that for myself one day.' But her voice was a little choked as she spoke, her chest tight with emotion as she realised that this woman had rocked the infant Roman, had held his little hand and watched as he'd learned to walk. And then she had been summarily dismissed from his life. 'Thank you for seeing me.'

Olga's still-beautiful eyes were a little faded, but they narrowed perceptively as her gaze took in the enormous emerald and diamond engagement ring which glittered on Zabrina's finger.

'You are Roman's woman?' she asked, very softly.

This was a tricky one to answer, but how could Zabrina possibly demand the truth, if she was not prepared to speak it herself?

'I want to be.' The words came out in a rush. 'I so want to be.'

Olga folded her hands together on her lap. 'I wondered when you might come.'

\* \* \*

Roman stared out of the window, but the sweeping beauty of the palace gardens remained nothing but a green and kaleidoscopic blur. He turned back to find Andrei regarding him with an expression of concern he hadn't seen on his aide's face in a long time. Probably not since he had masqueraded as Constantin Izvor on that fateful journey from Albastase to Petrogoria, he thought grimly.

'*Where*,' he repeated furiously, 'has she gone?'

'We don't know, Your Majesty.'

'What do you mean, you don't know? How can you not know?'

'Is the Princess not free to travel at will?' Andrei asked mildly.

Roman glared. 'Of course she is. It's just…'

Just what? Had he expected her to be pale-faced and remorseful over breakfast this morning, telling him she'd been too intrusive with her questions last night and promising him it wouldn't happen again? Yes, he had. Of course he had. For he wasn't blind to the effect he had on her—women were notoriously bad at hiding their feelings when they had begun to care deeply for a man, and he knew that cancelling their wedding was the last thing Zabrina wanted.

At first he had even been prepared to overlook her lateness, aware that she was going to have to lose face by backing down and was probably dreading making her entrance and her apology. But as his coffee had grown cold and the servants had hovered around the table anxiously, he had realised that she wasn't going to show up at all. Not only had she failed to appear, but she had neglected to do him the courtesy of informing him until much later. Wasn't such an act towards the monarch completely unacceptable?

He had gone to his offices and tried to lose himself in his work, but for once his grand schemes had failed to excite him. Even the prized Marengo Forest seemed to represent nothing but a cluster of trees which had forced him into making the most stupid decision of his life by agreeing to marry the stubborn and foxy Princess who refused to conform to his expectations of her!

Now it was getting on for midday and still she hadn't returned and his slowly ignited temper was in danger of erupting. He could hear Andrei talking quietly on his cell-phone and then the aide gently cleared his throat as he finished the call.

'Your Majesty?'

'Yes, what is it?'

'The Princess's car arrived back at the palace a short time ago and she—'

'Have her sent here as soon as she—'

'You don't have to have me *sent* anywhere,' came a voice from behind him. 'I came all of my own accord!'

He whirled around to see Zabrina standing there, a look of challenge sparking from her green eyes which matched the faint sarcasm underpinning her words. Her cheeks were flushed with roses, as if she had been outside in the fresh air, but there was no contrition on her face, he noted. No sense that she had offended him on so many levels he didn't even know where to begin.

'Where have you been?' he questioned coldly.

She opened her mouth as if to respond and then looked at Andrei.

'If you will excuse me, Your Majesty, Your Royal Highness?' said the aide smoothly, backing out of the double golden doors with indecent haste.

Roman wanted to demand that his aide stay, or that Zabrina return later, when he might deign to schedule in a slot to see her. Or even to suggest she wait until they were having lunch—because any of those propositions would demonstrate very firmly who was in charge. But the glint of determination flashing from her eyes made him realise that any such request would be futile. And besides, why not get it over with?

'So,' he said coolly, once the doors had closed behind Andrei. 'Are you going to answer my question and tell me where you've been?'

She made a big show of wiggling her shoulders so that her dark hair shimmered against the yellow blouse—the fine fabric hinting at the slender but muscular body beneath. Had she done that deliberately to emphasise her allure? he wondered achingly. To remind him how much in thrall he was to her agile physicality?

'No ideas, Roman?' she asked, with equal aplomb. 'You aren't going to accuse me of trying to seduce my new, Petrogorian groom?'

'Hardly,' he snapped. 'Since you were seen leaving by car, with Silviana!'

For a moment she looked as if she was about to smile, but then seemed to change her mind for her face took on a completely different look. Softer. Thoughtful—almost gentle. And that put the fear of God in him like nothing else, because gentleness was alien to him and he didn't trust it. Very pointedly, he lifted his arm to glance at his watch. 'Whatever it is, will you please hurry up and tell me because I haven't got all day?'

'Roman, I went to visit Olga. I found out where she lives.'

A barrage of feelings hit him. Cold fear, dark dread and anger. But anger was the overriding emotion which made him shoot out his response to her. Because wasn't it easier to focus on that, rather than confront the sudden blackness which was hovering at the edges of his mind? 'What the hell did you do that for?'

'Because I was confused by some of the things you told me.' She licked her lips. 'I guess I found it hard to believe that your mother never even wrote back to you.'

'You think all women are fundamentally good—and mothers in particular?' He gave a bitter laugh. 'In that case, I pity you your naivety, Zabrina. I lost faith in your sex a long time ago.'

But she shook her head as if he hadn't spoken. 'Some of the things you said didn't add up,' she continued. 'Why she used to hide away. Why she used to only come to you under cover of darkness. It seemed to me that Olga must have known something and she did. That was another reason why she was sacked.'

Roman's heart clenched as if some malevolent iron fist were squeezing it tighter and tighter. He wanted to turn and run, or to put his hands to his ears like a child and block out whatever was coming. But that would be the behaviour of a coward, and he was no coward. And hadn't he weathered the worst of the storm all those years ago? What could possibly be left to hurt him now? 'What did Olga know?'

She sucked in a deep breath and now he saw the flicker of fear and darkness in her own eyes. 'Your father used to abuse your mother,' she said. 'Mentally and physically.'

'No!' The word thundered from his lungs. 'That is not possible.'

'Why not?'

'Because I would have known.' He could hear the break in his voice as he shook his head in denial. 'I would have protected her.'

'No, Roman. You would not have known, because your mother wouldn't have wanted you to know. She wanted to hide her pain and distress from you. She wanted to protect *you*, which is a mother's instinct. And how could a small boy possibly save a woman from the wrath of his powerful and autocratic father? That would only have put you in danger and that was the last thing she would have wanted.'

He curled his fingers into his palms so hard that he could feel the deep imprint of his nails, but the sharpness of that didn't come close to the fierce stabbing of his heart. 'How could you possibly know what she wanted?' he raged. 'Are you the one who is now capable of reading minds?'

'No. But I have helped many women like your mother at my refuge in Albastase—'

'Poor women?' he demanded in disbelief.

'Yes, poor women—and some rich ones, too. As well as all

the others in between. Because abuse knows no age or class boundaries, Roman, and there are victims everywhere. Olga told me that your mother often used to have black eyes. That was why she would read your bedtime story in darkness and why she sometimes ducked out of sight if she saw you walking down the corridor. It was why she had to leave, because she knew she was incapable of being a good and loving mother towards you, if she was constantly being beaten down.'

'Then why...why didn't she take me with her?'

Zabrina heard the raw note of anguish in his voice as he whispered out that stark and heartbreaking question and she wanted so much to comfort him. To take him in her arms and hold him. But not now. Not yet. Because didn't he need to *feel* this? To *really* feel it—to have the ugly wound laid wide open after all these years, so he would be able to recover from it at last? Afterwards—maybe once he'd heard the whole story—that would be the time to offer him solace. If he still wanted her. 'She tried to take you,' she said simply. 'But, of course, your father discovered her plans and made sure she was spirited away in his private jet in the dead of night, while you were fast asleep. I don't know if you can imagine how different those times were, but a waitress from Missouri would have had no clout against one of the most powerful men in the world.'

'She never got my letters?' he questioned suddenly.

Zabrina bit her lip, because, oh, how she wished she could sugar-coat this one. But she couldn't do that either. 'I don't think so. I suspect the letters might have been destroyed as soon as you dispatched them,' she said. 'But she wrote to *you*.'

He narrowed his eyes and the flare of hope he was so desperately trying to repress made her heart turn over with love and sorrow.

'She wrote to you through Olga, but the letters only got through after your father died. I have them.'

There was a long silence while Roman digested this and he could feel the powerful thunder of his heart as he looked at the

Princess who stood before him, her green eyes wide with compassion. 'Why did I never receive them?' he demanded, but deep in his heart he knew the reason.

'Olga tried to contact you after your father's death,' she said gently. 'But she was blocked every time. By you.'

He nodded, painfully aware of his own contribution to what had happened. 'Because the thought of seeing and speaking to her again after all those years was more than I could endure,' he said slowly, almost as if he had forgotten she was in the room with him. Was that why he did nothing to conceal the bitter break in his voice? Or because he know that his Princess would understand? 'I couldn't bear the thought of reliving...' He swallowed. 'Of reliving all that pain.'

'I realise that,' Zabrina whispered. 'And so does she. She knows you were responsible for the anonymous donations paid into her bank account for so many years and she thanks you for your generosity.'

'I want to hate my father for what he did,' he said, his voice changing into a rasp. 'In fact, I *do* hate him.'

'Well, don't,' she whispered. 'Just let it go, Roman. For hate brings nothing of value to anyone's life and you don't know the truth about his own upbringing, I assume?'

He shook his head. 'No. No, I don't. He never wanted to discuss it. He never wanted to discuss anything.' His father had never *talked* to him, not properly. It had been like living with an automaton who had demanded increasingly high levels of perfection from his only child. Had he ever felt guilty about the way he'd treated the woman he had married? Could that have been the cause of the unexpected tears he had shed, just before shuddering out his final breath, his hand tightly clutching that of his son? Roman gave a heavy sigh because Zabrina was right. He needed to forgive, or there would be no peace in his own heart. His thoughts cleared and he looked into her clear, bright gaze, his mouth feeling as if it had been crammed full of stones as he asked the question he had been dreading.

'And my mother?' he asked, bracing himself for the inevitable reply.

'She's alive,' Zabrina said, very quietly.

He froze. 'Are you serious?'

She nodded. 'Totally serious. Your mother is alive and well, Roman. She sent you this.'

She bent and reached into her handbag and pulled out a small pouch and inside was a delicate necklace—a cheap silver chain with a blue enamel bird dangling from the end. 'It's a bluebird,' she whispered, as she let it spill into his open palm. 'The symbol of Missouri state, where she comes from. She sent it to Olga, with one of her first letters. She wants to see you. We could invite her to the wedding, if you like. Or you could go and see her on your own, if...if you don't want the wedding to go ahead.'

His fingers closed around the little locket. 'You're saying you want to call it off?' he husked.

Zabrina closed her eyes in despair as she watched him replace the necklace in the pouch and put it in his pocket. How could he be so *dense*? How could he fail to see the evidence which was before his eyes, that she wanted him so much she would walk to the ends of the earth for him? But deep down she knew the answer to that. Because he hadn't been shown enough love in his life—that was why he couldn't recognise it. His trust in love had been destroyed and this was her chance to help him rebuild it, and she had to take it, no matter what the outcome. Even if he felt she now knew too much about him, to be comfortable with them sharing a life.

'Calling it off is the last thing I want to do,' she said. 'I want to be your wife more than anything in the world, because I love you, Roman. I think I've loved you from the first time I saw you, when you were Constantin Izvor. I loved you as the man, not as the King, but I love the King too—if that makes sense. You make me laugh and you bring me joy, and, yes, you can be infuriating at times but I'm sure I can, too.'

'Zabrina—'

'No. Let me finish, because this bit is important,' she said in a low voice which, infuriatingly, had started shaking. 'When I told you all those things about what I expected from our marriage, I was wrong. When I said I would turn a blind eye if you wanted to have affairs with other women, I don't know what I was thinking. Well, I do actually, but I wasn't being honest with myself. Because the truth is that I would be beside myself with jealousy and rage if you ever touched another woman. I want you exclusively, Roman, maybe even a bit possessively. So if that isn't your idea of what you want out of a royal marriage, then—'

'Zabrina, Zabrina, Zabrina.' He pulled her into his arms and smoothed his thumb down the side of her face as if he were seeing it for the first time. 'I never wanted that kind of marriage and the thought of you being with anyone other than me repels me. In fact, the idea of you being jealous is rather reassuring— because we both know that I'm capable of feeling it, too.' He paused and his voice was a little unsteady. 'Except that I will never give you cause to be jealous, because I love you, Princess.'

'You don't have to say that,' she whispered.

'I know I don't. I'm not in the habit of saying anything I don't mean and I don't intend to start now. But learning how to express myself is a whole new skill set, so you will have to make allowances for me.'

She smiled. 'Oh, I think I could manage to do that, my darling.'

She touched her fingers to his jaw and Roman could see the wonder shining from her face and her sweet expression smote at a heart which was already full and somehow all the pain was just draining away from him, leaving him feeling as if he'd shed a heavy burden he hadn't even realised he'd been carrying. It would have been so easy to kiss her and allow their bodies to help heal the pain and take away the sense of time wasted, and a mother's love denied. But this was too important to take the easy way out. He needed to find the right words to say to her and make sure she believed them. 'Just like you,' he said slowly, 'I fell in love the first time we met and wished you weren't a princess so I could just go ahead and seduce you.'

'But you seduced me anyway!'

'So I did.' He sighed. 'I don't know if you can appreciate just how out of character that was for me, Zabrina—to shrug off my sense of duty and make as if it didn't matter. And I resented you for that. I resented your power over me.'

'You never wanted a woman to have that perceived power over you again,' she guessed slowly. 'Because you didn't want to risk being hurt again. I understand that. But I will never hurt you, Roman—certainly not intentionally—and if I do, then you must tell me and we'll talk about it.'

He felt his heart lurch. 'I want to marry you,' he breathed. 'If I could marry you here and now, then I would. And because these words do not feature in the official Petrogorian ceremony I will say them to you now. You are the most beautiful woman I've ever met—both inside and out. You are brave and strong and caring and I am blessed to have you in my life. I love you with every fibre of my being, Zabrina. Believe me when I tell you that.'

'Oh, I do,' she whispered, the break of emotion in her voice fracturing her response. 'I so do.'

## EPILOGUE

'OH, ZABRINA, YOU look so beautiful.' Eva clapped her hands over her mouth as she stared up at her big sister. 'Like a real queen!'

'That's because,' said Daria, glancing at the diamond-encrusted watch which had been a bridesmaid gift from her future brother-in-law, 'in approximately an hour's time she will *be* a queen! Are you nervous, Zabrina?'

Zabrina shook her head so that her tulle veil shimmered. 'Not nervous,' she said softly. 'Just happy.' She sighed. So very happy. Because Roman made her happy every second of every day. Soon she would legally be his wife and she couldn't wait. She wanted to start on this new phase of life with him. The two of them, together, as man and wife. She heard the sound of distant trumpets playing a triumphant Petrogorian fanfare and, turning to both her sisters, she gave a smile so wide it felt as if it might split her face in two. 'Shall we go?'

As they nodded, she reached out and took the fragrant white bouquet from Silviana, the gilded doors were flung open and she began to make her way down the aisle towards her beloved King. Embroidered with over one thousand tiny pearls, the train of her dress was heavy, which meant she had to walk slowly. But she *wanted* to walk slowly. She wanted to make the most of every second of her wedding day to her one true love. To the powerful soulmate who had emerged from all the turmoil and heartbreak as a different man, once all the barriers with which he'd surrounded himself had come tumbling down. She could see him standing waiting for her beneath an arch of flowers, his pewter eyes dark, a gleam of anticipation in their depths as he watched her approach.

Faces turned as she walked—some she recognised but many she didn't. Her parents were there, of course. Her mother sitting bolt upright in her recently cleaned 'best' crown and her father paying rather too much attention to the busty redhead seated at the end of the row. Zabrina found herself wondering how they would adapt to being grandparents. Maybe a brand-new generation would bring a little light and freshness into their cynical relationship. You could but hope.

Along the aisle she moved, watching heads incline and women curtsey. There were members of the Albastasian aristocracy alongside their Petrogorian counterparts—as well as royals from Maraban, from Greece and from Britain. There were A-list actors and academics—and a devastatingly handsome but rather dangerous-looking Sheikh called Zulfaqar, whom Daria had been flirting with all during the rehearsal last night. Zabrina intended have a stern word with her sister after the ceremony and warn her off, because apparently the desert King had a terrible reputation with women. But for now, she just wanted to reach her beloved Roman and say her vows.

Her heart was beating very fast as she handed her bouquet to Daria, and as she saw Olga sitting in the front row, with three of her grandchildren, Zabrina felt a great tremble of emotion. Maybe she *was* more nervous than she'd thought. But the moment Roman grasped her fingers within the warmth of his, she felt nothing but a powerful sense of excitement and contentment filling her heart.

'You look beautiful,' he murmured.

She could feel her cheeks grow warm. 'Beautiful for you.'

His eyes narrowed as he looked down at her and she realised that he wasn't seeing the spectacular white gown, or the white tulle veil held in place by a glittering diamond crown. Instead, his gaze was fixed on the chain which hung from her neck. A cheap little silver chain from which dangled a tiny bluebird. Her 'something blue', worn by every traditional bride.

Roman's mother hadn't come to the wedding. During a very exciting video call, she had explained that it was *their* day and she didn't want to take any attention away from that. But they were planning to visit Missouri during their honeymoon and Zabrina's brother was very jealous because Kansas City was the setting of one of his favourite films. And Roman was still getting his head around the fact that he had three half-brothers!

He had also invited her three siblings to stay during the long vacation and said he intended to do this every year if they were keen—and to instruct Alex in the art of kingship at the same time. He was also quietly intending to put a diamond mine in trust, so that her brother should have no financial woes, should he ever inherit a large national debt.

And when Roman had revealed that the priceless emerald and diamond necklace she'd worn on the night of the ball—and which she *hated*—had been a placatory gift intended to make amends for his deception on the train, Zabrina had wasted no time in chiding him. But not for very long. She had asked if she might sell it and use the funds raised to open a women's refuge in Rosumunte and Roman had agreed. As she had observed, the world was going through a bit of a crisis at the moment and people like her needed to lead by example. Because she didn't need *things*. The only thing she needed was him.

He lifted her fingers to his lips and as the trumpets gave their final flourish, he spoke against her skin, but so softly that only she could hear.

'You bring me utter joy, Zabrina. Do you know that?'

'Sssh,' she said. 'The congregation will be reading your lips.'

'I don't care—let them read to their heart's content. I need to say this and I need to say it now. I think you know how much I love you, my Princess. Just as I think you know I always will.'

Blinking back tears, she nodded, trying to compose herself in preparation for the sacred vows she would shortly make. Later, she would bring him even more joy when she told him about the baby growing beneath her breast. A baby they hadn't planned quite so soon, but something told her Roman was going to be a wonderful father.

She wanted to laugh and she wanted to cry. She was caught in the crossfire of so many powerful and conflicting emotions that suddenly she didn't care about lip-readers either.

'I love you too, my darling Roman,' she whispered. 'I love you so very much.'

And a single tear of happiness rolled all the way down her cheek and dripped onto the tiny enamel bluebird.

\* \* \* \* \*

# Queen By Royal Appointment

## *Lucy Monroe*

**Books by Lucy Monroe**

**Harlequin Modern**

*Million Dollar Christmas Proposal*
*Kosta's Convenient Bride*
*The Spaniard's Pleasurable Vengeance*
*After the Billionaire's Wedding Vows...*

**Ruthless Russians**

*An Heiress for His Empire*
*A Virgin for His Prize*

Visit the Author Profile page
at millsandboon.com.au for more titles.

*USA TODAY* bestselling author **Lucy Monroe** lives and writes in the gorgeous Pacific Northwest. While she loves her home, she delights in experiencing different cultures and places in her travels, which she happily shares with her readers through her books. A lifelong devotee of the romance genre, Lucy can't imagine a more fulfilling career than writing the stories in her head for her readers to enjoy.

For my bestie and the sister of my heart, Carolyn.
I'm just so grateful to have you in my life.
Much love!

# CHAPTER ONE

LADY NATALIYA SHEVCHENKO stood outside the private reception room in the Volyarus palace, feeling more like she was entering a war tribunal than going to the family meeting her "uncle," King Fedir, had decreed she attend.

And she was the one about to be on trial for Acts Against the State.

Only, legally, she'd done nothing wrong. Morally, she hadn't either, but she did not expect "Uncle" Fedir to agree.

King Fedir wasn't actually her uncle. He was her mother's cousin, but the two had been raised as close as siblings and he had always called himself Nataliya's uncle.

Taking a deep breath and centering herself, calling on a lifetime of training and all her courage, she indicated with a nod of her head for the guard to pull the ornate door open. His very presence indicated that there were more people in that room than her family.

Unless palace security had changed drastically, family only meant guards at either end of the hall, which there were, so this one meant more dignitaries inside.

Two guesses for who those dignitaries were and she would only need one.

Head held high, Nataliya walked into the luxuriously appointed room. No one would mistake this space with its silk wallpaper, and gilt and brocade furniture, for anything other than a royal's.

Her heels clicked against the marble, before stepping onto the lush carpet that filled the center of the room.

King Fedir sat in an ornate armchair that might as well have been his throne, for all his regal bearing. Except that glower he was giving her. That didn't look so much regal as just really, really annoyed. To his right sat Queen Oxana, her expression entirely enigmatic.

Nataliya's own mother was there too. First cousin to the King and Oxana's best friend, Solomia, Countess Shevchenko, nevertheless occupied a seat of no distinction.

Further from the royal couple than the youngest son of Prince Evengi of Mirrus, the other major player in this farce of judgment, Nataliya's mother sat in an armchair away from everyone else. Whether that had been by her choice or the King's, Nataliya would figure out later.

Right now, she surveyed the other occupants of the opulent room. Prince Evengi, former King of Mirrus, and his three sons sat opposite King Fedir and Queen Oxana. Although Prince Evengi had abdicated his throne to his eldest son, Nikolai, nearly a decade ago, there was no doubt that he was the driving force behind the contract Nataliya and her parents had signed.

A contract that stipulated, among other business and private concerns, that Nataliya would wed the second son to the House of Merikov, Konstantin.

Rumored to be descendants of both Romanov and Deminov blood, the Russian family had established their kingdom on an island between Alaska and Russia, like Volyarus, but Mirrus was in the Chukchi Sea.

They had another thing in common with Volyarus. The basis of their economy had started with mining rare minerals and was now just as profitable a worldwide concern, if not quite as stable as Yurkovich-Tanner, the company that supported Volyarus' economy.

Despite the Ukrainian heritage of Volyarus and its not so amicable history with Russia, King Fedir was determined to cement a family and business alliance with Mirrus, even ten years after that draconian contract was signed.

The only other two occupants of the room were her "uncle's" sons, Maksim, Crown Prince, and his elder brother, the adopted Prince Demyan.

There was a time that their families had been very close.

Although, Nataliya worked for Demyan and saw Maks and his wife on occasion when they were in Seattle, that closeness had been gone for many years.

Breaking protocol, Nataliya ignored the assembled Kings present and smiled her first greeting to her mother. "Hello, Mama. You look well."

"Thank you, Nataliya. It is always good to see you." Mama smiled back, but the expression did not reach her worried eyes, the same warm brown as Nataliya's.

Nataliya was not surprised her father had not been summoned. He was, for all intents and purposes, a nonentity in her life and still very much a persona non grata in Volyarus.

Fifteen years ago, his decision to abandon his Countess and their child to pursue marriage to his most recent mistress had broken the cardinal rules of discretion and putting duty to country above personal considerations.

He had brought ugly attention to the royal family and the throne, and for that, Nataliya doubted he would ever be forgiven.

After greeting her mother, Nataliya gave King Fedir and Queen Oxana her full regard, dropping into a perfect curtsy between their two chairs. "Uncle Fedir, Aunt Oxana, it is a pleasure to see you again."

That might be stretching the truth a bit. And under the circumstance, she had no doubt the man who was in actuality her first cousin, once removed was regretting not rescinding the courtesy title of uncle long before now.

"Nataliya..." King Fedir actually looked at a loss for words, for the first time in Nataliya's memory. He certainly hadn't been the last time they'd spoken.

That time during a phone call, she'd had to schedule two weeks in advance.

She might call him *uncle*, but she didn't enjoy family privileges any longer.

When the silence had stretched, Queen Oxana gave an unreadable look to her husband and stood.

In a move that shocked Nataliya, the Queen approached her in order to give Nataliya the traditional kiss of greeting on both cheeks. "My dear, it is good to see you." The Queen's voice held no insincerity. "Come, you will sit beside me."

The Queen gave a look to her son Maksim, indicating with a regal inclination of her head a couple of equally elegant flicks of her wrist what she wanted done. Despite being Crown Prince, Maks immediately jumped up and oversaw the moving of chairs so that Nataliya's mother sat on her other side, thus cementing in the minds of everyone present just where the Queen stood on the issue to be discussed.

Nataliya's scandalous behavior that had not in fact been scandalous at all.

The King did not look pleased by this turn of events, but Nataliya did not care.

His lack of true concern for her and her mother had been shown fifteen years ago, when they had been forced to emigrate to the States to *protect the good name of the royal family*. Though neither were responsible for the gutter press dragging their names through the mud.

No one spoke for several interminable minutes while both of the older Kings looked on at Nataliya in censure. King Nikolai had a better poker face than even Oxana, however.

Nataliya had no idea what the current King of Mirrus thought of the proceedings and what had prompted them, but even his unreadable regard did things to Nataliya's insides she wished, for the hundredth time at least, it did not.

And because she never lied to herself, she did not try to believe she did not care what that was. He was not the man she was supposed to marry, but he was the only man in the House of Merikov whose opinion carried any weight with her.

When she did not let the clearly strategic silence force her into speech, King Fedir frowned. "You know why you are here?"

"I prefer not to guess."

"You signed a contract promising marriage to Prince Konstantin."

"I did." Though if any man did not live up to his name, it was the one she was not engaged to, but still expected to marry one day. "Ten years ago," she added, letting her tone tell them all what she thought of a decade-long wait for that contract to be fulfilled and yet her being here because she'd done what? Gone on a few dates?

Not that she hadn't wanted just this reaction, but seriously? Get real.

A very unroyal-like sound came from Prince Evengi. "Then explain yourself."

Nataliya stood and gave the King a curtsy, acknowledging him formally, before returning to her seat. One must observe the niceties. "What would you like me to explain?" she asked.

"Do not play obtuse," he barked.

King Nikolai said something in an undertone to his father and the older man yanked his head in acknowledgement.

Prince Konstantin, current heir to his brother's throne, frowned at Nataliya. "You know very well why you have been summoned here, why we have all had to take time from our busy schedules to deal with this mess."

"What mess might that be?" she asked, unimpressed.

Had she curtsied to him? No, she had not and the ice cap on Mount Volyarus would melt before she did.

This man lived and breathed the company that made up the majority of his country's economy. The time he'd taken for his affairs had been negligible and Nataliya had felt no actual envy toward the women he'd taken to his bed and done nothing else to romance.

Ten years ago, she had signed that draconian contract for two equally important reasons. Ten years in which this man had not even made enough time in his schedule to announce the engagement. Ten years during which Nataliya had lived in a stasis that had not upset her all that much, honestly.

Her mother's limbo, she was not so sanguine about. Because one of the clauses of the contract was that Countess Solomia would be able to return to Volyarus upon the marriage of her daughter to the Prince of the House of Merikov.

Without the formalized engagement, much less a marriage, that had not happened.

Her second reason had been no less successful. Nataliya had hoped that by agreeing to marry Konstantin, her inappropriate feelings for his married brother would go away.

While she'd gotten over Nikolai, it wasn't because of her commitment to Konstantin.

"This mess." Konstantin threw down the fashion magazine that had run the "50 First Dates for a Would-Be Princess" article.

"Are you hoping to claim that in the past ten years, you have not dated anyone, Prince Konstantin?" she asked him, with little interest in his answer and aware that the term *date* was in fact a misnomer. "Only I have a whole file full of pictures that would indicate otherwise."

"You had me followed?" he asked with fury, surging to his feet.

Only his brother's hand on his arm kept the angry Prince across the room.

She should probably be intimidated, but anger and posturing held no sway with a woman who had endured years in her father's household. She could have told her erstwhile intended that.

His position as Prince was no more impressive to Nataliya. She'd been raised as part of the royal family of Volyarus until the age of thirteen and had never ceased being the daughter of nobility.

"Perhaps you would like to explain, Uncle Fedir?" she prompted, her own anger a wall of cold ice around her heart, making her voice arctic.

And she did not regret that. At all.

The King of Volyarus winced as his own family and that of the other royal family present gave him varying looks of anger and condemnation.

"Of course we kept track of Prince Konstantin, but it was in no way nefarious." He made a dismissive gesture. "I have no doubt you had your interests watched, as well." He indicated Nataliya with a tip of his head.

She wasn't offended being referred to in that manner. The King's ability to hurt her had passed years ago.

"You shared your investigator's findings with your niece?" Nikolai asked, his voice laced with censure, but no shock at the other royal's actions.

If he'd given a bit of that censure to his brother, Nataliya would have respected him more. And something in her expression must have told him so because he gave her a strange look.

"I did not," King Fedir denied categorically.

"Then how?"

"I believe I can answer that," Prince Demyan, who had remained silent up until then, said.

Interesting that her mother and Queen Oxana were the only other women who had been invited to this ludicrous tribunal.

King Fedir stared at his other son. "How?" he barked.

"You know I use hackers to watch over our interests," Prince Demyan said, clearly unafraid of making such an admission in the rarified company.

Not one of these royals would voluntarily share *anything* being said in this room right now.

King Fedir nodded with a single jerk of his head.

"Nataliya is one of those hackers."

"The best one," Nataliya added. "Not to put too fine a point on it."

Demyan actually smiled at her, but then they were still friends, if no longer as close as siblings. "Yes, the best one."

"You did not assign her to watch over her own errant fiancé," the King asked, obviously appalled at the idea.

"He is *not* my fiancé," Nataliya said fiercely.

"No!" Demyan said at the same time.

"Then how?" Her uncle looked at her. He had asked her the first time she'd brought the photos to his attention.

She'd avoided answering then, not wanting a lecture about her actions to derail the reason for their discussion. She'd still hoped he would put her happiness somewhere in the realm of his priorities three months ago. Now she had no such illusions.

She shrugged. "I like to practice my skills. I was looking through files and noticed one with his name on it."

Everyone in the room seemed shocked by her actions.

"You hacked into your King's private files?" Nikolai asked, nothing in his tone indicating what he thought about that.

But his deep voice reverberated through her being nonetheless. If she could have chosen one person *not* to be here for this farce, it would be King Nikolai of Mirrus.

"Not exactly. I hacked into Demyan's files." She frowned. "In fact, I was looking for security breach points. To shore them up. I *like* Demyan. I did not want him to be vulnerable to other corporate or politically motivated hackers."

"Thank you," Demyan said amidst gasps and condemnation by others.

"And so because you were angry my son had not paid you enough attention since signing the contract, and in a misguided fit of jealousy and feminine pique, you thought to embarrass him into action?"

She stared at the old King of Mirrus, flabbergasted at his interpretation of her actions.

"You think I was *jealous*?" she asked in icy disbelief she made no effort to soften.

"Naturally," Konstantin said, ignoring her tone as he had her person for the past decade. "Only you miscalculated my reaction."

"Did I?" she asked, doubting very much that she had.

"Your weekly online auction of the items I sent to you in my effort to court you prior to announcing our formal engagement made me look the fool."

The *wooing* gifts had started arriving exactly one month after her appeal to King Fedir to renegotiate the terms of the contract, no doubt prompted by him. Konstantin's attempt at courtship had been as impersonal as the greeting between strangers at a State function and with even less effort put behind it.

"The proceeds go to a very deserving charity," she pointed out, not at all unhappy with the direction this conversation was heading, and not particularly bothered that Konstantin had found her disposal of the gifts inappropriate.

Maksim swore, a pithy Ukrainian curse that shocked the people around him. But he was looking at Nataliya with reluctant respect. He knew.

Nataliya couldn't help smiling at the man who had been as close as a brother until she was thirteen years old, and her entire family was ripped from her. She even winked.

He laughed.

"You find this amusing?" Prince Konstantin asked with angry reproach.

"I find this situation laughable, yes," Maksim said without apology in his manner, or tone.

And Nataliya wondered if the future King of Volyarus was

more reasonable than his father and understood how over-the-top everyone's reaction was.

Not that she had not relied on that extreme reaction, but she still found it archaic, chauvinistic and not just a little ridiculous. Her manipulations would not have been possible if a gross double standard did not exist in the minds of almost every male in this room.

"You think your cousin is amusing, though her actions have destroyed our families' plans of a merger?" Konstantin asked furiously.

"Oh, there will be a business merger," Demyan said before his brother could answer. "Both our countries will benefit, but more to the point, Mirrus cannot afford to back out. The repercussions would be devastating for Mirrus Global and your country's economy."

"I will not marry her," Konstantin said implacably.

His father looked pained, and his brother, the King, frowned, but Nataliya felt elation pour through her. She had won. Because regardless of what the rest of the people in this room wanted, his words had just released *her* from her promise. And ultimately, that was all that mattered to her.

She'd only been eighteen, but she'd signed the contract in good faith and had been unwilling to simply renege. Her integrity would not allow it. She was not her father.

King Fedir suddenly looked old, and tired in a way she'd never noticed before. "That is exactly what you wanted, though, wasn't it?" he asked her.

"I could have done without the name calling and disgusting double standard, but yes."

King Fedir shook his head, clearly confused by her reaction. "I thought you wanted your mother settled back in her home country."

"Ten years ago, I wanted that more than anything. *I* wanted to come home, or at least be able to visit often."

"And that has changed?" King Fedir asked, sounding as fatigued as he looked.

"My mother has finally found peace with her life in America."

Queen Oxana looked wounded. "You don't want to come home?" she asked her best friend of more than thirty years.

Mama drew herself up, her dignity settled around her like a force field, making Nataliya nothing but proud. "My home is in America now."

"You do not mean that." Queen Oxana had the effrontery to sound hurt when she'd done nothing to stop Mama and Nataliya's exile fifteen years ago.

"I do."

"She does," Nataliya said with satisfaction, and was so happy about that she could cry. "You and your husband exiled my mother and me for the sins of my father. And though he knew how important that clause in the contract was to us both, he made no effort to press for fulfillment of the marriage merger." Now it would not happen at all.

Queen Oxana's expression was troubled. "You were too young to tie down to marriage when it was signed."

"But not too young to sign it? Not too young to be used as a political and business pawn?" Nataliya shook her head in disbelief.

"We all have duty we must adhere to," the Queen said, though with less fervent conviction than she used to.

"Our duty included exile. Looking back, I realize that asking more of my daughter was obscene." Mama could do regal disapproval as well as any queen.

"You know why we had to ask the sacrifice of you," King Fedir said to his cousin.

But Mama made Nataliya so proud yet again when she shook her head. "No, I never understood your decision to sacrifice me, a woman who was a better sister to you than Svitlana ever was.

I spent years grieving the loss of my homeland, but I grieve no longer."

"And so you decided to break the contract?" Nikolai asked, this time his opinion clear for any to hear the disapproval and disappointment in his tone.

Nataliya met his gaze squarely. "My mother told me five years ago that she was not sure she would move back to Volyarus permanently, even if she could."

His brows drew together in a thoughtful frown. "Then what prompted your dating and the very public rejection of my brother's attempt to court you?"

"There is so much wrong with that question, I don't even know where to start." Was he as draconian as his father?

Nataliya had never believed it of Nikolai.

"Try. Please."

It was the *please* that did it.

"One, I was *never* engaged to your brother. I was contracted to be engaged and married at a later date, which was never specified. Not exactly good contract negotiations," she criticized King Fedir. "So, I *could* have been dating all along."

Heck, she could have been sleeping around. She'd had no legal or moral obligation to go to her marriage bed a virgin, and the stipulation of her chastity or lack of romantic social life until the marriage had not even been alluded to in the contract.

She'd read it through, all thirty-six pages of it, before embarking on the dating article.

"But you did not date before this." Nikolai's words made it very clear that his family had in fact had her watched.

She shrugged, not particularly caring that a *lady* was never supposed to be so dismissive. "I did not want to risk developing an emotional attachment that would have made keeping my promise difficult, or possibly even impossible."

Nikolai nodded in approval of her words. "Very wise."

"So, by converse, you consider that your brother has been foolish?" she asked, unable to resist.

Konstantin cursed.

Nikolai looked at his brother and then back to her. "Considering the outcome of his choices, I would say that is a given."

"My choices?" Konstantin demanded with umbrage. "I was doing my best to protect and expand the business interests of our country so that we did not lose our independent status. How does that make me the bad guy here?"

Nataliya might have agreed with Konstantin, except for two things. One, he'd had affairs, if not dates. Two, he'd acted like an ass about *her* innocent dating.

If he hadn't, she might have even felt compelled to honor the contract.

But Nikolai ignored him. "You said *one*, there are other things wrong with my question?"

"Second, it is obvious that what prompted my actions was my desire *not* to marry a man who so obviously had no more personal integrity than my father."

"I am not like your philandering father." The Prince took clear offence with the comparison. "We were not engaged!"

Nataliya looked at Konstantin with a frown. "If that is your attitude, then how do you explain refusing to marry me because I *dated* other men while you were having *sex* with other women?"

Konstantin's mouth opened and closed without him saying anything.

"Anything else?" Nikolai asked her.

"Do you believe that waiting ten years to fulfill the terms of a contract is keeping good faith in that contract?" she asked instead of answering.

"There were circumstances," Nikolai reminded her, almost gently.

She nodded in agreement. "Your father's heart attack, followed by your own ascension to the throne and your brother having to take over more business responsibility."

"Yes."

"That was eight *years* ago."

"Our family was in mourning," Konstantin said snidely. "Surely you did not expect a formal announcement during that time."

He was referring to the death of his brother's wife, the new Queen, and trying to make her feel small doing it, but Nataliya wasn't going to let anyone in this room make her feel less than. *She* wasn't the one who had dismissed finer feelings or responsibilities.

"It is customary to observe a period of mourning for one year."

And it had been five. It didn't need to be said. They all knew. Again, the timing did not justify the ten-year wait.

For her, or her mother.

"No one from Volyarus approached me about formalizing the engagement," Konstantin pointed out, like that was some kind of fact in his favor.

"Are you saying that you only fulfill the terms of a contract when you are pushed into doing so?" she asked, not impressed and letting that show.

Konstantin glowered. "You have all but admitted you don't want the marriage," he accused rather than answer her question.

She wouldn't deny it. "I do not." While she'd never actually *wanted* to marry this man, she had wanted Mama to be able to return to the bosom of her family.

Nataliya had come to realize both she and her mom were better off without a family that could eject them from their lives so easily, but that was not how it had been ten years ago.

"If you had realized you didn't want to marry my son, surely you should have taken less scandalous steps to insure it." Prince Evengi sounded more baffled than angry at this point. "You could simply have reneged on the contract."

She cast a glance at her uncle before answering. "I approached King Fedir with my desire to do just that."

"And?"

"And he threatened to remove financial support of my mother."

"You are not worried he will do that now?" Nikolai asked her with a frowning side glance toward King Fedir.

"He could try, but I think everyone in this room is aware of how far *I* am willing to go to protect her."

"Are you threatening me, child?" King Fedir asked her, sounding more hurt than worried.

She gave him a cool look, hoping it conveyed just how very little she cared about his hurt feelings after all he had put her mother through. "I am telling you that all actions have consequences and I guarantee you do not want to live with the ones that would come from you doing something so reprehensible."

"Solomia, talk to your daughter!" King Fedir demanded, his shock palpable.

"I am very proud of you, Nataliya, you know that, yes?"

"Yes."

The King frowned. "That is not what I meant."

"You are upset because she carries the ruthlessness that is such a strong trait in our family?" Mama asked her cousin, their King.

Nikolai looked at Nataliya, his expression assessing. "But you did make a promise. *You* signed that contract," Nikolai said.

"I did." Nataliya could wish she hadn't been so eager to *make up* for her father's sins at eighteen, but she couldn't deny she had signed the contract.

"And you take your own promises very seriously."

"I do." Hence her need to get Prince Konstantin to back out of the contract.

Nataliya might no longer feel it was her responsibility to compensate for her father's behavior, but she still understood duty only too well. And she may have been exiled, but her integrity as a member of the royal family was still very much intact.

"She was willing to renege on the contract," Konstantin pointed out. "Her personal ethics cannot be that strong."

King Fedir drew himself up, his expression forbidding. "On the contrary, my *niece* came to me and asked me to negotiate different terms, sure that if the suggestion came from me, you would be more than willing to do so. At no time did she intimate our family should simply *renege*."

Nataliya didn't know what the point was of her cousin harping on how he thought of her as a niece. She would have thought King Fedir would want to distance himself from her at this point. Just as he'd done fifteen years ago.

Nikolai nodded his understanding. "But you refused?"

"I did, more the fool I."

Personally, Nataliya agreed with him. Her uncle had been a fool to think that she would sit meekly by, when in her estimation, she should never have been asked to sign the darn thing in the first place.

"But we raised a lot of money for Mama and Aunt Oxana's favorite charity," she pointed out, not entirely facetiously.

The charity that helped families stay near their children receiving treatment for cancer and other life-threatening illnesses was very dear to Nataliya's heart, as well. However, no one else seemed to find that the benefit she did, if all the gloomy faces were to go by.

"All that aside, you still consider yourself bound by the terms of the contract, do you not?" Nikolai asked her.

She stared at him, not sure what he was trying to get at. "Prince Konstantin has verbally repudiated his willingness to abide by its terms in front of witnesses."

"He did."

She smiled, relief that the current King of Mirrus wasn't going to try to push her to marry his brother despite either of their desires.

"The contract, as it is written, still stands," Nikolai said, his tone brooking no argument.

Shock made Nataliya lightheaded as dread filled her. "Your brother denounced the contract," she reminded him, even though she shouldn't have to, because Nikolai had just agreed that was the case. "I am under no obligation to marry him now."

"But you *are* under obligation to marry a prince of the House of Merikov," Nikolai said implacably.

Gasps sounded, his father demanded what he meant, but Nikolai ignored it all, his attention focused entirely on Nataliya.

Her brain was whirling, trying to parse out what he meant. Her gaze skittered to the youngest Merikov Prince. Dimitri, called Dima by his friends of which she counted herself one, though they'd met on only a few occasions, they had chatted more via text and email than she had with Konstantin in past years.

Not even out of the university yet, Dima was looking with utter horror at his eldest brother.

"I will not enter into such a bargain with a child," Nataliya vowed, knowing being called a child would prick her friend and unable to pass up the chance to tease him.

"You were four years younger when you signed that contract ten years ago," Nikolai pointed out without correcting her use of the term *child*, earning a frown from Dima.

"And still desperate to return home. I'm not that teenager any longer either." And she would not allow done to Dima, what had been done to her. She *liked* the twenty-two-year-old Prince.

"Regardless of what your reasons were for signing the contract, you did so. And while you were only eighteen, you were not a minor. You are obligated to its terms unless both parties agree to different ones."

"I will not marry either of your brothers."

"I am glad you did not include me in that categorical refusal." His smile was more like an apex predator baring its teeth.

# CHAPTER TWO

"You?" Nataliya asked faintly.

No, Nikolai could not be saying what Nataliya thought he was saying. "You're not a prince." The contract stipulated a prince. "You're a king," her voice rose and cracked on the word *king*, but seriously…?

He had to have lost his mind.

Ten years ago, she would have jumped at the chance to marry this man, but he had only had eyes for the beautiful socialite he had ended up married to. Naively believing that marriage to his brother would cure Nataliya of her adolescent feelings for the unattainable Crown Prince, she'd signed that stupid, bloody, awful contract in good faith.

"But you were married." To the beautiful, sophisticated woman who had become his Queen. Perfect for him in every way, she'd died tragically in a skiing accident. Only later had anyone realized the new Queen had been pregnant at the time.

"And left a widower five years ago."

A widower who would always love the wife he had lost. The fact that he had shown no interest in another woman since the young Queen's death showed that. Nataliya could not imagine a less appealing marriage to her.

"But…" She didn't know what to say. This was insane.

"You cannot want to marry this woman," Nikolai's father said, voicing Nataliya's own thoughts.

And probably the thoughts of everyone else in the room.

Only Demyan was nodding and Maksim looked satisfied. King Fedir looked astounded. Queen Oxana looked enigmatic, like always. But Nataliya's mom? She looked worried. And that, more than anything, solidified the sense of impending doom settling over Nataliya.

Her *mom* thought he was serious.

"I cannot?" Nikolai asked imperiously.

"She's made a spectacle of herself with that ridiculous article and the accompanying blog posts." Prince Evengi almost looked apologetic in the glance he cast at her. "She's dated no less than ten men, that we know of!"

"She has not had sex with any of them."

"How can you know that?" Prince Evengi asked.

But Nataliya wanted to know too. She *hadn't* had sex with any of them. Or anyone at all. But how could Nikolai know that?

She'd made sure that even if she was being followed by someone on behalf of the House of Merikov, like Demyan had kept tabs on Prince Konstantin, circumstances would be ambiguous enough that no one could be certain. She'd let two of her dates stay the night. On the sofa, but they hadn't left her apartment until morning.

So, there was no way he could *know* she hadn't had sex.

Only he seemed arrogantly sure of himself.

King Nikolai gave her a measuring look before returning his regard to his father. "Because her integrity would not allow her to do so when the contract is still in place."

"You heard her—she doesn't consider the contract a deterrent," Prince Konstantin said derisively.

"She knows *you* didn't consider it such—that does not mean she has not."

"You expected me to be celibate the last decade?" Konstantin asked, shocked.

Before Nikolai answered, the old King cleared his throat meaningfully. "This is not the place, or time, for this discussion." He turned to his eldest son. "You are not obligated to fulfill the contract on behalf of your brother."

"On that, I do not agree."

And something became very clear to Nataliya, besides the fact that being spoken about like she wasn't there was *extremely* annoying. But this man had an entirely different code of ethics and standard of integrity than his brother.

In truth, Nataliya had never doubted it, but then she'd always thought the best of the man who had become King to save his father's life. The man who she had fallen in love with at age fifteen and had only stopped pining for when she was about twenty.

Funnily enough, it had been his wife's death that had finally severed Nataliya's unrequited yearning. She'd hurt for him. Grieved from afar on his behalf at the loss of his beloved wife and unborn child and somewhere in the grief, she'd been able to put away her own longing.

It had just felt so selfish. So wrong.

"I can't marry you," she said in a voice much weaker than her normal assertive certainty.

"Oh, but you can, and you will."

The room erupted into pandemonium.

Even Queen Oxana voiced her disbelief at the turn of events. But Nikolai? Just sat there, looking immovable.

"The contract stipulates a prince of your house," Nataliya reminded him, ignoring everyone else. "You cannot insist I fulfill it by marrying you."

"I was a prince when you signed it, therefore the terms referred to me equally to my brothers."

"No. That's not right."

He just looked at her.

Suddenly, Queen Oxana stood and put her hand out to Nataliya. "That is enough discussion on this topic for present. You and your mother can join me in my apartments."

Nataliya might have argued, but her mother stood and somehow she found herself swept out of the reception room between the two women.

"I can't believe they made you sign that contract!" Gillian, wife to Crown Prince Maksim, exclaimed. "You were just a baby."

"I was eighteen."

"Too young to sign your life away."

"Welcome to life in the royal family," Nataliya said.

She'd left Mama and Oxana to themselves, knowing the two women needed to have a talk that had been fifteen years coming, and had searched out Gillian and her adorable children, finding them taking advantage of the summer sunshine in the palace gardens.

Nataliya loved watching the children play, knowing that the *normalcy* surrounding this very royal family was all down to Gillian's influence.

Gillian frowned, her expression going rock stubborn. "My children will be forced into that kind of agreement over my dead body. They won't be making any decisions about marriage until they are mature enough to do so."

"And when might that be?" Maksim asked drolly as he walked up. "When they are fifty?"

"If they aren't ready to make the decision before then, then yes!" Oh, Gillian was mad. "It's despicable that Nataliya was pressed into signing away her life at such a young age."

On Nataliya's behalf. And Nataliya couldn't say that didn't feel good.

Even her beloved mother had wanted her to sign that contract ten years ago.

Maks looked at Nataliya, something like apology in his brown eyes. "I offered to renegotiate the contract on more favorable terms for Mirrus Global if your participation could be removed from it."

"And?" Gillian demanded when Nataliya remained silent.

"His Highness refused. He considers it a point of family honor for him to fulfill the contract. He's livid with both his father and his brother for the way they spoke to you."

"So, he doesn't agree with the whole misogynistic double standard?" Gillian asked, having gotten the whole story from Nataliya.

"No. He says that neither Nataliya, nor Konstantin were under constraint not to date before a formal engagement was announced."

"Nice of him to absolve his brother too," Nataliya couldn't help saying.

"Did *you* expect him to be celibate?" Maks asked, sounding like he thought it was unlikely.

"I was," Nataliya reminded him.

Maks opened his mouth, but Gillian forestalled him. "Think very hard before you speak again, Maks, because my respect for *your* integrity is on the line here."

He stared at his wife, like he couldn't believe she'd said that.

"I know you are arrogant, but are you seriously going to try to say that Nataliya should have been happy to live in limbo while Prince Konstantin was not?"

"No. That's not what I was going to say at all. I agreed with King Nikolai that neither Nataliya, nor his own brother were under constraints not to date."

"But if I had slept around, what would you have said?" Nataliya couldn't help asking.

Maks's mouth twisted wryly. "That would have depended on the results, wouldn't it?"

"What do you mean?" Nataliya asked.

Maks looked to where the children played, a soft smile curving his usually firm mouth. "Our firstborn child is testament to how unexpected results can come from a night of passion."

"And if the little surprise had been the result of one of Konstantin's many..." Nataliya paused, unsure what term she wanted to use.

Indiscretion implied that Konstantin shouldn't have been having sex with those women. And she wasn't sure she wanted to imply that.

She only knew she didn't want to marry a man who had had so many sexual partners during the ten years he had not made any move to fulfill the terms of the contract they had both signed. Whether Konstantin liked it, or not, to Nataliya, that indicated a man who was both a womanizer and who did not keep his promises. Like her father.

"Sex partners?" Gillian offered, bringing a gasp of outrage from her royal husband.

Gillian rolled her eyes. "Don't be a prude, Maks."

"You are a princess now, Gillian. Maybe you could remember that."

"And this is the twenty-first century. Maybe *you* could remember *that*."

Nataliya found herself grinning despite the stress of the day. "She's got your number, Maks."

"And does King Nikolai have yours?"

"What do you mean?"

"He's completely convinced that you will adhere to the contract."

She didn't want to admit that he might be right. Integrity and honor were every bit as important to her as they were to the King of Mirrus. "I just don't understand why he's saying he wants to marry me."

"Well, he has to marry again at some point," Maks pointed out prosaically.

"But *me*?"

"Perhaps, I could answer that." Nikolai's voice hit Nataliya in the center of her being.

She spun and found him watching her with an implacability that sent a shiver through her.

"I wish you would. This idea that you have to fulfill the contract in place of your brother is ridiculous."

His enigmatic regard turned forbidding. "My honor is not a matter for ridicule."

"But it's not *your* honor in question."

Satisfaction gleamed in his steely gray gaze. "So, you acknowledge that it *is* a matter of honor."

"Prince Konstantin was the Prince referred to in that contract. Everyone knows that," she said, sidestepping the honor issue.

The King settled quite casually onto the fountain rim beside where Nataliya sat. "But it was not in fact, my brother who signed the contract."

"Why wasn't it?" She'd been required to sign on her own behalf and had only noticed that the former King had signed it on behalf of his son, when she'd read it before embarking on her dating campaign.

"In contracts of that sort, it is quite natural for the reigning sovereign to sign on behalf of his house. When I was crowned King, all promises made by my father in matters of state became mine to fulfill."

"So, renegotiate the contract." He had just said he had the power to do so.

"After leaving you and your mother's lives in limbo for ten years? I think not."

"But I don't mind."

"I do."

"I'm not queen material."

"If you marry me, you will be a princess. The title of Queen is bestowed only at my will."

And of course the wife he didn't love wouldn't be worthy of the title, not like the woman he had married and lost. "You know what I mean."

"But I do not agree."

"I'm a computer programmer, not a princess."

"You are a member of the royal family of Volyarus."

Like she needed reminding. "Not so you would notice. Not for the last fifteen years."

Maks made a sound of disagreement, but Nataliya just gave him a look. "When your father exiled me and my mom for my dad's indiscretions, we effectively lost our family. It's no use pretending anything different."

"Nevertheless, you *are* of royal blood, a lady in your own right," Nikolai pressed.

"No one calls me Lady Nataliya." At least no one in her current life.

"I'm sure that's not true. Protocol is observed here in the castle."

"I don't spend time here."

"And yet here you are."

"To answer for crimes that were not in fact crimes at all."

His smile did not reach his eyes. "No, not crimes, but you knew exactly what you were doing when you embarked on that article."

"It was for a perfectly respectable fashion magazine, not a scandal rag."

He nodded. "Well written and the tie in with fashion that you do not in fact have a great deal of interest in was clever."

"My friend thought so."

"Your friend?"

"The contributing editor who wrote the article and blog posts."

"I wondered how you had arranged the article."

"Jenna wanted to do the article but she's in a committed relationship, so she couldn't do the dates."

"Commendable."

"I thought so."

"Yes, you would."

"What is that supposed to mean?" she asked belligerently.

He spread his hands in a gesture of no offense. "You are a

woman of definite integrity. Your standards for acceptable behavior match my own."

"How can you say that?" she asked, shocked by how he viewed her. "I hack computers for a living."

"But not for nefarious purposes or your own gain."

"No, of course not." What did he think, she was a criminal?

No, she realized. It was that very certainty that she had *standards* that made her appealing to him.

"Plenty of women who would love to be a princess have integrity," she pointed out dryly.

"But you are the one who signed a contract promising to marry a prince of my house."

"But you aren't a prince."

"We've been over this."

"I just don't understand how you can say you want to marry me."

"Ten years ago, you were vetted and found acceptable."

"For your brother!"

"For any prince of the House of Merikov. That was the way the contract was written."

"That's not how I read it."

"It is standard language for such a contract," Maks pointed out, almost apologetically.

"But that's draconian." Gillian sounded shocked.

Neither the Crown Prince or the King looked particularly bothered by that condemnation.

Nikolai brushed the strands of hair away that the gentle wind had blown across Nataliya's face. She wondered if he even realized he'd done it, but she'd noticed. To the very core of her, a place she'd thought dormant.

Nataliya no longer thought about him *that* way.

But the simple act of him sitting down beside her, close enough she could feel the heat of his body, sparked undeniable sexual desire.

She realized he was watching her as the silence stretched.

One of the children started to cry and both Maks and Gillian went over.

Nataliya and Nikolai weren't alone, but it felt like they were.

"You agreed that you signed the contract in good faith." His words didn't register at first.

She was too busy staring into his gorgeous gray eyes, but then her brain caught up with her mouth and she said, "And your brother reneged in front of witnesses today."

"But not on behalf of our house, only himself."

Nataliya surged to her feet. "I'm not eighteen anymore—no one is pushing me into fulfilling that darn contract."

"If you are the woman I believe you to be, you will convince yourself of the rightness of doing your duty."

"To marry you?" she asked in disbelief that simply would not go away.

"To marry me."

"Good luck."

His smile was even more dangerous this time. "I never leave anything to chance."

Ignoring manners and protocol, she turned on her heel and headed back into the palace without another word.

A blooming orchid with tiny buds indicating more flowers to come was sitting on the table in her room when she reached it. Nataliya stopped and stared.

What was this?

She picked up the card sitting beside it and felt a shiver go down her spine at the slashing writing.

*With my compliments, Nikolai.*

In his own hand. Not typed like the ones she'd had delivered from Konstantin.

She recognized the orchid too, from the very distinctive pot it was planted in. She'd been to the castle in Mirrus for the funeral of Nikolai's wife.

There was an orchid room where his mother used to grow

the plants, now overseen by a world-renowned horticulturist. All of the orchids in that room were planted in the same style of pot with the Merikov crest in fine gold against the eggshell white of the ceramic.

Nataliya had spent a great deal of time in the orchid room during her three-day stay at the castle five years before. And she had learned that every orchid growing there had a special history and most were incredibly rare specimens.

Nikolai had caught her there more than once, because as he'd told her, he found comfort in the room his mother had spent so much time in.

Nataliya had offered to leave, but the young King had refused, asking her to keep him company. And that's what she'd done, sitting in silence with a man who was grieving the loss of his wife and unborn child.

Nataliya could not make sense of the orchid being here. As gifts went, it was very special. But he couldn't know that she'd started growing orchids after that visit. Nothing nearly so impressive as the Merikov collection, but lovely plants that gave her peace and joy caring for them.

Even if he had known something almost no one else did, Nikolai could not have gotten the plant delivered since the recent confrontation. Not even with a helicopter or the palace's personal jet.

Nikolai couldn't have known he planned to take his brother's place before the meeting today, so why the orchid?

Whatever the reason, the plant was beautiful and she knew how very special it was that he'd given it to her. She grabbed her phone and texted the number no one but his closest family and advisors was supposed to have.

Thank you for the orchid. It's beautiful.

His reply came back only seconds later.

I'm glad you like it, my lady. It was one of my mother's favorites.

Why did that *my* feel like it should be bolded? Like he was staking claim? And his assertion this had been one of his mother's plants? How was Nataliya supposed to feel about that?

Special. She felt special. And that was very, very dangerous.

Nataliya had the very distinct feeling that if the King decided to court her, it was going to be a different prospect than the past two months' worth of impersonal gifts sent via Konstantin's staff.

Nataliya remembered that fleeting thought a week later when she looked up from her computer to the sight of Demyan looking amazed.

It was not a look she'd ever seen on her imposing cousin's features before.

Needing a chance to come to terms with Nikolai's demand she fulfill the contract, *with him*, Nataliya had left Volyarus on her cousin's private plane before dinner the night of the big confrontation.

She'd been really grateful that Maks hadn't even blinked at putting his plane at her disposal. He'd assured her that he would smooth things over with his father and their royal visitors.

"You're still my family, Nataliya, and I can only apologize for not realizing that the exile to America was not voluntary on your mother's part. Had I known I would have redressed the issue."

She'd stared at him. "You were like my big brother. I thought you didn't care."

"My father told me that you and your mother needed space and distance to overcome the humiliation from your father. I believed him."

And then Nataliya had found herself being hugged by her cousin for the first time in over a decade and it had been all she could do not to break down and cry.

Demyan had come to her to say much the same thing when

he got back from Volyarus, adding that he'd never stopped considering her a close member of his family.

Now he stood there, with a really weird expression on his face.

"What?" she demanded.

"You got a new computer."

"So?" She hadn't asked Demyan for new hardware though.

"It's from King Nikolai."

Well, that was…*different*. "He gave me a computer."

Demyan nodded.

"Why do you look so weird?" she demanded.

"It's a prototype. Even I couldn't get my hands on this build with the new chipset."

That stopped her. "How did you know?"

"Because I had to sign an NDA just to take possession and you've got one to sign too. The company rep is waiting in the conference room."

This was crazy, but she couldn't pretend she wasn't excited. She *loved* new technology and like Demyan had said, this was something even he hadn't been able to finagle out of the manufacturer before early release.

There wasn't just one computer waiting for her in the conference room. There were two. The second was top of the line of available technology and came with a note. *Raise some more money for a very worthy cause.*

Okay, she was impressed. Not just that he'd chosen a gift she would love, her own prototypical, super-slim, ultrafast laptop, but because he'd seen what no one else had. How much she'd enjoyed raising money for the charity she'd chosen. And he was telling her, he wasn't intimidated by the idea she would auction off his gifts.

He expected it. But he provided gifts *to* auction. Over the next two weeks, every gift she received from him came with a personally written note and some kind of duplicate or equivalent item for her to put in the online charity auction.

He also texted her, several times throughout the day. Some innocuous texts. Some even funny. Others surprising, like when he asked her opinion of Dima's desire to take a gap year between university and graduate school. Apparently, when Prince Evengi abdicated his rule to his son, he'd abdicated all major family decisions, as well.

And then there were the texts that drove her batty.

How many children do you want?

Do you object to living in the palace after we marry?

As if her agreement was a foregone conclusion. It annoyed her, but there was this tiny frisson of excitement too. Nikolai was a really special guy and he wanted to marry her.

She knew he wasn't emotionally attached in any way, wasn't even sure if he found her sexually desirable, but he definitely hadn't backed down on his stance.

She knew his father wasn't happy about it. Konstantin wasn't happy. Demyan had told her, and he'd heard it from Maks. But Nikolai was a king and a king who apparently wasn't going to let anyone else dictate his future.

Not like he was doing his best to dictate hers, Nataliya reminded herself.

When the couture gown, shoes, jewelry and handbag arrived along with its auction equivalent and an invitation to dinner and a play two days hence, Nataliya could do nothing but stare in consternation at the boxes littering her desk.

Demyan stood, leaning against the doorjamb. "So, he's finally moving this courtship into the dating stage."

"Can you date a king?" she asked, a tinge of hysteria touching her voice.

"I guess you're going to find out."

"He thinks that stupid contract has me all sewn up."

"No, he thinks your sense of duty and integrity has you all

sewn up. But give the guy his due, he's setting the rest of his life up to fulfill his own sense of honor."

"I know you think duty is all there is to life—"

"Not since I married Chanel, but I won't pretend duty didn't play a big part in that."

"And that duty nearly destroyed your marriage." She'd been invited to the wedding. She'd seen the other woman's reaction before Chanel had disappeared from the reception without her groom.

And frankly, Nataliya had known all along what was going on. She was nosy and she had more ways than most of finding out what she wanted to know.

"We all make sacrifices for family and the good of Volyarus."

And she knew that despite how close he'd come to losing his wife, Demyan still saw duty in all capitals when he thought about it. Chanel just made sure that there was more to his life than a single concept.

"I made my sacrifice ten years ago, to provide a way for my mother to return home."

"And now she no longer wants to return to Volyarus full-time."

"But my sacrifice is still there, hanging over my head."

"Maybe it won't turn out to be such a sacrifice after all."

He could say that. Demyan's own sacrifice had led to the love of his life and children he adored. Hers could lead nowhere but heartache. Nikolai would never love her as he'd loved his first wife and even if she no longer felt the same things for him she once had, Nataliya didn't want to be trapped in a marriage to a man whose heart was locked in the past.

# CHAPTER THREE

NATALIYA WAS NOT at all surprised when her phone dinged with a text ten minutes before the limo was supposed to arrive for her.

Nikolai had texted updates on his schedule and arrival throughout the day.

Like he wanted to make sure she was ready, like he worried she might get the time wrong, or something. Or maybe, he just wanted to be sure she was going to show up. After all, not once had he actually asked her to join him for dinner and the play. No, just the delivery of the dress and tickets which she doubted very sincerely they would have to show to take their seats.

She had no doubt that between him and his security detail, they were taking up an entire box at the theater.

As a king, he was used to getting his way. And she'd been, oh, so tempted to simply not be here tonight, but the truth was, she and Nikolai needed to talk.

Nataliya needed him to understand that his honor would not be compromised by renegotiating the contract.

A sharp knock sounded at the door and Nataliya smoothed the opalescent gray designer dress down her long body. She had to admit that Nikolai had good taste in women's fashion. Though considering the perfectly coiffed fashionista he'd been married to, Nataliya should not be surprised.

"Showtime," said Jenna, her friend who had written the "50 First Dates for a Would-Be Princess" article.

She'd come over today to help Nataliya prep for her date with a king, doing Nataliya's makeup and hair, styling her so that Nataliya looked better than she had for any of those first dates.

Because Nataliya had not wanted to look like a consolation date in any of the pictures that were bound to be taken by the paparazzi.

Not because she wanted to try to look her best for Nikolai.

Nataliya opened the door to her condo and stepped back in shock that the King stood on the other side, two of his security detail hovering in the background. The others were no doubt securing the building.

"You didn't need to come up," she said, unable to hide her surprise at his presence.

Wearing a light custom-made charcoal gray suit that accentuated his six-foot-four, well-muscled frame, his presence sent a hurricane rioting through her senses.

Every part of her body suddenly felt more alive, more *present* and it was hard to take each new breath.

"May I come inside?"

She jolted, realizing she was letting the King of Mirrus stand in the hall like a salesman. "Of course."

Nataliya stepped back and he followed her inside, one of his security men accompanying him to do a routine sweep of her condo while the other pulled the door shut behind them to stand at attention on the other side.

Neither Demyan, nor Maks practiced such heavy security protocols when they were in Seattle.

But then, Nikolai was a king already, despite being only thirty-five years old.

"The dress looks every bit as beautiful on you as I thought it would." He took her in, his gray eyes going molten with an expression she had never expected to see in his eyes.

Desire.

"Thank you." She swallowed. "You could have sent a car for me to meet you at the restaurant."

Who had ever heard of a king calling for his date in person?

She'd made the mistake of telling him how impersonal and detached she'd considered his brother's overtures. And Nikolai had assured her, his would not be.

But seriously? Could he say *overkill*?

"Surely not." He reached out and brushed a proprietary finger along her collarbone. "This will be our first public appearance together. Calling for you at your door is only the most basic courtesy."

Heat whooshed through her body from that one small touch and Nataliya was momentarily unable to respond.

"Well, I'm impressed," Jenna said forthrightly.

Nikolai turned to acknowledge the other woman. "Jenna Beals, former college roommate and good friend of my intended as well as contributing editor for the fashion forward magazine that ran the article on my future betrothed, I believe."

Jenna gave a credible curtsy. "It's a pleasure to meet you, Your Highness."

Nikolai smiled, his gray eyes warm. "I liked the article and blog posts."

"You did?" Jenna asked in clear shock. "Really?"

"It was a clever concept, showing the fashion side of the modern dating game."

Jenna gave Nataliya a significant look. "He doesn't think you should be shamed for going out on a few dates."

"Not at all, but all future dates will be with me," he said with arrogant assurance.

"Because you have so much time to spend with me," Nataliya said with unhindered cynicism.

"And yet, here I am."

"But this is a one-off." Wasn't it? He was a king, he didn't have time to woo her.

Woo. What an old-fashioned word, but what else fit?

His honor demanded he fulfill the contract on behalf of his family and he was determined to convince her that marriage to him was what she wanted. Ten years ago, it wouldn't have taken any convincing.

But that was then and this was now.

The multi-Michelin-star restaurant he took her to for dinner was one she'd heard a lot about, but had never tried. The simple, elegant modern Japanese-style decor went perfectly with the Asian Fusion food on offer.

Among the diners on the way to their table, she recognized two prominent politicians, a football star and a television star.

Even the notable patrons' attention caught on King Nikolai and his entourage as they walked through the restaurant. Security took tables on either side of the one she and Nikolai were led to.

He held her chair for her, himself, his closeness impacting her in ways something so simple should not have.

Disconcerted, she blurted, "You don't have to do this over-the-top stuff. I'm a computer programmer, not a princess."

"You are Lady Nataliya and when we are wed, you will be The Princess of Mirrus."

"As opposed to *a* princess?"

He settled into his own seat across from her at the intimate table for two. "It is the distinction given to the wife of the King."

"I haven't said I'm going to marry you," she said quietly, not wanting to be overheard.

The expression on his chiseled features was untroubled. "On the contrary, you signed a contract that said that very thing."

She looked around and though no one was looking at them, that did not mean none of the other diners were listening. Though the acoustics in the restaurant and table placement made it unlikely.

"Why?" she asked him.

"Why?" He paused. "What?"

"You know what I'm asking. You turned down Maks's offer to renegotiate the contract at favorable terms for Mirrus Global."

"But I do not wish to renegotiate the contract. There are not terms more favorable than the ones we have now."

He could not mean what it sounded like he meant, that marriage to *her* was the most favorable term.

"You can't want to marry me." This she whispered nearly inaudibly, paranoid about being overheard as only the daughter of the notorious Count Shevchenko could be.

"You are mistaken."

That was all. *You are mistaken.* No explanation, but then this was not the place to have this conversation.

She should have brought it up in the limousine, but she'd been fighting entirely adult sexual feelings she had never experienced before. And he'd been happy to keep up the conversation with a charming urbanity that only increased his attractiveness to her.

Not one of the fourteen men she'd dated so far for the article and its accompanying blog posts had been even remotely as interesting, even the computer programmer who had developed an app that she loved to use.

"I am still obligated to go on thirty-six dates for the article," she apprised him, surprised at her own reticence about doing so.

"Thirty-five." His smile was way too appealing for her peace of mind.

"Thirty-five?"

"Tonight is one."

"But the photos of my style." That was the whole point of the article.

And technically, it *could* work, because Jenna *had* styled her.

"I will take care of it." He called one of his security people over with a jerk of his head.

A few low-spoken words and the other man went back to his table, his phone already out.

"A photographer will be here before we are finished with our dinner."

"I'm sure Jenna will appreciate that." Because honestly? Nataliya had made up sixteen different excuses for not scheduling a date the past two weeks.

"I will make sure we have a photographer on hand for the remainder of our dates."

"You're not going to take me out thirty-five more times." No way did he have the time.

"Some of those dates will have to happen after our wedding, but I fail to see why you are so surprised at the idea. You did not imagine that we would lead separate lives?"

"What do you mean *after* our wedding? When do you think we are getting married?" It took at least a year, usually two, to plan a royal wedding.

"Three months from now Mirrus is hosting a summit for small countries and monarchies. I would like the event to culminate in our wedding."

"Maks and Gillian did that, but she was pregnant. There was a reason for the rush."

He tilted his dark head in acknowledgment. "You have waited ten years for my house to fulfill its part of that contract. That is long enough."

"You're really stuck on this honor-of-your-house thing, aren't you?"

She expected him to get angry, or at least annoyed, by her snark.

But Nikolai smiled. "Yes, in fact, I am."

She sighed, acknowledging if only to herself, that he would not be manipulated as easily as his brother. "You're not going to be reasonable about this, are you?"

"If by reasonable, you mean change my mind, no."

She felt her own usually even temper rising. "You do realize you are a king, right?"

"And as such, I am accustomed to getting my own way."

She'd just been thinking that very thing, but still. "You're not supposed to admit that."

"I should lie?" he asked arrogantly.

"I don't know. Can you really see me as your Queen? Excuse me... I mean your Princess?"

"I have no trouble picturing that eventuality at all." The expression in his eyes was all male approval.

And it did something to her insides she did not want to admit. "I don't like dressing up."

"Yet you do so very well. I will never be anything but proud to have you stand by my side."

She frowned. He couldn't mean that. "I blurt stuff out before I think about it," she warned him.

"Do you? Thus far, I've noticed you being very careful about what you say and where you say it."

That was true in certain circumstances, like the few in which they'd met, but not always. "When I'm comfortable, I lose the filter between my brain and my mouth."

"I will look forward to you growing comfortable with me then."

"You don't mean that." How could he?

He didn't quite smile, but amusement lurked in his usually steely gray gaze. "You think I only want people around me who say what I want to hear?"

"You're a king."

"We've established that."

"You don't like people disagreeing with you."

"Disagreement is healthy." He gave her a look she thought might be intended to intimidate. "Disrespect is something else."

She wasn't intimidated, but she was curious. "What if you think I'm being disrespectful when I'm only being honest?"

"What if you think I'm being neglectful when I am only busy?" he riposted.

"I don't know."

"Neither do I. Marriage requires trust and compromise from both sides."

"Is that what you had with Tiana?"

Nothing changed in his expression, but there was a new quality of stillness about him and rigidity to Nikolai's spine. "My first marriage is not something I like to discuss."

"Okay."

His eyes widened fractionally. "Okay?"

"I don't like talking about my childhood either." Everyone thought they knew what her life had been like because her father had been in the tabloids so much.

No one but she and her mother knew about the Count's violent rages, about the mental and physical scars both she and her mother bore because of them.

His final desertion had embarrassed the royal family and torn their lives apart, but it had also come as a terrible relief. Once they reached the States, her mother had taken out a restraining order against her estranged husband and renewed it after their divorce became final.

Living in the States, she'd finally stood up for herself and her daughter in a way she'd never been willing to do when their lives were wrapped with the Volyarus royal family.

"Hearing you say that makes me very curious, *kiska*."

He could be as curious as the proverbial cat, but she wasn't talking about those dark years when her father had lived with her and Mama in Volyarus.

Not for anything. "I'm not a kitten."

"Oh, I think you are. You've proven you have sharp little claws, but you are not vicious with them and I am very much looking forward to petting you."

She choked on the wine she'd been sipping. "I can't believe you said that."

"I am a king, not a eunuch."

"But you don't want me."

"Don't I?" His heated expression belied her claim.

Suddenly, the air around them was charged and she pressed her thighs together under the table. "I don't look anything like Tiana," Nataliya blurted.

Dark brows raised, he said, "You look like yourself and I find you very attractive."

"Oh." She really hadn't expected that blunt declaration, much less the truth he'd have her believe was behind it. Unexpected heat suffused her face.

"Nothing to say back to me?"

"What do you want me to say?" she asked in a tone that was way too breathless.

"You could tell me if the attraction is one-sided."

"Of course, I'm attracted to you." He was smart, powerful, gorgeous, strong and just downright sexy. "Who wouldn't be?"

"I think I'm flattered." But he didn't sound too sure about that fact.

And for some inexplicable reason, that made Nataliya happy. She didn't like him taking her attraction to him for granted, despite the fact he had to know that most women would find him pretty much irresistible. "Don't be. You know who and what you are."

"Yes, but I was beginning to wonder if *you* appreciated my attributes."

He had to be joking. "I find that hard to believe."

She was no actress and right now, Nataliya couldn't stop thinking how much she wanted to kiss him and try things she'd never tried before with another man. It was all his fault too, the King who talked bluntly about stuff like *attraction*.

Which naturally sent her thoughts in a direction they never went. Except around him. And that had been a long time ago.

Only this was now and although she was no longer in love with him, Nataliya apparently still found Nikolai sexually irresistible.

And the King's expression said he knew it too!

A smile more predatory than amused creased his gorgeous lips. "The look on your face says that our wedding night will be very satisfying."

"Like you'd allow it to be anything else," she blurted with

more honesty than common sense. "You're the guy who always wins."

"It comes with the territory."

Satisfied with how their evening had gone so far, Nik slid into the limousine, taking the seat beside his future bride rather than the one across from her.

Although she was more stubborn than he'd given her credit for, Nik had no doubt that she would eventually agree to marry him.

Because Nataliya was that rare commodity in his world—a woman of honor.

When she made a promise, she kept it. Not like the faithless socialite he'd made his Queen. He'd made the mistake once of bestowing political and social power that rivaled his own on his wife and lived to regret it.

Nataliya had waited ten years on a contract that should have been fulfilled in half that time. And she had not allowed herself to consider getting out of her obligation to marry a prince of his house until she had discovered Konstantin's propensity for one-night stands.

Nataliya had very exacting standards and a highly developed sense of honor, both for herself and others. In her view, Konstantin hadn't lived up to those standards.

Nikolai understood, even if he did not agree fully. Her attitude was to his benefit.

And it was those traits that had first made Nik realize she would make his ideal wife. The low-simmering attraction he'd recognized in the agonizing days after his pregnant wife's death was also welcome. He had no desire to have an icy-cold marriage bed, but even he had not realized how deeply that attraction ran until he started spending more time with Nataliya.

He'd even been turned on during the confrontation at the Volyarussian palace.

Not that he would ever acknowledge such a thing.

Nor would ever lose control of his desire or allow it to drive his decisions.

He would not make the same mistakes with his second wife he had made with his first.

Starting with choosing a woman who had bone-deep integrity and absolutely no tolerance for infidelity.

Nataliya allowed Jenna to put the finishing touches to her makeup for the fifth date in three weeks with Nikolai.

He had stayed in Seattle that first week, managing to see her every day he had been in town.

The next week he had flown in to take her to the big technology expo. That would have been amazing enough, especially with the VIP treatment attending it with a king had provided. Yes, even Nataliya in all her pragmatism had been impressed. But somehow he had managed an invite for her to the super-secret hackathon she'd been trying to get into for the last three years.

*And* the King of Mirrus had not complained even a little when she'd immersed herself in learning new hacking technologies and going up against some of the biggest names in her industry for hours.

Tonight they were attending a fund-raiser ball for the children's charity she'd been donating the proceeds of her *Courtship Gifts for a Would-Be Princess* online auction to.

It was being held at one of the swankest hotels in Manhattan and Nikolai had arranged for a private plane to fly Nataliya, Jenna, the photographer and even Jenna's boyfriend to New York.

Jenna and her boyfriend were excited about going out on the town after Jenna finished styling Nataliya for her date and getting the information the junior fashion editor needed for her blog post.

"My boss is beside herself with joy in the amount of hits

we're getting on the blog from this series," Jenna said with satisfaction as she stood back.

Nataliya smiled at her longtime friend. "Good. You deserve recognition for your creativity."

"But it's your life that's making this possible. Everyone is keen to follow the courtship of a king and his would-be princess."

Nataliya was unwillingly enthralled herself. She spent too much time wondering what his next move would be and thinking about him between frequent texts and phone calls. "I think he's still expecting the wedding to take place month after next."

"Has he said so?"

"I got the mock-up invitations to approve this afternoon." But so far, she had not actually agreed to marry him.

He acted like it was a foregone conclusion. Because she'd signed that darned contract.

Jenna tried to stifle laughter but wasn't successful. "He's very confident you're going to agree, isn't he?"

"The word is arrogant."

"I'm pretty sure kings are allowed."

Nataliya smoothed a tiny wrinkle in the skirt of her dress. "And I'm *very* sure that he would be just as arrogant if he were the third son of the King's second cousin."

Jenna's laughter burst out and Nataliya couldn't help joining her, but she hadn't been joking. Not entirely.

Nikolai was always sure he was right and she'd yet to find an instance in which he was not. She couldn't even deny that she *would* ultimately agree to marry him.

She would like to say that was all due to her sense of duty and the contract she'd signed at the age of eighteen. And she could not deny that it did play a part, but that crush she'd gotten over?

Not so much in the *over* department.

Nikolai treated her like a person in her own right, not just an adjunct to his life. He didn't dismiss her job or put her down for loving what she did. Nor did he criticize her for having no personal clue about the latest fashions or being mostly ignorant of pop culture.

Nataliya wasn't interested in being *seen*, nor did she have any interest in playing on her current A-Lister status as Jenna called it.

Nikolai approved of her and supported Nataliya's interests and opinions in a way even her mom found challenging, Nataliya knew.

She was nobody's idea of perfect royalty.

So why did this King want to marry her?

What could *she* bring to the Royal House of Merikov? Other than her womb.

No question she would be expected to provide heirs *plural* to the throne. He'd been very frank about that fact. Just as he'd been, oh, so open on that first date about being attracted to her.

And yet he hadn't even kissed her. Not once. No kisses, no heated embraces.

Did he expect to use artificial insemination, or something, to get those heirs he was so keen on?

The thought was really lowering, but what else was she supposed to think?

He was so incredibly polite. And she? Wanted to kiss him and try all the things she'd ever read about with him. Sometimes he looked at her with what she thought was desire, but he never acted on it and she couldn't help thinking she'd got it wrong.

But did that stop her wanting him?

No it did not.

Stifling a sigh at her thoughts, Nataliya obediently looked in the mirror to check out Jenna's handiwork.

The dress was from an established design house but far from classic. Black lace over a nude slip that stopped midthigh, one shoulder was entirely bare and the other sleeve reached to her wrist. When she shifted, the slit that went right to the bottom of the slip showed her leg. The cut and style made the slit look like it went higher, but it did not in fact show anything but the pale skin of her thigh.

Thank goodness she did her muscle-toning elliptical every morning, or she would never show so much of her leg.

Biting her lip, Nataliya met Jenna's expectant gaze in the mirror. "It looks so risqué."

"But nothing that shouldn't be showing is."

"You can see the side of my breast."

"No, you think you can but the fashion tape and cut of the gown are both clever enough to keep you covered."

"Nikolai is going to have a fit."

Jenna rolled her eyes. "His Highness has been mixing with the glitterati for years while you've been happily moldering away at your computer keyboard. He's seen much more daring gowns."

More daring? What were they, see-through? When she asked, Jenna just laughed. "It has been known."

"This one looks like it's see-through."

"But it's not."

"The nude slip is an exact match for my skin tone."

"That was done on purpose," Jenna revealed with a tone of pure satisfaction. The clothes being provided by the fashion houses for Nataliya's dates were a serious coup for her friend. "The in-house designers were happy to provide a personalized gown for this event for you. You're an A-Lister now, hon."

"Only because I'm dating a king."

"Um…you do realize you just said that, right?"

Nataliya shook her head, but the image in the mirror was a woman who *could* date a king. Even she knew that. "You did good, friend."

"I had a great canvas to work with."

Now if only Nikolai would not just see Nataliya as a woman who could date a king, but one the said King would want to kiss. And perhaps do other naughty things with, *she* might feel like crowing.

# CHAPTER FOUR

NIKOLAI'S INITIAL REACTION was all that Nataliya could have wanted.

Steel-gray eyes turned molten with hot desire and she prepared herself for a kiss to blow her socks off.

Good thing she wasn't wearing any socks because no kiss was forthcoming and the King's expression shuttered almost immediately.

"You look beautiful," he told her, oh, so politely.

And Nataliya wanted to scream. "Thank you," she replied in kind, however, none of the frustration she felt bleeding into her voice.

"Once we are married, however, you will not be styled so provocatively." He gave her another cursory glance before leading her out of the hotel suite. "It is a good thing you are not enamored with this type of fashion. That will not be a loss for you."

Every word he spoke stoked the annoyance simmering inside Nataliya until she felt like a fizzing teakettle.

"*When* we are married?" she asked delicately. "Having you dictate how I dress won't be a hardship for me?" she inquired with even more precise syllables.

He stopped in the elevator, his gaze flicking to the security detail before coming to settle on her. "Naturally, my opinion on how you dress will be important to you."

"Oh, really?" she asked sweetly. "Because, and I know this is going to come as a surprise to you, but I have been dressing myself for years now and I have never once needed a man's opinion on what *I* choose to wear."

"You will be my Princess, and with that honor will come certain responsibilities," he said repressively, the buttoned-down King she'd gotten to know early on making a full appearance for the first time on one of their dates.

Somehow, with all the worries she'd had about the responsibilities of becoming a princess, none of them had ever centered around her wardrobe. "Responsibilities like letting you tell me how to dress?"

"Be honest—would you have chosen that dress on your own?" he asked, sounding like he knew the answer already.

"I don't wear high-end designer gowns on a regular basis, full stop."

"You could, though, if you wanted. I have never seen your mother wearing anything but."

"She accepts an allowance from her cousin." Hush money Nataliya had no interest in. "I live on the money I earn."

"Admirable, but when you are *The* Princess of Mirrus, you will dress in the top designers' creations and I do not believe that *you* will choose clothing as provocative as the dress you are currently wearing."

She had this crazy urge to wear nothing but sexually provocative clothing for the rest of her life. Comfortable, or not. "Let me make something very clear, Your Highness."

He waited without saying anything, his manners impeccable.

"I will wear the clothes *I* like regardless of who I am married to. That means that if I want to wear jeans from a department store, I will and if I want to wear dresses just like this one, I will. No one, not even a king, is going to dictate my choices like a petty fashion tyrant."

One of the bodyguards made a suspicious sound that could have been humor, but a look at their faces showed only impassive regard.

When Nikolai opened his mouth to speak, his eyes narrowed in clear irritation, she held up her hand.

"I am not finished."

"Then by all means, continue."

"You have not asked me to marry you. We are not engaged and speaking to me like that is a done deal when you haven't even given me the courtesy of that one small tradition is *not* making the outcome you so clearly want more likely." With that she set her not-so-happy gaze on the bodyguard nearest the door. "Open the doors—this discussion is over."

She'd noticed the elevator stopped moving, but the doors had remained shut. His security detail was always one step ahead of any potential problem. She admired that kind of cunning even if right now she wanted off that lift more than just about anything.

A small jerk of his head meant the doors remained closed. "Hardly a discussion when you have not allowed me to speak."

"No, you are right, it is *not* a discussion when the man who intends to marry me, despite having never gotten my agreement to that eventuality, starts laying down the law about the way I will be dressing in the future. I don't remember you asking my opinion on that, you are right."

With that she gave the bodyguard a look letting him know she meant business, but was sure the King had given his tacit approval, or the doors would not have swished open.

Uncaring of the why, Nataliya swept out of the elevator, heading for the front doors, certain their limousine would be waiting for her outside.

They were in the car and moving through city traffic before he broke the silence between them. "It was not my intention to offend you with my remarks."

"Wasn't it? But I'd always believed you were a top-drawer

diplomat," she said with no little sarcasm. Just what exactly had he intended if not to offend?

His mouth firmed. "I assumed that certain things had been made clear to you at finishing school as you were supposed to be prepared for eventual marriage to a prince of my house."

"Newsflash, I did not agree with everything my mentors said in finishing school and found the university far more to my liking." In fact, she'd only attended said finishing school so she *could* attend university and pursue a degree in computer programming and software design.

Something even her mother had insisted was unnecessary and would end up being useless to Nataliya later in life. Solomia had wanted her to get a liberal arts degree if Nataliya insisted on going to college. But Nataliya had fought for the future she'd wanted, while believing that part of that future was out of her control and had been since she was eighteen.

"The reports from the school do not mention a tendency to rebellion."

She wasn't at all surprised Nikolai had read Nataliya's progress reports from finishing school. She had no doubt he'd also read her college transcripts and all relevant commentary from professors and teachers alike.

"The fact I became a computer hacker rather than following a far more acceptable pursuit for a future princess didn't enlighten you?" she asked, revising her view of his powers of observation.

And not in a positive direction.

"Funnily enough, no."

"Because I never rebelled against the medieval contract I signed when I was eighteen?" she guessed.

The infinitesimal shift in his expression said she'd got it in one.

"I can't really explain that in terms of my sense of independent thought. It was just there, this knowledge I had promised to marry Konstantin."

"A prince of my house, not Konstantin per se."

"Well, he was the one I thought I was marrying and honestly? I wasn't keen to date or fall for someone and get hurt like Mama had been by my father."

"Theirs was a love match?"

"On her side, though their parents *were* instrumental in bringing them together." And like so many times in her mother's life, it was obvious *her* parents had placed their own social standing and prestige above what was best for their daughter.

Her grandparents hadn't argued against Mama's and Nataliya's exiles any more than anyone else had. Both had died, their daughter never restored to her place of birth.

"So you had family precedent."

"I'm a member of the royal family of Volyarus—of course I had precedent. Aunt Oxana married my uncle to give him heirs and he never let his mistress go. She made marriage for duty look easy." And somehow *right*.

Her aunt had never been *happy* in her marriage. She couldn't have been, but Oxana had never complained, had never shown regret for becoming Queen and giving birth to the heir to the throne.

"Your attitude has changed though?" he asked, not sounding happy.

"Not exactly." She may not have enjoyed finishing school, but Nataliya had been taught from birth to put duty to the royal family first.

She simply intended to do that without losing herself in the process.

She tried to put that into words and was surprised at the understanding that came over the King's features. Not only understanding, but approval.

"You have a strong sense of integrity and duty, but also an equally strong sense of self. Believe it, or not, Nataliya, I think that is a good thing."

"Even if it means I wear provocative couture one day and jeans off the rack the next?"

"It will be *my* preference that my wife dress appropriate to her station on all the days, but how to define that will naturally not only be for me to determine."

She wasn't sure she believed him. The guy who thought he didn't have to *ask* her to marry him despite her spelling it out to him. And she wasn't all that impressed with his belief it was *not only* his to determine, rather than *hers* in full.

Despite the argument that Nikolai insisted on referring to as a lively discussion, Nataliya enjoyed herself very much at the charity ball.

She was thrilled Nikolai had purchased an entire table's worth of tickets and then rather than filling the spots with dignitaries, he'd held a lottery for the employees of the charity to fill the seats. Each seat came along with the privilege of bidding on auction items up to a set amount that the House of Merikov would pay. In every way, he gave the seat winners a fairy-tale evening.

It was brilliant PR, but even with that aspect, she couldn't help being flat-out impressed.

Who wouldn't want to be with the guy so willing to make other people's dreams come true?

In his perfectly tailored dinner suit, he was also the best-looking man in the giant ballroom. She let herself fall into the fantasy as they danced after the auction to music slow enough to justify him holding her.

But the fantasy crashed and burned when a tap on his shoulder indicated another man wanted to break into the dance. That other man? Her father.

She gasped, anger filling her faster than the air refilling her lungs and then she jerked back in involuntary reaction to her father's nearness.

"No." She shook her head. "I am not dancing with you."

"You are making a scene," her father censured her. He gave his patented smile to the King. "Pardon my daughter, she has clearly spent too many years living like a commoner."

Panic tried to claim Nataliya, but she refused to let it take hold. Looking around them, she realized they were the center of attention among the nearest dancing couples. Soon it would be the whole room, but she *would not* dance with her father.

"You will have to excuse us, but I do not enjoy the opportunity of dancing with my intended often enough to relinquish her to another." Nikolai adroitly pulled her back into his arms and shifted so he stood between her and her father.

Shock coursed through her and she nearly stumbled.

No one had ever stood between her and her father. Not once. Not her mother. Not the security detail hired to protect her family, not her royal relatives.

The idea that Nikolai would risk making a scene to back up her refusal to dance with the Count was so astonishing, she had no frame of reference for it.

This was the man who had spent the beginning of their evening making it clear he expected her to dress the part of his Princess and yet when it came to actions, he was not allowing diplomacy to guide him.

But rather her expressed needs.

Her father tapped on the King's shoulder again, his smug smile still in place. "I really must insist. It has been too long since I have seen my daughter."

"No." That was all Nikolai said, but he did it with utter freezing civility and spun her away.

"Do you want me to have my security alert the authorities? Count Shevchenko is breaking the restraining order you and your mother have out against him, is he not?"

"You know about that?" Although when they'd first been exiled, her father had gone to Monaco with his latest flame, he followed Nataliya and her mother to Seattle when he ran out of money.

One trip to the ER later and her mother filed for divorce and the restraining order in the same week.

Her father had settled in New York, unwilling to risk jail time returning to Washington State.

"But apparently no one in your Volyarussian family does."

"Mama doesn't want anyone in her family to know." Her father's violent nature was never to be spoken of to anyone else. Mama had drilled that into Nataliya from her earliest memories.

While Mama had taken the order out and done more to break away from her toxic marriage than she'd ever done in Volyarus, Nataliya's mother felt deep shame for what her husband had done to her and their daughter. Mama had never wanted to talk about it, though she had started seeing a therapist.

Nataliya had learned young to carry the shame of her father's sins as if they were her own.

"Why?" Nikolai asked her.

And it took a moment for Nataliya to order her chaotic thoughts enough to realize what he was asking. "Because she's afraid they'll tell her she's wrong to have filed for it and kept it current? Because she's ashamed we need one? Because one simply does not talk about things like infidelity, much less abuse? Because she was made to feel like she carried the blame as much as he did for his actions? Take your pick."

"As you have been made to feel that his failings are yours?" Nikolai asked far too astutely.

"Does it matter? I know I'm not responsible for his actions."

"Maybe coming to realize that made you less willing to tolerate the claim the contract between our families had on you."

He could be right. Nataliya had grown less willing to play her part as future bride of Prince Konstantin from the time she'd realized she wasn't paying the price for her mother's happiness, but for her father's sins.

Remembering what else Nikolai had asked, she sighed. "No authorities. The order is filed in Washington, not New York. It would be a hassle and he'd talk himself out of it anyway."

"I will not let him near you."

"Why would you promise that?" How could he know that even her father's proximity sparked irrational panic in Nataliya?

"Did you know that he put his last mistress in the hospital?"

She shook her head, feeling guilt that was not hers to feel. Nataliya was not responsible for the actions of her father. Not now. Not in the past.

It had been a difficult lesson to learn, but she'd refused to spend her entire life feeling shame for her father's ugly choices.

"Neither you, nor your mother told your family what he was really like?"

"We were already so ashamed of his public behavior, we couldn't share what he was like at home."

"You were a child. She was the wife he did not honor." Nikolai's tone was certain. "Neither of you had any shame to carry."

"I know that in my head but getting my heart to believe has been a years' long process."

"I did not know he would be here."

"Me either. Do you think he knew I would be?"

Nikolai inclined his head austerely. "Our plans have been of utmost interest to the media."

"It's the fairy-tale story of the decade." Nataliya's mouth twisted cynically. "The King who's courting the lady who lives like a commoner."

"So you acknowledge I *am* courting you."

"I have never denied it."

"You simply refuse to confirm the outcome."

"Have you asked me to?" she asked, working not to roll her eyes.

"You're very much hung up on that issue."

"And you are very arrogant."

He shrugged. "It would be stranger if I was not."

"Haven't you heard? Humility is a trait to be admired."

"False humility has no appeal to me."

She huffed out a laugh, unable to stop herself. "Clearly."

"You think I should pretend not to know my own mind? Where is the integrity in that?"

"No, I don't think you should pretend. I think you should not be so sure you know best all the time."

"But I do."

"Hush. Just dance with me, all right? I've had an upsetting moment."

He pulled her just a little closer while remaining nothing but appropriate in how he held her. "Hushing."

"Do you always have to have the last word?" she asked, exasperated.

He just looked at her, as if saying, *No, see? Here I am not having the last word.*

In that moment, she wanted nothing more than to press her body into his and lay her head on his strong shoulder. Let him hold her and protect her, when she had never expected anyone else to protect her. When her entire life, all Nataliya could remember was doing her best to protect others.

She could still remember being no older than three or four and stepping between her mother and father, yelling at him to stop hitting her mama. He'd backhanded her so hard she'd hit the wall and she could remember nothing else from that night.

She didn't know if she'd been knocked out or it was just her spotty trauma memory at work again, leaving holes that often made little sense to her.

They were in the limousine on the way back to her hotel suite when she commented, "I think my father left early. It's not like him to give up so easily. I was sure he'd try to talk to me again."

"I had him escorted out."

"Aren't you worried he'll go to the press and accuse you of throwing your weight around?" That was exactly the kind of thing Count Danilo Shevchenko would do.

Nikolai did not look worried. "I think my reputation can

withstand anything a disgraced count could attempt to throw at it."

There went his arrogance again, but she admitted she liked it, if only to herself. "I'm sorry."

"You have nothing to apologize for."

"Would you be saying that if I refused to honor the contract?" she couldn't help asking.

"But you are not going to refuse."

"You're so sure." When she still wasn't.

"You have more integrity than any woman I know."

"I know loads of women with integrity."

"As do I, but not one of them is more honorable than you."

"Even Queen Tiana?" She wished she could take the question back the moment it popped out.

He'd said he didn't want to talk about his first marriage. Besides, it made Nataliya sound insecure and she didn't like that.

He surprised her by answering though. "Yes." He looked like he was thinking about what he wanted to say next. "Our marriage was not the perfect joining of two hearts the media painted it to be."

If the fact he'd answered was surprising, the answer itself shocked her. Nataliya remembered how in love he'd seemed when he'd married the daughter of one of the new Russian oligarchy. Nataliya had thought the other woman beautiful but spoiled.

And she'd felt bad for thinking that. She'd always assumed her impression of the other woman was skewed by Nataliya's own unrequited feelings for Nikolai. And she hadn't liked knowing that about herself.

"Thank you," she said now, not sure what else to say in the light of her own nosy question and his very unexpected, honest answer.

He shrugged, but his expression was forbidding. "I was not flattering you, merely speaking the truth."

"Still, it's a nice truth to hear. To be valued for something other than my womb and royal lineage is surprisingly satisfying." She wasn't going to mention the comparison with his dead wife where Queen Tiana came out second.

Or his admission his first marriage hadn't been perfect. That wasn't the important issue here anyway.

"I am glad you think so."

She bit back a sigh. It *was* nice to hear, but could his respect for her make for a strong marriage when he showed no actual desire for her despite having told her he thought she was attractive?

Biting her lip, she studied him and then finally asked. "Are you ever going to kiss me?"

There could be no doubt she'd surprised him. It showed on the handsome, strong features that rarely showed uncalculated reaction.

He gave her a repressing look. "I believe that should come after you have agreed to marry me."

"You don't think it might help me agree?" Or not. If they had no chemistry.

Which on her side she had no doubts of, but her doubts in his genuine attraction for her were growing with each date that ended without so much as a kiss on the cheek.

"I will not allow sex to influence my choices and would prefer you weren't under the influence of sexual need when you make yours."

"You do expect to have sex though? After we are married?" He didn't really anticipate using IVF to get her pregnant, did he?

She didn't realize she'd asked that last out loud until the look of shocked horror on his features told her she had.

"Yes, we will have sex. There will be no test-tube babies for us."

"Okay. Good."

"Your lifestyle to this point has not indicated a desire for sexual intimacy."

"I've already explained that to you." She made no effort to prevaricate.

For whatever reason, she didn't want Nikolai to believe she'd ever gone to bed with another man while she would have been perfectly happy for Konstantin to make that assumption.

"You have already told me you are attracted to me. Are you saying that is not true?" he asked her, like a man trying to figure out a very difficult puzzle.

It was all she could do not to give in to sarcasm. He could not be that dense. "It's not my attraction to you that I'm doubting."

"But I told you I wanted you," he said like that should be it. The final word on the subject.

"I think with some things, actions speak with more assurance than words."

"We are not having sex before our wedding night." He laid down the law like the King he was. "Our first child will be conceived within the bounds of marriage. As heir to my throne it would be grossly unfair for us to risk anything else."

"There are such things as birth control."

"We can wait."

She sat back into the corner of her seat, her arms crossed over her chest, feeling very put out and knowing he would not understand why *at all*. "Of course we can. Far be it from the King of Mirrus to act with spontaneity."

"I had my fill of spontaneity a long time ago." His expression said his memories in that direction were not good ones.

When he'd been married? Before that? After? She wanted to ask. So badly but knew she wouldn't.

Because as much as he'd guessed about her life as a child, she had no plans to ever share the memories that still haunted her nightmares.

With an imprecation, he grabbed his phone and sent a text, then crossed the limousine to join her on the leather upholstery on her side.

She stared up at him. "What's going on?"

"I'm letting my past dictate my present and that's as stupid as reliving it."

"You're not making any sense."

But the expression in his eyes was saying plenty. His gray eyes were molten with desire, his body rigid with self-restraint. And that's when she knew he wanted her too.

"You *want* to kiss me," she said wonderingly.

"Yes," he ground out.

"So, do it!" Why did men always make things so complicated?

She gasped in shock when he took her up on her offer. Nikolai's tongue was right there sliding between her parted lips. This was no polite peck of lips.

Nikolai took possession of her mouth with passionate domination and Nataliya fell into the kiss with every bit of desire coursing through her virginal body.

He pulled her close, one hand cupping her breast through the lace of her gown and she moaned. She'd never been touched like this. She'd never even been kissed with tongue.

And she liked it all. Every new sensation building something inside her so that unfamiliar tension coiled within her.

She put her hands on his chest, squeezing his pecs, then feeling down his stomach, wishing his shirt were not in the way.

He made a sexy growling sound deep in his chest and yanked her into his lap, deepening the kiss. Everything went hazy, passion burning all rational thought from Nataliya's brain as the kiss went on and on and on.

He carefully peeled the fabric away from her body, slid his hand into the bodice of her dress and cupped her breast, pinching her aching nipple between his thumb and forefinger.

She let out a little cry against his lips, overwhelmed by the amazing sensation, and the pleasure in her core spiraled tighter.

He rolled her nipple back and forth, sending pleasure zinging directly from there to between her legs and unfamiliar feelings built inside her until she felt like she would scream with them.

It was too much and not enough and she did not know how to ask for what she needed. But then he pulled her closer and she felt his hardness against her hip, through their clothes, and something about that intimacy just sent her pleasure skyrocketing. The most amazing sensations washed over her until her body went rigid with her climax.

She ripped her lips from his to let the pleasure out in a scream and he kissed down her neck and back up to her mouth.

"So perfect, so passionate," he said in a tone that only added to the pleasure floating over her.

She collapsed against him, awash with sensation but so lethargic she could not have moved for anything.

"Sexually compatible." This time his tone was pure smug arrogance.

And even that didn't turn her off.

"Last word again?"

"I deserve it, don't you think?"

"Maybe this time."

He rapped his knuckles on the window and that must have been some kind of signal because minutes later, the limousine slid to a stop.

The door did not open however and she was grateful. He helped her get herself back together and off his lap.

"I will see you tomorrow," he reminded her.

They had plans to go on a tour of Central Park, because she'd said she wanted to. Later, they were going to have dinner together again.

Another perfect date.

Maybe it would end with another perfect kiss.

# CHAPTER FIVE

KISSING NATALIYA HAD BEEN a good decision.

No way was she still worried that he did not desire her. As if.

If anything, his sexual feelings for her were so strong, he had almost dismissed his idea of fulfilling the contract in his brother's stead out of hand. Nikolai refused to be at the mercy of his libido. Again.

Only he'd realized that wanting her was not a bad thing. Having her would be a better thing. All he had to do was keep his emotional distance and never allow her to use his desire for her to control him.

Knowing that she wanted him, had always wanted him, even when she'd tried her best to hide it? That gave him the certainty that she would not withhold herself from him as Tiana had done. Would not use his desire as a weapon against him.

Nataliya was too honest and forthright to play those kinds of games, regardless.

He ignored the small voice telling him that all women were capable. He would not put himself in a position for sex to become a bargaining chip.

Never again.

But that did not mean he could not allay her fears on that score.

Nikolai was proud of both his superior decision making skills in sharing that intimacy with her. When she had climaxed in his arms, he'd wanted to shout in triumph. Nataliya had proven she could not withhold her reactions from him and that was something he needed to know after the pain of his first marriage, where sex had been a bargaining chip, a battleground, but never just pleasure.

And though her response to him had shot his libido into the stratosphere, he'd maintained the control he'd fought to hone.

He'd wanted to take her right there in the limousine, but he hadn't even undressed her. Nataliya's uninhibited passionate response had been deliciously surprising and nearly obliterating to his self-control.

But he *had* controlled himself and that was what mattered.

As he'd told Nataliya, his heir would not be conceived outside the legal bonds of matrimony.

A marriage he had no doubts *would* take place regardless of her posturing.

So, she wanted a proposal. He was a king, but he was also a man with superior intellect. He would give her the proposal of her dreams and she would finally agree verbally to what they both knew was a foregone conclusion.

Their marriage.

Nataliya was relieved that Jenna and her boyfriend were not back yet when she entered the hotel suite.

She needed some time. To parse what that kiss meant.

No way could she legitimately wonder if he wanted her. He'd been hard and she'd felt it. The fact he hadn't taken it farther than a kiss was a tick in the plus column. Nikolai could and would control his own sexual desires when necessary.

That boded well for the concept of fidelity.

Even so, she needed time to deal with the emotional aftermath of her first orgasm with another person and how vulnerable it made her feel.

Because as much as she respected that he hadn't pushed for more, the fact she was the only one who had come was a little disconcerting. She'd never seen herself as very sexual. Yes, she'd always wanted him, but in a vague, undefined way.

She'd experimented with toys, but her pleasure had taken longer to achieve and not been as devastating.

Far from having the slow fuse she'd always thought, with him, it was short and explosive.

Oh, man. So explosive.

It was time to do some research.

Research she should have done weeks ago, but she'd been putting off.

She didn't want to do a deep dive into Nikolai's life, but she wasn't marrying a man who had a long-term mistress like her uncle or a string of them like his own brother and her father.

She needed to know just how he lived his life now and if he was currently involved with another woman.

*You could just ask*, her conscience reminded her.

But Nataliya needed cold hard facts and as much as she knew Nikolai expected every word he uttered to be taken as gospel, her past made that kind of blind trust impossible.

She ordered a pot of coffee and pulled out the laptop that beat her desktop for speed and memory. It was a pretty cool betrothal gift. Sort of fitting she was using it to check out how smart betrothal to the King would be then.

Several hours later, Nataliya had some answers. And they were all good ones.

She'd hacked into his financial records, run his name and face through her personalized media and social media search engine. She'd checked out every single instance of travel for him in the past year, every expenditure in and out of country and done a less thorough but adequate search for the years since his wife's death.

Everything had come back empty. No apartments paid for by him but occupied by a woman. He'd had companions at some of the more prominent social functions, but he'd usually brought a cousin who was now married to one of his top aides. Nothing that would indicate he had liaisons, mistresses or even the occasional lover since his Queen's passing.

In short, on paper anyway, he was her dream guy.

For a woman, who had never thought to marry for love, that was a pretty big deal.

Nataliya woke after about four hours' sleep, still tired but feeling more solid about this royal courtship she was experiencing. She'd known Nikolai was not a carbon copy of his brother, but she'd needed to be sure.

About the fidelity thing. About the fact that there were no other personal contenders for the position of his Princess.

There would always be plenty of women with the right breeding and the desire for the role, but he had not been courting any of them.

Which meant what?

That he *wanted* her in that role? That the timing had been right, and he'd decided to remarry just when his brother was deciding to renege on the contract?

She couldn't dismiss the honor thing, because she'd come to accept that for Nikolai, maintaining family honor and fulfilling his house's terms in the contract were very important to him. Like obsession-level importance.

Whether he'd been raised with an overweening sense of integrity, or it was something innate in Nikolai. Either way, she no longer disregarded it as a very real motivation for him.

And that gave her hope for their future if they were to have one. A man that focused on maintaining family and personal integrity would not look at his marriage vows as multiple-choice options.

And he wanted her. He'd proven that.

Regardless of what others in her position might think, that mattered. As his Princess, Nataliya would lose all the trappings of a *normal* life she'd worked so hard to attain, but she would insist on having a stable and normal marriage, or as normal as possible married to a king who was also a billionaire business mogul.

That meant sharing a bed and a life. She was not Queen Oxana, and Nataliya would not spend her life finding satisfaction in her duty and her position.

There had to be more.

She'd seen that more in Maks's and Demyan's marriages, knew that even if her husband did not love her, he could give Nataliya more than what she'd seen between her aunt and uncle or her own parents, much less the other royals of that generation in Volyarus.

She would have more, or she would not marry.

No matter what she'd signed when she was eighteen.

Later, Nataliya was not at all surprised that they were going to have a horse-drawn carriage for their tour of Central Park.

Nikolai had a canny knack for knowing what she might enjoy most.

She was surprised, however, that the carriage looked so elegant and that it was drawn by two perfectly matched horses of the kind of quality she recognized as beyond the means of the average tourist company.

"Are these your horses?" she asked him in shock.

"They are now." He flashed her a slashing, arrogant smile. "I bought them from stables with an excellent reputation in Upstate New York."

"And the carriage?"

"Purchased for this occasion."

"You don't think that's a little over the top?"

"I am a king, Nataliya. I do not ride in conveyances that cater to the masses."

But to *buy* a carriage? "You sound really snobby right now."

"Not simply intelligent about my own safety?"

He was talking about assassination attempts. In his father's lifetime, the former King had survived one and she had no idea if Nikolai had ever been the target of such an attempt. She had no doubt that if he had, he would have kept it very quiet.

"I stand corrected," she acknowledged. "But I still think you have no clue how the average person lives."

"And you do." He said it with satisfaction.

Nataliya gave him a surprised look. "You like that?"

"Very much. Mirrusians live all over the globe in all walks of life. The royal family should understand them if we are expected to serve their needs."

"That's a very progressive view."

"I am a progressive man."

A man who was getting married based on a contract his father had signed? She did not think so. "Maybe in some things."

"I am no throwback."

"No, I'd say you are the inevitable product of growing up royal in the twenty-first century in a country that is still a full monarchy."

"Volyarus is also a monarchy."

"I am aware." She settled back into the comfortable leather squabs of the carriage. "What happens to this carriage after today?"

"It will be sold and the proceeds donated to the charity we've been supporting with our courtship."

"Konstantin didn't like my online auction."

"You hit at his pride."

"It was intentional," she admitted. "But you provide gifts *for* the auction."

"It is a worthy cause." He took her hand, in an unexpected public display of affection that should be entirely innocent.

Only she felt that touch go right through her and had to take a deep breath and let it out slowly not to give herself away.

His knowing look said she hadn't been all that successful. "So, going back to our earlier words, are you a proponent of constitutional monarchy?" he asked, but didn't sound worried or even shocked by the idea she might be.

"Power should always be checked."

"And those checks, do they always work?" He brushed his thumb over her palm, sending electric sparks along that nerve-rich center and up her arm.

She curled her fingers around his thumb to stop him so she could think clearly enough to focus on answering him. "No, but having them gives the people that power is supposed to protect more of a chance of actually enjoying that protection."

"Does your uncle know you have these prorepublic lean-ings?" Amusement laced Nikolai's tone.

"Technically, he is my second cousin."

"But he sees himself in a closer role. You call him uncle."

"Not anymore, I don't." It had taken her long enough, but she'd come to realize that family was more than a word. It was a relationship, and her "uncle" had removed himself from their relationship a long time ago.

Now that seemed to startle Nikolai, when her beliefs that *his* power should be checked by a parliament didn't. "Why not?"

"Fifteen years ago, he sacrificed me and my mother to protect his good name when the whole time he has been the biggest risk to scandal in the royal family." Mama had always known too.

Nataliya had only learned of her King's infidelity as an adult and quite by accident, but then she'd spoken to her mother about it, hurt and angered by the monarch's hypocrisy. She'd learned then that Mama had known since the beginning.

It had sparked one of their rare arguments.

"Because of his long-term mistress."

"Exactly." The woman he'd refused to marry because of her divorce but had never been willing to give up. "You know about their long-term affair. She's not the secret he believes she is. If the media starts digging, they won't have to go very deep to reach a royal scandal of epic proportions."

"You do not think King Fedir has things in place to protect the monarchy in such an event?"

"He may think he does, but his relationship is too long-standing for him to deny it with any chance at being believed. Too many people know about it. Too many bills have been paid for her through the palace accounts."

"I'm sure King Fedir has taken precautions so that those bills cannot be traced back to him."

"I traced them. And as we both saw at the hackathon, I'm good, but I'm by no means the only good hacker out there."

"You hacked into your uncle's financial records?"

"I hacked into the palace financial records."

"You didn't know about the mistress," he said in wonder.

"Before we left Volyarus, no I did not. In fact, I did not discover her existence until a few years ago."

"And realizing he maintained that relationship put a different complexion on his actions with you and your mother fifteen years ago."

"Yes. I realized that he expects everyone but himself to sacrifice for the sake of *his* throne."

"Isn't that a bit harsh? He has a whole country's well-being he must take into account."

"Not if it means giving up the woman he loves, but not enough to marry. If you can call the sort of selfishness that drives him love at all."

"You judge him harshly."

"I paid a high price for his pride, but Mama, who had already paid a terrible price for being married to my father, was forced to give up even more." And Nataliya wasn't sure she would ever forgive her King for making her mother pay that price.

"The Countess seems to have built a good life for herself in her exile."

"Mama has, but she should not have had to learn to live without her family and friends. It wasn't fair."

"Do you feel that way about the contract? That it is not fair?"

Nataliya thought about that for a minute, never having put the contract in those terms.

"I think me being pressured to sign it and accept the terms when I was eighteen was not fair. I would fight tooth and nail to stop my own child from doing the same."

He nodded but said nothing. Still waiting it seemed for her to answer the core of his question.

Did she think it fair that she was contracted to marry him?

Instead of answering that, she offered some truth of her own. "I did a deep dive into your life last night."

"I thought you looked tired." He took both her hands in his and smiled down at her, obviously not worried about her investigation. "Did you get any sleep?"

"A few hours." She licked her lips, her gaze caught on his mouth, wanting to taste.

His gray gaze darkened with desire. "A nap might be in order this afternoon."

Was he offering to take it with her? She shook her head. No, of course not.

"Is that all you're going to say?" Nataliya asked, stunned he wasn't offended.

"What do you want me to say? I cannot claim I did not expect you to use your skills to discover if I have any skeletons in my closet. Your main concern about marrying Konstantin was his tendency to have uncommitted sex with women."

"He wasn't in a relationship, not like my father."

"But it still gave you pause."

"You know it did."

"You would not have found anything similar in my background."

"Not even a discreet long-term mistress."

"I am not King Fedir either."

"No. You are kind of an anomaly among powerful men. I'd wonder if you had a repressed libido, but I felt the evidence of your arousal in the car last night."

Far from being insulted by her remark, he laughed. "I can assure you, my libido is everything you will want it to be."

"I don't doubt it." She looked to their tour guide-slash-carriage driver and only now realized he had earbuds in.

She probably should have noticed he wasn't giving a running commentary, but Nataliya had been so caught up in Nikolai, for once in her adult life, she hadn't paid the utmost attention to the situation around her.

His smile said he knew. "Just noticed he's in hear-no-evil, or rather *private discussion* mode?"

"Yes."

"That's not like you."

"I thought we were doing a tour."

"The commentary will start when I give him a signal."

"Your guards are in the pedicabs ahead of and behind us, aren't they?" She'd just noticed that too.

"They wanted to be riding their own horses, but you would not believe the regulations governing any and all activity in Central Park."

"Even a king has to submit to red tape."

He nodded, his expression rueful. "If I'd had more time…"

He'd had time enough to buy gorgeous matching horses and a carriage.

He did some more of that thumb brushing, this time on both of her palms and she shivered.

"You wouldn't have been sure of me, if I hadn't kissed you last night." He sounded very pleased with himself.

"Maybe. I'm not sure," she admitted. "I kind of see you as this larger than life man. Yes, you are a king, but you're not a despot."

"You don't think so?" he asked, like her opinion actually mattered.

"You're the kind of king that makes me not worry about you not having a parliament, unless I'm worried about you taking too much on and not having anyone else to help carry the burden." Why was she being *so* honest? She'd never have been this open with anyone else.

Nikolai's expression could be seen as nothing less than satisfaction. "King Fedir?"

"Would benefit a lot by having some checks of power in his life."

"So, you think I am a good king?"

"Yes."

"And a good man?" he asked.

"Yes." She'd always thought so, but she'd had to be sure.

"You have no questions about things you may have discovered last night?"

"I didn't discover anything. That's the point, isn't it? Were there things to discover?"

"About me? No."

"Then about who?"

"Does it matter?"

If his father, or brother, or someone else had done something she might have questions about? "No. I don't think it does, but you would tell me, wouldn't you, if there was something that would affect me?"

"Yes." Nikolai looked so stern when he said that, but not shifty.

So, she believed.

"I think if I were a different woman, raised in a different way, I might think the contract was unfair," she said, finally answering his initial question. "If *you* were a different man, you wouldn't feel the need to fulfill its terms on behalf of your house."

"Perhaps."

"But I am who I am. And honestly, I wasn't raised to believe in fairy tales and happy endings. I don't remember Mama ever suggesting she hoped I found true love." More like Solomia had hoped her daughter would not end up married to a man who would physically hurt her.

But even with that hope, Mama had still encouraged her daughter to sign that contract ten years ago, with no idea about what kind of man Konstantin was.

"I don't think the contract itself is unfair." Nataliya acknowledged as much to herself as to him. "I *did* sign it. I did agree to the terms. I never expected to marry a man I loved, but I won't marry a man I cannot trust."

"My brother is trustworthy."

"Maybe, but his double standard about dating and sex make it hard for me to see him that way." She didn't want to talk about his brother. "Regardless, if we marry and are blessed with children, then believe their well-being will be more important to me than that of Mirrus."

"But that is not how a royal thinks."

"Then I guess you'd better make sure I never have to choose between duty and my children."

"That's a heavy promise you want me to make."

"No. My promise to you is that if you don't succeed at that, I will not be browbeaten into doing something that could hurt those I love. Period."

"That is the perspective of the common man."

"A perspective you said the royal family needs."

"Yes."

"So, that implies you are going to take my opinions into consideration when making decisions for Mirrus."

"It does, yes."

"But you hardly know me."

"You are not the only hacker available to dive deep into someone's life."

"Plus your family has had me under surveillance for ten years." Someone paying attention could know a great deal about her.

"That is true."

"You've read the reports?" she couldn't help asking.

"All of them."

*All* of them? "That's a lot of reading."

"Deciding to enforce the contract and fulfill its terms was not a spur-of-the-moment decision. I do not make those." He said the last like his own warning.

"I believe it." Though at first that was exactly what she'd thought he'd done. "You came to Volyarus intending to put yourself forward as the Prince of your house referred to in the contract."

"I did."

"Did Konstantin know?"

"No. It is not my habit to take others into my confidence."

"I think I'll expect you to take me into your confidence, if I marry you."

"We are separate people. Our duties will live in harmony but not always overlap."

"Are you trying to warn me that I won't see much of you if I marry you?" That might actually turn out to be the deal breaker nothing else had.

His jaw went taut. "That will be up to you."

"What do you mean?" she asked, her brows drawn together in confusion.

"Though I travel some for diplomatic reasons, all business travel is Konstantin's purview. I spend most of my time in Mirrus."

"Wouldn't your wife do the same?"

"Tiana did not. She found life in Mirrus stifling and preferred traveling with friends in warmer climates."

That made no sense. No more sense that he would tolerate it. "But she was the Queen. Surely her duties precluded long vacations in Jamaica."

"Monaco was her favorite haunt, but as to her duties, she found those stifling, as well."

Nataliya didn't know what he thought about that. His expression revealed nothing.

"I am used to working long hours," she offered.

"Will you expect to continue with a career after marriage?" Something about that question made him so tense, she couldn't miss it, despite how he was so careful to maintain an expressionless mask.

"If I were to marry a king, I think the job of being his Princess would keep me sufficiently busy."

"Not all women would agree."

"Really? I can't imagine a single woman of my acquaintance who would attempt to maintain a full-time career as well as the full-time job of Princess."

"So you do see it as a job."

"Being a wife is a role, but being a princess? That's definitely a job."

"I'm very glad to hear you say that."

What else didn't she know about his marriage to Tiana? Nataliya had not known that Tiana spent so much time away from Mirrus, but she'd been careful in her research to respect Nikolai's personal privacy. Other than confirming that Tiana had not had a bunch of visits from the Palace Physician for unexplained injuries, Nataliya had purposefully not looked too deeply into his marriage.

Just because she *could* find out just about anything about a person's life, didn't mean she *would* do that. It was a matter of her own personal integrity.

They spent the rest of their tour talking about their families, getting to know each other on a level that no amount of reading investigative reports could achieve. Nikolai never did indicate their tour guide start his commentary.

And she didn't mind at all.

She wasn't surprised she enjoyed the King's company.

Nataliya always had.

He was the guy she'd had her first crush on and being older and wiser only made those feelings seem deeper. But she didn't love him.

Would not let herself.

She felt something for him though, that would make refusing marriage to him impossible.

Not that she was sharing that revelation with the arrogant King.

# CHAPTER SIX

NATALIYA DID END UP taking a long nap that afternoon because their dinner reservations weren't until eight.

Nataliya expected to be taken to an exclusive five-star restaurant with a month-long waiting list for dinner.

Because so far Nikolai had pulled out all the stops for this courtship.

So, she was a little surprised to find herself at Central Park for the second time that day. An eight-person security team surrounded them as they exited the limousine.

"What are we doing back here?"

"Having dinner."

"I thought we had reservations."

"I said dinner was at eight. And it will be." He sounded so complacent, almost smug, like he knew what he'd planned was going to please her.

She couldn't help wanting to push his buttons a little. Laughing, she said, "I'm not exactly dressed for a picnic with hot dogs from a local vendor," she teased.

The look of horror on his face was worth the tease. "Trust me—that is not what we are having for dinner."

"You're such a snob." She found herself reaching for his

hand and having to pull hers back before the telling movement gave her away.

He made it so easy to forget they weren't really dating. That this courtship was the result of a contract signed a long time ago.

"I am a king. I would and have eaten grubs in order not to offend my hosts in both Africa and Australia, but if the choice of venue is up to me? We are never eating from a food truck." He spoke with the conviction he usually reserved for matters of real import.

It made her smile. "I'm not sure hot dog carts are considered food trucks, but I get your point. Thousands of foodies would tell you that you don't know what you are missing though."

"I will live with the loss," he said dryly.

She shook her head, her smile undimmed. "You just watch. One day I'll convince you."

"Watch yourself, *kiska*. You are sounding dangerously like you are considering a future with me."

"Perhaps you should be the one watching out. Maybe I am," she admitted, some things having solidified inside her while she'd slept and rejuvenated that afternoon.

"I am very glad to hear that." He was the one who reached for her hand, bringing it to his mouth to kiss the inside of her palm.

She gasped, that small salute sending tingles of pleasure right to the core of her. It was not a carnal act, but her body's reaction was as basic as it got. Nataliya craved Nikolai like she'd never desired another man, and the more time they spent together the stronger that craving got.

It scared her and excited her at the same time.

Knowing that she was developing a need for him that only he would ever be able to fill frightened her, but the knowledge he wanted to marry her mitigated that fear.

If he were a man like her father, she'd run fast and far from both her feelings and him, but Nikolai would never betray her as the Count had betrayed Nataliya's mother over and over again.

They came into a clearing and unexpected tears pricked her eyes at what she saw.

It was so over-the-top, but even at first glance the amount of thought that went into setting it up was obvious.

Standing lanterns surrounded a table set with the official linens she'd only seen in the Mirrus palace. Eggshell white, they were embroidered in gold and navy blue with the coat of arms for the House of Merikov. Fine white bone china with the same design sat atop gold chargers she had no doubt were pure precious metal and the crystal on the table sparkled elegantly.

The eight-person security detail, rather than his usual four, suddenly made sense. The table settings alone were worth thousands, if not tens of thousands and the centerpiece looked like a vase Oxana had in her sitting room. Mama had told her as a child not to touch it because it was priceless.

When royalty used that term, they meant it.

But beyond the opulence of the setting was how much care had been taken to bring a taste of Mirrus to New York. A small, ornate, gold-leafed trinket box sat next to one of the place settings.

It didn't take a computer genius to know what was in that box. The official betrothal ring of the House of Merikov.

"It's beautiful," Nataliya said in a hushed voice, that trinket box taking her breath away.

Nikolai led her to the table, relinquishing her hand to pull Nataliya's chair out himself. "I have pleased you. I am glad."

"You've been pleasing me this whole courtship, and you know it." She made the mistake of looking up and found herself frozen by the molten depths of his gaze.

"I have tried."

Oh, man. She needed to get a hold of herself. Forcing herself to look away, she settled into her chair. "Enough with the false humility, Nikolai," she mocked, though she felt like doing anything but mocking. "You are a king. You do not consider failure as an option."

That ornate trinket box to the left of her plate affirmed that truth as much as it stole the very breath from her body.

He moved around the table and took his own seat, his attention fixed firmly on her. "And yet, to succeed, ultimately I need your cooperation."

"It's nice to hear you finally admit that."

His left brow rose in sardonic question. "I have never denied that your agreement is necessary."

"But you *have* acted like you assume you already had it." And why it should strike her that that kind of arrogance could be sexy, she did not know.

"You signed the contract, but only you can decide if you are going to fulfill its terms." He flicked his hand to signal someone.

A waiter came out of the darkness around them to shake out Nataliya's napkin and lay it smoothly across her lap before doing the same for Nikolai. Moments later, water and wine were poured in their crystal goblets and a starter of fresh prawns was served over a bed of arugula.

She savored a prawn before smiling at him, because she wanted to. "My favorite."

"I know."

"How?" she asked curiously, pretty sure she hadn't mentioned this weakness to him.

"A man reading your comings, goings and habits for the past ten years can learn a great deal if he wants to." And would be a fool not to, his tone implied.

After all the deep dives into someone else's life she'd done for Demyan, as well as the one she'd done on Nikolai, it felt strange to know that a *king* had spent so much time not only reading up on her but interpreting the very mundane details recorded by those who had watched *her* over the past decade. "And you wanted to?"

"Can you doubt it?"

"It just seems like overkill for you to pay such close attention."

"Does it? Didn't you do the same?"

"Not really, no. I only looked at certain areas of your life for the past couple of years." She'd been interested in patterns that would reveal behaviors she could not live with.

Nataliya had been content to learn his likes, dislikes and views through the more regular method of simply getting to know him.

"Believe me, after my first marriage, I had no desire to be surprised by any aspect of your life or nature." He made it sound like his first marriage had offered up some unpleasant surprises.

Remembering the way he'd been with his Queen, Nataliya found that difficult to believe.

But then, who looking at her family would ever have guessed her father was the violent man he had been with her and Mama?

"Doesn't that take some of the mystique out of it?" As she asked the question, Nataliya realized how foolish it was.

That kind of mystique belonged in romance, but their relationship was not based on anything so emotive.

His look said he was surprised by the question. "I do not think a marriage for a sovereign needs to have mystique."

"I would say you do not have a romantic bone in your body," she teased, covering her own embarrassment at the knowledge that very thing wasn't what they were about. "But this whole scenario says otherwise."

Which was no less than the truth, so maybe, he could take a little bit of the blame for how hard she found it to remember this courtship wasn't about romance.

"You deserve to be treated as the special woman you are, but that does not make me romantic," he said decisively.

Warmth unfurled inside her at his words, despite how surprised she was by his claim.

"You don't consider yourself romantic?" she asked, startled.

The man had been nothing but romantic in his courtship of her, despite the fact it was based on all sorts of things *besides* romance.

"Romance is based on illusion and I have no illusions left."

Okay. No question. His marriage had *not* been the perfect union she had always assumed, unless he'd had a relationship she didn't know about since Tiana's death.

"You sound so cynical, but that is not how you treat me." And she was glad.

"There is nothing about you which to be cynical about," he said with some satisfaction.

"I'm not perfect." Not even a paragon. She was after all the woman who had embarked on the first dates article in order to get Konstantin to back out of the contract when her King refused to renegotiate its terms to leave her out of it.

"No, but your integrity is bone-deep and your understanding of duty uncommon in the current age."

She found it interesting he believed so strongly in her honesty, knowing how she'd sought to manipulate his brother. But then she hadn't done anything *wrong* in her efforts to get out of the contract. Maybe more than anything, that revealed how much this King did not believe in the double standard of fidelity so many men in positions of power seemed hampered by.

Nevertheless, she reminded him, "We've had this discussion."

"Yes. You have promised that if it came between our children's happiness and duty, you would choose their happiness. That is not a deterrent to me."

"Apparently it's not." But she didn't understand how it wasn't. Did he think she'd give in when it came down to it?

He would learn differently if the situation ever arose.

"We share the knowledge that more than our own happiness rests on our shoulders, but the well-being of an entire country. That does not mean we will both not make every effort to see our children happy that we can."

That was good to hear, but too practically put to justify the squishy warmth inside her right now.

Doing her best to ignore those feelings, she acknowledged, "I was raised to understand my place in the world and that it was not the same place as Jenna's, or the other *normal* people like her."

Nataliya had done her best to have a normal life, but she belonged to the royal family of Volyarus and always would do.

He nodded. "Jenna, while a good friend, does not have the welfare of a country to consider when she decides how she spends her time."

"You're saying I do." Despite her ever-present knowledge of her place in the world, Nataliya had never really thought that she took that into account in *everything* she did, but she wasn't sure she could deny it either.

"You always have."

When she'd been little, Nataliya had known she could not talk about what happened in her home, not only because of the shame she and her mom felt, but because *a lady did not tell tales*. And she had known she was Lady Nataliya since she knew her own name.

As she'd grown older, that knowledge of who she was *had* continued to influence her. When she'd been tempted to test her hacking skills at the university in ways others did, she'd stopped herself, knowing if she got caught it could bring embarrassment to the royal family.

One of the reasons she was so good was that she'd had to be positive she could not be traced or trapped when she tried a hack. Her absolute need not to be caught had made her better.

Nataliya hadn't been born a princess, but she had been born into the royal family.

Because her father had been such an embarrassment to the throne, she and Mama had been forced to make choices for the good of Volyarus even other nobility of their country would not be required to make.

While those choices had hurt, Nataliya had never denied they were necessary.

The way the exile had been handled by King and Queen? That had not been okay.

The way she and Mama had been made into pariahs right along with her father? That had not been okay.

The fact that her mother's exile had never been lifted? That had not been okay either.

But Nataliya did not resent her place in the world or what it required of her to fill it.

"If it had been up to you, would you have left my mother living in exile for all these years?" she asked him as their soup course was laid.

"You mean, if I had been in your uncle's position? I should hope that I would show more concern for one of my subjects, much less a woman as close to me as a sister. It is true that in life we are sometimes called to pay the price for another's sin, but it is not my habit to dismiss that cost to others."

"Have you ever been faced with a similar situation?"

"Yes, I have." But he did not elaborate and then Nikolai frowned. "However, in a very real way, it was up to me. I did not pressure my brother into fulfilling the terms of the contract."

"Why not?"

"I was allowed to choose my wife."

"And you felt guilty that he had not."

"Yes." He paused, considered, like he was deciding how much he wanted to say. "That was part of it certainly."

"What was the other part?"

He approved the wine for the soup course and then met her gaze, his mysterious and dark. "When you were a teenager, you used to watch me like I was a football star."

"You knew about my crush?" She should have been embarrassed, but somehow she wasn't.

She wasn't ashamed of the feelings she'd once had for him, even if she never wanted to be that emotionally vulnerable again.

That crush had turned into unrequited love that she had not managed to stifle despite her best efforts until he'd lost his wife and his grief acted as a barrier to her heart she'd never been able to erect on her own.

"I did and I felt it was unfair on you both to press forward a marriage that would cause you both discomfort if not pain under those circumstances."

She'd never thought he'd noticed her obsession with him. Nataliya gave Nikolai a self-deprecating smile. "I thought I was so good at hiding it."

"Who of us as teenagers is that good at hiding anything?" he asked with some amusement.

"I'm pretty sure that even as a teenager, you were an expert at hiding any feelings you did not want to share."

"I had posters of…" He named a popular American film star. "All over my side of the room at boarding school."

"But she would have been old enough to be your mother!" Nataliya exclaimed, laughing.

"I thought she was everything sexy."

"And now?" Nataliya asked, wondering if he had another secret celebrity crush.

Nikolai gave her a sultry look. "My tastes have refined. I'm turned on by sexy computer hackers who forget dates."

"I didn't forget—I was late."

"Because you forgot."

How did a woman forget a date with a king? She didn't, but the first week of his courtship, Nataliya had gotten caught up in her work to the extent that Jenna's frantic phone call wondering where she was had been necessary.

"You weren't angry you had to wait."

"Naturally not. I find it admirable that you take your work so seriously."

"The duty thing again?" She sighed and knew she owed him the truth. "It's not about focusing so seriously on my job—it's that I really get lost in it and have no awareness of time passing or even people coming in and out of the room with me."

"I find that charming." His heated look said he found it something else too. Hot.

How? She didn't know, but she was glad. "Here's hoping that doesn't change because I'm unlikely to. It's a personality trait."

"You're very blunt."

Her mouth twisted in consternation. "Not a great trait for a diplomat, I know."

"For a princess who is a diplomat by role rather than career, I do not agree. I believe that your ability to be forthright will be a benefit to our House."

She laughed. Couldn't help doing so. "You're the only one who has ever considered that flaw a strength." Even her beloved mother found Nataliya's blunt manner something to censure.

"Honesty is not a flaw."

"Even when I say truths I shouldn't?"

"I have never heard you say anything you shouldn't," he claimed.

"Um, are you practicing selective memory, or lying?" she asked.

"Neither."

"But I offended your father and your brother during that little tribunal at the Volyarussian palace."

"And their attitude to you offended me."

"It did?" She thought about how Nikolai had responded in that confrontation. "It did."

"Yes. Nothing you said that day should not have been said," he repeated with an approving smile. "So, you too saw it as a tribunal?"

"What else? My so-called *uncle* and your father, not to mention your brother, were determined to put me on trial."

"And instead they found themselves on the wrong side of having to defend their own actions and attitudes."

Looking back, she realized that was true. No one had expected her to take them to task, but she had. And Nikolai, without condemning his own brother, had backed her up.

So had Oxana and Mama, in their own ways.

They ate in companionable silence for a few minutes before she said, "I've been thinking about what I would like to do careerwise if I were to become The Princess of Mirrus."

Subtle tension filled his body, like he had gone on alert. "Yes?"

"I would like to continue what I do for Demyan..." she trailed off when that subtle tension went overt.

His jaw went hard, his body going ramrod straight, but all he said was, "Yes?"

"I like what I do, but I wasn't sure there was a place for me at Mirrus Global."

The tension drained out of Nikolai and his smile was blinding. "You want to use your powers for my company rather than Yurkovich-Tanner?" His delight at the idea was unmistakable.

She grinned. "Yes, but only part-time."

"Because you understand that to be my Princess is in itself a job that requires time and attention? I could not have chosen a better lady to stand at my side if I had searched the world over."

The compliment was over-the-top, but she got the distinct impression he meant every word and that did things to her heart she didn't want to examine too closely. "You really are something special, you know that?"

"Because I like the idea of headhunting my own wife from my rival?" he asked, in full arrogant-guy mode.

She rolled her eyes at him. "Yurkovich-Tanner is not your rival. You are business partners."

"But I have been jealous of Demyan's hacker for years."

"You didn't know it was me." She didn't make it a question.

Nataliya and Demyan had done an excellent job of hiding her true role at Yurkovich-Tanner since she'd been hired on and he discovered her abilities as a hacker.

She was the one who had discovered the Crown Princess's pregnancy after Gillian and Maks broke up. Demyan had used Nataliya on the most delicate matters. Only now did she realize that was because he had always seen her as family, and he trusted her implicitly.

"I did not." Nikolai winked. "Once we found out at the *tribunal* I was worried you would want to continue working for your cousin."

That's why Nikolai had gone all tense just now? He'd been thinking about it even then?

"When I marry, my loyalty will belong first and foremost to my husband." She was still talking in couched terms, but it needed to be said.

"That is a great boon coming from a woman with such a formidable sense of loyalty."

She shrugged, a little embarrassed. "You're always so complimentary."

"I think very highly of you. I would have thought you would have realized that by now."

Coming from the man she admired above all others, that was kind of an amazing thing to hear. More than amazing, it touched Nataliya's heart in that uncomfortable way all over again and even filled it.

Everything around her went into sharp focus as something she had simply not allowed herself to see became glaringly obvious. This one man touched her emotions in a way no one else did, and with a simple compliment, because he lived in her heart.

She still loved him.

She'd never stopped, though she'd done a good job of pretending to herself for the sake of her own sense of honor.

She'd felt bad for loving a married man, and like a monster when he'd lost the wife *he'd* loved. Nataliya had also realized it was not fair to love one brother and marry another.

So, she'd convinced herself that her *crush* was over, that her feelings for Nikolai were nothing more than teenage hormones.

But this feeling inside her was so big, she could barely contain it. She adored the man who had always been her hero.

At first, she'd just had an almighty crush on the man, but she'd learned to respect so much about him from early on. Yes, he'd taken over as King for the sake of his father's health, but Nikolai had done so with a fully developed agenda that put the people of Mirrus first. He was a staunch conservationist and environmentalist which wasn't easy to manage with the economic needs of his country, but he did it.

He was respectful to others, didn't lose his temper or throw around his weight just because he could and he was loyal to his family. Loyal like her own uncle only pretended to be.

Had *he* been the reason she'd been so determined to end that contract? Had her subconscious finally realized that she simply could *not* marry his brother?

She couldn't be sure that it played no part and she wasn't sure how that made her feel.

Because her integrity was important to her.

"I think I still have a crush on you," she blurted. And while that was blunt it wasn't the whole truth, but telling the man who had made it clear he did not and never would love her that he owned her heart was not on.

He smiled at her, the expression unguarded for just a moment so she saw the difference between his normal smiles and this one. "I *really* like your honesty, *kiska*."

Everything inside her seized with the need to claim this man. "I'll marry you."

His smile fell away, but he didn't look unhappy, just really serious.

Silently, he stood up from his seat, and then he moved around the table to take one of her hands to pull her to feet, as well. "Will you marry me, Lady Nataliya?"

She stared at him in confusion. She'd just said she would. Then she realized what he was doing. Giving her the proposal.

And something else clicked. He'd *always* planned to propose tonight. That little trinket box had been a hint, but he had *not* intended for it to be the question.

She liked knowing that. A lot. She'd told him she wanted a proposal and because it was something he could give her, he had done. "Yes, Your Highness, I would be honored to be your Princess."

Then he kissed her, despite there being bodyguards all around. It wasn't a chaste kiss either.

His mouth claimed hers, his tongue sliding between her parted lips to tangle with hers. It was like the other night, but not.

She felt absolutely connected to this man and his arms around her in this very public place proclaimed she was his, as he was hers.

The kiss went on for long moments until flashes behind her eyelids made her open her eyes and she realized they'd drawn the attention of some enterprising paparazzi as well as park visitors using their camera phones.

"We're going to be viral by tomorrow," she husked.

"You were agreeing to be my wife—I do not mind the entire world knowing that."

"Me either." She sighed. "But I think we've given them enough fodder for gossip."

"Do you think so?" He lowered his head and kissed her once more.

Because he wanted to show he wasn't ashamed of claiming her? Because he was too arrogant to let her call things to a halt? Just because he wanted to?

She didn't know and didn't care as she responded with a passion-filled joy she'd never thought to experience.

# CHAPTER SEVEN

WHEN NATALIYA RETURNED to her hotel later that night, she called Mama to warn her about the formal announcement going out the next day.

Nikolai had never doubted Nataliya's answer even if he had been willing to ask the question.

"Are you sure this is what you want?" Mama asked, sounding worried.

"Why are you asking me that now? You didn't ask me ten years ago when I signed that contract if I was doing what *I* wanted." Nataliya didn't know where the words came from.

She sounded bitter, but she wasn't bitter. Was she? She'd never thought she was.

Her mother had done the best she could, but she hadn't been raised to stand up to family pressure, or even to stand against an abusive bully that called himself a husband.

Only it did feel like it was ten years too late to be asking Nataliya if she wanted to be a princess.

"Ten years ago, I was still desperate to go home, desperate to return to life as I knew it." Went unsaid was the truth that Solomia had been prepared to allow her daughter to pay the price to make that happen.

"And I was the conduit for that happening," Nataliya spelled out.

"You were born into a royal family—your life was never going to be entirely your own. No more than mine has been."

So, why ask if marriage to Nikolai was what Nataliya wanted now? "Did you ever want something different for me?"

"Why, when I believed that was the way life should be?" Her mother's sigh was clear across the phone. "I'm not the same woman I was ten years ago."

"So you don't still believe that?"

"If I could go back ten years, I would insist you *not* sign that contract," her mother said fiercely.

"Why?"

"Because at the time I didn't realize it could mean you would end up married to the King." And her mom's tone made that sound like the worst imaginable fate.

Nataliya didn't understand why. "Not because you didn't think an arranged marriage was a bad thing."

"No, actually. I didn't want you to love your husband like I loved your father. It made our relationship too inequal."

"You believe I love Nikolai like that," she said with dawning understanding.

Her mother was worried about Nataliya being hurt the way she had been.

"Don't you?"

"Nikolai is not anything like my father," she said instead of answering. Nataliya had never lied to Mother and she wasn't going to start now.

"You look at him with such fascination," her mother said, like that was a tragedy. "You always have done. Even before that contract. When the idea of you marrying Konstantin came along I thought I saw a way of protecting you from the pain of living with a one-sided love."

"Because you didn't think Nikolai could ever love me."

Her mother's scoffing sound was answer enough. And surprisingly hurtful. "He was infatuated with Tiana from the time he first laid eyes on her. They were of an age. She sexually enthralled him. I knew because I recognized the signs. I was enthralled with your father and I ended up badly hurt because of it."

"So you didn't want me to love my husband?" Nataliya asked with disbelief. "I think that's a little extreme."

"Not in the world I have always lived in. How many of our family's marriages are based on love, or even include romantic love, do you think?"

"Maks and Demyan both love their wives deeply."

"Your cousins have been very lucky and so have the women they married because incredibly, they share an abiding, reciprocal love."

"But you don't think any man would love me that way?" Nataliya asked painfully.

"My dear daughter, you are more comfortable with computers than people. You are no femme fatale, or even sexually aware socialite like Queen Tiana was. I love you with my whole heart—"

"But you don't think Nikolai ever will," Nataliya interrupted. "Well, that's fine. He wants me." She did not doubt that at all now. "And I want him. I don't need him to fall in love with me."

The secret hopes in the deepest recesses of her heart said otherwise, but no one else ever had to know about those.

"I sincerely hope for your sake, that is true. Just promise me…" She paused as if searching for words.

"Promise you what?"

"If he ever hurts you, with his fists or his infidelity, you will leave. The first time. Not the fiftieth."

As much as her mother's earlier words had hurt her, these showed just how deeply the Countess loved her daughter. Mama dove into the wedding preparations after that, insisting on flying to Mirrus and liaising with the official wedding planner in situ and Solomia planned to still be there when Nataliya arrived for her visit.

\* \* \*

Home in Seattle, Nataliya was happy to discover that Nikolai continued to text and call as often as his schedule allowed.

He also continued to send what he now called betrothal gifts for her online auction. And that touched her in ways she wouldn't have admitted to anyone else. Even Jenna.

They made plans for Nataliya to travel to Mirrus so that she could spend time with him and his family before the wedding.

"You are aware that I have known your family for a long time now," she said one evening on the phone as they discussed her upcoming trip.

"But not as my future bride. Both my father and brother need to come to terms with treating you like *The* Princess of Mirrus."

Nataliya wasn't surprised that neither the former King nor his second-eldest son, Prince Konstantin, were keen on her in the role. She'd offended them both and didn't regret that. So how could she regret that they *had to come to terms* with her as the future Princess of Mirrus?

"I notice you don't mention your younger brother," she teased, knowing full well that Dima liked her just fine.

"He thinks you're a goddess since you convinced me to allow him a gap year between the university and graduate school."

She laughed. "Does he know how easy that was?"

"And let him believe I'm *easy*? No chance."

"You'd prefer he think I have undue influence."

"Influence yes. Excessive amounts?" he asked with dismissive candor, no teasing in *his* voice. "Not likely."

He said stuff like that sometimes that made her think she needed to ask about his first marriage, but Nikolai clammed up whenever Tiana was mentioned in passing, much less asked about directly.

"Don't worry. I'm not in this for my influence over the King."

"Why are you in this?" he asked. Then sighed. "Forget I asked that. I know why you said yes to my proposal."

"You think so?"

"You would not go back on your word."

"So you think I said yes because I signed that contract?" she asked, wondering how he could be so blind to her feelings.

Of course she'd never voiced them, but he'd noticed her teen-age crush when she'd thought she'd done a much better job hid-ing it than the love that she could no longer deny she felt for him.

"Why else?" he asked, as if there really couldn't be another reason.

And she had to smile, though he could not see it. "Because I want to be *your* wife."

"You are good for my ego." His voice was rich with satisfac-tion, but more than that, Nikolai really sounded pleased.

And she thought that was definitely worth admitting that much of the truth. "I don't think your ego needs inflating," she teased.

"You might be surprised."

"Nikolai?"

"Yes?"

"Were you happy with Tiana?"

Silence pulsed across the phones for long moments. Then he sighed. "At first, I was deliriously happy. Later, I regretted ever meeting Tiana much less marrying her."

Nataliya had to stifle a gasp of shock. "Your marriage looked so perfect from the outside. You grieved her death. I know you did."

"I did, but relief was mixed with the grief. And I lamented the loss of my unborn child as much, or more than, my wife."

"I'm sorry."

"I was too, but that time in my life is over. You and I will start a new chapter."

"We already have." It was no less than the truth. For both of them.

Despite the shortness of their engagement, Nikolai found him-self unexpectedly impatient for the event in the weeks leading up to his wedding.

Far from assuaging his desire for his intended bride, the knowledge that she *would* be his soon only made him want her more.

He'd been surprised by how much he craved sex with Nataliya. Though lovely, she had none of the overt sensuality of Tiana, and the women shared almost nothing in common physically. Tiana had been a petite, curvy, blonde socialite. He'd *thought* she was his idea of sexual perfection.

Then he'd started looking at Nataliya as a potential bride and discovered that statuesque five-foot-nine innocence really did it for him. He could not wait to touch and taste her modest curves, to see how sensitive the nipples tipping her small breasts were. He wanted to touch the silky mass of her dark hair, to feel her body pressed all along his length.

She was going to fit him perfectly.

He had a purely atavistic anticipation of becoming Nataliya's first lover and spent more time fantasizing about their wedding night than he wanted to admit. He would certainly never allow Nataliya to know how much he wanted her.

He'd learned his lesson.

But that didn't mean he didn't crave her. He did. Nikolai had never had a virgin in his bed. Though he'd believed his first wife to be untouched until their wedding night.

She'd laughed at his surprise, telling him not to be such a throwback.

And he had taken her criticism to heart, realizing that it would be wrong to expect something from her he had not himself practiced.

Because although he had never found uncommitted sex the tension relief that Konstantin did, Nikolai *had* had a few partners when he was at the university.

In fact, he'd thought he was sexually sophisticated until he had married.

Tiana had been an expert at using her sensuality to tie him

into knots. Nikolai had made several decisions under the influence of his desire for her brand of sexuality.

He would never be so weak again.

His virgin fiancée was not going to play those kinds of
games, he thought with a great deal of satisfaction. Even if
Nataliya had enough sexual experience to know *how* to play
the *tease and withhold* game, she would not do it.

It was not only in physical appearance that his future wife
differed so strongly from the woman he had once made his
Queen.

Nataliya had all the honor that Tiana had lacked.

Nataliya would *never* take bribes in exchange for influenc-
ing her husband's political or business decisions. She had even
made it clear that their marriage would harbinger a shift in her
loyalties from the Volyarussian royal family to *his* family and
people.

Knowing how willing she had always been to sacrifice for
the good of the Volyarussian monarchy, he found a great comfort in that truth.

Yes, Nikolai had made a very good decision when he determined to make Nataliya his Princess.

# CHAPTER EIGHT

NIKOLAI SENT HIS personal jet to fly Nataliya to Mirrus for her visit.

That didn't surprise her. The social secretary and public relations consultant waiting on board for her did. Jenna had agreed to travel with her as her stylist.

The magazine was happy because Jenna was also doing a new series of articles on the personal fashions for *The* Princess of Mirrus, including an exclusive on her wedding dress and those of her attendants.

"We've both been hired on a trial basis, Lady Nataliya," the social secretary explained. "His Highness wants you to have final decision about the people who make up your team."

"Of course he does," Jenna said. She thought Nikolai pretty much walked on water.

Nataliya rolled her eyes at her friend. "Do you think I would tolerate anything else?"

"Well, you are fulfilling a draconian contract that most modern women would reject outright. Even if it is to marry King Yummy." Jenna waggled her eyebrows.

The PR consultant looked pained. "If we could refrain from mentioning the contract." She gave Jenna a stern look. "And from using terms such as *King Yummy*."

Unperturbed, Jenna just grinned. "Things like that contract don't stay secrets."

"The contract has never been a secret," Nataliya said with some exasperation. "And this modern woman is not naive enough to believe that everyone gets married for nothing but *true love.*"

"That is true, but we would prefer the international media pick up on the romantic element to your relationship with His Highness," the public relations consultant said repressively.

"What romantic element?" she asked.

It was Jenna's turn to look pained. "Please, Nataliya. Even I can see the sparks that arc between you two when you are in the same room."

"That's chemistry, not romance," Nataliya maintained. She might love her fiancé, but she was under no illusion the feeling was mutual.

The PR consultant looked like maybe she was regretting taking this job. Even temporarily. "His Highness has engaged in a very romantic courtship, my lady."

"Nataliya, please."

The consultant gave Nataliya a slightly superior look. "It might be a good idea to get used to being addressed by your title, before you become The Princess of Mirrus."

Nataliya's mouth twisted with distaste, but she nodded. The other woman was right, but that didn't mean Nataliya had to like it.

However, she did have experience with formal protocol as part of the royal family of Volyarus. And she was not unfamiliar with being addressed as *lady*, simply not enamored of it. But she'd have to get over that and she knew it.

By the time they reached Mirrus, Nataliya's new social secretary had briefed her on how her visit to the small Russian country would go. As the future Princess of their King, she would be greeted on landing with a formal procession and would be attending not one, but three royal receptions in the five days of her visit.

Nikolai had been right. It would be very different from the times she had spent in Mirrus before.

If Nataliya had been hoping for more time getting to know the man she planned to marry, she realized that wasn't going to happen.

He was there, with the officials, when her plane landed however.

Her social secretary sighed, the sound someone makes after watching a really sweet movie. "His Highness is smiling."

Her gaze locked on Nikolai's handsome countenance, Nataliya could do nothing but nod. He *was* smiling.

Which she realized wasn't something he used to do. Like at all.

But during their courtship, he'd graced her with that slashing brilliance often. And she'd basked in the warmth of it. Even as she was not consciously aware of how uncommon it was.

"Oh, that will make good copy," the PR consultant said.

And Nataliya's answering smile slid from her face.

Nikolai's brows drew together, and he took what looked like an involuntary step forward.

"Good grief. Lay off with the PR perspective, would you?" Jenna demanded of the PR consultant as she shouldered past the other woman to stand right behind Nataliya. "He wasn't smiling at you for public relations. He's happy you're here, friend."

"This is not proper protocol," the PR consultant reminded them. "Your stylist should not be in position to have photos with you."

Nataliya turned her head to look at the PR consultant. "Jenna is my friend before anything else and as such she is always welcome in the frame with me."

The other woman shook her head, actually taking hold of Jenna's arm to pull her back. "She can be your *friend* but not in optics. She's not from Mirrus. She's not from the nobility.

Miss Beals isn't the right sort of person for you to favor in the PR angle."

"Please, take your hand off of Jenna." Nataliya waited until the other woman complied. "We can discuss this later. I'm not sure your views and mine are on the same wavelength."

The look the other woman gave her said she agreed, but it wasn't the PR consultant who had it wrong. That was going to be a problem, but right now Nataliya needed to greet Nikolai.

She smiled and went down the stairs to the tarmac.

The King stepped away from the rest of the dignitaries and reached for her hand. "Welcome to Mirrus, Nataliya."

He didn't use her title and Nataliya's smile returned. "I'm very glad to be here. Nikolai."

Then he did something entirely unexpected. Nikolai leaned down and it seemed like he was about to kiss her.

Mesmerized by his nearness, she did not move. And then he *was* kissing her. In front of the dignitaries, the press and the special guests given permission to greet her plane.

All of those people faded from her consciousness as his lips played over hers. She leaned toward him and he let her, making no move to keep protocol-worthy distance between them.

Nikolai lifted his head, an expression of satisfaction stamped clearly on his features, but she did not understand its source.

"I think I'm going to have to let the PR lady go," she blurted. "We don't see the world through the same lens at all."

He nodded. "Okay."

"You don't mind?"

"Both she and the social secretary, Frosana Iksa, know they were hired on a provisional basis."

"The provision being that I approved them?"

"Exactly."

"I like Frosana. I think she'll make a good social secretary, but the public relations consultant called Jenna out for standing next to me."

"Jenna is your friend. Where else would she stand?" he

asked, showing that he understood life was about more than strict protocol.

"Exactly."

And maybe the PR consultant could change her perspective to more reflect Nataliya's, but somehow she doubted it.

That was the last moment they had for anything resembling private conversation as she was introduced to cabinet ministers and the C-level management from Mirrus Global.

She noticed that neither Prince Evengi nor Prince Konstantin were present.

But Nataliya did not allow that to bother her. If they were making a statement, that was not her problem. If they were too busy, again, not her problem.

She wasn't marrying either of them and if they had anything to say about her becoming The Princess of Mirrus, that was between them and Nikolai.

Since he'd made it clear he wanted her to marry him, she trusted the savvy, modern King to know his own mind. And how to handle opposition from within his own family when it came.

There were even dignitaries in the car with them on the way back to the palace, but Nataliya was pleased to see that Nikolai had arranged for Jenna to ride with them as well, cementing in the minds of those present her friend's role and the respect the royal family expected to be accorded to the best friend of the future Princess.

Nataliya's mother was with Prince Evengi at the palace when they arrived, the pair looking thick as thieves as they went over wedding preparations in the drawing room.

Mama gave Nataliya a warm hug and kisses on both cheeks before doing the same for Jenna. "I'm so pleased you could be here to support Nataliya, Jenna. You're a good friend to my daughter."

Jenna hugged the Countess back. "Are you kidding? I'm living the fairy tale without any of the angst."

Mama laughed, but Prince Evengi looked inquiringly at Jenna. "You believe Lady Nataliya is living a fairy tale?"

"Well she is marrying a handsome king," Jenna said drolly, showing no discomfort at being addressed by a king, but dropping into a curtsy as Nataliya had taught her to do even as she answered so frankly. Then she tacked on, "Your Highness."

"Ah, the Countess has coached you in protocol. That will help both your and Nataliya's acceptance now and in the future."

"Actually, it was Nataliya. She's perfect princess material. But you knew that, or you never would have signed that contract ten years ago."

Nataliya had to hold back her laughter at the look of consternation on the King's face.

"So I have reminded my father more than once in the last weeks."

Nataliya was a lot more shocked by Nikolai's willingness to air discordance with his father in front of others than by his championship of her. He was too strong willed to ever tolerate even the former King's second-guessing his choice of wife.

"I believe you were the author of the articles on Lady Nataliya's foray into dating," Prince Evengi observed to Jenna.

"I was. It turned out to be a nifty bit of PR for your son's courtship of my friend."

"It did at that." He frowned. "But that was not the intention of that article, was it?"

"No. The intention of the article was to highlight first-date styles for each season."

"And here I thought it was to embarrass my younger son into withdrawing from the contract," Prince Evengi said wryly.

"But how could that be when his older brother was not in the least embarrassed by the fact the woman he chose to court was attractive to other men?" Jenna asked innocently.

"You are quick on your feet," Prince Evengi said without a shade of irritation. "That will do you well if you choose to attend the receptions introducing Lady Nataliya."

"I'm invited?" Jenna asked, for once not sardonic, but surprised.

"Of course you are, dear," Mama inserted. "You are my daughter's best friend."

"I'm her stylist."

"Because she trusts you more than anyone else, or we would have a different stylist here for the week, but you still would have been invited to join her."

This was news to Nataliya, but she didn't doubt her mother's words. Mama was no longer the eager-to-please woman she had been when Nataliya was a child.

Prince Evengi took the news that Nataliya wasn't convinced the PR consultant would be a good fit with her with a frown, but one look from Nikolai and even the arrogant former monarch did not voice his evident displeasure.

"She came with the best of recommendations and had a great deal of experience working with royalty," Mama said musingly.

"I do not want a consultant who thinks every aspect of my life is a PR opportunity." Nataliya understood that her life had changed irrevocably when she agreed to marry Nikolai, but she was still a person in her own right with a life she intended to live happily.

"You have agreed to marry a king. Your life is no longer your own," Prince Evengi said but without reproach.

So, Nataliya did not take offence. Particularly since he only voiced her own thoughts. "No. It now belongs in a very real way to the people of Mirrus, but it will never belong to a PR consultant," Nataliya answered with spirit.

"And here I thought at least part of it belonged to me," Nikolai teased.

The varying looks of shock at his facetious comment made Nataliya smile. "Yes, just as yours belongs to me."

"But neither of us is willing to be bossed around by petty dictators masquerading as our personal staff." This time Nikolai's tone was nothing but serious and the look he gave his father and then the various staff members standing around left no one doubting he meant exactly what he said.

"Perhaps Gillian has someone she might recommend," Mama suggested. "I think you and she have similar viewpoints on the matter of public relations balanced with family and life."

Nataliya nodded to her mother's comment, her gaze caught by the look in Nikolai's gray eyes.

And for just a second, it was like they were alone in the room. Then Prince Evengi said something. Nikolai's expression veiled and a discussion of the finer details of the wedding ensued.

Nataliya and Nikolai did not have a private moment until after the formal dinner and reception that evening.

Nataliya had been introduced to a good portion of the Mirrus nobility, Prince Evengi doing the honors and exhibiting none of his reticence about her becoming the next Princess of Mirrus. Nataliya had met some of these people before when attending Nikolai's coronation and later Tiana's funeral, but of course they responded entirely differently to her in her new role.

There was a great deal of curiosity in the looks directed at her, though no one was gauche enough to give it voice.

But she *had* been intended for the second son and now she was marrying the King.

Despite the curiosity and the fact that formal functions had never been Nataliya's favorite thing, she managed to enjoy her evening. Mostly because while his father had taken on the role introducing her, Nikolai still contrived to be by her side for almost the entire evening, making it clear the wedding was not something he was being pressed into.

Nataliya and Nikolai were now walking in the private courtyard gardens. Nataliya found herself enchanted by them, lit beautifully to highlight the evening-blooming flowers and fountains.

"It's gorgeous out here." She had not seen this garden on her previous visits.

"My mother loved exotic flowers, not just orchids. She designed this garden as a private retreat for our family." Nikolai looked around as if remembering happy times. "There are both day- and night-blooming flowers."

"Don't they die in winter?" Nataliya asked while wondering what the gardens looked like during the day.

They were so magical now, she was almost afraid to see them and be disappointed.

"There is a retractable glass ceiling that is closed when temperatures drop."

"Amazing."

"And decadent, yes, but it made my mother happy and I find having a place in the palace that is reserved for family and only the closest of friends beneficial, as well."

"So, no using it to impress VIPs?" she asked, only half joking.

"No. Though my father argued doing just that many times with my mother, but she stood firm." Nikolai's smile was reminiscent.

"And he loved her enough not to gainsay her?" Nataliya asked, finding it difficult to imagine the arrogant former ruler in the role of adoring spouse.

"He respected her. I do not know if he loved her. That element of their relationship was not my business."

"He must have respected her a great deal not to start using it the way he wanted to once she was gone."

"Yes." Nikolai gave Nataliya a knowing look. "My mother was also formidable of nature. Much like someone else I know, she refused to be budged on matters that were important to her. I would not have put it past her to demand a deathbed promise from my father not to *desecrate* her garden."

Nataliya wished she'd had the chance to get to know his royal mother. She sounded like an amazing and strong woman. "Are you calling me stubborn?"

"Are you trying to imply you aren't?" he countered.

She shrugged. "You don't get far giving in." She'd learned that early.

"No, you do not."

"You're pretty stubborn yourself."

"And arrogant, or so you've said."

She couldn't deny it. "Was it all for PR?" Nataliya found herself asking, when in fact she'd had no intention of doing so.

Her mind had actually been on the promise she needed him to make her.

Nikolai led her to an upholstered bench with a back, its design in keeping with the Ancient Roman theme throughout the garden. He pulled her to sit beside him, the large central fountain in front of them, giving a sense of privacy that was probably false. But still, it was nice.

"Was what all for PR?" he asked her, genuine confusion lacing his voice. "I thought we'd just established this garden is not for public consumption, relations or otherwise."

Oops. "The PR lady said your courtship was a perfect romantic public relations coup."

"You are asking if my attempts at showing you how well suited we are were in some way motivated by a desire to look good for the public?" he asked, still sounding more confused than offended.

"Konstantin breaking the contract wasn't going to look good in the media." Nataliya sighed. "If I'd broken it, it wouldn't have looked any better. The press would have gone looking for the why and they might have found the same thing I did."

Nikolai looked surprisingly unworried by that prospect. "He might have been labeled the Playboy Prince, but I'm not as concerned about things like that as my father."

"You aren't?"

"No. I would be furious with either of my brothers if they married and then continued to play the field, but prior to marriage? I expect them only to behave with honor. And in answer to your question, no, my courtship of you was not a PR stunt."

"Courtship is a very old-fashioned word."

Nikolai's powerful shoulders moved in an elegant shrug. "In some ways, I'm a very old-world man."

She thought about his subtle change to her wording and smiled. "Yes, I think you are."

"In your own way, you are also very old-world."

She could not deny it. Perhaps it had been spending her formative years living with the volatile and pain-filled marriage of her parents, or simply being raised to respect duty and responsibility as paramount in her life, but Nataliya approached the world very differently than the friends she'd made in the States.

Even though she'd lived there more years than she had in Volyarus.

Nataliya's mouth twisted wryly. "Jenna calls the contract draconian."

"Haven't you thought the same thing?" he asked.

"Yes."

"But still, you honored it."

"My agreement to marry you had more to do with you than the contract," she told him with more honesty than might have been wise.

Nataliya had no intention of admitting her love for a man who didn't want it, but she wasn't going to have him believe she was more motivated by duty than she was.

Looking back, she wondered if she would have still backed out of the contract even if Konstantin hadn't proven himself to be a man she would never trust.

She could not imagine a wedding night with any other man than Nikolai.

"You do me a great honor saying so." The words were formal, but the look he gave her was heated.

Her body responded to that look in an instant, her nipples going hard and sensitive as they pressed against the silk of her bra. Nataliya pressed her legs together, the feelings in her core ones she'd only ever experienced with him.

The air around them was suddenly sultry.

"You have offered me the same assurance." Her voice came out husky and quiet, revealing the effect his intense regard was having on her. And there was nothing she could do about that.

They weren't kissing. Or talking about intimacy, but sexual desire was roaring through her body like a flash flood, drowning every other thought and emotion in its wake.

"You want me." His tone was filled with satisfaction laced by something like wonder.

Which made no sense. Considering what he knew of their history, he could not be surprised she wanted him.

Although the level of passion he drew out of her shocked even Nataliya.

She literally shook with the need to touch and to be touched by this man.

Nataliya leaned forward and tipped her head up so their lips were only a breath apart. "Of course I want you." And his un-hidden desire for her only fed that craving until she had no choice but to act.

Pressing her hands flat against his chest, inside his suit jacket, so she could feel the heat of his body through the fine fabric of his shirt, she let her lips touch his.

He growled deep in his chest but made no move to take over the kiss.

Nataliya's fingers curled into the fabric of his shirt while she moved her lips against his, teasing the seam of his mouth with her tongue as he had done to her.

His lips parted and his tongue came out to slide along hers, but it was not enough. She needed more.

More touch.

More of his mouth against hers.

More of his body and her body together.

More.

More.

More.

She climbed onto his lap, her legs straddling his hard thighs, the soft silky fabric of her cocktail dress cascading around them in a rustle of silk.

She pressed down against the hard ridge in his trousers, the layers of cloth between her most sensitive flesh and his no barrier to sensation. Without conscious thought, she rocked against him, increasing that sensation, driving her own pleasure higher.

He groaned, hard hands clamping on her hips.

For one terrible moment, she thought he was going to stop her, but he pulled her even closer, guiding her to a more frenzied rocking and suddenly she wasn't in control of the kiss anymore.

And she didn't care.

He knew exactly what she needed.

More of him.

And he gave it to her until the spiraling tension inside her made it almost impossible to breathe.

She broke her mouth from his. "Please, oh, please, Nik."

"Please what, *kiska*? Please this?" And one of his hands slid up her torso to her nape and then the hidden hooks holding the halter of her bodice together were undone and silk was sliding down bare and heated flesh.

Nipples already aching with arousal went so hard she hissed in borderline pain.

But he knew and he touched and squeezed and rolled and played before dipping his head to take one turgid nub into his mouth.

Nataliya cried out as ecstasy exploded in sparks through her.

Nikolai's mouth demanded nothing less than everything she had to give. And she gloried in the giving.

They rocked together, one of his hands on her hip and the other playing with her breasts. She kneaded his chest like the kitten he called her and gloried in the rising sensations.

Suddenly his hand on her hip moved to press against her bottom, increasing the pressure between their cloth-covered intimate flesh. His body went rigid and he groaned into their kiss like he was dying.

But he wasn't. He was experiencing the ultimate pleasure with her.

And knowing that was all her body needed to explode in the kind of ecstasy she hadn't known she could feel. Even after what she had already experienced with him.

These intense sensations were in a class all their own.

Her womb clenched and she knew that if he'd been inside her when this had happened, she would have gotten pregnant. It was too powerful not to have borne fruit.

She bit her lip and met his molten gaze. "And I can't wait for our wedding night. I used to think sex wasn't all that."

"You've never had it—how would you know?" he asked with an intimate smile.

"I never cared that I didn't have it," she told him. "And just because I never had sex with another person doesn't mean I didn't learn my own body's reactions."

"Hmm, I'd like to learn some more of your body's reactions." He frowned. "But not tonight." He looked around the garden. "I cannot believe we did that here."

"Do you regret it?" she asked.

"No." He helped her straighten her clothes. "But we are lucky we were not discovered. Although only family is allowed in these gardens, any one of them could have walked up on us."

"That would have been terribly embarrassing," she acknowledged, but she was still glad she had the effect on him that she did. "Sometimes I get the feeling you don't *want* to want me."

"Of course I do. Believe it, or not, but if I had not found you attractive, I would have found an honorable way around that contract."

"I believe it." But that didn't answer the truth that sometimes he said or did things that implied he refused to allow himself to desire her *too* much.

And maybe that was the key. The too much. Because Nataliya

remembered how he used to look at Tiana. And there had been no tempering in the desire Nikolai had felt for his first wife.

Whatever had happened between the two, it had taught this proud King that sexual desire that went too deep was dangerous.

Putting those thoughts aside because she could not change his past, or her own for that matter, Nataliya focused on their future. "I need a promise from you before we marry."

"Yes?" Nikolai shifted Nataliya so she was sitting sideways on his lap, but still so close to him their body heat mingled.

"I need your word that you will be faithful." Nataliya loved both her mother and her Aunt Oxana, but she had no desire to live their lives.

"Haven't I already given it?" His patrician brows drew together. "I asked you to marry me. And a promise of fidelity will be included in our marriage vows."

"Yes, but I need you to promise me personally. To say the words and mean them."

"You know I keep my promises." There was no little satisfaction in his tone at that truth.

"I do."

"And you want this one?" Nikolai confirmed.

"Among others."

"Very well," he said without asking what the other promises were. "I promise never to have sex with another woman while I am married to you."

"I promise never to have sex with another man," Nataliya offered, feeling something profound and right settle inside her.

His gray gaze flared with emotion and she knew she'd done the right thing.

Swallowing, Nataliya forced herself to continue. "I need you to promise that you would never physically hurt me, or the children we will have together."

She waited for Nikolai to get angry, but he didn't. He simply nodded.

"I promise to always use my strength to protect you and our

children. I promise never to strike you. I promise you will always be safe with me." He was so serious and she could hear the sincerity lacing his deep, masculine voice.

"I promise you will always be safe with me, too." A person didn't have to be stronger, or bigger to hurt someone else. Only willing to do harm. And she wasn't.

# CHAPTER NINE

THE REMAINDER OF Nataliya's visit to Mirrus went without incident, but there was also no repeat of the explosive passion in the garden.

She enjoyed meeting people at the receptions and was really happy with the plans in place for her wedding to the King. Her mom was over the moon about everything and that just added to Nataliya's sense of rightness about it all.

Yes, she had to live her life for herself, but knowing her choices were fulfilling some of her mother's dreams for her only child was nice.

Despite not being aware of Nikolai and Nataliya's time together in the garden, Prince Evengi and Mama contrived to make sure that Nikolai and Nataliya were not alone together for the remaining days of her trip.

Something Nataliya was seriously regretting as he escorted her to the airfield for her return to Seattle.

They were alone now; even Jenna was riding in another car, but the trip to the airport was not long enough.

"Are you sure you have to return to the States?" Nikolai asked.

His question startled Nataliya, because though he'd made it clear he was looking forward to their marriage, he'd never intimated he wanted her to move to Mirrus any sooner than planned.

Nataliya frowned, her own disappointment in the answer she had to give riding her. "Yes. I've barely started packing up my things."

"We could hire movers."

She smiled, liking his enthusiasm, but shook her head. "No. I need to sort through stuff and decide what to do with my furniture." It would be silly to move all of her things only to discard half once they reached Mirrus.

"Donate it."

She laughed. "I think I'll post pics to social media first and make sure none of my friends want anything."

"Your friends would want secondhand furniture?" he asked, sounding just a little shocked.

And Nataliya had to laugh. "Yes, Nikolai. Plenty of people are happy not to have to buy a new kitchen table, or sofa."

"Surely it will not take three weeks to dispose of your furniture." His handsome features were cast in frustrated lines.

And she wanted to smile again, but she held back, thinking he might take her attitude the wrong way. But he was a king and this near petulance was charming. "It will take me two weeks to work out my notice and get together with my friends to say goodbye. I'm actually coming back the week before the wedding. I thought you knew that."

He made a dismissive gesture with his hand. "I am glad of that, but I do not understand why you have to return to Seattle at all."

"I told you—"

"You have to work out your notice," he interrupted in a very unroyal-like way. "But Demyan will have to learn to do without you sooner, or later."

"In two weeks to be exact," she pointed out. "And there are still my friends."

"You're moving to Mirrus, not falling off the face of the

earth. You do not have to say goodbye when surely it will be a see-you-again-sometime moment."

"For some, it may be. Like Jenna. But others I probably won't ever see again. Their lives and mine won't cross."

"Are you upset about that?" he asked.

"I'm a little sad naturally, but if I moved to another part of the country for my job the same thing would happen. Life is full of change."

"Your mother isn't happy we're getting married so quickly."

"But she is *thrilled* we are getting married. Mama will adjust to the timing of it."

Nikolai grimaced. "She pulled me aside and asked if I realized that our expedient marriage would give rise to gossip."

"She's probably right." They'd been over this, or had they? They'd talked about so much.

"You're not worried about it?"

"No. I'm not." Nataliya had learned long ago that she could either live in fear of the scandal mongers or ignore them. She chose to do the latter. "If we *had* anticipated our wedding vows and I had gotten pregnant, it would not have been a tragedy."

Nikolai looked startled at that. "Because people are already speculating?"

"That's one reason."

"And the other?"

"I would not be embarrassed to walk down the aisle pregnant with your child."

"You're something of a rebel in the royal family, aren't you?"

Nataliya shrugged. "Maybe? My experiences have taught me what is important."

"And gossip doesn't make it on the list."

"No."

"I will miss you, Nataliya." Nikolai gave her one of his genuine smiles, the ones that melted her. "I enjoy your company very much."

"I'll miss you too," she admitted.

He kissed her then, a soft, tender kiss that said goodbye and see you soon and I'll miss you.

She was still in a daze of emotional wonder when she boarded the plane and strapped into a seat beside Jenna.

"I think I'm going to have to break up with Brian," Jenna mused in a light tone at odds with her words.

Nataliya jerked her head around so she was facing her friend. "What? Why?"

"Because his kisses don't affect me like that."

"What kiss?"

"Please. Why else would His Highness have wanted you to himself if it wasn't to kiss you goodbye without an audience?"

"He did kiss me."

"I figured. You came on the plane in trance."

"I wasn't in a trance."

"Close enough." Jenna searched Nataliya's features. "I understand you agreeing to marry him better now though."

"Because I get a little spacey after he kisses me?"

"Because you love him."

Nataliya went still. "It's not a fairy tale, Jenna."

"No, but you love the King and he's pretty darn into you."

"He doesn't love me."

"Does that bother you?" Jenna asked, curiosity but not judgement on her face.

"It should, shouldn't it?"

"I don't know. If you were someone who wanted to marry for *true love*, maybe. But you're not. Even though they had an arranged marriage, your mom fell hard for your dad and he claimed to love her back, but that wasn't a recipe for happiness for any of you."

"No, it wasn't."

"Look, I get it. I'm not sure about the love thing, but I know I'd rather be in a relationship with a man who could kiss me stupid than a man who I don't miss when I'm away from him for almost a week."

"You really are going to break up with Brian."

"Yep."

"I *do* love Nikolai and I think he needs to be loved."

"Whereas you need to be respected and appreciated and I don't think anyone after these past few days is in any question how highly your future husband esteems you."

That esteem was put severely to the test a week later when Count Shevchenko gave a "tell all" interview that barely side-swiped the truth.

Yes, he was her biological father and yes she had signed a contract that included marriage between the two royal houses ten years ago.

But from that point it was pretty much fabrication and fantasy, and nasty fantasy at that.

Furious that he had not been invited to the wedding and even more angry that his daughter's elevation to Princess would not mean a lift of his own personal exile from Volyarus, the Count gave chapter and verse on the personal aspect to the contract signed ten years ago. He implied that Nataliya had not been content to marry a mere prince and had set her sights on the widowed King.

He painted his daughter as a scheming manipulator whose only interest was in her social position and wealth.

Nataliya was still reading the four-page spread in one of the most notorious gossip rags with international circulation when her phone's ringtone for Nikolai sounded.

Demyan, who had provided the paper and voiced support for her before she started reading, asked, "Is it King Nikolai?"

She nodded, having made no effort to pick up the phone.

"Are you going to answer it?"

Nataliya shook her head.

"Why?"

"I'm afraid."

"He's not going to call off the wedding because your father is a cretin."

"Won't he?"

Demyan grabbed Nataliya's phone and swiped. "No." Then thrust the phone at her.

She pressed it to her ear.

"Nataliya, *kiska*, are you there?" It was Nikolai's voice.

Of course it was Nikolai's voice. He didn't sound angry, but then he was a king. He didn't go around yelling when he got mad.

"Nataliya?" he prompted in an almost gentle tone. "I can hear you breathing. Say something, *kiska*."

"I..." She had to clear her throat. "I'm here."

"Are you all right?"

"Have you read it?" she asked in turn, without answering a question she actually wasn't sure she had an answer to. Was she all right?

Her father was doing his best to upend her life. Again. The last time he got her exiled from her country and her family. This time? Would he destroy her chance at marrying Nikolai?

A heavy sigh. "Yes, I have read it. I want you to come to Mirrus. I can protect you from the paparazzi here."

"You want me to come there?" she asked, trying to understand that request in light of how ugly the publicity was likely to get.

"You are not a little girl, Nataliya. He cannot destroy your life again. No one will ever take your home or family from you again. I will not allow it."

"I don't have a home." She wasn't even sure where the words came from, except a tiny part of her heart that still held the wounds from her childhood.

Seattle had been her home for the last fifteen years, but her apartment was almost empty now, in preparation for her move to Mirrus. Only would Mirrus be her home now? After the article?

"He won't have only this up his sleeve," she warned Nikolai. "My father's probably planning to do a televised interview too."

"Your home is now the Palace in Mirrus and soon you will be my Princess. He can say what he likes, but nothing will change that."

"But he's always going to be a problem." She realized now how true that was.

Her father had no intention of staying quietly in the background. Apparently, he had no qualms about how he achieved the spotlight either.

"We will determine a plan of action for dealing with the Count, but I don't want *you* dealing with the intrusiveness of the media without my support."

Picturing just how intrusive things could get, Nataliya could feel the color draining from her face. Would the honorable thing to do be to withdraw entirely from her connection to Mirrus? And even her own royal family?

Her thoughts started spiraling and Nataliya felt dizzy with them.

"What's he saying?" Demyan demanded, putting his hand on her back and encouraging her to lean forward. "Breathe, Nataliya. Just concentrate on breathing."

"Hold on a second, please, Nikolai," she said into the phone as she attempted to take a couple of deep, calming breaths.

He cursed. "You are not all right."

Nataliya just took another breath as the world came back into focus. She sat up, all the while aware that Nikolai was barking out orders to someone on his end of the phone.

"You can call back later, if this is a bad time," she offered.

"Nyet. No. Do not hang up on me, *kiska*."

"Okay." She looked at Demyan and wondered what he was making of all this.

Her cousin's expression was grim, but he reached out to squeeze her shoulder. "It is going to be okay, Nataliya."

She just shrugged, not at all sure he was right.

"Put me on speaker, please, *kiska*."

"Why?" One of the protocols all the royals learned early was never to use the speaker function on their phones. Too easy to be overheard.

"I can hear Prince Demyan," Nikolai said. "I'd like to speak to him too."

She still thought it was odd, but Nataliya did as requested.

"What is going on?" Demyan demanded toward the phone.

But Nataliya answered. "Nikolai wants me to go to Mirrus, to avoid the media."

Something like relief flitted over her cousin's hard features. "That's a good idea."

"I'm not running away." Her father wasn't going to make her abandon her job or her plans.

She wouldn't let him.

"Coming home is not running away," Nikolai opined.

"Be reasonable, Nataliya," Demyan added. "The vultures aren't going to let you go to the grocery store without incident, much less anywhere else."

"I have commitments throughout next week." She took another deep breath and let it out slowly, reminding herself that she was not a little girl to be pushed around by her father's whims. "I'll be fine. I'll stay at Mama's." She'd been planning to do that anyway, for her last couple of days in Seattle, as the shelter she was donating her bed to was scheduled to pick it up then.

"But your mother is not there. She is here. And her home is not secure."

"Her condominium is in a gated community. They even have security that do rounds."

"A rent-a-cop in his golf cart?" Demyan snorted derisively.

Nikolai was worryingly silent.

"Nikolai?" she prompted when he had not replied several seconds later.

"Yes, *kiska*?"

"I'm going to be fine but thank you for worrying about me."

She had a lot of thinking to do and she knew she wouldn't make an unbiased choice if she went to Mirrus.

She couldn't simply consider what she wanted, but what was best for Nikolai and the people of Mirrus.

"You will be fine, yes. Demyan, please keep Nataliya inside the building until I arrive."

"Arrive? What do you mean arrive? You can't just drop everything and come here."

"Are you coming to Mirrus?" he asked.

"In a week." Maybe. "Nikolai, we need to think about how best to handle this and it might not be me coming to Mirrus in the near future." Or at all.

Demyan made a sound of disagreement.

Nikolai cursed again and then said, "I will see you in a few hours."

"But, Nikolai, there's no need." How was she supposed to make her mind up to break things off if he was there, tempting her?

"I know what you are thinking, Nataliya *moy*, and it is not going to happen. We are not breaking the contract. You are not backing out of this marriage." There was not a bit of give in Nikolai's aristocratic tones. "Prince Demyan?"

"I'll keep her inside, Your Highness."

Nataliya gave her cousin a look, but he just shrugged. "It makes sense, Nataliya, and you know it."

"Nikolai, you must realize that my uncle will want me to cancel the wedding to avoid further scandal," Nataliya said.

Demyan's grimace said he agreed.

"I repeat, we are *not* canceling our wedding," Nikolai said forcefully. "Any attempt to make you pay for your father's actions will be met with not only my disapproval, but retaliation."

Instead of looking annoyed by Nikolai's threat, Demyan grinned. "Good."

Nataliya was still trying to process that her fiancé was *not* looking for the easy way out of the scandal. Would not even hear of Nataliya backing away from their betrothal.

He'd been pretty adamant all along, but she found it incomprehensible Nikolai wasn't even considering it in the face of her father's behavior and the potential ugliness to come.

"I will see you in a few hours, Nataliya."

Nikolai and his larger-than-normal security team stepped off the elevator on the top floor of the Yurkovich-Tanner building in Seattle.

Prince Demyan was waiting, no doubt having been apprised of Nikolai's arrival. "She's in her office. Working."

The other man's tone let Nikolai know what he thought of that state of affairs and it wasn't approval.

"That sounds like Nataliya."

The Prince grimaced, but nodded. "My cousin has a full ration of our family's stubbornness."

"I have noticed."

"She'll pretend she's fine, but she's taking this hard," Prince Demyan warned as he turned to go down a soft carpeted hall. "Follow me."

Nikolai's security team took up different positions in the hall until only one remained at his side.

"That is to be expected," Nikolai said to Prince Demyan as they walked. "It is her father after all."

"Trying to ruin her life. The bastard."

"Indeed."

The Prince stopped outside a door and turned to face Nikolai. "You won't let her down, will you? She's going to try to sacrifice her own future for the greater good. I know her."

Prince Demyan's expression didn't bode well for Nikolai if his answer was anything but no. It didn't worry Nikolai because he had no intention of letting the very special woman be hurt any more than she had already been by her father's reprehensible behavior.

And she was going to be his Princess.

"You mean like she did ten years ago when she signed that contract."

"Yes."

"She wants to marry me." Of that Nikolai was entirely convinced.

"I agree, but are you going to let her go?"

"Never," Nikolai assured the other man. "I will stand by her as her own family did not all those years ago."

Prince Demyan nodded, his expression grim, nothing to indicate he had taken offense at Nikolai's words. "Our King did not do well by her or the Countess."

"No, he did not."

The Prince's demeanor stiffened. "Fedir and Oxana have made decisions that were difficult for the good of our country." As their unofficially adopted son, Demyan had always had leave to use the familiar address for the King and Queen.

"Even so, it is not a decision you would have made." Prince Demyan could be entirely ruthless, hence his marriage to the one woman who could have destabilized the economy of Volyarus, but he was fiercely loyal.

And Nikolai had learned that the Prince had ensured his wife-to-be was more than adequately protected with their pre-nuptial agreement. He was not the type of man to allow someone else to suffer unfairly.

Prince Demyan inclined his head and offered more truth than Nikolai was expecting. "Or that my adopted brother would make as sovereign."

"I believe that." Nikolai had done his homework on the entire family when he became King and his brother's betrothal became his responsibility and not that of their father.

"But that does not mean our King acted out of anything but duty and the belief that he was doing what was best for Volyarus."

"It would seem loyalty is a family trait."

"Nataliya is very loyal," Prince Demyan said, proving he knew exactly what Nikolai had meant.

Nikolai nodded. "It is one of the many things I admire about her."

"Good." The Prince opened the door and stood back to allow Nikolai entry.

Nataliya looked up from her computer, her face pale, her eyes haunted. "Nikolai! You're here."

"I told you I would be." He could only hope that his stubborn fiancée would cooperate with Nikolai's plan for dealing with the problem of her father.

"But you must have gotten on a jet almost immediately."

"I did." He instructed his remaining guard to wait outside the door and then closed it on him and her cousin.

Nataliya looked at the closed door with a worried expression. "I think Demyan wanted to talk strategy."

"You and I will do so. After."

"After?"

He crossed the room and pulled Nataliya from her chair and right into his body. "After we have greeted properly, and I have assured myself that you are all right."

"I'm fine."

He just shook his head and then kissed her.

She melted into him, no resistance whatsoever, kissing him back, her arms coming up and around his neck. Passion flared between them as it always did when they were this close, but he could sense a fragility in her that was not usually there.

And it was that fragility that allowed Nikolai to lift his head. "You are such a temptation, but I do not think you are fine at all."

"He said horrible things about me. I never did anything to him, but he never loved me." Nataliya snuggled into Nikolai, seeking comfort in a way that was both surprising and welcome. "I thought he couldn't hurt me anymore, but he can, and I don't like it. Mama will be so hurt. She's moved on with her life, but he's going to dredge everything up again. All the old pain while heaping on a new dose. It's just not fair."

"You have not spoken to her?" Nikolai knew the Countess had planned to call her daughter.

Nataliya shook her head. "I couldn't. She'll be devastated and it's all my fault."

"None of this is your fault," Nikolai argued, fury filling him that his sweet and loyal fiancée could take the blame for her reprobate of a father's actions. "All culpability lies one hundred percent with the Count."

Nataliya didn't answer, just leaned more securely into Nikolai, as if seeking strength. "I can't believe you came."

He was more than happy to share his with her, but knew she had plenty of her own. "I cannot believe you would think I would do anything else."

"But your schedule." Her head tucked perfectly under his chin, like she was made to fit against him like this.

"Can be adjusted," he reminded her. Nikolai rubbed her back, finding the action soothing and hoping she did too. "Just as yours must be."

Her head came up at that. "You're going to insist I return to Mirrus with you, aren't you?"

"I am hoping you have reconsidered that course of action on your own."

"And if I haven't?" she tested.

"I will leave it up to you to explain to my cabinet and my company why I am in Seattle when I am supposed to be in the palace for several important meetings prior to our wedding."

"You can't stay here!"

"I will not leave you alone to face the vultures of the press."

Nataliya sighed. "Demyan already told me that I didn't have a job to come to anymore."

"Did he?"

Her cousin went up a notch in Nikolai's estimation and he already respected the Prince.

"He said I was being recklessly stubborn."

"And what do you think?"

"I think you're both ignoring the most expedient course of action and I cannot figure out why. And in any case, I don't want to feel like a coward."

"There is nothing cowardly about coming home." He completely ignored her reference to expediency.

Their definition of that course of action wasn't going to match.

"And Mirrus is my home now?" she asked, her expression unreadable.

"You know it is."

She nodded and something in his chest loosened. "It is." She looked away from him. "I never thought I was weak, but I want to go back with you. I want to go through with the wedding."

Hearing the last loosened the remaining fear he had not wanted to acknowledge. She was not going to walk away from him. "No one could make the mistake of thinking you are weak," he promised her.

"You don't think so?" Nataliya was looking at him again, her lovely brown eyes shiny with emotion.

"No, but if they do, they are idiots."

"Why would a father be so cruel to his only child?" she asked, like she expected Nikolai to have the answer.

He didn't; he only had the truth he knew. "I am sorry, *kiska*, but your father is a cruel man all around. As to why the articles and why now, I do not think it is as simple as him wanting revenge for his continued exile."

That seemed to startle her. "What then?"

"Money."

"You think he hopes to extort money from us? But if that was the case, wouldn't he have threatened before going to the tabloids with his ugly allegations about my character?" Wasn't that how blackmail worked?

"He has done one interview in print, an interview that has

forced everyone involved to sit up and take notice. As you said earlier, he could do much more, but right now he believes his bargaining position is strong."

"But blackmail? He couldn't think he'd get away with it. With King Fedir, that might even fly. After all, there's a reason my father has been able to draw his allowance from the family coffers annually, but with you? He must know you will never pay him a penny."

Nikolai liked very much that she knew him that well. "You do not think so?"

"No." She rolled her eyes. "He'd have better luck getting blackmail payments out of a nun who'd made a vow of poverty."

"Interesting analogy, but you are right." Nikolai had plans where her father was concerned and not one of them included paying a single penny to the grasping Count.

"You're talking like you know the Count wants money."

"I do know. He made the demand while I was en route."

Nataliya's natural lovely tone went paste white. "What does he want?"

"Right now? A single large payment followed by a yearly stipend to ensure his silence in the future. He's getting none of that," Nikolai assured her.

Before Nataliya could respond, a knock sounded at the door.

"Come," Nikolai commanded.

It opened to reveal the Prince. "Your guests are waiting in the lobby."

# CHAPTER TEN

NATALIYA TRIED TO step back from Nikolai, but he wasn't having it. His arms remained firm around her as she tried to make sense of what her cousin had said.

"You never react like I expect you to," she told Nikolai.

Her proper King, who was known for his dignified demeanor, winked at her. "Just think, you will never grow bored with me."

There was an underlying seriousness to his teasing that Nataliya wished she understood better.

She patted his muscular chest, feeling daring with her cousin standing right there. "No chance of that happening."

"If we could suspend this somewhat nauseating chitchat, everyone is waiting," Demyan said sardonically from his place in the doorway.

"Give us a minute," Nikolai instructed her cousin.

Demyan nodded and left.

"Are you ready?" Nikolai asked her.

"Ready for what exactly?"

"We're about to give a press conference."

"What? Why?"

"We're going to detooth the tiger."

"But my uncle." No way had King Fedir agreed to such a thing.

"Is not the sovereign in charge here."

But King Fedir could be impacted in a very detrimental way. There was a risk her uncle's own long-hidden scandal would come out if her father decided to exact revenge, though she wasn't sure Danilo would risk losing what income he still received from the Volyarussian royal coffers.

Either way, her former King's actions were no more her responsibility than her father's had been.

"What is that sound you made?" Nikolai asked her, as if they weren't in the middle of an intense discussion.

"Surprise," she answered, with no thought of hiding her thoughts from him. "I just thought of my uncle as my former King."

"I am your King now." Pure satisfaction laced Nikolai's tone.

She smiled, her heart beating fast for no reason. Or maybe for every reason. "Yes."

"It is my honor and my privilege to protect you and your mother as members of my family. And I will do a better job than your former King."

"Your arrogance is showing again."

"Perhaps. Will you do the press conference with me?"

"You're asking me?"

"I am."

"Yes, but I'm not sure what we are supposed to say?"

"In this one instance, I would consider it a personal favor if you would follow my lead."

"Okay."

"There's something else."

"What?"

"Beyond the press conference, we have two legal options open to us. We can file criminal charges against the Count for blackmail. Even if he has a good lawyer, he'll spend some time in prison. In addition, you can sue for libel and drag him through the courts for the foreseeable future. We don't have to win the case to bankrupt him with legal fees. He lives beyond his means as it is."

For the first time, Nataliya had hope her father would not prevail. Why hadn't she considered legal recourse?

Because to do so would cause scandal, and that was anathema to the Royal Family of Volyarus, but there was no way past scandal in this situation. Even paying the blackmail wouldn't guarantee her father's silence. He was vindictive and cruel and not always smart.

He could get angry and do something that would harm himself more than her or Mama in the end, but it would still harm them. Just as his actions had with their exile.

"He could go to prison?"

"All calls to the palace and to my personal cell phone are recorded."

Which meant that they had recorded evidence of the attempt to extort the King. "He should have gone to prison for what he did to my mom when they were married. He's broken the law again and I think he should pay the consequences of that, but I need to talk to my mother before I decide."

"I would expect no less from you. The charge doesn't become any less serious waiting a day or two to file." Nikolai cupped Nataliya's cheek. "You understand that in trying to blackmail *me*, that even if we do not file a complaint here in the US, he is already guilty of treason against the Mirrusian Crown. If he ever attempts to enter our country, he will be detained, tried and most likely end up incarcerated."

Nikolai could have no idea how good that news sounded to Natalia.

Detooth the tiger indeed. "And the press conference?" she asked.

"We will set the story straight."

Jenna arrived then, for moral support, but also to help Nataliya get ready to face the press.

Again, Nikolai had thought of everything.

\* \* \*

When they reached the lobby, both Nikolai's security and that for Yurkovich-Tanner were in position. There was a table covered with a cloth and bunting in the colors of the House of Merikov. The Mirrusian Royal Crest was displayed prominently on the front.

The cavernous lobby was packed. News crews from the major networks were there along with journalists for reputable entertainment shows, magazines and newspapers.

Demyan stood to one side, along with people Nataliya did not recognize.

One of those people stepped forward, introduced themself as the press liaison for King Nikolai of Mirrus, thanked everyone for coming, gave a few instructions for holding questions and the like and then introduced Nikolai and Nataliya.

"I want to thank you all for coming," Nikolai said in confident tones. "Understandably my fiancée, Lady Nataliya of Volyarus, has been deeply saddened and upset by the spurious interview given by her father, the disgraced Count Shevchenko."

Nikolai smiled reassuringly down at Nataliya and whether it was for show or because he cared about her feelings in that moment, she felt better.

"The one thing the Count got right was that there was in fact a contract. Neither my people, nor King Fedir has ever tried to hide that fact."

Murmurs erupted in the room, but soon died down as it became obvious Nikolai would not continue until there was silence.

"That contract was not between Lady Nataliya and my brother."

"But she was expected to marry him?" a bold reporter called out.

He was shushed, but Nikolai answered. "That contract was signed ten years ago. If they intended to marry, I think it would have happened by now, don't you?"

Laughter erupted into the room.

Nikolai waited until it calmed down before going on. "The truth is that when I realized I'd mourned my deceased wife long enough, I looked around me and Lady Nataliya was the woman I saw."

Nataliya did her best to keep her smile and not show the shock she felt on her face. Did he mean that, or was it part of the damage control?

"My brother made his disinterest in fulfilling the contract official, leaving the way open for me to court the woman I wanted to stand beside me, but make no mistake, I had every intention of stealing Nataliya from my brother if he did not step aside."

Gasps sounded throughout the room, and the tap of furious typing on touch screens.

Even knowing how that all had come to pass, Nataliya almost believed Nikolai's version.

"So, the idea that Nataliya set her sights on me because I am a king when she was promised to my brother is a total fiction. The fact is, it was entirely the other way around. I set my sights on her and I courted her with every intention of success."

"How do you feel about that, Lady Nataliya?" a female reporter asked.

"Honored. And very pleased with the outcome. Anyone who thought Prince Konstantin and I would have a made a good couple doesn't know either of us very well."

"You don't like the Prince?" someone asked.

"I'll like him just fine as a brother-in-law," she promised.

Laughter erupted again.

The rest of the press conference was more of the same, and Nataliya's sense of unreality grew. How much of what Nikolai said was the truth and how much was *spin*? When the courtship had first started, it would not have mattered to her, but now?

Now that she realized she loved him, the answer to that question was of paramount importance.

* * *

More reporters and cameramen congregated on the walk outside the Yurkovich-Tanner building. These weren't the ones invited to the press conference. These were the ones who had read that sleazy interview with her father and wanted their pound of flesh.

Nataliya could see them from her seat beside Nikolai in the helicopter as it lifted off from the roof. They were traveling via helicopter rather than the jet he had arrived in because he had refused to allow her to be exposed to the clamoring press waiting like jackals.

She couldn't help feeling a certain satisfaction knowing the vultures had been deprived of their prey.

Not all journalists were bottom feeders. In fact, she was of the opinion *most* weren't. Her best friend being a prime example, and she'd been impressed by those who had shown up for the press conference.

But the ones hoping to get a word from, or a picture of, the scandal-tainted Lady Nataliya were the type who gave journos a bad name.

The rest of Nataliya's things were being packed up by movers and would be taken to Mirrus the following morning. Her social secretary, Frosana, was busy either canceling her final engagements with friends or rescheduling virtual get-togethers from the palace.

As they flew over the sea's choppy waters and Nikolai worked on his computer, dialing into meetings via a live feed from his laptop, Nataliya realized that her life had finally changed irrevocably.

The wedding was just a formality.

She no longer worked for Yurkovich-Tanner. Nataliya no longer lived in her own pretty condominium she had bought with her own money. She could no longer meet Jenna at their favorite coffee shop.

Nataliya would never again go shopping on her own, or go hiking by herself, or do anything alone again. Not really. Even when there was the illusion of privacy, it would only be that. An illusion.

From this point forward, she would always have a security detail. Though the wedding had not yet happened, she was already considered a part of the Royal House of Merikov.

Nataliya didn't have the title of princess yet, but this flight represented the end of her personal independence.

Maybe that was why she'd fought against going to Mirrus ahead of schedule.

Nataliya knew that this time, when she stepped foot on Mirrus soil, her entire life would change. Permanently.

Because of the man sitting beside her.

Her father had really picked the wrong victim when he'd tried to blackmail King Nikolai Merikov.

If there was a more stubborn person, as certain of his course, Nataliya had never met him.

Nikolai had decided that Nataliya would make a good wife and Princess to his people. And he had allowed no one to dissuade him, not his family, not his advisors, not even Nataliya herself.

Certainly, he wasn't going to allow a man like Count Danilo Shevchenko to undermine the King's plans.

Nataliya wasn't sure what Nikolai would make of her love for him, but she was sure it wasn't part of his plan.

Affection? Yes. She could see he wanted that, but a more consuming emotion? No.

Definitely not on his agenda to give or receive.

At first that had given Nataliya a sense of peace, but as her love grew she realized how difficult it would be to keep it to herself.

Especially when he acted like he had today, like her comfort and safety were *the* top priority. When he refused to give in to pressure and take the *easy* way to anything if it wasn't the *best* way.

He was such an honorable man.

Such a good man.

"What?" he mouthed to her.

"I'm fine," she assured him, knowing he would be able to read her lips, as well.

They weren't talking via the internal communication headsets because he was using his headset for the meeting he was dialed into via his laptop.

He clicked something and then his voice came through her headset. "You sighed."

"I did?" He noticed? While in a meeting?

"You did."

"Just realizing everything is different now."

"Everything became different the moment you agreed to marry me."

That was true. "But that difference wasn't real."

"And now it is?"

"Yes."

"Good."

She laughed. "No commiseration?"

"I am pleased you realize the weight of our choices. Your sense of honor and commitment are exemplary."

"You're such a sweet-talker," she said, tongue in cheek.

Unbelievably, color burnished his aristocratic cheeks. "I am not a romantic man." He said it like he was admitting a grave shortcoming.

Nataliya smiled, but shook her head. "I disagree. You put on a very romantic courtship, but even if you hadn't? Believe me, I could not imagine a more romantic gesture than for you to clear your schedule and come to Seattle to bring me home."

The press conference had been pretty amazing too. He'd done something she knew her uncle wouldn't have.

"You didn't sound like you thought I was being romantic this morning."

"I was still fighting the final change to my life, I think," she admitted.

His brows drew together, like the idea of fighting one's duty was incomprehensible. "You knew it was coming."

"In two weeks."

"You're a little set in your ways, aren't you?" he asked like he was just now realizing that fact. "Not fond of change."

Her smile was self-deprecating. "Yes, I can be. Change is inevitable but not always my friend."

"This change will be good."

"If I didn't believe that, I wouldn't have agreed to marry you." She gave him a reassuring smile. "And please don't think I need romantic dinners in the park to be happy. The way you stood up for me today? The way you wouldn't let anyone make me a scapegoat for my father, even when I thought I needed to, that's the kind of romance that secures affection for a lifetime."

It wasn't the declaration of love her heart longed to make, but it was more than she thought she'd admit before the day's events.

"I can hope situations like that do not arrive often, but be certain I will always take your part."

"I believe you." And that? Was kind of amazing.

She trusted him in a way she trusted no one else. Not even her mother, whom Nataliya adored.

"I am glad."

Nataliya noticed one of the men at the conference table on the laptop's screen waving like he was trying to get Nikolai's attention.

"I think they need you." She indicated his computer. "I'm fine on my own."

He nodded and clicked back to his meeting without another word, trusting her at her word and Nataliya realized she really liked that too.

# CHAPTER ELEVEN

THE DAYS LEADING up to her wedding were much busier than Nataliya had expected. Since she hadn't planned to be in Mirrus for several days, the fact she magically had a full schedule was another reality check.

Nataliya had always been aware that being a princess, especially The Princess of Mirrus, was a job. What she was coming to see was how much someone in her position had been needed.

The fact she was on call to Mirrus Global for her specialized computer skills took up some of her time, but so far she hadn't been pulled into anything really tricky or time-consuming.

She saw almost nothing of her fiancé during the day, their schedules both full without overlap. They dined together every evening, but even the dinners that were not State business offered no opportunity for her and Nikolai to talk privately.

He insisted on them spending an hour together each evening in the palace's private garden, but they never repeated the passionate kisses they had shared before she'd returned to Seattle.

She wasn't sure why.

It wasn't because he didn't want her. The sexual tension between them only got higher and higher as their wedding approached.

Nataliya didn't have enough experience with this sort of thing to know exactly what to do with that, but one thing she was not? Was a shrinking violet.

So, one evening a couple of days before the wedding, while they sat in the garden talking, like they had every evening for the past week, she reached over and laid her hand on his thigh.

Nikolai's reaction was electric. Her soon-to-be husband jumped up and moved several feet away before spinning around to face her. "What are you doing?"

Since she thought the answer to that question was more than obvious, Nataliya frowned and tried to make sense of his over-blown response. "What's going on, Nikolai? I thought we agreed there was nothing wrong with sharing our passion?"

"We did." He looked like he was in physical pain.

She let her gaze slide over him and couldn't miss the erec-tion pressing against his slacks. Did it hurt?

"Stop that!" he admonished.

"Stop what? Looking at you?" she asked with disbelief.

"Yes!"

This was just getting stranger and stranger. "Why?"

"I promised your mother," he gritted out.

"Promised Mama? That I wouldn't look at you?" That didn't make any sense.

"That I would not touch you again before our wedding night," he ground out.

Irritation filled Nataliya, both at her mother for asking for such a thing and at Nikolai for agreeing to it. "At all?" she clarified.

He shrugged.

"What does that mean?" She made no effort to hide the an-noyance in her tone.

He winced. "It means that I'm on a hair trigger here. If I touch you or allow you to touch me, if I kiss you…" He visibly shuddered at the thought. "This thing between us is going to explode and I will break my promise."

"That you made to *my mother*?" Nataliya's voice held a

wealth of censure. "*Why* did you make that promise?" He was too smart not to have known what a challenge it would be to keep.

For both of them.

"Because she asked me to."

"And that was enough?" Nataliya's voice rose on the last word.

The look he gave her from his steely gray eyes implied she should understand. "She's your mother."

"And *I'm* the one you are going to marry."

"Yes."

"So, why promise my mother something you had to know I would not like? Something that would be so difficult for us both?"

"At the time, I did not think you would be here on Mirrus until a couple of days before the wedding. It did not seem like a hardship."

"And now?"

He scowled, the look close to petulant.

"Not as easy as you thought, huh?"

"I would not make such a promise now."

"You thought, easy way to win some points with the future mother-in-law," she teased, her irritation evaporating, if not her sexual frustration.

"Something like that."

Even kings worried if their mothers-in-law approved. Who knew?

Even so. "You're usually better at foreseeing the potentially bad outcome. You didn't think, hey, this could backfire on me?"

"First, I do not think *hey* anything. Second, no, I did not foresee the potential for backfiring."

"You'd better have a pretty spectacular wedding night planned," she warned him.

His smile was devastating. "You are very demanding for a virgin."

"Maybe I wouldn't be so demanding if I had any choice about that status changing before our wedding," she grumbled.

"You could always seduce me," he offered.

She tilted her head to one side, studying him. "And that would not make you feel like you broke your promise?"

His expression said it all.

"That's what I thought." She nodded and then promised, "I will never knowingly undermine your integrity."

An arrested expression came over his aristocratic features. "That means a great deal to me."

"Why?" She shook her head. "I don't mean it shouldn't." She paused. "I think it just surprises me that you would not have taken it as given."

"There was a time when I did, but I learned I could not."

"With Queen Tiana?" Nataliya asked, bewildered by the possibility.

They had seemed so in love, but maybe she needed to re-think her belief on that.

*"Da."*

"You so rarely mention your first marriage." In the beginning, Nataliya had believed that was because he still grieved the loss of his wife.

Now, she wasn't so sure.

"Tiana was not above using her position as my wife and confidant for her own gains." Nikolai's voice was devoid of emotion.

But that confidence had to have cost him, in terms of pride, if nothing else. Nataliya could not wrap her head around his deceased wife using him, much less her position, in that way.

"That shocks you," he opined.

"Yes."

"Because you could not imagine doing such a thing."

"No." There was no point Nataliya trying to prevaricate. If it made her sound provincial rather than royal, that could not be helped.

"I believe you. And that makes me very happy." His tone

wasn't lacking in inflection now. It positively rang with satisfaction.

Nataliya smiled, pleased that in this way at least he saw her as superior to the beauty he had married. "I'm glad."

"We are going to have a good marriage." He sounded very sure of that.

But that was nothing new. He'd been certain from the beginning. It was Nataliya who had taken some convincing.

"With a really special wedding night."

His sexy laughter followed her into her dreams that night and she woke with a sense of hope and happiness that only increased as Nikolai played out the humorous role of paying the bride ransom the day before their official ceremony. Because of the security necessary and the guests who would be attending their wedding, some traditions were more royal than orthodox.

Nataliya wore a vintage gown for the wedding. Despite its short lead-up time, the affair had dozens of the world's elites as guests.

The other couple of hundred guests were by no means to be dismissed. Nearly the entire nobilities of both Volyarus and Mirrus were in attendance, along with billionaire business associates.

Jenna was there, and although she would cover the wedding in an article she would write later, her only role at present was that of maid of honor or *witness* according to the traditions of the church.

Nikolai's *witness* would be his brother Konstantin, which had been suggested by the fixer to show the younger man's support of the proceedings despite being the one Nataliya had first been intended to marry according the contract. Nataliya didn't really care who stood up with Nikolai.

She was simply happy Jenna would be by *her* side at the wedding. Mama still insisted on calling it a *crowning* according to church tradition, because of the religious crowns placed on both her and Nikolai's heads during the ceremony. Not to be confused with the Princess Coronation ceremony, where Nataliya would receive an official royal tiara.

That would happen *after* the wedding.

Jenna's fashion magazine's photographer represented the favored press presence and would be the only press allowed to photograph the official coronation, while having access to areas the other media guests did not, as well.

Nikolai had made known his displeasure with news outlets that had run stories based on her father's spurious allegations of Nataliya's avarice and scheming. Excluding them from the official coronation was only part of it.

Which was why Jenna's photographer was in the room with Nataliya now as the stylist Jenna had recommended put the finishing touches on Nataliya's *look*.

"You definitely look regal enough to be The Princess of Mirrus, *Lady Nataliya*," Jenna teased, using the title she never did when they were alone.

Nataliya had been pleasantly surprised when no one suggested she choose someone with a higher rung on the social ladder than Jenna to be her maid of honor and said so now. "I'm so glad you're here with me. I'm pretty sure I'd be a bundle of nerves otherwise."

"I think the fact you are marrying the man of your dreams has more to do with why happiness is overriding nerves, but who am I to say?" Jenna responded with a laugh. "And there never was any chance someone might argue your choice to have me as your only attendant. Your mom and King Hotty put the kibosh on any dissent before you even floated my name to the wedding planner."

"How do you know that?" Nataliya demanded.

"Because unlike you, my dear friend, *I* listen to gossip."

Nataliya just laughed and got ready to promise the rest of her life to serving the people of Mirrus, as their King's Princess.

* * *

The Russian Orthodox church that hosted the wedding had been built the first decade of Mirrus' settlement.

The gorgeous structure had been the setting for every wedding in the House of Merikov since. Like Saint Basil's in Moscow, Mirrus' cathedral had multicolored rather than gold conical-topped spires, but inside the gold-leafed icons were lavish works of art from another century, and the intricately designed floor tiles breathtaking.

Her gown a replica of the one worn by the first and most beloved Queen of Mirrus in the country's history trailed behind Nataliya down the center aisle in thirty feet of rustling satin train. The guests filling the church were in a hazy glow, but Nikolai, waiting at the front for her, was in sharp focus.

He looked unutterably handsome in his Head of State military regalia, but even wearing an off-the-rack suit, she knew this man would leave her breathless.

The expression in his steely gray gaze when she joined him at the front of the church was so intense, it sent goose bumps along her arms and made her breath catch.

This man had a plan and she was part of it.

During the *procession* Nataliya was glad she had practiced negotiating her train or this moment could have been an unmitigated disaster. She was even more relieved that she would be changing into a more modern gown created by a high-end Russian designer before attempting to circulate at the reception later.

She wasn't thinking about her dress, or her need to stay very still not to mess up the train, when the priest began to speak the words of the age-old ceremony in Russian. He repeated each vow in Ukrainian before Nikolai and Nataliya made their promises.

Her heart pounding in her chest, Nataliya was surprised at how profound the moment felt.

She knew she loved the man she was marrying. Accepted

that he did not love her, but she had not considered how bound to him the vows she spoke would make her feel.

She had anticipated the weight of her role as his Princess settling on her, but not this feeling that her heart and her life were irrevocably tied to this man. To a king.

The look in Nikolai's eyes said he felt a similar level of profundity.

Which perhaps should not have surprised her, but it did.

He kept his promises. Knew she kept hers.

It was a moment of total connection between them.

They were both making commitments they intended to keep. Absolutely.

As much as Nataliya was not a fan of big gatherings, she put on her game face, smiling until her cheeks ached as she was introduced or reacquainted with the upper echelon of society.

She accepted every good wish on her future happiness with a king with equal warmth, refusing to allow the hundredth thank you be any less sincere than the first.

However, when Jenna sidled up next to her and asked if she was ready to go, Nataliya wanted to shout, *Yes!*

She couldn't though. "We've got hours yet," she informed her best friend in an apologetic whisper.

"Not according to your husband, you don't."

Nataliya startled and looked around for Nikolai. "What do you mean?"

They'd spent more of the reception together than she had expected, but it would have been impossible to remain at one another's side throughout the evening.

And now, she couldn't see him anywhere.

"His Highness sent me to get you."

"Get me?" Nataliya felt like she wasn't tracking.

"He said something about a promise he made about your wedding night?" Jenna prompted.

Heat washed into Nataliya's cheeks. No way was she going to explain that particular promise to even her best friend.

"Where is he?" she asked.

Jenna nodded her head toward the south doors to the palace ballroom. "Come with me."

Somehow, Jenna, who had not been born to nobility, was negotiating the room like a seasoned campaigner. She had Nataliya in the corridor outside mere minutes later, explaining to anyone who impeded their progress that His Highness needed Princess Nataliya for something.

Unsurprisingly, a security detail waited, but neither of the men said anything as Jenna continued to lead the way to one of the hidden hallways used by the royal family to navigate the palace. Then they were going through a set of thick doors that led to the outside behind the palace where a sleek black limousine waited.

One of the security detail stepped forward to open the door and help Nataliya inside, still silent.

The interior of the limousine was empty but for her cell phone on the seat. She picked it up and settled onto the soft leather. It rang in her hand as she was reaching for the seat belt.

Nikolai's face flashed on the screen.

She answered. "Really? You changed my ringtone for your calls?"

"I thought it was appropriate." Amusement warmed his voice.

"Somehow I don't think of you when I think of modern hip-hop."

"And yet the song is very appropriate."

It was a modern ballad by a popular female artist about desire and fidelity. Not a song she would have thought he even knew. "Not exactly subtle." As all things royal should be.

In a hip-hop song. Who knew?

"You may want to change it later," he conceded.

And she smiled. He'd made the change as part of this special night.

"Where are you?" Should that have been her first question? Maybe.

"In the SUV in front of you."

She remembered there being an SUV in front of the limousine and one behind. A quiet cavalcade without the flags of station waving.

"Why there and not here?" she asked.

"You deserve a very special wedding night. Not for our first time together to be in the back of a limousine." The promise in his voice sent shivers of desire through her.

Nataliya's hand tightened on the phone. "And if you were here, it would be?" she goaded.

"Of a certainty."

How was it possible for the sexual intensity between them to be so hot? "Is it always like this?" she wondered aloud.

"No," he assured her in a growl. "It is not. What we have is uncommon."

But not love. Not on his side anyway. "Was it like this with your first wife?"

He inhaled, like the question shocked him, but he answered. "At first, something like it, but looking back I realize that it was never this intense. Maybe because Tiana and I didn't wait." He paused, like he was thinking. "I don't know, but as much as I desired her, there was never a time I thought I wouldn't be able to control myself if I was with her."

And he felt that way with Nataliya? She couldn't help liking that, but she didn't doubt that if *she* told him no, ever, he would control himself just fine. He meant he didn't think they could control themselves together.

"Like that first kiss in the garden." Neither of them had been showing any sort of control then.

"Yes."

"At first?" she asked. "Will it get less intense?"

"No," he said without hesitation.

"But you said that with Queen Tiana…" Nataliya allowed her voice to trail off.

He knew what she was talking about.

"What I had with my first wife was different," he said with certainty. "I was enthralled by her. She used sex to control, to manipulate, but I didn't realize it until we'd been married more than a year."

No question he was alone in the back of the SUV with the privacy window up. Just as she was. Or they would not be having such an intimate and revealing conversation.

Nataliya shifted, trying to alleviate the feeling of need that even talking about his dead wife was in no way diminishing. "Even if that's true, I cannot imagine she wasn't just as enthralled by you."

"Because you are." Nikolai sounded very satisfied by that fact.

"You know I am."

"We are well matched."

"Yes." She could not deny it. Nor could she deny that she wished he was with her, the setting of their first time sharing full intimacy be damned.

"Where are we going?"

"Somewhere we can have that spectacular wedding night you demanded."

"How long until we get there?"

"Only about forty-five minutes."

"Did you just say *only*?" she demanded.

"Relax, *kiska*, we will be there before you know it. I will keep you entertained." And he did, telling her his plans for the night ahead.

By the time the limousine stopped, Nataliya was so hot and bothered she couldn't fumble her seat belt open. When she finally got it, she surged toward the door with no sense of aplomb and even less reticence.

Nikolai was there to take her hand. He practically yanked her from the car and right into his embrace.

"Lost your cool, Your Highness?" she asked him breathlessly as her body pressed against his hardness, her own cool nowhere in evidence.

"*Da*," he growled out, reverting to Russian. He told her he wanted her, that she was too beautiful to resist, in the same language. Then he swept her high against his chest.

She gulped in air and tried to regain a little of her equilibrium. "I thought carrying the bride over the threshold was a western tradition."

He didn't reply. Didn't look at her, just focused on covering the distance to the door of the mountain chalet in long, impatient strides.

Something in the corner of her vision caught her eye and Nataliya gasped. "You brought me to a glacier?"

The chalet sat high on a craggy hill overlooking a pristine blue glacier.

"Tomorrow," he gritted out as the door swung open in front to them.

"Tomorrow, what?"

"Talking." He acknowledged the woman who had opened to the door with a nod, but no words.

Nataliya gave the older woman a little wave and received a warm, very amused, smile in return.

Nataliya nuzzled into the curve of where his shoulder and neck met. "You're in kind of a hurry, huh?"

His big body gave a shudder, but he didn't slow down as he carried her determinedly up the stairs. And then they were in a huge master bedroom, the solid door slamming when he kicked it closed.

She would have teased him about slamming doors, but suddenly *that* moment was upon her. They were going to make love...have sex. Whatever they called it, Nataliya knew it would change her forever.

Her King made no move to let her go.

Inhaling his delicious masculine scent, she pressed a kiss to his neck, letting her tongue flick out to taste.

Everything inside her tightened, the pleasant throb between her legs she'd had for the last thirty minutes of the drive up the mountain becoming a sensual ache.

With a groan, Nikolai released her and then quickly stepped back, putting distance between them that she did not want.

She moved to follow him, but he put his hands up as if warding her off.

"What?" she demanded.

"You are a virgin."

"So? Tomorrow, I won't be."

"Precisely." He turned toward the door.

She stood in stunned silence until his hand landed on the handle. "Where are you going?" she demanded.

"You need gentle."

That was debatable. Nataliya wasn't feeling *gentle* right now. She was *hot and bothered*.

"So?"

"So, I need some time."

"Why?"

"So I can give you gentle."

"I don't want gentle," she informed him.

He spun to face her. "You think that, but—"

"Stop, right there," she interrupted. "Be very careful before you try to claim you know more about what I want and need than I do. I am a twenty-eight-year-old woman. I am a virgin by choice, not because the men in my life knew what was best for me and protected poor little old me."

And being a virgin did not mean she was ignorant about sex, or her own body's needs.

"You will be a passionate advocate for the rights of women in Mirrus."

"Right now, I'm not thinking of anyone but us." She stepped

out of her shoes. "Either you respect me enough to let me make my own choices, or you don't."

She waited, wondering if she could have misjudged this man and his intentions so badly.

Air filled her lungs in a breath of relief as his hand dropped from the doorknob. "It is a matter of physical necessity, not believing I know your body better than you do."

It so was, but she could forgive him because he wasn't in possession of all the facts.

"I have toys," she told him baldly.

"What?" He stumbled back, like her words profoundly shocked him.

"I am a twenty-eight-year-old woman. If you have a fantasy of a naive virgin in your bed, we can play that scenario out sometime, but right now I just want *you*."

"What kind of toys?"

She rolled her eyes. "I'll show them to you sometime. Maybe you'll want to use them with me, but not tonight."

His already dark eyes flared with heated desire. "No. Not tonight."

Done with the waiting. Done with *any* delays, Nataliya reached behind her back and pulled the zip down on the designer dress she'd changed into for the reception.

He didn't ask what she was doing, or make any more sweet but inane comments about how she needed gentleness when Nataliya was so hot she thought she might combust if he didn't get inside her soon.

Nikolai stripped with more speed than finesse, baring his gorgeous body to Nataliya's eyes.

He was beyond fit. Muscles bulged on his biceps and chest, usually hidden by the formal attire of a king, his sculpted thighs showing why he'd found carrying her up the stairs so easy.

She let out a pent-up breath, her own dress a pool around her feet. "You are beautiful."

"I believe those are my words to you."

Her throat had gone dry and she couldn't reply with a witticism, just shook her head. He was everything she could have imagined wanting in an intimate partner.

She didn't need physical perfection, but it was standing right in front of her and she had no more words to tell him how turned on he made her.

The sight of his masculine body finished what his words on the phone had started and she *wanted*. She *needed*.

She went to shove her panties down her legs, but he was there just that quickly. His hands over hers. "Let me."

She nodded, her own hands sliding out from under his to press against his sculpted chest. She circled the eraser-hard nubs of his nipples, brushed her fingertips over them just as he undid the catch on her bra, releasing her breasts. Her already turgid nipples tightened as they were exposed to the air.

They both gasped.

He cupped her breasts, swiping his thumb over the hardened peaks. "You fit my hands too perfectly."

She moaned at the sensation coursing through her, but passivity was not on her agenda. Nataliya leaned forward and took one of his small male nipples delicately between her teeth, gratified by the groan of pleasure that came from her royal husband.

She'd read that some men loved having their nipples played with, some didn't like it, and some didn't care either way, but it did nothing for them. She was glad he was of the first type. She liked getting the kind of reaction she was getting from him.

His impressive erection jutted out insistently from his body, the head brushing against her skin and exciting her even more.

The years she'd fantasized about this man were nothing compared to the reality of having the freedom to touch as she pleased and the knowledge he wanted to do the same to her.

She kissed a trail upward until their mouths met again; all the while his hands were busy pulling sensual pleasure from her body with knowing touches to her breasts.

Without breaking the kiss, he pushed her panties down her

thighs. He waited for her to step out of them and then dropped to his knees to brush her thigh-high stockings down with caresses along her inner thighs, then pulled them from her feet with sensual mastery.

This man understood a woman's body and how to give intense pleasure.

Nikolai shifted back just a little and then looked his fill at her now naked body. "*Krasiva.*"

"I thought that was my word for you," she said breathlessly, her knees threatening to buckle.

"You said it in English."

She would have laughed, but he ran a probing finger between the folds of her most intimate flesh. A strangled sound came out of Nataliya as she was touched so very intimately.

Nikolai surged back to his feet, pulling her into his body, rubbing against her with no evidence of reluctance. His hands cupped both her breasts and squeezed. The air in her lungs left her in a whoosh and though she gulped in air, Nataliya couldn't catch her breath.

Not with the way he touched her.

No hesitation, no excessive gentleness. He played with her breasts while she mapped his body with her hands.

She tilted her head and then they were kissing again, the hunger between them voracious and unabated. They kept kissing and touching until they fell together on the bed, their bodies pressed so tightly together she could feel every nuance of the ridge of his erection against her stomach.

He rolled them and she spread her legs, encouraging him to shift so his steel hardness rubbed against her clitoris.

She tilted up, seeking more stimulation, but it wasn't enough.

He reached down and pressed a finger inside her.

Pleasure rolled over her, her womb contracting in a moment of ecstasy unlike any she'd ever felt on her own. He pushed upward with his finger, hitting that spot inside so rich with nerve endings. Her climax crested again and she screamed, the sound swallowed by his mouth.

He caressed her through the ecstasy, but even though she'd just had the most intense orgasm of her life, her body was craving more.

And he gave it to her.

Nikolai pushed her thighs just a little wider and pressed inside, stretching swollen and slick flesh with his rigid erection.

"Yes!" she cried out, the sensation of him inside her absolutely perfect.

The pain of him pushing through her virginal barrier was masked by the incredible sensual pleasure racking her body. Clearly trusting her to know what she wanted, he set a hard and fast rhythm. She tilted her pelvis upward, matching his movements, demanding more with her body.

Their bodies grew slick with sweat, their breaths mingling in panted pleasure and the ecstasy built again.

"Come for me," he demanded as he pistoned into her body with unfettered passion.

"You come for me," she gasped back.

Everything inside her contracted in a rictus of pleasure so strong she could not even scream. His body went rigid and Nikolai tossed his head back, a primal shout coming from deep in his chest.

Every little move of his body triggered aftershocks of pleasure in hers. His groans said he was experiencing the same.

"That was amazing," she said with panting breaths.

He didn't reply with words, but kissed her, his lips soft and perfect against hers in the aftermath of such a primal loving.

She didn't know how long they remained connected like that.

But eventually Nikolai rolled off her, his arm going around her waist. "I suppose you want to take a shower."

"I do?" she asked, having no thought of doing so.

"We are all sweaty."

"So?" Sex was supposed to be messy, wasn't it?

"You don't mind?"

"Do you?" she asked, really not wanting to move, even for a shower.

"No." He nuzzled into her shoulder. "I love that you smell like both of us together."

"How primitive of you," she teased.

He went to shift away from her but she followed, leaning forward to kiss his muscular chest. "I like it too. Let's be throwbacks together."

The rigidity that had come over his body relaxed. "You do?"

"Hmm mmm." She snuggled into her new husband. "Thank you."

"For?" he asked, like he didn't want to misunderstand.

"Listening to me. For treating me like a woman and not just a princess."

"I will always try to listen to you."

Even his promises were perfect. He knew he couldn't promise to always get it right. Only to try.

"And I will always try to listen to you."

# CHAPTER TWELVE

NIKOLAI AND NATALIYA lay together for a while, pressed together from chest to hip and Nataliya reveled in the intimacy of it.

But they had been on sexual edge for too long and the desire between them inevitably built again.

This time, he was gentle and teasing, showing her just how much pleasure he could bring to her body with a slow buildup. She returned his touches, learning what made him moan, what made him give that contented growl that said she was connecting to him more than sensually.

She wanted to be on top during their coupling this time and he let her without hesitation. Nataliya brought them both to another culmination of pleasure and collapsed onto him after.

Eventually, they did make it to the bath, where she learned the slide of naked bodies in the water could be terribly arousing.

The sun was rising over the glacier out the huge wall of windows when she and Nikolai finally settled into sleep, their bodies entwined.

They slept away the morning, but rose to have lunch together. The entire side of the chalet facing the glacier seemed to be made of windows, so the dining room overlooked the incredible view just as the master bedroom did.

"This place is amazing."

"It is our personal getaway."

"You mean the family doesn't use it?" she asked in surprise before dishing some more fruit onto her plate.

She was ravenous.

"Not without my permission and with rare exception, I do not give it. The people of Mirrus can visit the glacier from the other side of the chasm."

"Aren't tourists allowed?"

"No. The park is owned by the royal family and only open to the people of Mirrus."

Conservation was a big thing on the island, so she wasn't surprised. "But the chalet is *yours*, not the royal family's?"

"Yes." He placed another fluffy pancake on her plate, seeming to enjoy watching her eat so enthusiastically. "It is a retreat for the King."

Nataliya looked around herself with satisfaction. "It's the perfect honeymoon destination." It afforded the privacy that would be lacking in their daily life and she was really happy to know they had this retreat to come to when they needed it.

"I'm so glad you think so."

Something about the way he said it gave Nataliya pause.

"Didn't Queen Tiana like it?"

"She never came. Nature was not her thing."

"But it's so beautiful."

"Tiana had no interest in seeing the glacier. She refused to go anywhere she could not be entertained."

"You two weren't very well suited." Nataliya sucked in her breath and nearly bit her tongue in her chagrin saying something like that. "I'm sorry. It's not my place to judge your past relationship."

But he wasn't offended. Nikolai's smile was approving and warm. "If not you, then who?" He sipped his coffee. Black, no sugar or cream. So not how Nataliya enjoyed the bitter elixir. "You are right. Once we were married, I realized how little in common I had with my wife."

"That must have been hard, but still, you loved each other."
And Nataliya was just realizing how very much she wanted
that emotion from him.

"Love?" he mused. "I thought I did, but now I'm not so sure.
She had me sexually enthralled. *She* was enthralled by the idea
of being a queen."

"I'm sure she loved you." How could Queen Tiana have felt
anything else for this amazing man?

"Are you? I am not." He didn't sound like he was bothered
by that fact.

But she knew he had to be. She remembered how he'd been
with Queen Tiana. Whatever he thought now, Nikolai had loved
the other woman. And while that hurt Nataliya a little, she recognized that their marriage would probably be a much happier one.

Nikolai asked, remembered pain reflected in his steely gray
eyes, "If she loved me, would she have gone skiing on that dangerous slope, knowing she was pregnant with my child?"

"She was very athletic," Nataliya offered. "Her sports acu-
men was renowned."

Queen Tiana had been known for her skiing prowess as well
as her skydiving feats. She was very good at any sport she tried
and she always did the most challenging aspect of those sports.
The former Queen had been lucky right up until the end too,
never having broken so much as a pinky in all her exploits.

"I'm sure Queen Tiana never even considered it might not
go well for her to take that slope."

"I've never been sure. Yes, she enjoyed the adrenaline rush
of high-risk sports, but she was a queen, pregnant with the heir
to the throne." He looked at Nataliya with an expression she
could not read. "Tiana did not want to be pregnant. She had
wanted to wait to have children, but her birth control failed."

"All this time, I thought she didn't know," Nataliya admitted.
Everything in the media, every statement given by the pal-

ace, it had all said at the time that the tragedy was made worse by her taking a chance she hadn't realized she was taking.

"That she was pregnant? Oh, she knew. As I said, she wasn't happy about it. She refused to allow her pregnancy to curtail any of her pleasures."

Nataliya didn't know what to say. She couldn't imagine making the same choices as Queen Tiana, but those choices had been the other woman's to make. Even if they felt incredibly selfish to Nataliya.

"I could tell my brother absolutely no when he wanted to participate in extreme sports," Nikolai said, frustration lacing his tone. "He recognizes my role as his King. My dead wife? With her, I had no authority."

Nataliya got what Nikolai was saying. Konstantin had given up any hopes of participating in extreme sports because of his role as his brother's heir. Queen Tiana had disregarded not only her role as Queen, but the risk to her unborn child who would become the heir to the throne.

Even so. "Um… I don't really want you bossing me around like my sovereign either."

"What about as your husband? Do I have any sway over your actions in that regard?"

"Of course you do, just I expect you to listen to my counsel when something is important to me in regard to your actions. But ultimately, though we will listen to each other, we are still self-governing."

"You live in a monarchy now, you do realize this?"

"Yes. But you aren't the type of monarch to dictate the actions of your people."

"You think not?"

"I wouldn't have married you otherwise."

"Then I hope you will not be too disappointed to realize that I will not allow you to take the kind of risks Tiana did. Not with your own safety and definitely not with the safety of any of our future unborn children."

"You sound really stern right now."

"You do not sound intimidated, but I promise you. I learned my lesson."

"And I promise *you* that while I intend to make my own decisions, you never have to worry about me putting my own safety at risk or that of our children, born, or otherwise."

The only high risk she'd taken was the one to her heart by marrying him.

They went hiking that afternoon, the lush forest awash with summer plants and flowers. They didn't see as much wildlife as they might have done but for the security detail ahead of them and the one that came behind.

Too many people. Too much noise.

Nataliya didn't mind because nothing could detract from the beauty of Mirrus. And as much as she might enjoy seeing moose or even a wildcat, she wasn't keen to see a bear. Even a small brown one.

"I'm glad you haven't encouraged tourism to the detriment of this beauty," she told Nikolai as they walked.

"We have been fortunate that Mirrus Global and the other industries on the island have never been reliant on the tourist season."

"I know about the mining." Which posed its own challenges for conservation. "And the high-tech arm of Mirrus Global."

"Mirrus Global isn't the only high-tech company we have based here. One of the world's most advanced AI developers is a citizen and his company employs many others."

"I'd like to meet him."

"Of course you would." Nikolai smiled down at her with indulgence.

Since the barely banked desire was there as well, Nataliya didn't take offense.

"Nevertheless, a certain amount of tourism is beneficial." He took her hand and kissed the back as if unaware of doing so. "If for no other reason, than offering an opportunity for our people to meet potential partners from a new gene pool."

She laughed, thinking he was joking but realized he wasn't. "You're serious. That happens? A lot?"

"Enough to make the management of our tourism industry worth the headache it brings to environmental and resource management."

"Although the education system through high school is top-notch on Volyarus, Uncle Fedir has fought against building a university every time the issue comes up. Maybe that's why." She'd spent so many years living in the greater Seattle area that some of these nuances to a small, island country were new to her, despite having been born in Volyarus and being a member of its royal family.

Nikolai nodded. "We do not have a university for the same reason."

"But aren't you afraid young people won't return to the island?" she asked, thinking that had to be a real detriment.

But Nikolai shook his head. "We are both small countries, only able to support a finite population. Attrition is not always a bad thing. Voluntary attrition is preferred over involuntary."

Like her and her mother's exile?

But thinking about it, Nikolai's attitude about natural attrition made sense. If everyone stayed, both small countries would be very different places. They would be crowded. And the problems that came with higher populations would plague them. Higher crime. Unemployment. Poverty, etc.

"I never even considered that. Both countries have a lot of citizens working in other countries while maintaining their citizenship."

"Yes. And sometimes their children return to live."

"Do you allow immigration?"

"Our numbers are by necessity extremely low, but we have few requests for permanent residence. Living in a country that lacks the amenities of big cities because we do not have them and has months in the winter with only a few hours of sunlight isn't for everyone."

She considered that. "It is very isolated, but it's so beautiful."

"I am glad you think so. It is my hope you will find life here as fulfilling as I do."

They continued to hold hands as they walked, and Nataliya made no effort to overcome the illusion of intimacy and romance the small physical connection provided.

Their honeymoon lasted only a week, but Nikolai was a reigning monarch with duties even his father and brother could not perform in his place. And yet, during their honeymoon, he never once allowed state business to take precedence over their time together.

It was a heady feeling for Nataliya to be the center of her royal husband's attention.

And the sex?

Was off the charts. She learned he had no compunction about dragging her off to bed in the middle of the day. He learned that she was no retiring maiden, unwilling to initiate lovemaking.

They made love often and by the end of the week, Nataliya felt more connected to Nikolai than she ever had to another person.

Their first official state event as a married couple was the night after their return to the palace.

Nataliya did her best to maintain a cordial demeanor, but she spent most of the evening managing her response to subtle and even some overt bids to get her to speak to her husband on one matter or another.

She complained to Nikolai later as they were going to bed. "I don't understand what they hope to gain having me bring a topic up to you rather than them." Nataliya let the disgust she felt by the grasping behavior show in her tone.

"Perhaps they believe you will attempt to use my obvious affection for you to sway my opinion."

"Is your affection for me obvious?" She hadn't noticed him being all that affectionate since returning from their honeymoon.

In fact, his very dignified manner was taking some getting used to after such an intensely sensual week where they touched constantly, whether they were having sex, or not. He had been more overtly affectionate with her *before* their wedding than since their return to the palace.

Nataliya wished she knew what caused the difference. Because she'd look for a way to change it.

He looked chagrined whether by her question or his own thoughts, she couldn't tell.

"We have been home for thirty-six hours," he informed her like she didn't know. "In that time, I have texted you several times, eaten every meal in your company and called you for no other apparent reason than to check on your welfare."

"Um…you kept track?" She hadn't. Maybe she should have. Apparently that kind of communication indicated a *deep* affection on his part. Who knew?

His gorgeous lips twisted in grimace. "My aides have. And you can be sure that the gossip of my *besotted* state has spread like wildfire through the palace."

She crossed the huge bedroom they shared until she stood only a few inches away from him, but for some reason couldn't make herself reach out and touch him.

Perhaps them sharing a room was another indication of his regard? She knew her aunt and uncle did not, but she'd never considered their marriage all that healthy. At least not since becoming an adult and realizing her uncle had a "secret" lover.

"Did you share a room with Queen Tiana?" she asked out of curiosity.

"Naturally. This is not the nineteenth century."

She smiled. "No, it isn't. So, what do the gossips say about the *deep affection* I hold for you?"

He stilled, his hands on his unbuttoned shirt, his head swiveling so their gazes caught. "You hold me in *deep* affection?"

"Yes." It wasn't as if Nikolai didn't already know she had had feelings for him for a long time. She wasn't using the L word, might never use it, but he had to know her feelings ran deeply. "Didn't your aides point out my behavior?"

After all, she'd texted him just as often, answering any communication from him immediately, regardless what else she might be doing.

"No. They did not remark on it."

And it clicked. "They're worried about you."

"I believe so, yes." He went back to removing his clothes, his body shifting so he was turned more away from her than toward her.

"They know Queen Tiana influenced your decisions." And that must lacerate pride as deeply rooted as the King's.

He jerked his head in acknowledgment and then looked away, pushing his slacks down his thighs.

Refusing to be sidetracked by the sexy vision before her, Nataliya reached out and laid her hand on his arm. "You know I won't ever do that."

"I do." But he still wasn't looking at her.

"They don't."

"No."

"That is their problem," she pronounced.

He jerked back around to face her. "No, it is also my problem."

"No, it is not. You know I won't try to manipulate you. That's all that matters. Eventually, they will see that I'm not like her, but it is not on you to convince them."

"They have a right to be worried." And he hated admitting that.

That much was obvious.

"Sure," she acknowledged. "Just as my mom is going to

worry about how you treat me until she sees for herself you aren't going to change into a monster."

His brows furrowed, offense coming over his features. "I promised you."

"You don't think my father ever promised never to hit her again, never to hurt me again?"

"I am not him." This time his tone left no doubt he was offended. Deeply.

"No, you are nothing like him," Nataliya agreed. "You are everything I could have ever hoped for in a husband."

"Unlike my brother."

"Even if your brother was as wonderful as you are, he has the singular disadvantage of not being you. It wasn't fair of me to sign that contract when I knew I cared for you."

"You were a child."

"I was legally an adult and the feelings I had for you were very adult." Nataliya no longer felt guilty for those feelings.

She knew the difference between having feelings and acting on them. She never had because he had been married and then she had been promised to his brother.

But now? She could do as she liked.

"You are my wife. You get to act on those adult feelings," he said, as if reading her mind.

The kiss they shared was incendiary and the lovemaking after had an emotional quality Nataliya couldn't define. And really? She was too tired and sated to even try.

She just snuggled into her husband's muscular body feeling safe and held in very deep affection.

A couple of weeks later, Nataliya was in the study in their suite, looking for some research she needed for a meeting she was supposed to attend with the labor council.

She had some ideas for employment-driven voluntary expatriate living she hoped they would be willing to listen to, but she was prepared for skepticism. Because so far, that was all she'd met with when she attended meetings in her official capacity as The Princess of Mirrus and a member of Nikolai's cabinet.

She'd been shocked when he'd given her an official title and list of duties that showed he regarded her as equal to his brothers and father. Even so, his cabinet ministers, business associates and other politicos treated her ideas with indulgence rather than attention.

Her mother reminded Nataliya that she had to build relationships before she would get the trust and sometimes even the respect Nataliya knew she would need to do her job as The Princess of Mirrus effectively.

It had not gone unnoticed that Nikolai made no indication he would be bestowing the title of Queen on her as he had his first wife.

Some took that to mean he had married Nataliya for mainly breeding purposes. She found such assumptions offensive. Yes, she would be giving birth to the heir to the throne, but that didn't make her a brood mare.

She didn't need to be Queen to hold an opinion or have a brain and use it.

Not that her job as The Princess of Mirrus was something she'd ever aspired to, but she would do it to the best of her abilities. It was how she was made. How her mother had raised her to be.

Nataliya could admit to herself, if no one else, that she enjoyed her couple of hours each day on the computer working in the elite tech department of Mirrus Global more than all the luncheons and meetings where she was treated like a nominal figure.

But she couldn't make changes if she didn't stay the course. And she'd noticed some changes that needed to be made.

For instance, as forward thinking as she considered Nikolai, she had done some deep digging and discovered a discrepancy in pay to female and male staff in senior positions both in the

Mirrus Global and the palace staffs. She planned to address those with him in their meeting the following day.

She grabbed her papers and knocked a folder to the floor. Nataliya picked it up and recognized the logo for Yurkovich-Tanner.

Feeling no compunction about reading it, she flipped the folder open and started thumbing through the pages. It was a joint business proposal for the high-tech divisions of Mirrus Global and Yurkovich-Tanner, written by her cousin Demyan. So, it had been created with serious intention.

Demyan didn't put his name on anything he didn't believe in fully.

She would ask her husband what he thought of the proposal at their meeting the next day, as well.

Nikolai's administrative assistant showed Nataliya and her own personal assistant into the King's spacious office.

Nikolai stood on her entrance and indicated a set of sofas and chairs on the far side of the office. "Let's sit over here."

The dark paneling and nineteenth-century-style furniture gave off a decidedly royal vibe, but the hints at high-level tech-nology were there to see if you recognized them.

Now that she was The Princess of Mirrus, Nataliya had an entire staff and her own set of offices, but all meetings with her husband were held in his.

Protocol.

It would be daunting if she hadn't been prepared for the changes coming into her life. At least that's what she told her-self.

Nikolai took a seat kitty-corner to her, but far enough away to maintain professional distance. Again…protocol.

Someone came in with a coffee tray, but Nataliya didn't need more caffeine, so she ignored it. So did Nikolai.

He pulled out his tablet, looked down for a minute and then

back up at her. "I've looked over the report you sent over. I agree we need to hire an equity auditor."

That had been easier than she expected, but she didn't make the mistake of saying so in front of their staff. She'd thought they'd have to take the report to the appropriate HR people. It was good to be King.

She smiled. "Thank you. Would you like me to take care of that, or did you have someone else in mind?"

"My staff will contact the firms you suggest in the addendum to your report."

She nodded. "That's wonderful." She was careful to monitor her enthusiasm, but Nataliya was thrilled and tried to let him know with her eyes.

His own eyes crinkled at the corners in a smile that did not reach his mouth. "We cannot allow such wage inequalities to continue."

"I agree."

They talked over some other things and he asked her opinion on taking Mirrus Global into a certain technology area. Offering her opinion also gave the opportunity to segue into asking what he was going to do about the combined venture proposal she had seen the day before.

"How did you know about that?" he asked, sounding wary.

She tilted her head, studying him and wondering where the wariness was coming from. "You left the prospectus on the desk in our study."

"I see." Rather than looking upset she had read it as she might have expected from his cautious reaction, tension leached from Nikolai's stance and expression. "And you thought, what?"

"On the face of it, it seems to be a win-win for both Mirrus Global and Yurkovich-Tanner, not to mention the two countries."

"Provided you trust Yurkovich-Tanner in their dealings with some of our most proprietary software."

"Well, yes." She frowned. "Don't you?"

"I make it a policy never to trust anyone outside my inner circle that completely."

That was not surprising. She'd be a lot more shocked if he was any other way. "That is understandable, but if you look at their track record, Demyan's office has never been responsible for a data leak." She smiled. "And he is your family now."

"Family are not always trustworthy," Nikolai said repressively.

Like Nataliya needed that reminder. "I am aware."

He nodded. "Good."

Not thrilled by his apparent lack of sensitivity where her dealings with her father were concerned, Nataliya nevertheless was ready to tackle the subject. "You said you had an update on the situation with the Count."

Nikolai jolted, like he was surprised by something. But she could not imagine what. Surely he expected her to ask?

After speaking with her mother, Nataliya had decided to press criminal charges against her father as well as filing a civil lawsuit against him.

"The first update is that he is no longer a count. While he has maintained his citizenship in Volyarus, he is no longer recognized as a member of its nobility and his exile has been formally extended to lifetime status."

"My uncle did all that?"

"You are calling him uncle again."

After a quick look at the staff and the security in the room, Nataliya nodded. "I have realized that life, not to mention our personal motivations, is complicated."

Nikolai inclined his head.

But Nataliya wasn't going to get any more private with her thoughts in front of an audience. "Is that all?"

"No. Danilo has been arrested and charged with attempted blackmail. He will be tried in Washington State. Both Mirrus and Volyarus have levied charges against him for crimes against the monarchy."

Chills ran down Nataliya's spine. "You insisted on that, didn't you?"

"Yes."

"Thank you." Her father would not be allowed to hurt her mother again and that was the most important thing to Nataliya. "I'm surprised my uncle went along."

"I am not. He had more to lose refusing than to risk by doing what he should have so many years ago."

"Do you think the civil suit is still necessary?" she asked, thinking pretty strict measures had already been taken.

But Nikolai nodded. "The charges against him do not carry a life sentence. Although he will never be allowed on either Mirrusian or Volyarussian soil again unless he wants to face a trial for those charges, he could still do you and your mother damage from America."

"And you think a civil suit will prevent that?"

"Winning a civil suit against him will go a long way in preventing him filing charges against either of you."

"For what?"

"You need to ask? Danilo will manufacture whatever tale he needs to in order to pursue his own ends."

Nataliya frowned and nodded. It was nothing less than the truth. "You're right."

Nikolai smiled a politician's smile, not a lover's and asked, "Did you want to discuss anything else?"

"No, but I would like to make sure we have time to walk in the garden tonight."

He looked startled.

"I miss you," she admitted baldly.

Also, she *liked* him texting her throughout the day and calling her when he had the chance. She didn't want that to stop because his staff thought she was less invested than he was in their time together.

"I will make sure my schedule permits."

* * *

Though she was tired, their walk in the garden was everything Nataliya needed it to be.

Nikolai held her hand and reverted to the more openly affectionate man she found so hard to resist.

Not that she needed to resist him.

He might not trust her cousin implicitly, but Nataliya trusted Nikolai. She loved him. So much.

Her unusual exhaustion was explained later when she realized she'd started her monthly.

Her first couple of days always left her nearly comatose with tiredness. She took vitamins to combat the symptoms, but the supplements only helped so much.

She was practically falling asleep as she slid into bed late that evening. There had been another State dinner and they'd come up to their suite later than they usually did.

He reached for her and she snuggled into his body, but when he started to touch her intimately, she stayed his hand with her own. "Not tonight."

His reaction was electric. He sat up and the light went on. "So, this is it? This is how you react to me telling you no about something that benefits your family?"

"What are you talking about?" she asked, even his uncharacteristic response unable to wash the tiredness from her brain. "I just want to sleep."

"Last night, you did not want to sleep."

"Last night I wasn't having my period," she informed him with more honesty than finesse.

"You're having your monthly?" he asked, like the idea was a foreign concept.

"Yes. Sorry, no royal babies just yet."

He waved his hand like that wasn't important when in fact it was incredibly important. Especially to everyone else. Even her mom wanted to know if Nataliya was pregnant yet.

She'd only been married three weeks!

"I thought…"

"What did you think?" she asked, not sure she even wanted an answer.

"That you were angry I said no to Demyan's proposal."

"Did you say no to it?" She didn't remember Nikolai saying that.

"Well, not yet, but my plans are to turn it down."

"Okay."

"Okay?"

"Only I'm really tired. Can you hold me and let me sleep?" she spelled out for him.

He settled back down beside her, pulling her upper body onto his chest, his arms wrapped securely around her.

She went boneless against him, making a soft sound of approval.

"You don't care about the joint venture?" he asked into the darkened bedroom, something strange in his tone.

"Not enough to talk about it now. Can we talk in the morning?"

He kissed the top of her head. "Yes."

Nataliya woke with a sense that something wasn't right.

Nikolai's arms were still around her, though they were spooning now. Which was definitely *right*. It was the light coming in through the windows.

"What time is it?" She tried to move his arm so she could get up. "We overslept!"

How was that possible? Nikolai *never* overslept and frankly, neither did she.

His hold on her tightened. She wasn't going anywhere. "Do not stress yourself. I arranged for our morning meetings to be moved."

"How?" Both their schedules were set in stone as far as the staff was concerned. "When?"

"How? I called my administrative assistant and had her call

*your* personal assistant and social secretary. When? Last night after you fell asleep. I don't think a foghorn would have woken you, much less my voice talking on the phone."

"I was pretty tired." She felt a lot better that morning, her supplements and the extra sleep having done wonders. "It's always like that the first couple of days of my period. I'm sorry."

He grunted. It was not a kingly sound. At all.

But it carried a wealth of masculine meaning. "*You* have nothing to apologize for."

"But you do?" she asked as she turned in the band of his arms to face him.

His gorgeous cheekbones were scored with color. "I do."

"What?"

"I doubted you."

"What did you doubt?" She did her best to remember the night before and tried to figure out what he was talking about. He'd been weird all right, but she'd been too tired to worry on it then.

"Last night when you turned me down, I thought you were withholding sex to get your way." He looked and sounded as embarrassed as a king could be.

Good. He should be.

Withhold sex? From him? Chance would be a fine thing!

"My way about what?" she asked in confusion.

"The business venture with your cousin."

"I have a *way* about that?" she asked, still not sure she got where the disconnect was coming from.

"I thought you wanted me to say yes and were making sure I did so."

Nataliya sat up, giving him a look so he would loosen his arms. "We talked about that. I promised I would never do it. You said you believed me."

"I did believe you. I do believe you."

"Then what was last night about?" The things he'd said made a lot more sense now.

"It was about bad memories."

Nataliya got that. She really did. "I am not her."

It was his turn to sit up. They faced each other in the big bed. "No, you are not. You could hurt me so much more than Tiana ever did."

"What are you saying?" How could that be possible?

He was implying Nataliya had some emotional hold on him.

"I have come to realize that while I was sexually besotted with Tiana, I never really loved her. My grief on her death had more to do with what could have been than anything that was."

"Okay."

"I realized on our honeymoon that *I do love you* and knowing the depth of my feelings for you when you do not feel the same has made me…" He paused, took a deep breath and then offered. "Insecure."

"You love me?" she asked, the shock of such a possibility making her heart race and her face go all hot.

"With everything in me. My staff and cabinet are right to worry. I would move heaven and earth for you."

"But Nikolai, I do love you. I have since I was a teenager."

"That was not love. You felt attracted to me like I was attracted to Tiana. Love is a much deeper emotion."

"Do you remember what we learned on our wedding night?" she asked.

"That we are insanely sexually compatible?"

"That I know myself better than you do. After all, I am living in my skin."

"Yes, of course."

"So, when I say I love you, I mean it."

"You mean it?" The smile that came over his features was so vibrant it almost hurt to see. "You mean it! You love me."

"I do."

The intimacy that followed was shocking. She didn't know they could have sex this time of month, but showers were an amazing thing.

Later, they shared a leisurely breakfast on the balcony to their palace suite.

"Did you love me when you accepted my proposal?" he asked.

She refrained from rolling her eyes. Barely. He'd been asking questions like this since they sat down. "Yes."

"Did you *know* you loved me?"

"Yes."

"And when you made your vows…"

"I meant every one. Nikolai, I love you."

"Enough to forgive me for doubting you?"

"I was never actually angry."

"But—"

"Nikolai, we both brought damage into this marriage."

"Your damage doesn't have you accusing me of things I would never do."

She was glad he recognized she would never use him the way Tiana had. "My damage made it impossible for me to admit my love before you acknowledged yours."

And that shamed her. They'd both suffered pain because of her inability to offer emotional honesty.

"I did not tell you right away either."

"You realized you loved me on our honeymoon. Your timing has mine beat by a mile."

He grinned. "I do not care. You love me. That is all that matters to me."

"I've loved you half my life, it feels like. It's a permanent condition."

"Nothing could make me happier."

He named her Queen of Mirrus on their first anniversary and she wore a dress and robes that had to be accommodated for her tiny baby bump. They made it into the media spotlight often because the love between the King and Queen of Mirrus had the world enthralled.

It was the romance of the century.

Nataliya never cared about stuff like that, but waking every morning with the knowledge she was loved so completely made each day better. Her very dignified husband showed an affectionate side no one thought he had.

A side he had never shown another.

Nataliya was honored to be his Queen, but she adored being his wife.

And Nikolai made it clear every single day, in small and big ways that he adored being her husband.

\* \* \* \* \*

Keep reading for an excerpt of
*The Millionaire's Melbourne Proposal*
by Ally Blake.
Find it in the
*Local Bestselling Authors Collection 2024* anthology,
out now!

# CHAPTER ONE

FACE TILTED TO the bright spring sky, Nora Letterman absorbed her daily dose of Melbourne sunshine as she moseyed her way along the beaten-up Fitzroy footpath.

A tram rattled past, rails screeching, sparks shooting skyward from the wires overhead, drowning out the music playing through Nora's earbuds. She danced out of the way of a smiling couple as they all squeezed between a lamppost and a young girl walking four small fluffy dogs.

As moments went, it was pretty perfect, actually; one of a zillion lovely mental keepsakes she'd tuck away for when she left this little pocket of wonderfulness behind.

Which she would do. Any day now.

The eighteen months she'd spent there were the longest she'd stayed in one place. Ever. And she loved it dearly. But at her core, Nora was footloose and fancy-free. It even said so, in faded, scrawling script on the inside of her right arm, alongside a delicate dandelion, petals breaking away and drifting with the breeze.

"Nora!"

Nora looked back over her shoulder as Christos the fruiterer threw her a mandarin, which she swiped out of the air. Spinning to walk backwards, she put a hand over her heart.

Christos called, "The Tutti Fruiti website is such a hit, Nora. Lots of compliments from customers, which I accept on your behalf. Are you sure I can't pay you in fruit?"

"Not unless the phone company accept payment in kind," Nora called back.

Christos grinned. Then he shot her a salute before turning to flirt with the next customer.

Cheeks full with smiling, Nora meandered on, absorbing the cacophony of sensory delights that made this patch of Fitzroy infamous: incense and coffee, flowers and pre-loved clothes, street art and graffiti, multicultural foods and the lingering scent of smoked herbs that might or might not be legal.

Sure, there was a chain chemist or two along the strip, an American burger behemoth on the corner, but for the most part the shopfronts were generational, mum and dad stores, or young entrepreneurs stepping out into the fray. People having a go. Which was why she'd fitted in so quickly.

The fact that so many of them had readily snapped up the services of *The Girl Upstairs*—Nora's fledgling online creative business—for a website dust-off, virtual assistance, or a vibrant social-media overhaul was yet another reason her time in this place had been so golden.

Gait loose, mind warm and fuzzy, her time her own, Nora slowed outside Vintage Vamp.

Misty, the elegantly boho business owner who'd refused to hire Nora as she believed the internet would cause the downfall of civilisation, mumbled under her breath as she reworked a clothing rail full of brightly coloured kaftans flapping in a sudden waft of breeze.

"Hey, Misty!" Nora sing-songed.

Misty turned, her eyes lit with genuine fondness, before she remembered herself and frowned. "Thought you'd have left us in your dust by now."

Nora rolled her eyes. "Do you really think I'd go without saying goodbye?"

"Good point, Little Miss Sunshine. Not a chance of that. Now, help me. Do I retire these things?" Misty waved a hand over the colourful kaftans. "Or leave them here, in memory of our Clancy?"

As one, both women blinked, breathed out hard sighs, then looked across the road, to the row of terrace houses on the far corner.

Some facades were overgrown with weeds, paint peeling, fretwork rusting; the tenants mostly students and artists who had gravitated to the area. Other properties had been meticulously renovated till they were worth an utter mint. But Nora's and Misty's gazes were caught on the cream-and-copper-hued terrace house right in the middle.

Neither dilapidated, nor pristine, Thornfield Hall—as it had been lovingly dubbed by its long-time owner—was tidy and appealing. It was also the house in which Nora had been lucky enough to live as the single upstairs tenant for the past year and a half.

Its downstairs sitting room was well known around the area as a safe, warm space for book clubs, widows' groups, and a widows' book club. Always open for a quick coffee, a listening ear, a place to grieve, to vent, to go for laughter and company.

Though it had gone quiet in the days since Clancy Finlayson—eighty-something, raucous, divine, and the owner of Thornfield Hall—had fallen ill. She had passed away before any of them had had the chance to ready themselves for the possibility.

"Any news?" Misty asked. "About the new owner?"

Nora shook her head. "Still no word."

It was all anyone had asked since Clancy had passed.

Knowing Clancy as she had, the house might have been left to some distant relative, or the local puppy shelter.

While Nora had kept Clancy company during her final days at home, she had no more of a clue than anyone else. She'd focussed, as she always did, on the good not the bad, the happiness not the suffering: reading *Jane Eyre* aloud, telling funny stories she'd picked up in the neighbourhood, playing Clancy's favourite records, and making sure Clancy's hair and nails were *en pointe*.

After Clancy had passed, the lawyers had been frustratingly tight-lipped about it all, citing privacy laws, and Nora didn't know where else to turn.

Which was how she'd found herself in her current state of limbo, ready to move on but unwilling to walk away and leave the beautiful old house untended, abandoned to fate, local squatters or graffiti gangs.

There was also the fact that she'd promised Clancy as much.

In those quiet, final hours, with Nora no longer able to hold back the ache that had been building inside her from the moment Clancy had announced she was sick—her insides crazing faster than she could mentally patch up the damage—in a rare fit of poignancy she'd promised Clancy that she'd take care of her beloved house till the new owner took over.

Clancy might not have been lucid, might not have heard a word, but Nora had been on the receiving end of enough broken promises in her life, a promise *from* her was as good as placing her beating heart in someone's open hands.

So she would stay. Bags packed. Money put aside to cover her interim rent. Ready to hand the house keys to the new owner the moment they showed their face. And only then would she move on, leaving behind nothing but warm feelings and pleasant memories.

After all Clancy had done for her, it was the very least she could do.

Misty cleared her throat and shook herself all over. Pathos was not her natural state of being. "Loved the woman to bits, but I'm never going to move these damn things without her."

Nora dragged her gaze and thoughts back to the rack of floaty, wildly coloured garments now flapping in a growing breeze, the Melbourne weather having turned on a dime as it tended to do.

"May I?" Nora asked, bringing out her phone to take a photo.

Misty waved a *whatever* hand Nora's way.

Nora stood back, found the best angles and took a slew of photos, which she'd edit, filter, tag and post later on her *The Girl Upstairs* pages, which had gathered followers like lint on felt from near the moment she'd set them up as a showcase for her clients. If a half-dozen kaftans weren't snapped up within the day she'd eat her shoes.

Thus distracted, she was too slow to move when Misty grabbed a moss-green kaftan with hot pink embroidery and purple fringing and thrust it up against Nora's person. "You must have it. And when you wear it, you'll think of Clancy."

Beneath the sway of the lurid pattern, Nora's hemp platforms poked out from under her frayed denim flares. If she ever wore such a thing, she'd more likely be thinking she looked like a seventies boudoir lamp.

Nora caught Misty's eye, and the gleam of commerce within, then handed over the twenty bucks anyway. It was Nora's mission in life to leave any place, conversation, and moment brighter than when she entered it and if selling a kaftan made Misty feel a little happier, then so be it.

Kaftan draped over her arm, Nora backed away. "Friday night drinks?"

"If you're still here."

"If I'm still here."

With that, Nora waited for a break in the meandering traffic and jogged across the road.

When she reached the front gate of Clancy's old house, she ambled up the front path; past the Japanese myrtle, to the front patio, its fretwork dripping with jasmine, pale green buds just now starting to show. The elegant facade was a little worn around the edges, but still strong and purposeful, like a royal family who could no longer afford servants, but still wore tiaras to dinner.

Using her key, she jiggled the old lock till it jerked open, then stepped inside.

Dust motes danced in the muted afternoon sunshine pouring through the glass panels in the front door. In the quiet it was easy to imagine Clancy's Chloé perfume on the air, Barry Manilow crooning from the kitchen speaker, the scent of Clancy reheating something Nora had cooked on the beautiful old Aga.

A slice of sadness, of *loss*, whipped across her belly, so sudden, so sharp she let out a sound. Her hand lifted to cover the spot but it took its sweet time to ebb.

*This*… This was the biggest reason why she had to get the house sorted and move on as soon as possible. As strongly as Nora believed in the deliberate collection of happy moments, she'd made a concerted effort in her adult life not to put herself in situations that might bring on sadness, emotional pain, the sense of missing something, or someone.

Connections, friendships, and traditions felt nice, superficially, but they were so dangerous. They made a person feel as if such things might actually last. Shuffled from foster home to foster home as a kid, promises had been made to Nora, hopes raised, then summarily dashed, again and again.

There was no room for hope, or guilt, or expectations, or regret; not if she wanted a happy life. That lesson had been learned, until it was as indelible as any tattoo. And Nora *really, truly, deeply* wanted a happy life.

And so she woke up smiling, worked hard, kept little in the way of possessions, was nice to people and expected nothing in return, so that when she moved on, no part of her was left behind. Only a fond lustre, like the kiss of the first cool breeze of autumn at the end of a long summer.

The sudden clackety-clack of toenails on the hardwood floor split the silence, then stilled, snapping Nora back to the present.

"Magpie?" she called, her voice wavering just a smidge. "Pie?"

Pie was a bad-tempered, one-eyed, silky terrier; the latest in a long line of dogs Clancy had fostered in the time Nora had lived there. He'd been due to go back to Playful Paws Puppy Rescue around the time Clancy had passed. But after hearing the news, they'd said it was no rush getting him back.

This wasn't their first rodeo.

So, she was not only stuck looking after a house that wasn't hers, but also a dog that didn't much like her. Which mucked with her head more than she liked. This had better get sorted... and soon.

Nora reached slowly into her tote for the baggie of dried meat she'd picked up at the whole-foods market. "I got you a little treat, Pie. Want some?"

She earned a distant growl for her efforts, before the flap of the doggie door gave her reprieve.

Stepping deeper inside the house, her foot caught on the mail that had been slipped through the mail slot in the front door.

A couple of department store mailers, Clancy's subscription to *Men's Health* magazine—for the articles, she'd always claimed—and an official-looking envelope. The latter was thick and yellow, the Melbourne address of a London law firm etched into the top left corner.

And it was addressed to Nora.

Heart kicking till she felt it in her neck and in a flush across her cheeks, Nora moved to the steep stairs leading up to her first-floor apartment, and sat, popping her tote and new kaftan beside her. Then she opened the envelope without ado.

As expected, it was news of Clancy's will, as it pertained to one Nora Letterman.

She knew nothing would be left to her; she'd made Clancy promise after the older woman had made noise about leaving her a sideboard she'd admired. Unless it would fit in her ruck-sack, it would only be a burden. From what Nora could ascertain from the legalese, Clancy had listened. Apart from a few charitable bequests, the house and everything Clancy owned had been left to one Bennett J Hawthorne.

An answer. Finally!

Though while she felt the expected relief, hot on its heels came a wave of uncomfortable tightness in her belly.

Bennett J Hawthorne. *Bennett*. It had to be Clancy's adopted grandson who, from the little Nora had gleaned, had lived with Clancy from when he was quite young.

Poor guy. What rotten news. And to find out his adoptive grandmother was gone while so far away. Actually, where was he again?

The dozen odd times his name had come up someone had always changed the subject, so she'd never heard the story behind his adoption. Since mere mention of Bennett had always made Clancy maudlin, which was the opposite of Nora spreading sunshine wherever she went, and in her experience "family" was as often considered a dirty word as not, she'd happily let it be. And never thought more of it.

Now she wished she'd pressed. Just a little.

Rubbing a finger and thumb over her temple, she searched her memory banks for the times she'd heard mention of his name.

Once a month or so, Clancy would answer the phone, her face pinched, her shoulders tight, and she'd quietly take the phone to her bedroom. One of those times Nora had heard Clancy say, "Bennett" just before the bedroom door snicked shut.

Was that it?

Then it hit her.

Bennett. *Ben.*

Deep into the night, near the end, perhaps even the very last time Clancy had been in any way lucid, she had muttered, "Ben." Then, louder, more insistent, "*Ben? Is that you?*"

"*Ben?* Ben who? Would you like me to find him?" Nora had asked, not realising at the time Clancy had meant Bennett, the prodigal, *hush hush* adopted grandson. "Ask him to come?"

*"No,"* Clancy had shot back, her face twisting as if in pain. "Leave him be."

*Leave him be.* As if asking a guy to take the time to visit his ailing grandmother was too great a burden.

Nora shifted on the stair, the skinny plank of wood with its threadbare patch of old carpet biting into her backside, her initial feelings of *poor guy* having morphed into *what the heck?*

This was the person Clancy had left her beloved Thornfield Hall to? Seriously, what kind of man treated a person that way? Never visiting, calling but rarely. Especially someone as vibrant and loving and wondrous and accepting as Clancy?

Nora allowed herself a rare moment of indulging in feeling all the feelings—the gutting sorrow, the flutters of rage—letting them stew till they coagulated in an ugly ball in her belly before she sucked in a deep soothing breath and reduced them to a simmer.

It took longer than she'd have liked to let it go. But she managed. Letting go of ugly feelings was something she'd long since learned to do with alacrity and grace.

*Happiness over suffering.*

This was the news she'd been waiting for, unexpected outcome or no. Bennett Hawthorne could come and grab the keys, she'd politely talk him through the vagaries of the old home— the upstairs window that had been painted shut, the noisy downstairs pipe, the wriggly front door lock—then she could draw a nice clean line under what had been a wonderful chapter of her life.

Before the place got its claws into her any deeper. Before this pile of bricks, this street, these people, began to feel like something as insidious and treacherous as *home*.

Nora lifted the papers in her hand, flipped the page and read on, hoping to find a timeline as to when Hawthorne might finally show up so she could be ready.

But then she reached a section that left her a little stunned, as if she'd been smacked in the side of the head.

While the house would go to Bennett Hawthorne, Clancy's will also declared that one Nora Letterman, aka *The Girl Upstairs*, had the right to stay on in the house for a period of up to two months from the date of Clancy's death.

A cleaner would be paid for by the estate. All upkeep and utilities as well. And Nora was not to pay a cent of rent.

The house was not to be open for inspection, put on the market, or in any way renovated during the time Nora was in residence.

She was—of course—welcome to leave sooner if she desired. But the rooms were hers, for two months, if she needed them.

All of which, apparently, suited Bennett Hawthorne, as the reason the letter was from the Melbourne office of a London law firm was because the guy was London-based and thus would not be able to inspect the property in person any time soon.

"Oh, Clancy." Nora breathed out audibly, the letter falling to her knee, her gaze lifting to glance into the kitchen.

The kitchen said nothing in return. Though, in the silence, the clackety-clack of tiny doggy claws echoed somewhere in the big empty house.

Clancy *knew* Nora was a wanderer. They'd often chat about where Nora might end up next; Clancy wistfully sighing over Nora's stories of camping out on other people's sofas, slinging coffees in a train station café for a day in order to be able to afford the fare to get her to the next place, as if that life were something to aspire to rather than a case of needs must.

So what had she been thinking, sneaking this into her will?

Nora felt the slightest twinge tugging on her watch-out-ometer, as if she'd somehow found herself swept up in some larger plan. But she quickly shook it off. Clancy didn't have it in her to be so manipulative. She'd been good, through and through. The best person Nora had ever known. And now she was gone.

"Dammit." Nora rubbed a hand over her eyes, knees juggling with excess energy as she mentally gathered in all the parts of herself that were threatening to fly off into some emotional whirlwind.

Breaking things down into their simplest forms:

Clancy was simply being kind.

But staying was impossible.

So this Bennett guy *had* to come back. Now.

Irresponsible or no, on the other side of the world or not, whatever the story, he was one of Clancy's people. And Clancy never gave up on her people. He'd know what this house meant to his grandmother. And would take care of it.

If not…

While Clancy had loomed large in Nora's life these past months, had treated her with such kindness, respect, and fierce support, she wasn't family. So, it was actually none of Nora's business.

Ignoring the latest twinge *that* brought on, Nora grabbed her phone and searched for Bennett Hawthorne, but she had no clue what he might look like and, since he was adopted, she couldn't even look for a similarity to Clancy. A plethora of images and articles popped up, all the same, most regarding the sweet-looking, elderly mayor of some small town in America who'd tried to make it so that dogs could legally marry one another. Ah, algorithms.

Figuring it mattered little—the guy was who he was—she popped her phone away, grabbed the legal letter, took it upstairs, turned her Taylor Swift playlist up nice and loud, and emailed the lawyers.

# Subscribe and fall in love with a Mills & Boon series today!

You'll be among the first to read stories delivered to your door monthly and enjoy great savings.

WE
SIMPLY
LOVE
ROMANCE

# MILLS & BOON